Sisterland

Curtis Sittenfeld

W F HOWES LTD

This large print edition published in 2013 by
W F Howes Ltd
Unit 4, Rearsby Business Park, Gaddesby Lane,
Rearsby, Leicester LE7 4YH

1 3 5 7 9 10 8 6 4 2

First published in the United Kingdom in 2013
by Doubleday

A CIP catalogue record for this book is available
from the British Library

ISBN 978 1 47123 963 2

Typeset by Palimpsest Book Production Limited,
Falkirk, Stirlingshire
Printed and bound by
CPI Group (UK) Ltd, Croydon, CR0 4YY

MIX
Paper from
responsible sources
FSC
www.fsc.org   FSC® C013604

For my aunts,
Ellen Battistelli and Dede Alexander,
who are Missouri natives

PROLOGUE

December 1811
New Madrid, Louisiana Territory

The first earthquake wasn't the strongest – that would come later, in February 1812 – but it must have been the most astonishing. It occurred shortly after two in the morning, and I imagine it awakening the people of New Madrid: the farmers and fur traders, the French Creoles and Indians and American pioneers. More men than women lived in the river town, and few families; the population was probably less than a thousand. The people were lying in their beds on this cold and ordinary night when without warning a tremendous cracking sound interrupted the quiet, a growing thunder, followed by the impossible fact of the quake itself: the rocking not just of their beds or floors or houses but of the land beneath them. Whether they stayed inside or hurried out, they'd have heard their animals crying, heard trees snapping, the Mississippi roaring up; so much fog and smoke filled the darkness that they would have felt the roll of the earth before they realized they could see it, too, undulating like the ocean. In some places, the ground split apart and flung up water, sand, and rocks, entire trees it had swallowed shortly before, and in turn it devoured horses and cows. Rising out of the cracks and holes was the smell of sulfur, like the wicked breath of the devil emanating from deep underground.

For hours, the convulsions didn't stop, and when eventually their bewildering rhythm changed, it was not to decrease but to intensify: Twice more, at seven in the morning and again at eleven, the earth exploded anew. And daybreak had not brought light. Still there was the chaos of vapors, the bleats and squawks of domesticated and wild animals, the collapsing trees and spewing land and mercilessly teeming river.

Only around noon did the earth settle, and only gradually. But what was left? The people's homes – one-story log or frame structures – were leveled, as were the town's stores and churches. The land was broken, the river roiling. The banks of the Mississippi had simply plunged into the water below, carrying with them houses, graveyards, and forests; canoes and keelboats had vanished under thirty-foot waves, reappeared, and vanished again.

Though it must have seemed, on the afternoon of December 16, 1811, that the world was ending, more destruction would follow. In this same remote area, another powerful quake occurred on January 23, 1812, and two weeks later, on February

2

7, the last and biggest. In just months, whole towns disappeared not only from the Louisiana Territory – soon to become the Territory of Missouri – but also from the Mississippi Territory and Tennessee. People claimed that the Mississippi River ran backward and that the effects of the quakes were felt hundreds of miles away: that clocks stopped in Natchez, chimneys collapsed in Louisville, and church bells rang in Boston.

But perhaps these myths were merely that, embellishments more irresistible than accurate. Magnitude scales wouldn't exist for another century, so calculations of the New Madrid quakes came long afterward, and though the highest estimates placed them above 8.0 – stronger than the 1906 earthquake in San Francisco, the strongest of any continental earthquake in United States history – other guesses were closer to a magnitude 7. Which would have made them frightening, certainly, but not unprecedented.

My husband would say that such distinctions matter, that there are ways of conducting research and establishing hypotheses based on credible evidence. My sister would disagree. She would say that we create our own reality – that the truth, ultimately, is what we choose to believe.

CHAPTER 1

September 2009
St. Louis, Missouri

The shaking started around three in the morning, and it happened that I was already awake because I'd nursed Owen at two and then, instead of going back to sleep, I'd lain there brooding about the fight I'd had at lunch with my sister, Vi. I'd driven with Owen and Rosie in the backseat to pick up Vi, and the four of us had gone to Hacienda. We'd finished eating and I was collecting Rosie's stray food from the tabletop – once I had imagined I wouldn't be the kind of mother who ordered chicken tenders for her child off the menu at a Mexican restaurant – when Vi said, 'So I have a date tomorrow.'

'That's great,' I said. 'Who is it?'

Casually, after running the tip of her tongue over her top teeth to check for food, Vi said, 'She's an IT consultant, which sounds boring, but she's traveled a lot in South and Central America, so she couldn't be a total snooze, right?'

I was being baited, but I tried to match Vi's

5

casual tone as I said, 'Did you meet online?' Rosie, who was two and a half, had gotten up from the table, wandered over to a ficus plant in the corner, and was smelling the leaves. Beside me in the booth, buckled into his car seat, Owen, who was six months, grabbed at a little plush giraffe that hung from the car seat's handle.

Vi nodded. 'There's pretty slim pickings for dykes in St Louis.'

'So that's what you consider yourself these days?' I leaned in and said in a lowered tone, 'A lesbian?'

Looking amused, Vi imitated my inclined posture and quiet voice. 'What if the manager hears you?' she said. 'And gets a boner?' She grinned. 'At this point, I'm bi-celibate. Or should I say Vi-sexual? But I figure it's all a numbers game – I keep putting myself out there and, eventually, I cross paths with Ms or Mr Right.'

'Meaning you're on straight dating sites, too?'

'Not at the moment, but in the future, maybe.' Our waitress approached and left the bill at the edge of the table. I reached for it as soon as she'd walked away – when Vi and I ate together, I always paid without discussion – and Vi said, 'Don't leave a big tip. She was giving us attitude.'

'I didn't notice.'

'And my fajita was mostly peppers.'

'You of all people should realize that's not the waitress's fault.' For years, all through our twenties, Vi had worked at restaurants. But she was still regarding me skeptically as I set down my

6

credit card, and I added, 'It's rude not to tip extra when you bring little kids.' We were at a conversational crossroads. Either we could stand, I could gather the mess of belongings that accompanied me wherever I went – once I had been so organized that I kept my spice rack alphabetized, and now I left hats and bibs and sippy cups in my wake, baggies of Cheerios, my own wallet and sunglasses – and the four of us could head out to the parking lot and then go on to drop Vi at her house, all amicably. Or I could express a sentiment that wasn't Vi, in her way, *asking* me to share?

'I believe in tipping well for great service,' Vi was saying. 'This girl was phoning it in.'

I said, 'If you feel equally attracted to men and women, why not date men? Isn't it just easier? I mean, I wish it weren't true, but—' I glanced at my daughter right as she pulled a ficus leaf off the plant and extended her tongue toward it. I had assumed the plant was fake and, therefore, durable, and I called out, 'No mouth, Rosie. Come over here.' When I looked back at Vi, I couldn't remember what I'd wanted to say next. Hadn't I had another point? And Vi was sneering in a way that made me wish, already, that I'd simply let the moment pass.

'Easier?' Her voice was filled with contempt. 'It's just *easier* to be straight? As in, what, less embarrassing to my uptight sister?'

'That's not what I said.'

'Don't you think it would be easier if black

7

people hadn't demanded to ride in the front of the bus like white people? Or go to the same schools? That was so awkward when that happened!' This seemed to be an indirect reference to my friend Hank, but I ignored it.

'I don't have a problem with gay people,' I said, and my cheeks were aflame, which I'd have known, even if I hadn't been able to feel their heat, by the fact that Vi's were, too. We would always be identical twins, even though we were no longer, in most ways, identical.

'Where's Rosie's baloney?' Rosie said. She had returned from the ficus plant – thank goodness – and was standing next to me.

'It's at home,' I said. 'We didn't bring it.' The baloney was a piece from a lunch-themed puzzle, a life-sized pink wooden circle on a yellow wooden square, that Rosie had recently become inexplicably attached to. I said to Vi, 'Don't make me out to be homophobic. It's a statement of fact that life is simpler – it is, Vi – don't look at me like that. It's not like two women can get married in Missouri, and there's a lot of financial stuff that goes along with that, or visiting each other in the hospital. Or having kids – for gay couples, that's complicated and it's expensive, too.'

'Having kids period is complicated!' Vi's anger had taken on an explosive quality, and I felt people at nearby tables looking toward us. 'And this whole making-life-simpler bullshit?' she continued. While I flinched at the swear word in front of Rosie, it didn't seem intentional – there was no question that Vi sometimes liked to provoke me, but it appeared she was swept up in the moment. 'Children are nothing but a problem people create and then congratulate themselves on solving. Look at you and Jeremy, for Christ's sake. "Oh, we can't leave the house because it's Rosie's naptime, we can't be out past five forty-five P.M." or whenever the fuck it is—' I was pretty sure Rosie had only a vague notion of what these obscenities, or anything else Vi was saying, meant, but I could sense her watching rapt from beside me, no doubt even more enthralled because she'd heard her own name. 'Or, "She can't wear that sunscreen because it has parabens in it" – I mean, seriously, can you even tell me what a paraben is? – and "She can't eat raw carrots because she might choke," and on and on and on. But who asked you to have children? Do you think you're providing some service to the world? You got pregnant because you wanted to – which, okay, that's your right, but then other people can't do what they want to because it's too complicated?'

'Fine,' I said. 'Forget I said anything.'

'Don't be a pussy.'

I glared at her. 'Don't call me names.'

'Well, it seems awfully convenient that you get to speak your mind and then close down the discussion.'

'I need to go home for their naps,' I said, and there was a split second in which Vi and I looked

9

at each other and almost laughed. Instead, sourly, she said, 'Of course you do.'

In the car, she was silent, and after a couple minutes, Rosie said from the backseat, 'Mama wants to sing the Bingo song.'

'I'll sing it later,' I said.

'Mama wants to sing the Bingo song now,' Rosie said, and when I didn't respond, she added in a cheerful tone, 'When you take off your diaper, it makes Mama very sad.'

Vi snorted unpleasantly. 'Why don't you just toilet train her?'

'We're going to soon.'

Vi said nothing, and loathing for her flared up in me, which was probably just what she wanted. It was one thing for my sister to fail to appreciate the energy I put into our lunches, the sheer choreography of getting a six-month-old and a two-year-old out of the house, into the car, into a restaurant, and back home with no major meltdowns (never in my children's presence could *I* have ordered a meal as intricately, messily hands-on as a fajita), but it was another thing entirely for Vi to mock me. And yet, in one final attempt at diplomacy, as I stopped the car on the street outside the small single-story gray house where Vi lived, I said, 'For Dad's birthday, I was thinking—'

'Let's talk about it later.'

'Fine.' If she thought I was going to plead for forgiveness, she was mistaken, and it wasn't just because we really did need to get home for Rosie and Owen's naps. She climbed from the car, and before she shut the door, I said, 'By the way?'

A nasty satisfaction rose in me as she turned. She was prepared for me to say, *I didn't mean to be such a jerk in the restaurant.* Instead, I said, 'Parabens are preservatives.'

Fourteen hours later, at three in the morning, our squabble was what I was stewing over; specifically, I was thinking that the reason I'd made my points so clumsily was that what I really believed was even more offensive than that being straight was easier than being gay. I believed Vi was dating women because she was at her heaviest ever – she'd quit smoking in the spring, and now she had to be sixty pounds overweight – and most lesbians seemed to be more forgiving about appearances than most straight men. I didn't think I'd object to Vi being gay if I believed she actually was, but something about this development felt false, akin to the way she'd wished, since our adolescence, that she'd been born Jewish, or the way she kept a dream catcher above her kitchen sink. Lying there in the dark next to Jeremy, I wondered what would happen if I were to suggest that she and I do Weight Watchers together; I myself was still carrying ten extra pounds from being pregnant with Owen. Then I thought about how most nights Jeremy and I split a pint of ice cream in front of the TV, how it was pretty much the best part of the day – the whole ritual of relaxation after both children were asleep and before Owen woke up for his ten P.M. nursing – and how it seemed unlikely that half a pint of fudge ripple was part of any diet plan. This was when the bed in which Jeremy and I slept began to shake.

I assumed at first that Jeremy was causing the mattress to move by turning over, except that he wasn't turning. The rocking continued for perhaps ten seconds, at which point Jeremy abruptly sat up and said, 'It's an earthquake.' But already the rocking seemed to be subsiding.

I sat up, too. 'Are you sure?'

'You get Owen and I'll get Rosie.' Jeremy had turned on the light on his nightstand and was walking out of the room, and as I hurried from bed, adrenaline coursed through me; my heart was beating faster and I felt simultaneously unsteady and purposeful. In his crib, illuminated by a starfish-shaped night-light, Owen was lying on his back as I'd left him an hour earlier, his arms raised palms up on either side of his head, his cheeks big and smooth, his nose tiny. I hesitated just a second before lifting him, and I grabbed one of the eight pacifiers scattered in the crib. As I'd guessed he would, he blinked awake, seeming confused, but made only one mournful cry as I stuck in the pacifier. In the small central hallway that connected the house's three bedrooms, we almost collided with Jeremy and Rosie, Rosie's legs wrapped around Jeremy's torso, her arms dangling limply over his shoulders, her face half-obscured by tangled hair. Her eyes were open, I saw, but barely.

'Do we go to the basement?' I said to Jeremy. The shaking had definitely stopped.

'That's tornadoes.'

'What is it for earthquakes?' In retrospect, it's hard to believe I needed to ask, hard to believe I had reached the age of thirty-four and given birth to two children without bothering to learn such basic information.

Jeremy said, 'In theory, you get under a table, but staying in bed is okay, too.'

'Really?' We looked at each other, my husband sweet and serious in his gray T-shirt and blue striped boxer shorts, our daughter draped across him.

'You want me to check?' He meant by looking online from his phone, which he kept beside the bed at night.

'We shouldn't call Courtney, should we?' I said. 'They must have felt it if we did.' Courtney Wheeling was Jeremy's colleague at Washington University – his area of study was aquatic chemistry, hers was seismology and plate tectonics – and she and her husband, Hank, lived down the street and were our best friends.

'It doesn't seem necessary,' Jeremy said. 'I'll look at FEMA's website, but I think the best thing is for all of us to go back to bed.'

I nodded my chin toward Rosie. 'Keeping them with us or in their own rooms?'

Rosie's head popped up. 'Rosie sleeps with Mama!' A rule of thumb with Rosie was that whether I did or didn't think she was following the conversation, I was always wrong.

'Keeping them,' Jeremy said. 'In case of aftershocks.'

In our room, I climbed into bed holding Owen, shifting him so he was nestled in my right arm while Jeremy helped Rosie settle on my other side. I wasn't sure whether to be alarmed or pleasantly surprised that Jeremy was all right having the kids sleep with us. In general, he was the one who resisted bringing them into our bed; he'd read the same books in Rosie's infancy that I had, half of which argued that sharing a bed with your kids was the most nurturing thing you could do and the other half of which warned that doing so would result in your smothering them either figuratively or literally. But I liked when they were close by – whether or not it really was safer, at some primitive level, it felt like it had to be – and the thought of them sleeping alone in their cribs sometimes pinched at my heart. Besides, I could never resist their miniature limbs and soft skin.

Rosie curled toward me then, tapping my arm, and I turned – awkwardly, because of how I was holding Owen – to look at her. She said, 'Rosie wants a banana.'

'In the morning, sweetheart.'

Jeremy had gone to the window that faced the street, and he parted the curtains. 'Everyone's lights are on,' he said.

'A monkey eats a banana peel,' Rosie declared. 'But not people.'

'That's true,' I said. 'It would make us sick.'

Jeremy was typing on his phone. After a minute, he said, 'There's nothing about it online yet.' He looked up. 'How's he doing?'

'He's more asleep than awake, but will you get an extra binky just in case?' Surely this was evidence of the insularity of our lives: that unless otherwise specified, whenever Jeremy or I said *he,* we meant our son, and whenever we said *she,* we meant our daughter. On a regular basis, we sent each other texts consisting in their entirety of one letter and one punctuation mark: *R?* for *How's Rosie doing?* and *O?* for *How's Owen?* And surely it was this insularity that so irritated Vi, whereas to me, the fact that my life was suburban and conventional was a victory.

Jeremy returned from Owen's room with a second pacifier, handed it to me, and lay down before turning off the light on his nightstand. Then – I whispered, because whispering seemed more appropriate in the dark – I said, 'So if there are aftershocks, we just stay put?'

'And keep away from windows. That's pretty much all I could find on the FEMA site.'

'Thanks for checking.' Over Owen's head, I reached out to rub Jeremy's shoulder.

I felt them falling asleep one by one then, my son, my daughter, and my husband. Awake alone, I experienced a gratitude for my life and our family, the four of us together, accounted for and okay. In contrast to the agitation I'd been gripped by before the earthquake, I was filled with calmness, a sense that we'd passed safely through a minor scare – like when you speed up too fast in slow highway traffic and almost hit the car in front of you but then you don't. The argument with Vi, inflated prior to the quake, shrank to its true size; it was insignificant. My sister and I had spent three decades bickering and making up.

But now that several years have passed, it pains me to remember this night because I was wrong. Although we were safe in that moment, we hadn't passed through anything. Nothing was concluding, nothing was finished; everything was just beginning. And though my powers weren't what they once had been, though I no longer considered myself truly psychic, I still should have been able to anticipate what would happen next.

CHAPTER 2

Our routine in the morning was that we'd awaken around six-fifteen either to Owen's squeaks on the monitor on my nightstand or to Rosie chatting with herself on the monitor on Jeremy's nightstand. I'd go nurse Owen while Jeremy showered, then he'd take both children downstairs to eat while I showered. When I joined them, they'd have moved into the living room, which was also our playroom, and I'd be only halfway down the steps before Rosie began making excited announcements about my appearance – 'Mama has a blue shirt!' – or describing her own activities. As I reached the bottom step, she'd fling herself into my arms, as if we were reuniting after many years apart. (How flattering motherhood was, when they weren't smearing food on my clothes or sneezing into my mouth.)

On this morning, Rosie squatted by the bookshelf and shouted, 'Rosie's driving a school bus!'

Jeremy, who was holding his phone and Owen, said, 'The earthquake had a magnitude of 4.9, and the epicenter was in Terre Haute, Indiana.'

'Have you talked to Courtney yet?' I asked.

He shook his head. 'I'll wait until I see her at school. I'm guessing she's already fielding calls from the media.'

As soon as I sat on the couch, Owen began kicking his legs and reaching for me. I lifted my arms, and as Jeremy passed him over, he said, 'By the way, your dad just called. He wants to know if you can take him grocery shopping tomorrow instead of today.'

'Is everything all right?'

'Well, he said he felt the earthquake, but he didn't seem worked up about it.'

'Since when does my dad call at seven A.M.?'

'Go call him now if you're worried.'

I held Owen back toward Jeremy. He began to cry, and as I walked to the kitchen, I heard Jeremy say, 'Really, Owen? Am I really that bad?'

From our cordless phone, I called my father's apartment. After he answered, I said, 'So you felt the earthquake, too?'

'Just enough to know what it was,' my father said. 'I'm afraid I have to postpone our trip to the store this afternoon. Will tomorrow work for you?'

'Tomorrow's your birthday dinner, Dad.' My father still drove – he wasn't supposed to at night but was fine during the day – but even so, since my mother's death ten years before, I'd taken him grocery shopping once a week. We'd get deli meat and sliced cheese for his lunches and plan out his dinners, for which he'd buy himself only the cheapest cuts of beef and pork.

'I hope you're not planning anything fancy,' my father said.

'I promise it'll be very low-key. What do you have to do this afternoon?'

'I'll be giving a lift to your sister. I'm sure you know she has a date.' Though my father didn't sound like he was complaining, irritation gathered in me. About a year before, around the time my father's doctor had told him he could no longer drive at night, Vi had stopped driving period. She said she'd had enough of all the jackasses jabbering on their cellphones while going eighty miles an hour; also, not driving was greener. But Vi rarely recycled an aluminum can of Diet Coke, even when a bin was two feet away, and it was obvious that the real explanation was that she'd developed a phobia. I'd meant to get online and do some research, but many months had passed without my doing so. I did get online on a daily basis, usually in the afternoon when Rosie and Owen were both asleep, but once in front of the computer, I'd forget everything I'd meant to do and end up either on Facebook or reading about pregnant celebrities. Meanwhile, Vi showed no inclination to start driving again, and socializing with her and my father, especially during the evening, continued to require elaborate planning.

'Dad, she can take a taxi to her date,' I said. 'She's not destitute.' Vi was always thousands of dollars in credit card debt, as I had once been, too, but surely she could scrape together cab fare.

'I don't mind,' my father said. 'She doesn't think they'll be more than an hour.'

'They're meeting in the afternoon, not at night?'

'At three o'clock, at a Starbucks in Creve Coeur. Not too far off 270, I believe. Vi said I'm welcome to come in and sit at another table, but I'll just bring the paper and make myself comfortable in the car.'

'That doesn't sound like much fun for you.' My father had also said nothing to suggest that Vi had revealed the gender of her date to him. It was so like my sister to have our almost-seventy-four-year-old father drive her, even to be okay with him following her inside, yet not to bother explaining to him either online dating or her nascent lesbianism. (The first I'd ever heard of Vi being involved with a woman was two summers before, when she'd met someone named Cindy at a spirituality conference in Illinois. Cindy was our age but wore a long gray-and-green batik skirt with a matching flowing shirt and the kind of sandals you'd go river rafting in, and thirty seconds after meeting me, she said in a faux-sympathetic tone, 'You give off a very, very tired energy, and you need to make more time for yourself.' When of course I was tired – I had a six-month-old baby! Vi hadn't introduced Cindy to our father, and a few weeks later, Vi had told me she and Cindy were no longer on speaking terms. Since then, Vi hadn't, to my knowledge, dated anyone.)

I said to my father, 'I have a question for you about tomorrow. It's just as easy for Jeremy to grill salmon or steak, and since it's your birthday, you should decide.'

'Oh, heavens, I'm not picky.' He was quiet before adding, 'Vi seems well these days, doesn't she? She's come into her own.'

My father tended to speak in code, which had to do, I believed, with his midwestern decorum, a discretion so extreme that it precluded direct mention of a wide range of topics. Perhaps the worst thing Jeremy had ever said to me, when we'd been together about six months, was that my father was cold. Jeremy had made this remark after we'd invited my father to hear the symphony and he'd declined without giving any reason, and the way Jeremy had said it had been as if this view was a shared understanding we had instead of a scathing observation on his part. 'Well, I've never heard him say "I love you,"' Jeremy had added. 'I've never heard him give you a compliment.' When I began to cry, I think Jeremy was shocked. But to me, my father had always been the kind, warm parent. He was reticent, yes, but he wasn't cold.

In this moment, however, I truly had no idea what my father was talking about when he said Vi was doing well: Her job, which I had long assumed was as much a source of discomfort for him as it was for me? The fact that she had a date?

I said, 'I guess she does seem good.' That she and I had had a fight wasn't worth burdening my father with. 'All right,' I added. 'So Jeremy will get you tomorrow at five o'clock.'

Back in the living room, I said, 'My dad is driving Vi to her date, but I don't even think Vi's told him it's a woman.' The night before, I had recounted to Jeremy my disagreement with Vi at Hacienda, including the part where she'd declared that children were a problem people created then congratulated themselves for solving, at which point Jeremy had laughed and said, 'She's right.'

I said, 'I assumed the woman was picking her up, but they're meeting this afternoon at a Starbucks in Creve Coeur.'

'How romantic,' Jeremy said.

'I know, right?' Even though I wasn't exactly rooting for a thriving lesbian romance for my sister, she'd be better off meeting the IT consultant at night for a drink. How could you possibly fall in love off Interstate 270, on a Thursday afternoon? As I dropped to my knees and began picking up blocks that were strewn across the rug, I said, 'So I think for his birthday dinner, my dad wants steak.'

A few minutes after twelve, Rosie pounded on the Wheelings' door while I unfastened the various harnesses keeping Owen strapped into his half of the double stroller. From the porch, I could hear the television in their living room, which was never on in the middle of the day. Hank had an odd expression – both perplexed and amused – as he held open the door. 'So do you know or do you not know that your sister was just on Channel 5?'

22

'What are you talking about?'

'Do you ever feel like there are only six people in St Louis?' Hank said. 'And we're either married or related to half of them?'

'If you think that, try having grown up here. Why was Vi on TV?' Although Hank didn't seem perturbed, my pulse had quickened. *Please let it just be a man-on-the-street interview,* I thought. *Something about the Cardinals or the Highway 40 construction.* I followed Rosie inside with Owen in my arms.

'Hey, Rosie the Riveter,' Hank said, and Amelia, who was Hank and Courtney's three-year-old daughter and who was standing on the couch, called out, 'My mom is on TV!'

I turned back to Hank. 'What's going on?'

'Courtney and Vi were in the same news segment about the earthquake.'

'Why would Vi be—' I started to ask, and Hank said, 'I think it's better if you just watch. I DVR'd it for Courtney.'

'Is it good or bad?'

On the wall in one corner of their living room was a large flat-screen TV, and Hank held the remote control toward it. 'It's not that it's bad,' he said. 'But you'll think it is.'

I tried not to grip Owen too tightly as I faced the screen. The segment began with a young brunette reporter describing the earthquake that had occurred during the night and providing an overview of the region's geology. 'San Francisco gets more attention,'

23

she said, 'but heartland dwellers know that one of the strongest continental earthquakes ever recorded in the U.S. had its epicenter in the Missouri Bootheel, just a few hours south of St Louis.' Courtney then appeared on-screen, Courtney as in Hank's wife and Jeremy's colleague, sitting behind the desk in her office. 'In fact, it was a series of between three and five seismic events, the first of which was in December 1811 and the last in February 1812,' she said, and she sounded calm and authoritative. COURTNEY WHEELING, WASHINGTON UNIVERSITY PROFESSOR OF GEOPHYSICS, it said in black letters at the bottom of the screen. 'At this point, we don't know if the second and third events on December 16, 1811, were quakes or aftershocks. As for the question of whether we're living in an active seismic zone right now—'

Before Courtney could finish, the reporter said, 'According to one area woman, the answer is very much so.' Hank laughed, presumably because it seemed obvious that Courtney had been about to say the opposite, and then Vi filled the screen. Seeing her, I flinched. The big, loose purple tunic she wore had seemed unnoteworthy at Hacienda but now appeared garish, and even if she hadn't been in the same clothes, I'd have guessed she hadn't slept the night before: There were shadows under her eyes, her face was puffy, and she didn't have on makeup. I had never been on television myself, but I knew you at least needed foundation.

'Another earthquake is coming soon. A powerful, powerful earthquake.' In voice-over, as footage showed Vi giving a tour of her living room – the iron candelabra set on the windowsill and the Tibetan prayer flags strung across one wall and the little fountain in the corner, with water bubbling over a pile of stones – the reporter said, 'Violet Shramm, a self-described psychic medium living in Rock Hill, claims that the tremors St Louis residents felt earlier today were a prelude to a much bigger earthquake. No, she doesn't have proof, but in 2004 she helped Florissant police find nine-year-old kidnapping victim Brady Ogden, she publicly predicted Michael Jackson's death in June – and she says she had a hunch about the quake that happened early this morning.'

'I did a reading for a group last night,' Vi told the camera, 'and the last thing I said to them was, "Be careful, because Mother Earth is very restless right now."'

I glanced at Hank. 'I thought you said it wasn't that bad.'

'Well, I wish they weren't pitted against each other. I'm sure Courtney had no idea.'

'She looks deranged,' I said and added, as if it were necessary, 'Not Courtney.'

'Shramm knows she'll have her skeptics,' the reporter was saying, 'but she believes that staying quiet could do more harm than good.'

'If I can save just one life,' Vi said, 'that's what's important.'

The shot shifted to an image of a map with a pulsing red circle over the border between Missouri

25

and Arkansas on one side and Kentucky and Tennessee on the other. 'No doubt about it, we're in a hot zone,' the reporter said. 'But according to Washington University's Wheeling, the Big One could come tomorrow – or never.'

'It's no likelier to happen next week than fifty years from now,' Courtney explained, and she looked, I noticed this time around, impeccably tasteful in a gray blouse, a black suit jacket, small silver earrings, and well-applied foundation; her short blond hair was neatly brushed. 'Does it hurt to keep emergency supplies in the basement? Not at all. But in terms of daily threats for St Louisans, I'd say something like obesity far outranks earthquakes.'

'Oh, God,' I said, and Hank said, 'Yeah, she could have chosen a different example.'

'Every year, GPS instruments record hundreds of instances of seismic activity on and around the New Madrid fault line, yet we feel virtually none of it because it's not that strong,' Courtney was saying on-screen, and she sounded serene and wise and not sleep-deprived. 'The reality is that if you're using seismometers, you'll see earthquakes occurring.' She smiled. 'The earth is always busy.'

The brunette reporter reappeared in front of Vi's house, though blessedly without Vi herself anywhere in view. 'For St Louisans rattled first by recent events and now by future predictions, let's hope not *too* busy,' the reporter said. 'Back to you, Denise.'

Hank paused the screen, and I turned to him and said, 'That was awful.'

'So Vi's eccentric,' Hank said. 'It's not illegal.'

'Kate, Owen spit out his binky.' Amelia was pulling on my hand. 'He spit it on the floor.' She held the pacifier up toward me, and I rubbed it against my shirt and stuck it back in Owen's mouth. I glanced at Rosie, who was setting a blanket over a row of Amelia's stuffed animals, and I wondered if she realized her aunt had just been on television.

'Vi must have called the station herself, right?' I said. 'I mean, how else would they have found her? It's not like she's an expert on earthquakes.' No, the earthquake expert – that was Courtney. The feeling that gripped me in this moment was similar to what I imagined the relatives of an alcoholic must experience when they learn that their parent or child or sibling has gone on another bender: that mix of anger and disappointment and lack of surprise, a blend so exquisite, so familiar, it's almost like satisfaction. Of course. Of course Vi had had a premonition about something big, and of course, instead of taking the time to think it through, she'd called a television station, and of course she'd let herself be interviewed while wearing no makeup. Why did she always get in her own way? I was embarrassed, yes, but my embarrassment was mostly for her, not me. After all, we no longer had the same last name, no longer looked identical. People I was close to knew I had a twin sister, but acquaintances – my former co-workers, or our neighbors other than the Wheelings – wouldn't connect me to this strange woman in her purple shirt, with her weird prediction. I said, 'I'll never understand why she likes drawing attention to herself.' After a beat, I added, 'And the reason you think Vi is delightfully eccentric is that you're not from here.' Hank, Courtney, and my husband had all grown up on the East Coast: Courtney outside Philadelphia, Hank in Boston, and Jeremy in northern Virginia.

'Oh, I'm not arguing that there aren't some small-minded yokels in the Lou,' Hank said, and I realized with self-consciousness that a black man married to a white woman probably didn't need to be reminded by me of how conservative a place St Louis could be. 'But—' Hank paused and mouthed, *Fuck 'em.* 'Seriously,' he said aloud.

'What about Courtney, though?' I said. 'She must have been appalled by Vi just now.'

'She hasn't seen it yet.' Hank checked his watch. 'She teaches until one-fifteen. But I'm sure she'll be okay being the yin to Vi's yang.'

You mean the rational to Vi's crazy, I thought, but even in my head it sounded too mean to say. Besides, I didn't believe Vi was crazy. I believed she sometimes seemed crazy, and that on a regular basis she exercised bad judgment, but I didn't believe she *was* crazy; I never had. 'Should we get going?' I said.

Amelia attended preschool in the morning three

days a week, at a place I was planning to put in an application for Rosie for the following fall, so on those days, we met up post-lunch and pre-nap. Our default plan was to walk first to Kaldi's, where Hank and I would get coffee and the girls would split a scone, and then to backtrack to the park – officially known as DeMun Park, though Hank had been greatly amused when Vi told us that everyone who'd ever worked in the row of restaurants along DeMun Avenue referred to it as MILF Park.

As we left the Wheelings' house, it occurred to me that I should call my father, to check if he'd watched the news, but after his comment that morning about Vi coming into her own, I couldn't bring myself to do it; in case he hadn't seen her, I wanted to give him a few more hours of not knowing.

Outside, Amelia and Rosie skipped in front of us, and Hank walked beside me as I pushed Owen in the stroller. Amelia slapped her palm against a lamppost, and when Rosie mimicked the gesture exactly, I thought, as I often did, that Amelia and Hank were like mentors to Rosie and me: Amelia was always beckoning Rosie toward the next developmental stage, while Hank was the person who'd most influenced me as a parent. It was from Hank that I'd learned to give Rosie her own spoon when I'd fed her jar food, so that she wasn't constantly grabbing the one I was using. Hank had told me to put Triple Paste on her when her diaper rash got bad ('Way more than you think you need, like you're spreading cream cheese on a bagel,' he'd said), and to buy a Britax car seat after she outgrew her infant seat, and to go to the Buder library for the best story hour. The way Hank was with Amelia – affectionate and relaxed, unconcerned with getting mud or food on his clothes – was the way I aspired to be with Rosie, and the way Hank answered the questions Amelia asked, which was succinctly but accurately (and definitely not cutely, not in a winking manner for the benefit of another adult), was the way I tried to answer Rosie's when she began asking them.

As we turned onto DeMun Avenue, I said, 'Courtney looked good on TV. How's she feeling?'

'Not too bad. She wants to get the results of her CVS, just for peace of mind, but she hasn't been nauseous for a while.'

Courtney was eleven weeks pregnant, expecting in April. When we'd gotten to know the Wheelings, they'd been in agreement that they were having only one child, and in fact, Rosie had been the beneficiary of Amelia's pricey hand-me-downs, which Courtney had told me with such certainty they'd never want back that I hadn't worried when Rosie ripped or stained them. And then, the summer after she got tenure, Courtney decided she wanted another child. Not only wasn't it difficult for her to persuade Hank, it was so easy that I suspected he'd have preferred two kids all along. Courtney was then thirty-seven, and when they hadn't conceived within six months, she began taking Clomid; after another six months, she decided to have IVF but hadn't yet started the first cycle when she discovered she was pregnant.

I'd had Owen during the time Courtney and Hank had been trying for a second baby, and I had never spoken to Courtney about their fertility troubles; Courtney herself still hadn't told me she was pregnant, and everything I knew had made its way to me via Hank. Courtney also hadn't broached the subject with Jeremy, though they were closer than Courtney and I were. Once it had seemed slightly strange to me that our friendships with the Wheelings broke down not along gender lines but along professional ones – like me, Hank was the stay-at-home parent – but these days I rarely thought about it.

'So this morning Amelia wakes up at five-fifteen,' Hank said. 'Not like wakes up crying in the night, but *wakes up* wakes up, in a great mood, wanting to eat breakfast. And she'd slept through the earthquake, but Courtney and I had been up then, too, so I was so tired I felt hungover. It was like all the downside of a hangover without any of the fun. I started thinking about getting up in the night with a newborn, and I seriously don't know if I have it in me again.'

I laughed. 'I think that train has left the station.'

'It's been a while for us,' Hank said. 'And we aren't spring chickens anymore.'

'Oh, please.' Hank and Courtney were only four

31

years older than I was, and they were in great shape. Every Wednesday afternoon and Saturday morning, they saw a trainer together, and they had met because they'd both played varsity squash as Harvard undergrads, a fact I was glad I hadn't known until my friendship with Hank was established – not the squash part, though it was a sport with which I was totally unfamiliar, but the Harvard part, which made Hank not quite the same breed of stay-at-home parent I was.

'Call me when you turn thirty-five,' Hank said. 'I swear something changes.'

'All right, geezer.'

'I will say this: Your son is an excellent advertisement for babykind.' Hank stepped around the stroller, so he was facing Owen, and started walking backward. 'We want to order one just as easygoing as you, O,' he said.

'Not to confirm your fears, but you know he's not sleeping through the night yet, right?' I said. 'He still nurses every three or four hours.'

'For real?' Hank looked incredulous. 'You've got to let him cry it out.' Hank was still walking backward in front of the stroller, and he said to Owen, 'You don't want your mom to get a good night's sleep, huh? Kate, you should see the shit-eating grin your son has on his face right now.'

I laughed, though beneath the levity of the moment, I felt a sudden uneasiness that wasn't related to our conversation. It was the realization I hadn't allowed myself to have earlier, choosing instead to be distracted by how disheveled Vi had looked on the local news: My sister had received a warning that something bad was going to happen. I wasn't yet entirely convinced that there would be another earthquake, though I wasn't convinced there wouldn't. Either way, she'd sensed something.

I said to Hank, 'Do you and Courtney keep emergency supplies?'

'Not a one. Do you guys?'

I shook my head.

'You planning to go buy a generator now?'

A generator, no, but maybe a crank radio, and definitely water and canned food. Aloud, as if the possibility amused me, I said, 'I might.'

'I have a confession,' Hank said, and I felt a kind of tingle, a nervous anticipation. I was both surprised and unsurprised when he said, 'I know how you feel about Vi's whole gig, but there's a part of me that believes in that stuff. ESP, psychic predictions – the world's a pretty weird and cool place, so why is it impossible?'

Again trying to sound lighthearted, I said, 'Don't let Courtney hear you say that.'

'Ehh—' He shrugged. 'She cuts me slack for being artsy.' Before Amelia's birth, Hank had worked as an art teacher at a private high school, and he made oil paintings, or at least he intended to even if he didn't have much time these days. The attic of their house, where I'd never been, was his studio. He added, 'My only point is that it's hubris to claim there aren't unexplained phenomena out there.'

Hank and I had been friends for just over two years, which wasn't that long, but we'd seen each other almost every day during this time, and there were ways in which he knew more about my daily life than Jeremy did. Yet every time Hank and I had headed in a direction that could have opened onto the topic of psychicness, of *my* psychicness – conversations about our families or our child- hoods or about secrets, even conversations once or twice about the paranormal – I'd always let the opportunity to tell him pass. I'd imagined that I'd immediately wish I could take the admission back. The last person I'd revealed the truth to was Jeremy, because I'd thought I owed it to him. But if I wasn't marrying Hank, was it unreasonable that I wanted to seem to him like a regular person? Growing up, from adolescence on, I had assumed that I couldn't live in St Louis as an adult because my past would always follow and define me. I'd been pleasantly surprised to discover that I might be wrong. To have settled in my hometown with a husband from elsewhere, to have friends from elsewhere – this was a version of life I hadn't been able to envision as a teenager. Why would I disrupt this fragile balance just for the sake of self-disclosure? Hank and I knew each other well; we didn't need to know each other completely.

And yet my withholding of information, which had previously felt only like discretion, abruptly seemed to be verging on dishonesty. We'd arrived at Kaldi's, and I pulled the brake on the stroller. Amelia, who was standing with Rosie by the café's front door, called, 'Daddy, can we have a raspberry scone?'

'Hang on, sweetheart,' Hank said.

'I'm sure Vi will be glad to have you in her corner,' I said.

'But does she have you?' Though Hank's tone was casual, he was looking at me so intently that I wondered what he suspected. Surely this was the moment to say, *Of course she does, because we're exactly the same.* Or we had been, until I'd deliberately destroyed my abilities.

Instead, like a coward, I said, 'Of course she does. She's my sister.'

CHAPTER 3

Vi and I were born in August 1975, less than a month before our parents' first wedding anniversary. At thirty-seven weeks, we were considered full-term, which was and still is unusual for twins, but the truly notable fact of our arrival was that our mother didn't know until the day of her delivery that there were two of us. Twenty-three years old and slim, she had gained seventy pounds during her pregnancy; by her second trimester, her hands and feet were so swollen every morning that the doctor told her to remove her wedding ring or risk needing to have it cut off.

Apart from her dramatic weight gain, our mother had experienced what she understood to be a normal pregnancy. It was at a routine appointment on a hot morning in mid-August that our mother's obstetrician ordered an X ray because he was considering revising her due date based on her size. (Sonograms existed then, but they were still uncommon.) During the X ray, the technician saw right away that there were two babies, announced the news to our mother, then pleaded with her to act surprised when the obstetrician told her. But she didn't have to act – she was stunned. How would she take care of twins? She had moved to St Louis a year and a half earlier from the tiny town of Risco, Missouri, and she knew no one who could help her. She'd grown apart from the girl she'd lived with before marrying our father, she was estranged from her family in Risco, and she no longer had co-workers.

The doctor, who didn't want our mother carrying twins beyond thirty-seven weeks, told her to call our father and have him pack a bag and meet them at the hospital. Once there, the doctor broke our mother's water – she said he used a hook that resembled a crochet needle, a detail that as children, Vi found fascinating and I was disturbed by. After several hours, the doctor decided that our mother's labor had progressed enough, and he had an anesthetist administer an epidural. As soon as it took effect, our mother realized only half her body was numb. She needed another dose, she told the nurse, but the nurse explained that the anesthesia just hadn't kicked in yet and our mother should wait. An hour passed, and our mother, with increasing desperation, told the nurse she still was numb on only one side of her body. After the doctor examined her, he said she was too close to delivering to receive additional medication. This meant that while the left side of her body remained desensitized and immobile, the right side was wild with pain; one arm and leg writhed as the other lay inert. She was trapped, and she also was alone; our father sat in the waiting room.

When Vi emerged, our mother felt as if she'd been turned inside out. A nurse whisked the baby away, and as the contractions continued, another nurse told our mother to keep pushing, which our mother thought she already was doing. I emerged eight minutes later and was similarly whisked away. Our mother had neither held nor even really seen us; she was hyperventilating, and though she soon stopped, she felt flattened, overwhelmed by what she had just been through. She lay motionless in the hospital bed and swore that she would never have another baby.

As for Vi and me, after our Apgar scores confirmed that we were healthy, we were weighed (Vi was six pounds, nine ounces and I was five pounds, eleven ounces), then cleaned, wrapped in blankets, deposited in bassinets, and taken to the nursery, where we were introduced to our father. Vi was asleep, he said, and I was awake, and he went about memorizing our faces. Vi had been named, but I hadn't. For the next five days, though the nurses and our father repeatedly inquired about our mother's preferences, she declined to answer. Having expected only one baby, she had planned on Violet for a girl and Victor for a boy. What about Violet and Victoria, our father suggested, but our mother shook her head. She had spoken very little since our birth; she did not breast-feed us. Violet and Margaret? (Margaret was the name of our father's mother.) Our mother shook her head again. Violet and Daisy? our father asked, and our mother shrugged. He took this as assent, and we became Violet Kimberly and Daisy Kathleen. Our mother later claimed that Kimberly and Kathleen had been maternity ward nurses, but our father denied it, saying the nurses had merely helped him select our middle names.

As little girls, Vi and I loved hearing about our arrival in spite of the fact that we didn't have a mother who concluded this narrative with lavish expressions of affection. In retrospect, I'm not sure why we were so enthralled by this story, aside from the fact that we possessed the guileless self-absorption of most children. But it took having babies myself for me to understand just how lacking, how depressing even, the story of our births was, with its absence of any hint of joy on our mother's part. She had looked forward to having one child, was my interpretation of events when I became an adult, but having two did not double her excitement; rather, it extinguished it. Our mother was neither a happy mother nor a happy person. It's impossible for me to know if she was unhappy before she had us, but I suspect she previously must have been able to enjoy herself at least a little or I doubt that my father would have married her. And not only married her but been so smitten that, as a thirty-nine-year-old bachelor, he'd proposed to her within three months of their meeting and left behind a life in

Nebraska to move to St Louis for this beautiful woman seventeen years his junior.

It also took having babies of my own for me to truly imagine what that experience in the hospital must have been like for my mother, how difficult: At twenty-three, she was almost a decade younger than I was when I delivered my first child; her husband wasn't in the delivery room to support her; and the combination of the ineffective epidural and the still surprising fact of there being two babies to push out must have been, in the clinical sense, traumatizing. And things did not improve much, particularly with regard to her isolation, when the hospital discharged the three of us.

That morning, our mother had changed, for the first time since our arrival five days earlier, from a hospital gown to a dress, and she was shocked when she looked in the mirror. Between giving birth and shedding the water weight that had made her swollen, she had lost at least thirty pounds; her legs were so skinny that she reminded herself of Minnie Mouse. And this, in a way, *was* the happy ending of our birth story, a happiness Vi and I surely intuited, and celebrated, even if it had little to do with either of us – that in spite of everything she'd been through, on the day she left the hospital, our mother once again looked pretty.

We lived in Kirkwood, Missouri, a suburb twelve miles southwest of the St Louis Arch. The blue shingled house on Gilbert Street that my parents had bought when they married was the one they stayed in until after I'd graduated from college, and for all that time my mother complained about it. She said that the house was drafty in the winter, that the street smelled of exhaust from trains on the nearby tracks, and that the neighbors were nosy and low-class. The real problem, however, wasn't the house; it was a simple and terrible fact that none of us ever discussed because we didn't need to, which was that our mother didn't like our father. In her crossed arms, the exhalations of her nostrils, the pinch of her lips, she showed us every day that she didn't enjoy his company, didn't find him interesting, and didn't respect him. Part of it seemed to be that she held him accountable for the disappointments life had dealt her, though it was always easier to see that she *was* disappointed than to understand exactly why. (Not that my father was alone in having let her down. Almost everyone my mother encountered fell into one of two categories: low-class or snobby. Only very occasionally would she bestow her most prized compliment, reserved for a rich person who had pleasantly surprised her: *He didn't put on airs,* she'd say. *He acted the same as you and me.*)

Our parents had met when our father, who lived in Omaha, traveled to St Louis on business – he was then a salesman for a commercial carpet manufacturer – and my mother was working at the front desk of the Clayton hotel where his employer put him up. He stayed in the hotel for two nights, and on the second, he invited her to go with him to a French restaurant. Our mother never suggested that he outright lied during these initial interactions, but she conveyed that he'd led her to believe he occupied a more senior position in the company than he did, and that he was more worldly than he turned out to be. (Of course, I thought later; he was trying to impress her.) Once a month for the next three months, my father returned to St Louis to woo my mother – she was living with a roommate on Wydown Boulevard, and he stayed at the hotel – and on these trips they attended a Cardinals game, strolled in the Missouri Botanical Garden, and toured the Anheuser-Busch Brewery, where my mother purchased a tiny beer stein for her charm bracelet, an accessory that in elementary school Vi and I would fight to try on. On his third visit, my father arranged a ride in a hot-air balloon, an outing that so frightened my mother that they asked the pilot to land after just a few minutes. Back on earth, my father proposed, and my mother accepted. In Omaha, my father gave notice to his boss, moved to St Louis, found a job as a salesman for a lighting fixture company, and married my mother in the late morning of September 5, 1974, at the St Louis County Courts Building on Carondelet Avenue in Clayton. She wore a sleeveless twill dress with a pattern of interlocking green and black hexagons, and he wore a carnation boutonnière; they went out for a steak lunch afterward, and then they both returned to work.

Why did my mother make things unnecessarily hard? That's the main question I ask myself in retrospect. Our lives weren't glamorous, but they weren't so bad; they were ordinary, and there are many worse ways to be. Though looking back, I see my father's complicity, too. If I were to fault him for falling for my mother, I'd be wishing away my own existence. But I was fairly sure he proposed to my mother, perhaps without really knowing her, for a foolish if time-honored reason, which was that she was beautiful. In photographs from around the time they married, her straight blond hair is parted in the center and falls past her shoulders; her lips are thin but flirtatiously upturned; her cheekbones are high, her eyes big and blue, her lashes accentuated with mascara. She was five-five, the same height Vi and I eventually grew to, but outside of pregnancy, I don't think she ever weighed more than a hundred and ten pounds. She favored snug blouses, dresses that cinched at her small waist, jumpsuits with flared pants. In a photo Vi and I especially liked, our mother stands in front of the Arch holding our father's hand. She wears a belted orange wool jacket with an oversized collar and a matching orange beret; he has dark sideburns. Both of our parents are beaming.

That my mother turned out to be difficult as well as beautiful was likely a result of her upbringing. In Risco, she had grown up poor on a small farm, the third daughter in an extremely religious Baptist family, and after graduating from high school, she'd remained at home and gotten a job at a newly opened rice-processing facility twenty minutes away. For three years, she secretly saved money, and as soon as she could afford to, she and her friend Jeanine bought bus tickets to St Louis; my mother carried with her a single suitcase containing her clothes, toothbrush, and Christmas records. Although St Louis was just three hours north of Risco, neither of them had ever been, and most of what they knew, or thought they knew, about the city was that they shouldn't go north of the Delmar Loop because that was where the black people lived.

Given that both the civil rights and the women's rights movements seemed to have entirely bypassed my parents, I never understood why it was my father who joined my mother in St Louis rather than my mother moving to Omaha; perhaps this decision reflected the more invested party in the relationship. My mother quit her job the day after they married, and they soon bought the house that would evolve from a source of pride to one of disappointment.

I was four years old the night I woke up screaming. Vi and I shared a room, and by the time our mother came to me, Vi was sitting up in her bed. In a dream, I had seen a house on fire, flames soaring and billowing from all the windows; the house was orange with light and terrifyingly alive.

Even after our mother's arrival, I remained inconsolable. There was an impatience to the way our mother dealt with Vi and me that was surprisingly effective, implying as it did that whatever had upset us wasn't important. But in this case, anything she could have said, any tone she used – it wouldn't have mattered, because the house would still have been consumed by fire. I am sorry to say I remember this feeling well not only because the image of the house was so vivid but also because that dread has returned regularly throughout my life, almost always when I awaken during the night: an anxious kind of certainty, an awareness of the world's menaces that feels like a recognition of the truth, and an awareness of my own vulnerability – of everyone's vulnerability.

As I continued shrieking, my father joined us, and I heard my mother tell him I'd had a nightmare. He sat on Vi's bed; light from the hallway cut into our room. My mother, who had taken several minutes to decipher what I was trying to tell her, kept saying, 'But if there was a fire, we'd smell smoke.'

'Should we sing a song?' my father asked. He began to hum, then to sing the words to 'I See the Moon,' and Vi joined him. Our vulnerability continued to clutch at me; hearing their voices, it clutched at me in a different way. How could our parents protect Vi and me from anything? For the first time, I realized that there was no guarantee that they could protect themselves. But then, as my father and Vi sang, the familiarity of the lyrics was comforting. My mother pulled my covers up before she left, and my father stayed in the room; he continued singing until Vi and I were both asleep.

The next night, a house halfway down our block burned to the ground. My parents, Vi, and I were awakened by the sirens, and the flashing lights from the fire trucks and the police cars reflected on our walls. Though our parents didn't let us go outside, our father went to confer with neighbors. Vi and I couldn't see the fire because the house was on the same side of the street as ours, but I already knew what it looked like. The people who lived in the house were an older couple.

A few months later, we were eating a family dinner when Vi said, 'Why does Aunt Erma's heart hurt?' She asked this in a neutral tone rather than a distressed one, but our parents exchanged an alarmed look. Aunt Erma was actually our great-aunt, our paternal grandmother's sister, and lived in Grand Island, Nebraska; we had met her perhaps three times in our lives.

'What do you mean, Vi?' my father asked.

'She fell down,' Vi said without emotion, and took another bite of pork roast.

That time, more than a week passed before my father's mother called on a Sunday morning to say that her sister had died of a heart attack. I didn't overhear my father on the phone, but he repeated the information to our mother when he came into the kitchen. Vi and I were playing Candy Land at the table while our mother washed the breakfast dishes.

It was Vi's turn, and I was watching our father as he said, 'It's not just Daisy then. It's Violet who has the senses, too.'

Our mother's expression when she turned to look at our father was sour. She was wearing yellow rubber gloves, cleaning a pan in which she'd cooked bacon, and she didn't turn off the faucet. She said, 'What do you suggest I do about it?'

CHAPTER 4

Owen woke up from his afternoon nap before Rosie, and I nursed him sitting on our living room couch. As I burped him afterward, the phone rang, and I knew without seeing the caller ID panel that it was Vi.

I set Owen on the floor with a little wooden car – he was just beginning to sit on his own – and when I answered, Vi said, 'Courtney Wheeling is finally preggers, isn't she? Which is a miracle because she's so fucking skinny I can't even believe she was getting her period.' This was generally the way it went when my sister and I fought. After a day or two, I'd call her and say, 'I never realized until right now that coriander and cilantro are the same thing. Did you?' or she'd call me and say, 'I'm looking out my window and there's a totally perfect cobweb in the railing on my front steps. It's like the platonic ideal of a cobweb.' Neither of us would formally apologize.

'Hank and Courtney haven't told people yet, so don't bring it up with them. She's only eleven weeks along.' I hesitated before adding, 'Do you really think there'll be a huge earthquake?'

'No, but you know how I love attention. Yes, Daze,

I do. I mean, sorry.' She sounded more serious. 'But that's what came through, loud and clear.'

'And how soon is soon? Tomorrow? Six months from now?'

She exhaled. 'That part I'm not sure of.'

'But you're confident it's an earthquake and not something else, like a tornado? Or, I don't know, a building being imploded?'

'No, it's an earthquake. Especially after the one last night – it all feels connected. Anyway, I didn't have a visualization. I just got the message.'

I could tell that we were perilously close to her mentioning the spiritual guide she believed was the source of such messages, whom she called Guardian. Vi usually didn't bring up Guardian around me because she knew the topic made me uncomfortable, but surely if I was the one peppering Vi with questions, he was fair game.

I said, 'If you get a sense about a specific date, will you tell me? Just with the kids, you know, I'd rather be prepared—'

'Of course.' Not only did Vi not gloat over her power, but she sounded kind, protective even, as if she'd never have considered anything else. Then she said, 'Was it just me or did Courtney come off as completely uptight?' Adopting a British accent that sounded like neither Courtney nor an actual British person, Vi said, '"Let me tell you about the statistics that my extensive research has uncovered. Did I mention I have two degrees from *Haaarvard?* And that I hate fat people?"'

'How did you end up getting interviewed?' I asked. 'Did you call the station?'

'I thought maybe they'd blow me off, but I was put right through to the producer. I probably should have brushed my hair this morning, huh?' Vi laughed. 'But it all happened so quickly. One minute I was on the phone with the producer, and the next they had that girl standing in front of my house with a microphone. Did you notice her double D's, by the way? I'm surprised those things fit inside the newsmobile.'

'Have you talked to Dad?'

'Not yet, so I assume he didn't see it. Although doesn't he usually watch Channel 5?'

That she hadn't heard from him didn't, in my opinion, mean he hadn't seen it. 'Wait,' I said. 'Shouldn't Dad be there to take you on your date?'

'Not till three.'

'Vi, what time do you think it is now?' My own watch said two fifty-two. 'Have you taken a shower?'

'Shit, I didn't realize how late it'd gotten.'

'Hold on,' I said quickly, and I heard Vi on the other end of the phone, pausing. 'Wear your dark jeans and your black beaded V-neck shirt,' I said. 'And those patent leather flats. Don't wear Birkenstocks.'

After we'd gotten Owen and Rosie down to sleep, Jeremy and I made a stir-fry for dinner; because we'd become accustomed to eating at five forty-five, dinner at eight o'clock felt almost European.

I poured sesame oil into a pan and used a knife to sweep onion pieces from the cutting board into the oil as Jeremy removed two beers from the refrigerator. He opened them both and passed a bottle to me – while nursing, I allowed myself one cup of coffee during the day and one beer per night – and he tapped his bottle against mine. 'Cheers,' he said. 'We survived another day.'

Thinking of Vi on television, I said, 'Barely.' But it was nice to be in our bright kitchen together, nice to have Jeremy home from work and Rosie and Owen asleep, and I added, 'No, you're right.' I knew he'd watched the Channel 5 news segment online at his office, and I said, 'So what'd you think of Vi and Courtney?'

'Your description was accurate. Probably not the finest hour for either of them.'

'Are you embarrassed to be married to me?' I'd thought I was making a joke, but aloud it didn't sound like one.

'Of course not.' Jeremy leaned in and kissed my forehead. 'I know you think Courtney came off well, but she was fuming because they edited her to look like she believes the New Madrid Seismic Zone is an active threat, and she doesn't. She thinks it's basically dead. Besides the fact that the New Madrid isn't even where last night's earthquake was – it was in the Wabash Valley.'

'Do you think Courtney will tell other people in your department that the psychic weirdo is your sister-in-law?'

'No, but who cares if she does? It was a three-minute piece in the middle of the day on the local news, and no offense to Vi or Courtney, but who even watches that?' He reached out and took a slice of bell pepper. Then, because for him the topic was finished, he said, 'How was Vi's date?'

I rolled my eyes. 'I haven't heard yet.'

'Let's say for the sake of argument that you're right. She's in no way attracted to women and is just dating them because it's easier for her to find a girlfriend than a boyfriend. Here's my question for you: So what?'

I was quiet for a few seconds – Jeremy had a point – then, rather lamely, I said, 'I just think it'd be confusing to our dad. For someone from his generation, if she says, "I'm dating a woman. Oh, no, I'm not" – that's a big deal. It's kind of unfair to make him accept that and then to change her mind again.'

Jeremy took a sip of beer, watching me, and said, 'Unfair to him or to you?' I didn't answer and he said, 'Even if your identical twin turns out to be a lesbian, it doesn't mean you're secretly one, too.' He smiled. 'Let's hope. So I got asked to give a talk at Cornell.'

'When?' Quickly, I added, 'That's great.' It wasn't at all great logistically – Jeremy hadn't been out of town since Owen's birth, and the idea of it didn't thrill me – but because Cornell was where Jeremy had earned his PhD, I knew he'd be pleased by the invitation.

'Lukovich said this semester, and I might as well

go sooner rather than later and avoid getting stuck in a snowstorm.' George Lukovich, head of Cornell's Department of Earth and Atmospheric Sciences, had been Jeremy's adviser, and he and his wife had attended our wedding.

I added the pepper to the pan of onions, along with broccoli Jeremy had already chopped, then wiped my hands on a paper towel. 'You couldn't do it in the spring? Or at least wait until November?'

'You don't mean because of Vi's prediction, do you?'

'She did say the earthquake would be soon.'

We looked at each other, and neither of us spoke. Then Jeremy said, 'You remember that my AEPS conference is in October, right?'

It wasn't just that I hadn't remembered that the conference was in October; after five years of being married to Jeremy, I still couldn't even remember what AEPS stood for. 'When is it again?' I asked.

Jeremy walked to the calendar on the wall and lifted the month of September; in the grid for October, he had indeed made note of his conference. I squinted to see that it was in Denver and would run from Thursday, October 15, to Sunday, October 18.

'And you're presenting?' I said.

'On Sunday morning, when everyone is hungover, probably to a crowd in the single digits.'

'So it's a really worthwhile use of your time, and I'm sure it'll be a piece of cake to take care of Owen and Rosie by myself. It's a win-win.'

'Sweetheart . . .' Jeremy paused, and I could tell that he was proceeding carefully. 'The fact that Vi predicted another earthquake – it *could* happen. Of course it could. And I could be run over in the Schnucks parking lot this weekend.'

'That's reassuring. Thanks.'

'Or I could buy a lottery ticket and win a million dollars. But we have to live our lives with the information available to us. We can't make decisions based on remote possibilities.'

'What makes you so sure Vi's prediction *is* remote?' I said. 'She isn't usually wrong.'

Jeremy swallowed, and I knew he was trying to seem respectful, not sarcastic, as he said, 'Is it her spirit guide who told her there'd be an earthquake?'

'I didn't get into that with her, but I assume so.'

'And you believe her? You believe that this ghost or whatever told Vi about an upcoming geological event, and therefore it's true?'

To be asked to defend a situation that I more than anyone wished weren't part of my life – it felt not quite fair. Furthermore, in acting as if Vi's psychicness was unconnected to me, weren't we failing to acknowledge certain facts? I said, 'So you feel like you can completely dismiss her premonition?'

Jeremy was still standing by the calendar and I was at the stove and because he was short for a man, just two inches taller than I was, and I had on clogs, we were the same height as we faced each other. While the silence between us grew, I had the troubling thought that maybe I'd married him because he didn't entirely believe in something about myself that I hated; that maybe he'd married me because he wasn't worried about, wasn't deterred by, what he didn't entirely believe in; and that both of us had mistaken our marriage for consensus. But compatibility and agreement, it struck me suddenly, were not the same.

I said, 'I'm not claiming that she's definitely right. But if the weatherman says there'll be rain, why not take an umbrella? And if he's wrong, better safe than sorry.'

'But what's the umbrella in this scenario? Saying no to Cornell? Canceling my plans for AEPS?' Jeremy was still calm, as if the idea that we were having a disagreement hadn't occurred to him.

'What if you go to the conference but postpone Cornell?' I forced a smile. 'And then neither of us gets our way and we can both feel resentful.'

He smiled, too. 'Has anyone ever told you that you're a world-class negotiator?'

'Lukovich isn't trying to recruit you, is he?' I said. It was well-established between us that I didn't want to leave St Louis as long as my father was alive.

'They do have a job opening this year, but Lukovich knows where we stand on moving. This would just be a colloquium, not a job talk.'

'Will they pay you?'

'Let me put it this way: Yes, but it probably won't be enough to cover a trip to Target.'

After a minute, I said, 'If Vi's right, then I guess her prediction's not embarrassing, but I'd rather be embarrassed and safe.'

'I know you would,' Jeremy said.

As we were cleaning up after dinner, there was a knock on the back door – this wasn't the one we, or anyone else, usually used – and when I looked over, Courtney Wheeling was making a blowfish face against the windowpane. I opened the door, and she said, 'I saw the light on back here. Late-night dining, huh?'

'Come on in,' I said, though I wasn't entirely sure why she was at our house. We hung out with the Wheelings all the time, but we generally called or texted each other first. In spite of the fact that Courtney was wearing shorts, running shoes, a T-shirt, and an unzipped hooded sweatshirt, the force of her personality – her intelligence and confidence and will – emanated from her. Although Courtney was pretty, her prettiness was never the main thing I noticed about her. Her hair was blond, like mine, but very short – she'd once told me she got it cut every three weeks – and even in her haircut her confidence was obvious; the same was true of her glasses, which had aggressively nerdy thick black frames. I liked Courtney, and I was impressed by her, but I didn't always find myself able to relax in her presence.

'I'm sure you're feeling weird about the Channel 5 thing today, but you shouldn't,' she said. 'That's what I came over to say. It's not your fault if you have a wackadoodle sister.'

Was I supposed to thank her? I glanced at Jeremy, who was wringing out the sponge, and his expression was impassive. I said, 'What a weird coincidence, huh?'

'That poor newscaster wouldn't know seismic energy if it bit her in the ass,' Courtney said. 'Which tends to be the norm with the media. Did Jeremy tell you he got invited to give a talk at Cornell?'

'I did indeed,' Jeremy said.

Courtney took a seat at our kitchen table. 'Cool, right?' she said to me. Then, to Jeremy: 'Did you read Leland's email yet?'

'I skimmed it,' Jeremy said. We made eye contact, and he said, 'Nothing interesting. Department politics.'

'So Amelia is agitating to eat meat,' Courtney said. 'Which I knew would happen eventually, but I didn't think it'd be this soon.' Both Courtney and Hank were vegetarians.

'I was wondering about that,' I said. 'At the park today, she was pretending to cook ham.'

Courtney wrinkled her nose. 'Gross.' As if I were a pig farmer, she added, 'No offense.'

'None taken,' I said.

She said, 'There's just something extra-revolting about ham. It's so fleshy. But we've always said if Amelia wanted to try meat, we'd let her, so I'm thinking we should all go out for dinner and you carnivores can show her how it's done.'

Jeremy looked amused. 'I'm guessing if she's got molars, she's good to go.'

'Okay, then you can provide moral support to her parents.'

'You mean molar support?' Jeremy said, and Courtney and I rolled our eyes at each other.

Courtney said, 'Kate, did you hear that Justin Timberlake and Rihanna are hooking up?'

'I saw that online, but I'm not sure I believe it.'

'I want it to be true. They'd make beautiful babies.' Early in our friendship, I had wondered if I should feel patronized by Courtney's tendency to bring up celebrity gossip with me, but I had soon realized that her interest in the topic was unabashedly sincere; in fact, her knowledge far eclipsed mine, though I still wasn't sure when she had time to study up. Courtney stood then. 'I'm thinking Saturday for meat night. You guys free then?'

Jeremy and I looked at each other, and I said, 'I'm pretty sure.'

'You can tell Hank tomorrow,' Courtney said to me. 'And we're cool on the whole TV news showdown? No hard feelings?' When I nodded, she said, 'Tell your sister nice prayer flags.'

When Courtney had left, I let a minute pass, which probably was long enough for her to be halfway home, before saying, 'I kind of feel like she was trying to trick me into being on her side.'

Jeremy shook his head. 'Courtney's just being Courtney.'

We both were quiet, and I said, 'I can understand

her being bummed out about Amelia wanting to try meat.'

'Why? Meat's delicious.' Jeremy was grinning.

'But doesn't it make it seem like all our children are growing up so quickly?'

'Am I allowed to remind you of that when Owen wakes up at two in the morning?' Then he said, 'What if you go do your thing in the living room and I bring out some ice cream for us? Will that make you feel better?'

What Jeremy meant by doing my thing was that every night after the children were asleep, I took a few minutes to set the diaper bag by the front door, checking that inside it were not only diapers and extra clothes but my wallet with my health insurance card; I also charged my cellphone in the closest outlet.

'I'm leaning toward a chocolate-pistachio blend tonight,' Jeremy said, and I thought, as I did at least once a day, how lucky I was that he was my husband; it hadn't been a foregone conclusion that I'd marry someone kind, because I hadn't understood how much it mattered.

I said, 'You really think I'm a person of simple wants, don't you?'

Jeremy grinned again. 'Isn't that why you settled for me?'

CHAPTER 5

In April 1989, the spring Vi and I were in eighth grade, I got invited to a slumber party at Marisa Mazarelli's house and Vi didn't. While I wish I could say that I considered declining out of sisterly loyalty, the truth is that when Marisa called our house, I raced to ask my mother, and when she granted permission, I accepted with an excitement that I tried to conceal more from Marisa than from Vi. I was surprised and flattered to have made it onto Marisa's guest list – Marisa of the long, dark, curly hair, Marisa of the large, newly constructed house with a hot tub, Marisa of the scary power over most of the girls at Nipher Middle School. Marisa was the daughter of the owner of an eponymous pizza chain in eastern Missouri and western Illinois. She had started wearing lip gloss in fifth grade. And at a dance the previous fall, she had, during the last song of the night – Poison's 'Every Rose Has Its Thorn' – brazenly made out on the dance floor with a boy named Chip Simmons. I'd already heard about the Mazarellis' hot tub, even though I'd never been to Marisa's house, and when she told me over the phone to bring a bathing suit to the party, I felt the thrill of confirmation.

It wasn't until a few hours after Marisa's call, when Vi and I were getting ready for bed, that the first wave of uneasiness struck me. We had just emerged from the bathroom and were headed toward the bedroom we shared. (The third bedroom in our house was kept as a guest room, its double bed pristinely covered by a white spread with cream-colored satin borders, unslept in and unsullied by actual guests from one year to the next.) Our room, which was usually a mess, had a sign on the door that Vi had posted when we were in fourth grade and neither of us had taken down since:

SISTERLAND

POPULATION 2

DO NOT ENTER WITHOUT PERMISSION!

'I could ask Marisa to invite you, too,' I said.

'I saw her cheating on the math quiz yesterday,' Vi said. 'She was copying off Dave Stutz, and he didn't even know it.'

I said nothing, and Vi added, 'Marisa is a rich bitch.'

Coming on top of the cheating comment, this was too much. 'It's not my fault if you're jealous,' I said.

If asked during elementary and middle school, I would never have claimed that Vi was my best friend. I might not even have said I liked her that much.

For one thing, I was unsentimental as a child, and for another, I had no frame of comparison. Did I like living in Missouri? Did I enjoy having ears?

In any twenty-four-hour period, it would not have been uncommon for us to be apart only during a few classes at school. Otherwise, we were almost always in the same room, side by side on chairs in the school cafeteria or at our kitchen table, watching television in the living room with our heads on the cushion we'd moved from the couch to the floor, taking turns hanging upside down from the mulberry tree in our yard, the backs of our knees hooked on the lowest branch and our shirts flying over our faces. We participated in no organized sports or other extracurricular activities – our mother's general suspicion of the world extended to doubts about the value, financial or otherwise, of music or dance lessons – and we were often unsupervised.

We made up many of the games we played. One that irritated our mother involved, in its entirety, lying with our heads on opposite arms of the living room couch, the soles of our feet meeting up in the middle, and pumping our legs back and forth as if riding a bicycle while singing, over and over and over, 'There's a place in France / Where the naked ladies dance / And the men don't care / 'Cause they wear their underwear.'

Around fifth grade, Vi and I invented Commercial, which we played only outdoors, in the backyard, and which entailed assigning each other imaginary

62

products that we then pretended to advertise; for the most part, these products were related to sex or farting. (Vi once made me come up with a commercial for what she called a vagina wig, and it was one of the great shocks of my life, years later, to learn in a college history course of the existence of merkins; I almost stood up in the middle of the professor's lecture and walked out to call my sister.) Vi and I also played Person, which was the name we gave to a game much like Twenty Questions, except without the questions: One of us would think of either a celebrity or someone we knew – our music teacher, Mrs Kebach, for instance – and the other of us would get three guesses to figure out who it was, though we usually got it on the first or second try. Our mother disliked this game even more than she disliked our singing, 'There's a place in France.' The first time she ever heard us playing, when Vi and I were in the backseat while she drove us home from the dentist's office, she turned around and said, 'Stop it! Stop it right now! That's a bad game!' We still did play, but not in front of her.

None of us attended church, and my mother, despite her own upbringing, didn't seem to be religious, but she was superstitious; if we spilled salt, she made us throw some over our left shoulders, and if the sun came out while it was raining, she'd say it meant the devil was getting married. My mother's one great happiness was her Christmas records, the ones she'd brought up on the bus from Risco: Perry Como singing 'O Holy Night,' Bing Crosby and Nat King Cole and Frank Sinatra. We listened to them from mid-November to mid-January.

On the weekends, our father would drive Vi and me to P.S. Video on Jefferson Avenue, where we each got to select one movie to rent. We could spend easily half an hour considering our options, picking up and returning various empty cardboard cases to the shelves – the actual cassettes were stored behind the cash register – and there are movies from this time period that I never saw but still feel a kinship for just from holding their cases in my hands: *Good Morning, Vietnam* and *Mannequin* and *Rumble Fish.* Often, the movies we picked were ones we'd already seen: *The Secret of My Success,* which featured a young and handsome Michael J. Fox, or *Class,* which featured a young Rob Lowe, who was so far beyond handsome, so perfect in every possible way, that it hurt to watch him. In a scene in which he bit into an apple, the juice clung to his lips in a way Vi and I found devastatingly sexy; we'd rewind the video several times per viewing just to torment ourselves.

During the week, after school, Vi and I watched vast quantities of television. By middle school, our two favorite shows were *Divorce Court* and the soap opera *Santa Barbara,* both of which we viewed while eating either Cool Ranch Doritos, Wonder bread toast topped with butter and cinnamon sugar, or tiny pieces of American cheese melted in the micro-wave onto Triscuits. We shared a radio-cassette player on which we listened to Y98, and there were certain songs we'd become obsessed with – 'Take My Breath Away' and 'Walk Like an Egyptian' – and try to tape, though we rarely succeeded in pressing the Record button until several seconds into the songs. Soon after getting our ears pierced in sixth grade, we began pleading to get our right ears double-pierced, which our parents let us do as a twelfth-birthday present just before the start of seventh grade, and around this time, Vi also wanted an asymmetrical haircut – it would be chin-length on the left side of her face but cropped above her ear on the right – which our mother said she was allowed to do only if she lost ten pounds. Toward this end, Vi intermittently did sit-ups in front of the television, which I'd join her for because it felt more festive that way, though what's notable to me about the bargain in retrospect, when I look at old photos, is that Vi wasn't heavy then. She weighed ten pounds more than I did, but I was skinny.

It was also in seventh grade that one night at dinner, Vi said, 'Want to hear a clean joke? Bob took a bath with bubbles. Want to hear a dirty joke?' Without waiting for anyone to respond, she said, 'Bubbles was the lady next door.' There was a long silence, and then my mother leaned forward and slapped Vi's face.

'That didn't hurt,' Vi said, and my mother said, 'Go to your room, you spoiled brat.'

I got up with Vi, and neither of our parents objected.

In late October, Vi gave herself an asymmetrical haircut, and the first thing I thought when I saw her was that our mother would forbid her to attend the Halloween dance and I'd have to go alone, but Vi wasn't punished. Instead, my mother just pursed her lips before saying, almost with pleasure, 'No boy will want to dance with you like that.'

Vi and I had only one real friend, a girl named Janie Spriggs, who lived a block away and regularly joined us to play Commercial; in turn, Vi and I would go to Janie's house to ride her mother's stationary bike and try on her mother's fur coat, sometimes doing both simultaneously. Janie had an older brother named Pete who had Down's syndrome – Vi and I referred to him as retarded, as did our parents – and every time he saw us, by way of greeting, Pete would say in a singsong, 'You're twins because there's two of you.' Interestingly, though, Pete could always tell us apart, long before the asymmetrical haircut and the weight difference, back when many of our teachers and the other students couldn't.

Vi and I were included in classmates' parties only when everyone was invited, but I didn't feel the sting of rejection; after all, I wasn't staying home alone. I think our classmates considered us a benign oddity. Twins weren't nearly as common then as now – this was prior to widespread fertility treatments – yet we'd been going to school with many of the same people since kindergarten, which meant that we were both familiar and strange. Until

Marisa, we also were viewed, I'm pretty sure, as a package deal; if another girl were to have one of us over, she'd have to have both of us, and we weren't beloved enough to be worth two guest slots.

But it wasn't as if we invited anyone to our house besides Janie. Our birthday usually fell during the week in August when we drove to visit our father's relatives in Omaha, so we had cake there and never held a celebration back at home. When Vi and I were younger, I suppose it was our mother who didn't initiate social activities on our behalf, and when we were older, we didn't initiate them because we had realized, without ever speaking of it, that we were colluding to conceal a certain fact about our family. This was not the fact of our 'having senses,' as Vi and I called it from a young age. Rather, it was that, from the time we arrived home after school until a few minutes before our father arrived home after work almost three hours later, our mother remained in bed with the door closed, the shades drawn, and the lights off. Vi and I referred to what our mother did in our parents' darkened bedroom as napping, though we understood that she wasn't asleep – often the TV was on, sometimes set to the same program Vi and I were watching in the living room – and in rare instances, we'd knock on the door to ask her a question.

The first time we came home from school to find our mother in bed, Vi and I were eleven, and this turn of events made us decidedly nervous; we inquired as to whether she was sick and when she ignored the question, we heated a can of chicken noodle soup and carried the steaming bowl into her room on a tray. Our father returned every evening from work at five forty-five, and that evening, when it got to be five o'clock and our mother showed no sign of emerging, we took matters into our own hands. Using a recipe from one of the index cards our mother kept in a white tin box on top of the refrigerator – she herself had copied the recipe by hand from the *Post-Dispatch* in 1977 and made it frequently – we prepared broiled chicken breasts, as well as buttered rice and an iceberg salad with Kraft ranch dressing. Optimistically, we set the kitchen table with four places but were surprised when, at five-thirty, our mother appeared before us, fully dressed, seeming like an only slightly more pre-occupied version of her usual self. 'Oh,' she said when she saw that dinner was almost ready. 'Well, good.' When our father arrived home, we ate as if it were a normal night. At the end of the meal, he wiped his mouth with a napkin and said, 'That was good, Rita.' This was what he said at the end of every dinner, and none of us corrected him.

Astonishingly, this pattern continued every week-night for the next six years, until we left for college, by which point we'd long ago forgotten how odd it was that our mother spent each afternoon in bed and that Vi and I pretended – to ourselves, I think, as much as to our father – that she'd cooked dinner when she hadn't. Vi and I rotated among three dishes: the broiled chicken breasts of the first night, creamed chicken breasts, and orange juice pork chops. These other two recipes were also ones that had been our mother's staples and were located in her tin box. Our sides were always – and I truly mean always, 100 percent of the time – the iceberg salad with ranch dressing and either the rice or baked potatoes. On Friday nights, we ordered pizza; on Saturday nights, our father grilled steak; and on Sundays, our father took us without our mother – ironically enough, so that she could rest – to either Hacienda for Mexican food or King Doh for pot stickers and General Tso's chicken. (Our mother didn't care for what she referred to as un-American food.) At some point when Vi and I were at school, usually on Monday or Tuesday, our mother went to the grocery store, an act that, in retrospect, seems to me to deepen her complicity in the unspoken pact to deceive our father. In high school, after Vi joined the tech crew for school plays our freshman year, I'd cook dinner alone for weeks at a time while she was at rehearsal.

Once, shortly after Jeremy and I moved in together, I decided to make him the orange juice pork chops. As they baked, I opened the oven door, and the hot, meaty, orangey smell assaulted me, the smell of my adolescence, of my parents' house, of my mother's depression that we never called depression. I wanted to turn off the heat and dump the chops in the trash, but to do so would have been melodramatic. Instead, I let them finish cooking and served them on beige plates.

When Jeremy and I were seated at the high little table we used before we had children, I cut a small piece with my knife and fork, speared it, put it in my mouth, and began to cry. 'Sweetheart?' he said. It took me a while to explain, and after I had, he picked up both our plates and set them in the sink, saying, 'We'll never eat pork chops again.'

'It's not all pork chops,' I said. 'Just this recipe.'

'Life's too short.' He reached into the pocket of his pants and jingled his keys. 'Come on,' he said. 'Let's go get sushi.'

Surprising as the invitation to Marisa Mazarelli's slumber party was, I did understand its genesis, and that genesis was fraudulent. Two weeks earlier, in a performance conceived of, choreographed, and directed by Vi, she and I had lip-synched and danced to Billy Joel's 'You May Be Right' in the Nipher Middle School talent show. Because I had so little to do with the act's creation, I feel that I can say without bragging that we brought down the house. The song started with the sound of glass breaking, then the ramping up of the electric guitar, then Billy, as Vi and I called him, singing in his bravado-filled way about crashing a party. Per Vi's vision, she was dressed as a fifties greaser, in penny loafers and white socks, jeans rolled at the cuff, and a white T-shirt; her hair was slicked back, and she wore mirrored aviator sunglasses. I, meanwhile, was supposed to channel Marilyn-Monroe-over-the-grate, except that instead of relying on a subway, I was responsible for swishing my own skirt; I wore a white halter dress of our mother's from the seventies, and fake-leather white high heels, also our mother's, with socks stuffed in the toes, and I'd applied heavy makeup and used a curling iron to create ringlets. The real coup of our performance was that Vi had convinced our science teacher, Mr Dummerston, to let us use his motorcycle as a prop; he himself was waiting in the wings with us before we went onstage so he could help wheel it out, and as soon as the lights went up and the students saw the motorcycle – he was the only teacher who drove one, and it was immediately recognizable because of its yellow frame – they began to scream. Then there was that thrilling sound of breaking glass and Vi strutting around the stage, fearlessly inhabiting her greaser persona: getting down on her knees and gesticulating forcefully with her arms, pleading with me to give her a chance; being wounded by my rejection, stalking away, then returning to plead some more. All I had to do was dance in place, shake my head dismissively, wag my index finger, and bat my eyelashes like I was conceited, which, of course, the more I could feel the enthusiasm of our audience, the more I really was. Every time the chorus came on Vi and I would seek each other out and dance together, waving our arms, nodding our heads from side to side, linking hands and stepping forward then backward, in exactly the way we'd practiced night after night for the last two months.

A feedback loop occurred wherein I was aware

of the audience's perception of us shifting from *I never really noticed the Shramms before* to *They sure look like they're having fun* to *Oh, I wish I were a twin!* And it was true – we *were* having fun, being a twin *was* a great thing – and having an audience for the greatness only made it truer. To receive adulation just for being ourselves, albeit our costumed and choreographed selves, was both disorienting and miraculous.

When the song was over, we got the only standing ovation of the night. The next person to go on was a seventh-grade boy performing a magic act, and a minute in, as he was fumbling with playing cards, a good-looking soccer player named Jason Trachsel yelled, 'Bring back the twins!'

After the talent show's conclusion, there were cookies and juice and mayhem as the teachers chaperoning tried to get the students to fold chairs before all the kids dispersed to their own or one another's houses. Vi and I were going home; our father would be waiting outside in his Buick to pick us up. I'd put on a sweatshirt over my mother's halter dress but was still wearing my heavy makeup, which made me feel glamorous as Vi and I were mobbed by classmates and even teachers wanting to congratulate us. And the fraudulence first dawned on me as I accepted these congratulations: It wasn't just that Vi and I got equal credit for a performance that had been in almost every way her idea. Rather, I received more credit for the sole reason that I had played the girl and she'd played the guy.

Marisa Mazarelli, whom I hardly ever talked to, shoved aside two seventh-grade girls who'd approached to examine my curled hair and high heels. 'That was awesome,' she said.

I smiled. 'Thanks.'

She gestured toward Vi, who was standing a few feet away talking to Janie Spriggs, and said, 'I never realized before tonight that you're the pretty twin.'

There were, I see now, insults for both Vi and me embedded in this comment, but I was so caught off guard that all I could say, in genuine confusion, was 'But we're identical.'

Marisa shook her head. 'Barely.' Twelve days later, she called to invite me to her birthday party.

As I discovered, a hot tub was the least of the Mazarelli family's treasures. A vast, lushly carpeted basement rec room also contained an enormous television set opposite a three-sided brown leather sectional sofa, ping-pong and pool tables, a player piano, a jukebox, a pinball machine, a gumball machine, and a dartboard whose bull's-eye was the tomato icon of Mazarelli's Pizza. Fourteen guests including me were in attendance, and the slumber party started with a pre-dinner staking out of sleeping bag locations (I hadn't expected to land the prime real estate near Marisa herself and therefore wasn't troubled that I didn't) and proceeded with Mazarelli's pizza for dinner, the boxes carried out with a kind of showy fake humility by Marisa's father; a sundae bar set up

73

along the Mazarellis' dining room table; the ceremonial unwrapping of presents; a ten P.M. dip in the hot tub, which entailed much shrieking and the revelation that Marisa wore a yellow string bikini; a post-hot-tub viewing of *The Exorcist* (I spent large chunks of it with my eyes closed, reconstructing in my mind the plot of the first *Back to the Future*); and finally the time at which some girls started falling asleep just as others caught their second wind. There was talk of prank-calling boys, but instead Marisa brought down from the living room the Ouija board she'd been given a few hours before by Abby Balmer.

I was on my way to my sleeping bag after using the bathroom adjacent to Marisa's bedroom – of course Marisa had her own bathroom – when I paused by a handful of girls who'd clustered around the Ouija board. They sat on the floor next to the pool table, and soon I found myself sitting, too. Marisa was cross-legged on one side of the board and Abby was on the other, their fingertips not quite meeting on the planchette, which was made of plastic and shaped like an upside-down heart with a circular window near the top. I didn't know what question they'd asked before my arrival, but I watched as the planchette slid over the letters O-N, followed by a chorus of squeals. Although I'd heard of Ouija boards, I'd never seen one. But I knew immediately that they were using it wrong – they were forcing the letters, picking them, instead of allowing the letters to be picked.

'Ask it Jason Davis or Jason Trachsel,' said a girl named Beth Wheatley, and Marisa gave her a withering look.

'Obviously, it's Jason Trachsel,' she said. *Who likes me?* That must have been the question Marisa had asked the board. Jason Trachsel was the agreed-upon best-looking boy in our class – his mom was Korean and his dad was white, which meant he was the only Asian person in the eighth grade, and he was already expected to make the varsity soccer team the following year as a freshman at Kirkwood High School – while Jason Davis was a quiet boy with a center part. 'Does he want to kiss me?' Marisa asked.

At the top of the board, flanked by a menacing sun and a gloomy moon, and separated from each other by a skeleton head with wings and devil horns, were the words *yes* and *no*. As we waited, *yes* appeared beneath the planchette's window in Gothic script.

'Does he want to go all the way with me?' Marisa asked.

Yes.

She glanced around at us and said merrily, 'Not that I would.'

'Does he have wet dreams about Marisa?' cried out Debby Geegan. Neither of my parents had ever initiated a birds-and-bees conversation with Vi and me, and Debby was the person who in fourth grade had explained to us the meaning of the line 'They keep their boyfriends warm at night' from the song 'California Girls.'

Yes, the board told us, and all the girls exclaimed with disgust and delight. But I wasn't caught up in the excitement. I felt distracted by whatever it was – the energy – that had been summoned by the Ouija board; the girls had invited the energy in, and their invitation had been accepted.

'When will he try to kiss me?' Marisa asked.

V-E-D-R-Y, the board spelled out. As Marisa and Abby's hands kept moving, Beth Wheatley said, 'Does that mean Wednesday?'

'Shh!' Marisa said.

S-O-O-N.

'Oh,' Beth said. 'It just misspelled it.'

'Beth.' Marisa had lifted her head to look at Beth directly. 'Shut up.' Beside me, I felt Beth flinch.

'Ask if anyone likes me,' said Debby.

'Nobody cares if anyone likes you,' Marisa said. She smiled. 'Who here tonight will be the first person to die?' As the other girls gasped, I did it without deciding – my hand shot out, stilling the planchette.

'No,' I said. 'Don't.'

'Because you think it's you?' Marisa said.

It wasn't me. It was Brynn Zansmyer, who at that moment lay on the far side of the rec room in her sleeping bag. She wouldn't die immediately, but it wouldn't be in such a long time, either. The energy, the presence, told me this without using words.

'Because it's sad,' I said. Marisa and Abby wouldn't have come up with Brynn's name except

76

by coincidence. That was the irony, that they believed they wanted to know the answers to their questions, but they weren't listening.

'Fine,' Marisa said. 'Then how about this: Is it true that Violet Shramm gave Mike Dornheiss a blow job behind the cafeteria?'

Right away, and not because of the presence, I knew. *But a blow job?* I thought. *An actual blow job? And Mike Dornheiss?* Mike was pale and red-haired and freckly and on the seventh-grade field trip to the Daniel Boone Home in Defiance, Missouri, on the bus ride out, he had been sitting across the aisle from Vi and me and had lifted his backpack from the floor by his feet, unzipped it, vomited inside, then zipped it up. And besides all that, why hadn't Vi told me? I was myself completely sexually inexperienced, which had the effect of causing me to withhold judgment – a blow job wasn't much more foreign or hypothetical than a kiss.

'I'm going to bed,' I said.

'Me, too.' Beth stood as I did, and Marisa said, 'You guys are lame.'

I had made a mistake in sitting down by the Ouija board, but my bigger mistake had been attending the slumber party in the first place. Marisa was, as Vi had warned me, a rich bitch, though mostly just a bitch. Standing in the rec room, at what had somehow become almost four in the morning, I wished I were at home and that I'd spent the evening lying on our living room floor with Vi, watching Rob Lowe bite into an

77

apple. Gesturing toward the board, I said, 'You should be careful with that.'

'You're scared of it, aren't you?' Marisa said.

'Ask if I should quit violin,' Debby said.

Marisa looked at me. 'You are scared. Your sister is a penis licker and you're a scaredy-cat.'

'Here's a question,' I said. 'Is Marisa's dad having an affair?' As in the moment when I'd set my hand on the planchette, it didn't feel like I'd decided to blurt this out before doing so.

Very quickly, Marisa overturned the entire board. 'Fuck you, Daisy,' she said. She seemed to be biting back tears, which I had never seen her do and which made me feel panicked rather than triumphant. Then she said, 'Fuck all of you.' She stood, whirled around, and stomped up the basement stairs, leaving us hostessless.

Beth, Abby, Debby, and I hardly spoke after Marisa's departure; we retreated to our sleeping bags, but none of us had shut off the rec room lights, and I could feel their brightness when I closed my eyes. I lay there for more than an hour, listening to the breathing of the girls around me, wanting to undo this last section of time – why had I stopped on my way back from the bathroom? – and then I climbed out of my sleeping bag and went upstairs. Marisa's room was at the front of the second floor. Her bedroom door was closed, and I opened it quietly. She was asleep in a double bed, lying on her back with her mouth open, and

I saw how even Marisa Mazarelli was vulnerable. This was what I knew but sometimes forgot: the vulnerability everyone shared.

I tapped her foot, and she startled.

'I'm sorry for the question I asked,' I said. It didn't occur to me that she might apologize in return, and she didn't. I had ruined her birthday party, whereas she had merely been her usual self. I added, 'I really liked the sundaes.'

'I'm sleeping,' she said.

'I don't think you guys were using the board right anyway,' I said. 'That means the questions don't count.' Not that the final question, my question, had even been answered.

'Get out, Daisy,' she said.

'Vi and I have ESP,' I said into the dark room, and it would be impossible to overstate how desperate this disclosure was. Though our parents had never explicitly cautioned us against discussing our senses, they hadn't needed to. But I was thirteen years old, it was getting light outside, I still hadn't slept, and Marisa terrified me. The worst part was that my announcement worked. Right away, I could tell that Marisa became alert.

'If you want to know stuff, about Jason or whatever, I could help you,' I said. 'Usually I just know things because I dream them, but I could try using the Ouija board. We could use it together.'

When Marisa finally spoke, she sounded neither mean nor excited but only curious. 'Is the ESP because you're twins?'

'I guess so,' I said.

'And that's how you knew about my dad?'

'We don't have to talk about it.' I had felt his affair when Mr Mazarelli came downstairs carrying the pizza boxes, while Mrs Mazarelli hovered nearby with a camera and they didn't interact. The skin on Mr Mazarelli's face was ruddy, and he had a smug, unselfconscious grin, and he wore a gold pinkie ring. The affair was inside his grin.

'*Does* Jason like me?' Marisa asked.

I tried to feel the answer, to let it float toward me like seaweed in a calm incoming tide. But the information wasn't as close as it had been when we were sitting around the Ouija board; the presence wasn't in Marisa's room. Nevertheless, I heard myself say, 'I'm sure he likes you. Doesn't every guy in our class?'

It seemed I'd responded wisely. She shifted a little with pleasure. Then, in a darker tone, she said, 'Are my parents getting a divorce?'

Foamily, the tide slid in and out. 'That's hard to say.'

She had started to doubt me, I could tell, and I wasn't surprised when she asked, 'What's something about me that no one else knows?'

This was too easy. 'You cheated on the math quiz last week,' I said. 'You copied the answers off Dave Stutz.'

She laughed. Then she patted the mattress. 'You can sleep up here if you want,' she said, and gratefully, I climbed over her, into the empty space.

For a brief time, I became Marisa Mazarelli's best friend. It was five weeks total, from the middle of April to the end of May. Before, I had walked home from school each day with Vi; now I would trot alongside Marisa as she rode a blue ten-speed with white handlebars to her house. Instead of eating melted cheese on Triscuits, we'd drink Diet Coke, which we carried to the rec room for our Ouija sessions. Usually but not always, the presence from before was there when we used the board, and it guided our hands. When the presence wasn't there, I was just guessing, though sometimes Marisa was clearly pushing the planchette, and I never stopped her. At almost five each afternoon, I would depart from her house, which left me just enough time to make dinner with Vi before our father arrived home.

Marisa's family wasn't around in the afternoons. Her father was working, her mother played tennis, and her older brother, Todd, was away at the University of Kansas. Based on what I could discern from photos and passing remarks, Todd appeared to be merely normal, even a glasses wearer, and not a member of the superspecies to which Marisa belonged.

I had figured out on my own, by watching him during an assembly, that Jason Trachsel was not actively interested in Marisa. But he was persuadable, and Marisa and I spent many hours consulting the Ouija board about his preferences. Perfume, yes. Smoothly shaved legs, yes. Tank tops and big boobs, which meant Marisa had more going for her in the former category than the latter; she looked good in her string bikini, but she wasn't spilling out of it. Another of Jason's likes was when girls had sweat above their upper lips, which surprised us. He thought girls' periods were disgusting and that girls who played video games were cool, and this was how Marisa eventually lured him and Brad Wennerle over one afternoon. We kept the Ouija board hidden, and the four of us played Super Mario Bros., and after an hour Marisa and Jason went up to her bedroom. She had shaved her legs that morning and was wearing perfume and a tank top. Brad and I switched from Super Mario Bros. to pool. I felt mildly hopeful and mostly fearful that he would try to kiss me, but he seemed more interested in poking the stucco ceiling with his pool cue and causing tiny particles of paint to rain down on us. The longer this activity went on, the less I experienced of either hope or fear. Putting a stop to the ceiling poking felt like my responsibility, as if I were babysitting, but I wasn't sure what to say to Brad. He went home before Marisa and Jason reappeared, and then it got to be five o'clock, six after five, ten after five, and I climbed the two staircases to the second floor and stood outside the closed door of Marisa's bedroom. I was considering knocking when I heard Jason say, 'What if I only use one finger?' I turned and fled.

This was three weeks into my best-friendship with Marisa, and she had, as was to be expected, less time for me once she and Jason became a couple. On the days Jason didn't show up, we still used the Ouija board; on the days he and Brad or someone else came over, we didn't speak of it. The second time a boy named Alex Cooke accompanied Jason to Marisa's, he kissed me during a commercial for a local car dealership, while we sat together on the sectional sofa. Then we continued watching *Divorce Court,* then he kissed me again during the next commercial. Alex was decently cute, and I couldn't wait to tell Marisa about this development – I was thinking about telling her even *while* I was kissing Alex – but once again, it got to be five and she and Jason were still in her room and I had to leave.

That night at nine forty-five, after Vi and I were in bed with the light out, the phone rang, and I leapt for it. Unlike some of our classmates, Vi and I didn't have our own line.

'Does Jason love me yet?' I heard Marisa ask.

In the dark, Vi was watching me from her bed. 'I'm not supposed to be on the phone right now,' I said, which wasn't true. Our parents weren't strict; strictness would have required more energy than our mother could or would exert, and our father deferred to her. To Marisa, I said, 'But let's ask the board tomorrow.'

She was pushing the planchette toward *yes,* and I let her. But Jason hadn't come over that day, and Marisa was clearly in a bad mood. There had been only one Diet Coke left in the refrigerator, and she'd said, sighing, 'You can have it,' and I'd said, 'Oh, that's okay,' and she'd said, 'Good,' popped the tab off, and taken a long swallow. She could have offered to split it, I thought. (I drank Diet Coke – way too much of it – for the next eighteen years. I quit only when I got pregnant with Rosie, which is to say that perhaps all that aspartame was Marisa Mazarelli's true legacy in my life.)

As we sat with the Ouija board between us, Marisa asked, 'Does Jason think Abby is hot?'

Yes, appeared beneath the planchette, but again, Marisa was pushing it.

'I knew it,' she said. We both were quiet. Really, she'd already asked so many questions about Jason that there was little left to discover. Meanwhile, I rarely posed questions and I never posed ones about myself. This was only partly because I recognized that my role was to assist Marisa; it was also because I didn't feel the urgent curiosity she did, except on her behalf. If anything, the future seemed overly knowable to me, pressing up against the present.

Then Marisa found inspiration. 'If he wasn't going out with me, who would he go out with?'

The planchette dipped downward and stopped on GOOD BYE.

Marisa lifted the planchette, held it in front of her face, and said, 'What's wrong with you today?'

'Do *you* love Jason?' I asked.

She opened her mouth and released a huge, prolonged belch – a belch worthy of a smelly old man and therefore all the more delightful for its emergence from the mouth of a pretty fourteen-year-old girl. She said, 'That's what I think of love,' and we both laughed. 'Let's put on fake tanner,' she said.

I still ate lunch with Vi, Janie Spriggs, and a few other girls we'd known since elementary school, and at our table the next day, Vi was talking about how cockroaches can survive decapitation – she claimed they died not from their heads being severed but from starving – and I thought of asking her to stop, but I was barely listening anyway. I was trying to figure out how to intercept Marisa in order to deliver the information that had waited for me as I'd awoken that morning.

When Marisa stood from her table and dumped the remains of her lunch in the trash bin, I stood, too, hurrying. By the time I caught up with her, she was outside, walking with Debby Geegan and two other girls.

'Marisa, I need to talk to you,' I said. 'It's important.'

She turned to the other girls. 'Wait here.'

We walked toward the chain-link fence. 'Jason is

cheating on you.' I was so overwrought that I was on the verge of either smiling inappropriately or bursting into tears; presumably, Marisa's reaction would help guide my own.

Her eyes narrowed. Her voice was firm as she said, 'No, he's not.'

I'd imagined that she might be upset or angry or perhaps even grateful to me. But I hadn't anticipated that she'd simply deny what I was telling her. 'Maybe you should ask him,' I said.

'Maybe you should shut the fuck up,' she said, and she walked away.

For the first time in more than four weeks, I didn't go home with Marisa. At my own house, I was surprised to discover that Vi wasn't there. Walking up Gilbert Street, I'd almost been able to taste the melted cheese on Triscuits, but when I found the kitchen empty, I lost interest. I poured ginger ale from a two-liter bottle into a glass, but the soda was flat and in any case a poor substitute for the dark magic of Diet Coke. I could hear my mother's television, and I went into the living room and turned the TV set there to the same channel – the end of *Santa Barbara*. I hadn't been watching for more than a few minutes when I was seized by the blazing obviousness of the situation. It did not require any extrasensory powers; in fact, it seemed that only willful blindness had prevented me from knowing until then.

For twenty minutes, I peered out the living room

window that faced the street, waiting for Vi, and when she walked into view, I hurried outside to meet her. 'You have to stop,' I said.

She grinned.

'Vi, I'm serious.'

'Why? It's a free country.' This was a favorite expression of hers then.

I looked at her and she did, I realized in that moment, fulfill all the criteria: She wore tank tops and perfume (the brand she liked was Primo!, which was supposed to smell like Giorgio but you could buy it at Walgreens for $7.50), and she shaved her legs and she had big boobs and her upper lip got sweaty. But the legs in question were pale white, not nearly as shapely as Marisa's, and clad in pea green cargo shorts from the army-navy surplus store in Webster Groves; below the shorts she wore black Doc Martens without socks. And the big boobs were because, as if to justify our mother's criticism, Vi was getting big overall. By that point, she weighed perhaps eighteen pounds more than I did, weight that seemed concentrated primarily in bras that were two cup sizes bigger than mine, and in her belly, the soft flesh of which was discernible beneath her shirt.

I said, 'If Marisa finds out, she'll kill me. Or you.'

'Oooh!' Vi clapped her palms against both her cheeks and made her eyes big. 'I'm terrified!'

'You don't know Marisa.'

Vi looked at me. 'What is it she has over you?'

'And you don't even like Jason,' I said. 'Do you?'

Vi shrugged. 'He's not my type, but he's cute.'

Vi had a type? We were only thirteen! Who had my sister become, and when? Lowering my voice, I said, 'Did you give a blow job to Mike Dornheiss?'

Vi laughed. 'Did Marisa tell you that? Because it would explain things. Listen, Daisy. Jason came to me.'

'So yes or no about Mike?'

'No.' She looked indignant, and then she smiled. 'I gave him a hand job.'

For the second time that day, the first having been when I'd told Marisa that Jason was cheating on her, I felt as if I might cry. I said, 'You're going to get a reputation,' which was surely something I'd heard one person say to another in a movie.

'Who cares?' Vi said. 'Unlike you, I'm not trying to join Marisa's little club.' All this time, we'd been standing on the sidewalk, and she turned toward the walkway that led to our front door. 'Did you start dinner?'

I shook my head and followed her inside.

We made creamed chicken, and just after she'd set the pan in the oven, Vi turned to me. 'Don't flip out,' she said. 'You promise?' Then she whispered, 'I did give a blow job to Jason.' Her expression was half bashful and half proud. 'We sixty-nined.'

'Oh, Vi,' I said.

Certainly Marisa might have believed I'd made up my abilities, that all along I'd been in cahoots with my sister. This was what I'd have preferred for Marisa to believe, but I already knew, even then, that my own preferences had little bearing on the outcome of events.

I avoided her for the rest of that week, but apparently Jason did, too. On Monday afternoon, she marched to his house, entered via the unlocked front door, walked up to the second floor, found his room – she had never been to the Trachsels' before – and discovered him straddling my sister in his bed, leaning in to lick her ample boobs. 'We had our shorts on,' Vi told me later, as if this fact restored all dignity to the encounter.

On Tuesday, as Marisa and I and a few dozen other girls were changing before PE, she yelled 'Hey, Daisy.' When I looked over my shoulder, I saw that she already had on her PE clothes and was standing by the sinks, about fifteen feet away. All the conversations that had been occurring ceased at once, and I could feel, before she said anything else, that it was going to be bad. And Vi wasn't in school that day; she was faking sick, and I was alone. I forced myself to turn in Marisa's direction.

'How's your ESP today?' she called out.

My heart slammed against my rib cage. The presence from the Ouija sessions – it was here, too, in the locker room. It was egging Marisa on, even if she wasn't aware of it. And then I understood, as I never had before, that it was a malevolent presence. Did we think we could simply ask it question after question and give nothing back? No. It wanted something from us in return.

'Did you guys know that Daisy is psychic?' Marisa's tone as she looked around the locker room was filled with a brutal cheer. 'And Violet, too,' she continued. 'Although I wonder if Violet's so busy being a slut that she doesn't have time to predict the future.'

There was a shift in the air, a dawning comprehension on the part of the other girls. This was a takedown. Which was probably what they'd suspected, but the way Marisa had started had been confusing to them.

'They talk to the devil,' Marisa said. Except for a dripping faucet, the locker room was silent. 'That's who tells them things.'

Later, it felt like I should have offered an explanation, stating facts to our audience: *We've been using a Ouija board Marisa got for her birthday, but now she's mad because she found out she and Vi both have been hooking up with Jason Trachsel.* But I said nothing, and Marisa added, 'Daisy and Violet are devil-worshipping witches, and if you don't watch out, they'll put a spell on you.'

From out in the gym, I heard the sound of Ms. McKee's whistle summoning us. In the locker room, the girls remained quiet. What was it that the presence wanted? And then I thought that maybe Marisa was right; maybe it *was* the devil. If I never asked it anything else, would it leave me alone? 'We're not witches,' I finally said, and my voice was small.

Marisa walked toward me, and I braced myself, as if for a punch. Instead, she leaned in close to my face, brought her hands up, clenched them, and popped them open as she shouted, 'Abracadabra! Ooga booga!' Laughter erupted as she kept walking.

I turned back to my locker, and I remained facing its metal door for more than a minute. The other girls began murmuring, then they began talking at a normal volume, and then they, too, walked into the gym. When I turned around again, only a handful were left, conversing as if I weren't there.

That weekend, my mother dropped Vi and me off to spend the afternoon at the West County mall. In the food court, Vi went to buy a cheeseburger from McDonald's while I got in line at Sbarro. I felt a tap on my shoulder, and a girl I had never seen, a girl who didn't go to our school, said, 'Are you one of the witches?' Her voice was mostly bright, almost friendly, but with a filigree of cruelty probably attributable to the fact that she was accompanied by three other girls. Variations on this interaction played out for Vi and me for the rest of eighth grade and all through high school.

On the last day of middle school, the eighth graders went to Six Flags, and that evening there was a pool party at Mandy Jurenka's house that I didn't go to; all that summer, I hid at home. One day in July, a letter arrived for me in the mail, my name in all caps on the envelope, as if to disguise the handwriting – as if I wouldn't know immediately who it was from. Inside was an unlined piece of paper with ten words on it: *You are a FREAK and you are going to HELL!*

When Vi returned before dinner from watching a movie at Janie Spriggs's house, I was lying on my bed looking at the paper. I immediately set it to one side, and she grabbed for it, held it up, and snorted. 'I *should* put a spell on her,' she said. Whatever had been going on between Vi and Jason was long finished, and when we'd run into Beth Wheatley one Sunday at King Doh – she was with her family, and Vi and I were with our father – she'd mentioned that Jason was going out with Marisa again. I later heard that Jason told people that when Vi had lain on top of him, he'd felt like he was being smashed, but this may have been a rumor circulated by Marisa because it didn't sound to me like what a boy would say.

I doubted our parents had any inkling of what had transpired that spring – they were even more socially isolated than Vi and I were – but one evening shortly after I received the freak letter, on another night when Vi was at Janie's, my father knocked on the open door of our bedroom. He said, 'I thought I'd get an ice cream cone. Would you like to come?'

My mother was watching TV in the living room as we left the house. Neither my father nor I said a word during the eight-minute walk downtown, and we spoke little as we waited in line at Velvet Freeze, then placed our orders; he asked for chocolate and I asked for peppermint with rainbow sprinkles. When we had our cones, we went back outside, and after we'd found an empty bench, my father said, in a mild way, 'I didn't much care for junior high. I hadn't had my growth spurt yet, and kids that age can be cruel.'

I kept licking my ice cream and said nothing, and my father didn't speak again, either. He finished his cone first, then I finished mine, then he said, 'Shall we?' and we walked back home, also in silence.

In my first month of ninth grade, at Kirkwood High, a senior boy named Dan Edwards approached me in the hall and said, 'You're Daisy, right?'

I tensed, waiting for the inevitable.

He said, 'Some of us are going bowling on Friday, and you should come.'

I blinked.

'I can pick you up at your house,' he added.

He was medium height and skinny, with a narrow head and moderately bad skin. He was on the fringes of the popular crowd in the senior class, which was how I knew his name – he was thought by guys to be very funny, though his was a *Monty Python* and *Blues Brothers* brand of humor that I never exactly got. Dan did, however, turn out to possess a private kindness not commonly associated with allegedly funny high school boys.

Standing by the lockers that afternoon, I said, 'I live on Gilbert Street near the train tracks,' and

I experienced an unexpected surge of optimism, as if I were a trapeze artist letting go of one swing and lunging hopefully toward the next. Might it be possible for me to transform myself from an unacceptable high school type – a freak – into an acceptable type: a freshman girl dating a senior boy? And surely this was no colder a calculation than the one made by Dan. Not being all that attractive, his best bet for landing a girlfriend was the well-established method of using his senior status to pursue somebody younger.

In late December of my freshman year, after Dan and I had been going out for three months, we lost our virginity to each other in his single bed, under tan-and-white striped sheets, while his parents were driving his grandmother back to Rolla after Christmas. If the sex didn't hurt as much as I'd feared, I also wouldn't characterize it as pleasurable, possibly because we were using not one but two condoms. But Dan's gratitude and nervousness made me feel very tender toward him. The next day, he gave me a thin gold necklace with a pendant of peridot – my birthstone, though I'd never known it – and a card that read, *Dear Daisy, I care about you a lot. Love, Dan.* The sweetness of these words was almost – almost – a counterbalance to *You are a FREAK and you are going to HELL!* Also, the fact that Dan couldn't bring himself to write *I love you,* even though clearly he wanted to, was a relief because I didn't think I loved him back.

Dan and I kept going out after he left for Grinnell, until the spring of my sophomore year, when I was wooed by a classmate named Tom Mueller. Tom was better-looking than Dan, and a proud Republican; once after he used the term 'welfare queen,' he and Vi got in a fight that culminated in her throwing a Lucite salt shaker from our kitchen table at his head.

Although I had, unbeknownst to myself, become a serial monogamist – for almost a decade, until after my mother died, I wasn't without a boyfriend for more than a couple weeks at a time – I hadn't totally succeeded, back in high school, in going from Witch to Girlfriend. In our junior year, Vi, Marisa, and I all ended up in the same English class. The teacher was Mr Caldwell, who was in his mid-thirties and had blond hair, a blond beard, and flushed cheeks that became even pinker when he spoke about the genius of Melville and Faulkner. He had a PhD from Yale, which made it a feather in the cap of Kirkwood High that he was there; after earning his doctorate, he'd moved to St Louis because his wife was a native who wanted to come home. Everyone loved Mr Caldwell, and many girls had crushes on him, though I found his unusually rounded hips and buttocks womanly. But I did think he was a great teacher, and the force of his personality, his enthusiasm for American and British literature, made his the one class I was in with Marisa during high school that was tolerable; Mr Caldwell made Marisa irrelevant.

And then, in January of our junior year, Mr Caldwell came down with the flu and a substitute teacher showed up. She took attendance by calling out our last names, and when she got to Shramm, I raised my hand and said, 'Here.'

She looked again at the list. 'There are two Shramms. You're which one?'

'No,' Marisa said immediately. 'She's Witch Two.'

The class broke into laughter; Vi gave Marisa the finger; I sat in my chair facing forward, not turning my head. There was then, for weeks, a resurgence of our identity as the witches, and once when I got excused from chemistry to use the bathroom, I passed a popular freshman boy named Kevin Chansky in the otherwise empty hallway. He smirked and said, 'Hey, Two,' and I whirled around. Perhaps this was the last straw because Kevin was younger than I was or because he was sure enough of himself to taunt me with no one watching. In any case, I grabbed the back of his sweater, pulling him toward me, and said, 'Don't ever talk to me again, you piece of shit.' He looked terrified, which was gratifying, but I was shaking as I continued down the hall. I wasn't so sure I'd done the right thing – in Kevin's retelling, I might seem weirder than I was already thought to be – but when I described the incident to Vi, she gave me a high five.

I wondered sometimes what my boyfriends made of the rumors surrounding Vi and me. To Dan, I think they seemed like freshman silliness. He once said, 'You're not really psychic, are you?' and I said, 'No,' and he said, 'Too bad, because I was hoping you could tell me if I'll get into Northwestern.' (In fact, I did know – he wouldn't.) I always felt that my reputation preceded me, that every time I talked to someone I hadn't talked to before, every time I drew any attention to myself, which I did only when I couldn't avoid it – I would participate in class if it was required but under no circumstances would I have made an announcement at assembly – I was proving one thing: *Look how normal I am. Look how not creepy.*

I earned B's in high school, was accepted in the spring of my senior year by four colleges, including the University of Missouri – Mizzou – and introduced myself as Kate when I arrived on campus in the fall of 1993. *Daisy* had always seemed like someone else, someone fanciful and lighthearted. But, as with my decision to date Dan Edwards, my reasoning also reflected calculation. Other people from my high school attended Mizzou, and though I could, with a student body of over thirty thousand, mostly avoid them, I didn't want to take chances. If someone I knew from St Louis told someone else at the university, 'Did you know Daisy Shramm is a witch?' I wanted the other person to say not 'She is?' but 'Who?' For no particular reason, I majored in political science. I also joined a sorority and spent forty minutes a day climbing to nowhere on a StairMaster in the gym.

Vi had gone out to Reed College, in Portland,

97

Oregon; she and my father had flown west the same day my mother and I made the two-hour drive from our house in Kirkwood to Columbia, Missouri. But Vi did not last long at Reed, and I've wondered if her departure from the school was the first in the series of events that propelled her not toward a degree, not toward the kind of steady career she was certainly smart enough for, but instead onto the fringes of society. Or maybe she was already headed that way all along.

Marisa Mazarelli stayed in town for college, going to Saint Louis University, which was a Jesuit school downtown. I didn't attend high school reunions or informal get-togethers held by our classmates, so I didn't see her for more than fifteen years following our graduation. I heard that her father had moved out a few months after we finished high school; for years, he'd been having an affair with a waitress at one of his restaurants. After college, Janie Spriggs told me that Marisa was engaged, and then that the wedding had been called off, but I didn't know if the decision had been made by her or her fiancé, or even who her fiancé was.

Brynn Zansmyer, the girl whose name had come to me that night at the slumber party when Marisa asked the Ouija board which of us would be the first to die, was killed in a hiking accident in California in August 1998, when she was twenty-four; she tripped on a narrow path on a cliff and fell a hundred and twenty feet into a ravine. I didn't go to Brynn's funeral, but she was the first person I knew to die young, and I felt – I shouldn't have, but I did – shocked by her death. So consumed had I been by the other events of that slumber party and their aftermath that I had never again considered the information I'd received about Brynn until nine years later. I wondered then: Should I have warned her? Would she have thought me insane, or would the rumors of my demonic powers have made my claims plausible? Even if she'd believed me, though, what would I have said? Vi and I hadn't been raised in any church, and my understanding of concepts such as fate and destiny was decidedly murky, influenced by *Back to the Future* as much as anything else. But what was clear, what had always been clear, was that I was not powerful. Thus I could feel guilty, and deeply sad for Brynn, without the conviction that I could have changed the outcome of her life.

Brynn had had large brown eyes and very long hair that in elementary school she'd worn with bangs and a middle part. On either side of her part she wore what we called friendship barrettes – little metal clips into which we wove two colors of skinny ribbon. We all made these, but Brynn's collection was the most extensive. She also had a pet rabbit, Marshmallow, whom we had the opportunity to hold at her eighth-birthday party, in second grade. In middle school, she turned suddenly pretty, which I suppose was why Marisa had tapped her to be in her coterie. About a month after my show-down with Marisa, following a PE class in which

Ms. McKee had had us do push-ups on the pavement outside – this was one of the last days of eighth grade – we were changing clothes in the locker room, and Brynn said with concern, 'Daisy, your leg is bleeding.' I looked down to see a two-inch cut below my left knee. 'I have a band-aid,' Brynn said. But instead of passing it to me, she ripped the wrapper herself, pulled off the tabs, and knelt to apply the band-aid to my skin; the gesture was both sweet and weirdly intimate. As she stood, she said, 'When you get home, you should have your mom put Neosporin on it.' This was something I thought of after Brynn died. We were, after all, in eighth grade and certainly old enough to apply our own antibiotic, but apparently she lived in a house where her mother still did such things. Later I was glad for this – for all the indications that poor pretty Brynn, with her barrettes and her rabbit and the little pink zippered vinyl case in which she'd kept band-aids, had during her short life been well-loved.

CHAPTER 6

For the second night in a row, I had trouble falling back to sleep after Owen's two A.M. nursing; I was determined not to think about Vi's earthquake prediction, which was soon indistinguishable from thinking about it. The real question was whether I'd be cheating, breaking the pact I'd made with myself when Rosie was a baby, if I tried to figure out if Vi was right. Was I even capable of figuring it out at this point? And if I did, if I invited senses to come back in this way, then what? Hadn't I learned that I couldn't just glean one useful tidbit, then slam the door on everything else?

So no. No, I would not attempt to find out whether there would be an earthquake. But what was permissible – because wouldn't any other mother do the same? – was to think through a strategy for if an earthquake happened. I imagined being in the yard with Owen and Rosie, the blue sky and sharp sun and the dry, curled leaves blowing off the trees. And then, from nowhere, would come the shaking, the power of the land asserting itself. I would press my children to the ground and cover them with my body.

Inside our house, dishes would slip from cabinets and lamps would tip over; I didn't want this, of course, but to sweep up broken glass would be manageable. Or maybe it would be worse: Trees would fall and roads would buckle. Or in the most terrible version, if the earthquake was as strong as the New Madrid ones centuries earlier, houses would crumble, cars fly skyward. If Rosie and Owen and I were in the house, on the first floor, we'd climb under the dining room table, and on the second floor, we'd – I wasn't sure. Get in the tub, or the closet Jeremy and I shared? Lie down in our bed again? I needed to look up online what was safest.

Or, I wondered, should we just leave St Louis altogether? But for how long and where would we go and what would happen to Vi and my father? Jeremy would never agree to canceling his classes. If staying meant certain death, then of course I wanted to leave, but if staying merely meant being temporarily inconvenienced, then I wanted to stay. Unlike a hurricane, an earthquake, even a bad one, wouldn't last long.

And after it was over, we'd pick ourselves up. Maybe we'd be completely unscathed, or maybe there'd be several days of inconvenience and atypical neighborly chumminess while the electricity was out and tree trunks blocked the street, or maybe it would be the beginning of real, sustained chaos, society as we knew it breaking down. But wasn't this ludicrous to consider? An earthquake in St Louis, even a devastating one, would be significant for only a tiny portion of the American population; it wasn't going to render the dollar worthless or lead to pillaging.

I just had to keep Owen and Rosie safe during the shaking, I thought; if I could do that, we'd all be fine. With this resolved, I fell asleep.

'I had a revelation this morning in the parking lot of Schnucks,' I told Hank as we stood together at the edge of the Oak Knoll playground later that day. Amelia and Rosie were running back and forth across the bridge that connected the towers on the larger of the two play structures, and Owen perched in a baby carrier on my chest. He was facing out and I could feel him watching the girls as raptly as if they were finalists in a tennis tournament. 'I want a minivan,' I said.

Hank snorted, but not meanly.

'Will you go with me to a dealership to do reconnaissance?' I said. 'Not right away, but maybe after all the earthquake stuff? I feel like I need to have the facts in order to make my case to Jeremy.'

'Jeremy's too cool for a minivan?'

'What would you do if Courtney said she wanted one?'

Hank grinned. 'As if I haven't been emasculated enough with our his-and-hers Priuses.'

I said, 'When we were at the grocery store, I'd just put Owen and Rosie into their car seats and Rosie was screaming her head off because I hadn't let her get a cookie – I mean, it wasn't even nine A.M. – and

103

I was cramming the groceries into the trunk, but they didn't all fit because the double stroller was back there.' Another reason they hadn't all fit in my sedan was that I'd bought six gallons of water, along with batteries and extra diapers, which I planned to store in the basement; in addition, I'd withdrawn three hundred dollars from the ATM, not that it was clear to me what I'd do, in an emergency, with the money. I said, 'I had to put bags in the front seat next to me, and then that sensor thing on the dashboard thought a person was sitting there who wasn't wearing a seat belt and kept dinging. And as I pull out of the parking lot, I pass this woman loading up her minivan all placidly, and there's room for everything, and she has two children in car seats, too, but they're both very calm.'

'You know a minivan doesn't guarantee that Rosie won't scream for cookies, right?'

'Also, we could all go places in one car,' I said. 'Like if you and I wanted to take the girls to Grant's Farm, we wouldn't need to drive separately.' Before Owen's birth, Hank and I would drive together, but neither Hank's car nor mine could fit three car seats. I said, 'Is the dealership you guys used last time the one out in Hazelwood?'

'Yeah, but what if they're so persuasive that I come away with a minivan, too?' Hank said. 'Then what? You'll have a lot to explain to Courtney. Here's what I really want to know, though. When the seat-belt sensor was going off, did you buckle up your bag of bread and milk?'

'If we'd been driving more than half a mile, I would have, because it was so annoying. But no.' Amelia had moved to the center of the bridge, its lowest point, and she began jumping in a way that made the bridge shake; Rosie clung to the metal railing and shrieked with joy. I said, 'I let the bread and milk live dangerously.'

As soon as Owen and Rosie were down for their naps on Friday afternoon, I began making my father's birthday cake, and I'd just set the pan inside the oven when the phone rang. Seeing that it was Vi, I said, 'Did you figure out when the earthquake will be?'

'Daze, you'll be the first to know if I do. But Jesus, you need to relax.'

'You're the one who went on TV warning people about a life-threatening natural disaster.'

'Well, I don't think your time is up. Do you?'

'I hope not.'

'I was calling to ask if you got Dad a present yet, and can I go in on it?'

'You can, but it won't seem like it's from you. We got him a Wash U sweatshirt and a picture of Rosie and Owen in a frame that says WE LOVE GRANDPA.'

'You always have to make me look bad.'

'Give him an IOU for a fun activity, like you'll take him out for brunch.'

'That's what you give your dad when you're twelve.'

'Then do what you want.' *But do not,* I thought,

ask me to pick you up right now and drive you to the mall.

'Jeremy's coming to get me at five-fifteen, right?' Vi said. 'You think we could swing by the Galleria and I'll run into Brookstone for literally three minutes?'

Which is the same amount of time it would have taken you to order something online two weeks ago, I thought. Aloud, I said, 'That won't work because Jeremy's picking up Dad, too. I'm sure Dad doesn't care if you give him a present. He probably won't even notice.'

'So says the good daughter with multiple gifts.'

'You can put your name on our card,' I said.

'Yeah, and maybe I can Photoshop my face into the picture of Owen and Rosie.'

'So did Dad have fun on your date?'

'Very funny. He didn't come inside. The woman was okay but kind of intense.'

'So are you.'

'Yeah, but I hadn't even finished my coffee when she's like, "I'd like to see you again. How about dinner on Saturday?" I said I needed to check my calendar, but don't you think that's weird not to wait until the end of the date? Or she could have sent an email after.'

'It's flattering,' I said. 'She must like you.'

'Well, I *am* irresistible.' Vi sighed. 'You really don't think an IOU for Dad is lame?'

'You could make it for something he'd never do on his own, like getting massages together at a spa.'

'Dad would hate a massage,' Vi said, which was probably true.

I'd set Owen and Rosie's monitors side by side on the kitchen table, and just then, from Owen's, there was an unhappy yell.

'Wow,' Vi said. 'I guess the pleasure of your teats has been requested.'

The phone rang again as I was changing Owen's diaper, and I answered it without looking at the caller ID panel; I assumed it was Vi.

Instead, Hank said in a tight voice, 'So Courtney just got a call from her doctor about the CVS, and it looks like the baby has Down's.'

'Oh my God,' I said. 'I'm so sorry.' Was *I'm so sorry* even an appropriate response? 'Is there anything we can do?'

'Courtney's coming home from work now, and she's pretty upset.'

'They think the baby has Down's or they know?'

'Well, we meet with a genetics counselor next week, but if there's an extra chromosome 21, that's Down's. I guess the question then is how severe.'

I thought of Janie Spriggs's brother – *You're twins because there's two of you* – and I wanted to say something to Hank about how sweet Pete had been, but again, I wasn't sure of the protocol of this moment; maybe mentioning that I'd known a nice retarded person was akin to announcing that some of my best friends were black. 'How about if we drop off dinner tonight?' I said.

'Nah, I'm sure you've got your hands full with your dad's thing.' Hank sounded miserable as he said, 'Tell him happy birthday from the Wheelings.'

When I'd hung up, I called Jeremy.

'Wow,' he said. 'Poor Hank and Courtney.'

'You don't want to come home early, do you?'

He hesitated. I was asking because Hank's call had made my heart clench – it was a particular kind of nervousness I thought of as anxious heart – and because Jeremy's presence in the house calmed me, even if he was upstairs reading or grading and I was downstairs with the children, and these were facts that both of us understood without discussion. When Rosie had been five months old, she'd gotten very sick – she'd been in the hospital for three days – and sometimes, even though more than two years had passed, the panic I'd felt then abruptly came back to me, the nauseous fear that something terrible was happening or about to happen; if anything, now that we had Owen, when the panic surged, it was worse because there were two of them and (Pete Spriggs's proclamations notwithstanding) only one of me. What Jeremy and I also didn't need to discuss right then was his belief that he ought not to accommodate my every flare-up of anxiety, a belief I mostly agreed with, though more in theory than at specific times such as this one. Nevertheless, knowing he'd be home in a few hours and that in fact nothing about Rosie or Owen's well-being had changed since Hank's phone call, or for that matter since Vi's earthquake prediction, I made myself say, 'It's fine if you can't.'

'I'm supposed to meet with a couple students.'

'No, it's fine.'

'You got the steaks for tonight, right? I don't need to stop by Schnucks?'

'I have everything. The cake's baking as we speak.' I could feel Jeremy's attention turning, and I blurted out, 'You know how I didn't want biological children?'

'Was that you?'

'Seriously,' I said. 'If this had happened to us, I'd have felt really guilty.'

'They're not responsible. It's a matter of genetics.'

'The chances of Down's increase the older you are.'

'Sure, but the great majority of women over thirty-five still have healthy babies.'

'No, I know.' I paused. 'I wonder if they're considering—' I couldn't bring myself to say the word *abortion* in front of Owen, though apparently I didn't mind announcing to him that I once hadn't wanted biological children.

'I'm sure they're in shock right now,' Jeremy said. 'But will you do me a favor? Will you take a deep breath?'

Rosie awakened and started talking nine minutes before the timer for the cake was set to go off – over the monitor, I distinctly heard her say, 'The baloney has a pee-pee in she's diaper' – and my heart was still clenching. Before taking Owen upstairs to get Rosie, I called Vi back. When she answered, I said, 'If you're ready right now, we'll come over and take you to the mall.'

The Galleria was crowded pretty much all the time, and on a Friday afternoon it was mobbed; we had to park at the far north entrance beyond Dillard's. Rosie didn't want to ride in the double stroller, and I ended up mashing her down into the seat and snapping the buckles around her waist as she writhed up. 'Mommy is a bad Mommy,' she howled. 'Rosie does *not* like Mommy.'

'Tell us what you really think, Rosie,' Vi said. 'Don't hold back.'

Inside Dillard's, I let Rosie out and said to Vi, 'Feel free to go ahead and we'll meet you.'

'But I need your advice.'

'I thought you had something specific in mind from Brookstone.'

Quickly, Vi said, 'There's a few possibilities.'

By the time we'd made it across the mall, up the elevator, and into the store, and Vi had dawdled in the way of the childless as she considered whether our father would prefer a shower radio or velour slippers, it was after four. The double stroller was too wide to push inside the store, so I'd left it near the front, carrying Owen while I chased Rosie around, righting the picture frames and alarm clocks she knocked over, returning the wine openers and noise-canceling headphones she'd grabbed to their rightful shelves.

The cashier who rang up the slippers Vi decided on was a short, sandy-haired man who took Vi's credit card then glanced back and forth between us. I was so sure that he was going to say *Are you twins?* that I was already half-nodding (*She is. By eight minutes. Yes, identical*), but what he said instead, looking only at Vi, was 'You're the psychic, aren't you? I saw you on Channel 5.'

'Oh,' Vi said, and the energy of the encounter shifted; she became the most important of the three adults present. 'Yeah, that was me.'

'You predicted a big earthquake?'

Vi's brow furrowed; the excitement of being recognized was suddenly imbued with the seriousness of what she'd predicted. 'I hope I'm wrong,' she said. 'I really do.' This was such a perfect response that I silently begged her to say nothing else; when she plucked a business card from her wallet and passed it to the cashier, it was impossible to know whether she'd chosen to ignore my plea or been unaware of it. 'If you'd like to talk about your own path, this is how to reach me,' she said to the man. 'Issues with loved ones, romantic and career guidance, what your true purpose is – really, anything you're confused about, I'd be happy to help.' I wasn't hearing her spiel for the first time, but still, the irony was so rich, and she was so oblivious to it. She added, 'I do private consultations for seventy-five dollars and group sessions for thirty per person.'

The man set the card on top of a clipboard next to the cash register – he wasn't obviously disgusted – and I averted my eyes so I wouldn't see the card's background, which featured a peach-tinted sunset and, on the left side, a mountain; next to the mountain it said VIOLET SHRAMM, PROFESSIONAL PSYCHIC MEDIUM and had not just her phone number and email but her home address, which was where she conducted her sessions.

Outside the store, as I wrangled Owen and Rosie back into the stroller, Vi said, 'I just want to get a Diet Coke in the food court and then I'm done.'

'I need to make the icing for Dad's cake.'

'Homemade icing, huh? Eat your heart out, Martha Stewart.' But Vi was already walking away, and she called over her shoulder, 'I'll hurry.'

'Meet us at the car,' I yelled. Three teenage girls passing by looked at me.

A solid twenty minutes later, beaming and entirely unapologetic, Vi opened the front passenger-side door. Owen and Rosie were both in their car seats and the stroller was put away; I was in the driver's seat with my own seat belt fastened and the car's motor on. As Vi climbed in, a twenty-ounce cup in her hand, she said, 'You'll never believe who just called me.'

I said nothing as I backed out of the parking space, and Vi said, 'You can't give me the silent treatment right now. This is way too exciting.'

112

'I'm not giving you the silent treatment. I'm trying to get us out of the parking lot.'

'Fine. I won't tell you if you don't want to know.'

The truth was that I wasn't that curious, and certainly not enough to beg her. I suspected her allegedly juicy tidbit would be along the lines of the cousin or mother-in-law of some Rams player requesting a reading.

From behind me, Rosie said, 'Rosie wants a straw.'

'You can use your cup with the straw at home.'

'Rosie wants that straw.'

'It's Aunt Vi's.'

'Does she want a sip?' Vi asked, and I gave her a look and shook my head; Rosie had never had soda. We were driving east on Clayton Road, passing Hanley, when Vi said, 'You really don't want to know who called me? It's major.'

'Tell me if you want to.'

'Not if you're not interested.'

I ignored the bait. 'When we get home, will you set the table on the patio while I frost the cake?'

'Rosie wants a sip!' Rosie yelled, and she kicked my seat as I made a left off Clayton Road, onto DeMun. When we turned onto San Bonita, Jeremy's car was parked on the street in front of our house, and he and my father were walking across the yard toward the door.

After Jeremy set the steaks on the grill, he closed the lid and said, 'Kate, we're probably T minus fifteen minutes if you want to take Owen up.' We were all outside on the patio. My father sat in a chair, drinking beer from a clear glass mug, and accepting Rosie's offerings of twigs and leaves. Vi was also drinking a beer except out of the bottle and sitting in the recliner with her legs extended, and I was standing next to the table, holding Owen on my hip.

The temperature had been in the mid-seventies during the day and was now in the high sixties, the light softening, and the loveliness of the evening made me wish I hadn't let things turn even slightly ugly in the car with Vi. Then I thought, But hadn't the whole outing, squabbling included, served its purpose? It had distracted me from Courtney and Hank's test results.

Owen's little face was right next to mine, and when I turned my head toward his, we touched noses, which delighted him. 'Are you ready for night-night?' I said.

My father held up one finger. 'Might I get a picture of the whole family first?'

'Of course,' I said. My father still used a standard camera he'd acquired when Vi and I were in high school, and I had no idea where in the year 2009 he went to buy film or have it developed.

I called to Rosie, who was lying on her stomach in the grass, and she looked up at me brightly and said, 'Rosie's swimming.'

'Grandpa's about to take our picture. Can you come over here?' Because Jeremy had gone inside to wash his hands, I said to Vi, 'Will you watch

Owen?' Without waiting for an answer, I set him on Vi's lap and walked toward Rosie.

When I scooped her into my arms, she patted my cheek and said, 'It's nice to meet you, Mama.'

'It's nice to *see* you. We already know each other.'

Vi and Owen were still nestled on the recliner, and – I hadn't planned this – I said, 'That's a cute shot right there. Dad, want to get Auntie Vi with her nephew?' This was, I was fairly sure, my apology to Vi. Or perhaps, if what I was apologizing for was driving her to the mall and waiting in the parking lot while she bought a Diet Coke, it was my affirmation that I was a doormat.

I set Rosie down on the bricks and stood next to Jeremy, who had come back outside. 'You doing okay?' he murmured.

'I keep thinking of Courtney and Hank,' I murmured back, at which point I became aware that my father had taken our picture. 'I don't think I was smiling,' I said.

'It's a candid,' my father said. 'Now, the umbrella casts a bit of a shadow, so for the group shot, if you all want to stand to the right of it—'

I took Owen from Vi, and as we arranged ourselves, Vi somehow ended up between Jeremy and me; Rosie formed the front row by herself. 'Jeremy, I feel like your sister wife,' Vi said, and Jeremy said, 'I should be so lucky,' and I loved him a little bit extra. Then my father clicked the camera several times, until without warning Rosie shrugged off the hand I'd set on her shoulder and raced back across the yard. 'I hope you got one with all our eyes open,' I said.

Upstairs, Owen fell asleep while nursing, and he sighed a little as I set him down in the crib, what sounded like a sigh of contentment. His eyes remained closed, and I watched him, feeling that sprawling, bottomless love.

When I returned outside, Rosie was sitting in a booster seat on top of a patio chair, eating macaroni with her fingers, while everyone else cut their steaks.

'This is delish, Jeremy,' Vi said. 'You've outdone yourself.'

'You can thank Kate for picking the meat,' Jeremy said.

I set Owen's monitor on the recliner and took a seat in the vacant chair at the table, but I hadn't even unfolded my napkin when Vi tapped her fork against the neck of her beer bottle. 'So I have an announcement,' she said. 'Not to steal your birthday thunder, Dad.' She wasn't going to tell our father about the woman she was dating, was she? Over dinner, in our backyard, with Rosie sitting next to her? But no, Vi looked too pleased, too unambivalent, to be coming out of the closet. And then she said, 'Guess who got invited to be a guest on the *Today* show next week?' She grinned and pointed both her thumbs up toward her own face.

'Seriously?' I could hear how my voice sounded

accusatory rather than excited. 'Because of the earthquake stuff?'

Vi nodded. 'One of their producers heard I was on the news here, and now they want to interview me, too. Not in New York, they'll do it by satellite, but still – not too shabby, huh?' She looked directly at me and said, 'And you didn't even want to know who'd called me at the mall.'

'My word, Vi,' said my father.

'What day?' said Jeremy.

'They think Wednesday.' Vi made a fake-nervous expression, setting her top teeth against her bottom teeth and inhaling while raising her eyebrows, and I understood that she was beyond thrilled; this was very likely the greatest thing that had ever happened to her, her reward for persisting on her authentic life journey while the assholes we knew from high school had all paired off and become accountants. She added, 'And they're doing it at my house, so I guess I better vacuum!'

'Well, hey, Vi,' Jeremy said. 'The *Today* show is the big time.'

Who was most horrified, I wondered? My father, in his distant way, or me with my dread of exposure and my complete lack of confidence in Vi's ability to act in her own best interest? Or maybe it was Jeremy, who had to know that ultimately he'd be the one to bear the brunt of my agitation.

'I hope Ann Curry interviews me, because I know she'll keep it classy,' Vi was saying.

'Is that the black lady?' my father asked.

'Is she black?' I said. 'I thought she was something else.' My steak, which I hadn't yet touched, had become inedible. The *Today* show was viewed by how many millions of people with whom Vi would share her insane-sounding, panic-inducing, wholly sincere vision? What I wanted to tell her was that being on the news in St Louis was bad enough, but surely there would be consequences of a different order if she repeated her prediction on national television. And yet – it had to do with our father's presence – I couldn't say this at all. The bargain my father and I had struck at some point in the last five years was that we would withstand our discomfort at Vi's having become a professional psychic, and preserve our relationship with her, by simply not talking about her job except in terms of logistics. *I know Vi has to work this Thursday night* – that was an acceptable thing to say. However, if I said, *But you'll become a national laughingstock,* it would be a violation of our agreement; I'd be explicitly acknowledging who Vi was, who in some ways I was, too. Plus, given Vi's palpable excitement, I'd be acting like a killjoy. And yet, because I couldn't bring myself to say *This is wonderful!* what I finally said, in a tone that I strove to keep free of judgment, was 'What do you think you'll wear?'

Vi laughed. 'Of course that's what you want to know.'

CHAPTER 7

I can't recall any of the speeches at my high school graduation, but what I do remember from the ceremony is that our robes were red, that Vi won a prize for a poem she had written about the expedition of Lewis and Clark from the point of view of Sacagawea (senior year, Vi had taken creative writing with our beloved junior-year English teacher Mr Caldwell), and that the name of the girl who tripped walking across the stage to receive her diploma – I'm pretty sure there's always a girl who trips – was Gabrielle Rhoads. I felt bad for Gabrielle, but I also was glad that it hadn't been me or Vi.

Following the ceremony, which was in Queeny Park, a bunch of parents were hosting a casino-themed party at the Town and Country Racquet Club. After the party, around three A.M., the seniors would drive back to campus for a big breakfast set up outside. Before we left Queeny Park, in the fading evening light, our father took pictures of Vi and me in our caps and gowns, and our mother, in what was her version of a compliment, said to Vi, 'I didn't know they gave prizes for writing a poem.' The prize itself was a small square glass box with KIRKWOOD HIGH SCHOOL engraved on the lid.

My father was still taking pictures when we were joined by Vi's friend Patrick, a scrawny but good-looking blond guy whom my parents seemed to assume Vi was romantically involved with – they'd gone to prom together, at least until they skipped out after the first hour – although I felt pretty sure Patrick didn't like girls. If I was right, then despite her precociously slutty leanings in middle school, Vi had had no real boyfriend during high school. I wasn't even sure she'd had sex. In any case, for the last four years, Vi and Patrick had both been on the tech crew of school plays; dressed in black, they emerged between acts in *Guys and Dolls* and *The Pajama Game* and moved sofas.

My own boyfriend, Tom, briefly came over to greet my parents, but when I said he should bring his mother and father over, too, he hesitated. I had thought our agreed-upon plan was that we'd intro-duce our parents at graduation; they'd never met, though Tom had spent the last twenty-six months at our house on Gilbert Street, having sex with me on an old single cot in our basement before my father got home from work on weekdays and on weekends after my parents had gone to bed. Tom was a big, genial, not intensely smart basketball player whose father was a pulmonologist and whose mother – the first person I ever met who'd had a face-lift – ran Kirkwood High School's Mothers' Club and didn't like me.

A few weeks after Tom and I had gotten together, on an evening on which we'd stopped at his house to do shots of his dad's bourbon before going to a party hosted by a kid who lived in Glendale, I emerged from the downstairs bathroom and found Mrs Mueller standing right outside it; I hadn't realized she was home. 'I hope you know you're just a fling, Daisy,' she said. 'Tom would never be serious about a girl who doesn't go to church.'

I had believed that when Mrs Mueller finally met my parents, she'd understand that I wasn't a Satan worshipper or whatever it was she'd heard but that I came from a respectable middle-class family. However, after the graduation ceremony, when I pressed Tom to get his parents, he said, 'My mom's really busy with stuff for the party. She might have left already for the Racquet Club.'

'I see her right there.' I gestured ten yards away, toward where Dr and Mrs Mueller and Tom's brother Laird were all talking warmly to our principal.

'Well, she's about to leave,' Tom said.

I scowled at him, and he said, 'What?' and then he said, 'Don't get mad, but she doesn't want to meet your parents. I'm sorry. I swear I tried.'

My parents were at this point just a few feet from Tom and me, my father taking pictures of Vi and Patrick as they pressed their heads side by side and held the tassels from their caps above their mouths like mustaches; my mother was observing them and frowning. And in this moment I felt a welling

121

combination of shame and fury on my family's behalf, a fear that my parents, while innocent of Mrs Mueller's suspicions, were still too odd and socially inept to convince anyone otherwise.

I was close to crying, but I tried to conceal it as I said to Tom, 'Your mom's a snob.' Really, I was about a second from tears. 'And you're a wimp.'

'Daisy—' He seemed less offended than concerned, and before my face collapsed, I turned and ran in the other direction. But I had no plan, I realized when I found myself on the outskirts of the throng of graduates and their families; my plan had been for Tom to chase and soothe me, but he wasn't cooperating. I was at least five miles from home, wearing heels and a dress under my ridiculous red gown, but I couldn't come up with a better idea, so I began walking. Mason Road ran along the east side of the park, and I knew it intersected with Manchester, which would eventually lead me back toward Kirkwood.

I'd been walking for twenty minutes, it was completely dark out, and I'd developed blisters on both heels when I heard frantic honking that I briefly felt sure was coming from Tom's Jeep before I saw Vi driving our father's Buick and gesturing wildly. She pulled over, and I ran across Manchester Road. 'What the fuck are you doing?' she called out her open window.

'I got in a fight with Tom.' I had thought Patrick would be with her, but she was alone. I said, 'Did Mom and Dad wonder where I went?'

'We assumed you'd left with Tom, but then I ran into him, and he asked me where you were.'

'I hate his mom.' When I saw that Vi was looking over her shoulder, preparing to make a U-turn, I said, 'Can you take me home?'

She glanced at me. 'What did Tom do?' Just about everyone – even Vi and Patrick – planned to attend the after-graduation party. It was the kind where you couldn't go back in if you left early, but almost no one left early, either.

'I'm not in a party mood,' I said. 'My feet hurt.'

Vi laughed, but she kept driving east. We rode in silence, except for the radio, but first Vi didn't make a left on North Geyer, then she didn't make one on Kirkwood Road, either.

'Where are you going?' I said.

'I'm seeing where the wind takes us.'

'Seriously,' I said.

'If you're not going to the party, I'm not, either.'

'You don't have to skip it.'

'Well, I'm *so* crushed,' she said. 'I'll probably regret it for the rest of my life.'

We were quiet again, and at Hampton Avenue, she got on the highway.

'Don't take us to East St Louis,' I said.

Vi grinned. 'Relax.'

By the time we were downtown – which wasn't reputed to be quite as dangerous as East St Louis but also wasn't known as a hangout for suburban white girls, especially at night – my agitation about Tom and his mother had been replaced with wariness of whatever it was Vi and I were doing. Vi parallel-parked on Fourth Street and reached in the backseat for her bunched-up graduation gown and mortarboard cap. She climbed from the car, donned them both, then ducked her head back in to look at where I still sat in the passenger seat. 'Come on,' she said. 'And put your hat on.'

I'd almost thrown it in the trash on my way out of Queeny Park, but instead I'd carried it with me, and even though I wasn't sure why I was doing so, I obeyed Vi. We walked north on Fourth, then cut right on Market, and all at once, the Arch was before us, huge and luminous and impossibly curved. We crossed the street and entered the grounds of what was officially known as the Jefferson National Expansion Memorial. 'Aren't there park hours?' I said.

Vi scoffed, holding up her gown. 'These are our immunity. Because it's our special, special night.'

There were no people nearby, though I could see in one direction two men standing beside an overloaded grocery cart and in the other direction a figure of indeterminate gender squatting by the curb. We followed the inclined sidewalk, then turned onto the grass, and then we could no longer see the Arch because we were standing under it; beyond the grass, down the steps and across the street, lay the dark mass of the Mississippi River. Vi looked up and said, 'Okay. This is the place.' Soon she was lying flat on her back. Her mortarboard cap fell

124

off, and she tugged it back on; when it fell off a second time, she adjusted it so her head rested on it like it was a pillow.

Under her gown, Vi was wearing a navy blue rayon dress printed with large brown flowers; it was knee-length, and as the gown parted and the dress rode up, I saw that beneath it, like a girdle, she was wearing spandex bike shorts. It had been years since I'd seen her either wear a dress or ride a bike.

She patted the grass and said, 'Make yourself at home.' As I lay down next to her, she withdrew a pack of Camel cigarettes and a plastic lighter from a side pocket in her dress; she tapped out two cigarettes, held them in her mouth as she lit them, and passed one to me. 'It's a little-known fact,' she said, 'that if you make a pilgrimage to the Arch on the night of your high school graduation, and if you lie down under its highest point, then any wish you make will come true.'

'What about picking up homeless-man germs?' I said. 'Is that part of the tradition?'

'You know what they say. Until you've had gonorrhea, you haven't really lived.' In fact, as we lay there and smoked – I smoked only at parties and had gotten through high school never purchasing a pack – there was something pleasant about being stretched out on the grass in the warm night. Above us, the underbelly of the Arch glowed, and past the Arch was the infinite sky; it did not seem so hard to believe, in this moment, that a wish you made here could come true.

'That's cool about your poetry prize,' I said. 'You didn't know, right?'

'You mean *didn't know* didn't know or didn't have a sense?'

'Either.'

'Well, I'm pretty sure Mr Caldwell decided single-handedly, so it doesn't exactly count.'

I turned to look at her; I could have asked what she meant, but I didn't.

After a minute, Vi said, 'You think Mom will start cooking dinner again when we're at college?'

'I've wondered that.'

Vi inhaled on her cigarette. 'I have a present for you.'

'Really?' It hadn't occurred to me to buy one for her.

'Don't worry. I didn't pay for it. It's a story Patrick told me, and I've been saving it to tell you because it's awesome. You know his cousin Mary in Kansas City?'

I nodded.

'She works at a coffeehouse that sells biscotti. The pieces aren't wrapped, they're just in a jar with a lid next to the cash register. And every night when the employees close up, they play a game called Naughty Biscotti. They each take a piece, put it in their butt crack, and see how far they can walk before it falls out. Whoever walks the farthest wins. Then they put the pieces back in the jar.'

'That is *not* true,' I said.

'Mary swears.'

'Bullshit,' I said. 'Maybe she swears, but it's still not true.'

'But will you ever eat unwrapped biscotti again?' Vi laughed. 'See? You believe it. Okay, want to hear my first wish?'

'That the cafeteria at Reed sells butt crack-flavored biscotti?'

'Oh, I already know they do. That's why I decided to go there. My second wish is that Mrs Mueller's face-lift starts melting. And my third wish is that after college, I get into the Peace Corps and I fall in love with a dashing African tribesman and become his wife.'

'Why don't you just fall in love with another Peace Corps volunteer?'

After consideration, Vi said, 'Okay. And then I'll go to law school at Berkeley. But who will you marry? Don't say Tom.'

In fact, despite Tom's mother, he and I were planning to stay together after I'd left for Mizzou and he was at DePauw in Indiana. And yet I swear that in this moment – a breeze rose, and I could hear it passing through the ash trees – I saw Jeremy; truly, I saw him. Not up close but at a distance, in profile, as if across a parking lot. This wasn't how I'd see him when we would actually meet, but I think it's how I recognized him. And though I could, on the night of graduation, feel his kindness, the image of him made me nervous. I was seventeen, and he was a strange, grown-up man.

I said to Vi, 'Compared to most of the guys in our class, Tom has a lot going for him.'

'Well, sure – in the land of the blind, the one-eyed man is king. Okay, how about this? At Mizzou, you'll meet a nice country boy named Fred who'll sweep you off your feet and take you back to his family farm. You'll have eight children. Every night you'll cook meat loaf, put the kids to bed, and you and Fred will make passionate yet gentle love.'

'What, while he chews on a piece of hay?' Then – I had never said this aloud, I hadn't even realized I'd decided it – I said, 'I don't want to have children. I want to adopt so they don't have senses.'

'Really?' Vi looked genuinely interested. 'That's the only reason I *would* want kids. But why do you even think senses are hereditary? I've never met anyone more clueless than Mom and Dad, so they sure as shit don't have them.'

'But we know nothing about Mom's family. Obviously, something weird happened between her and them.' Vi was quiet – I could feel her skepticism – and I said, 'I'll be like the Garretts.' These were neighbors I babysat for, a white father who worked at Monsanto and a white mother who ran a catering company and their two Chinese daughters, Lucy and Anna, who were four and five.

Vi wrinkled her nose. 'Those girls are annoying.' She never babysat; in the summers, she worked at a frozen yogurt place that would be closed by the mid-nineties.

I said, 'The reason Mrs Mueller doesn't like me is because of senses. And all the stuff with Marisa Mazarelli – I'd never want to put my children through that.'

'Marisa's an ignoramus,' Vi said. 'And you still haven't wished for anything.'

'Have you?'

'The Peace Corps and law school. Oh, and my cool husband. I think he'll be named Theo. That's a cool name, right?'

What I wanted sounded so pathetically unambitious that I almost didn't say it, but then I did. I said, 'I wish to live anywhere besides St Louis.'

Back in the car, we were headed west on 40 until Vi got off on Grand. 'Where are you going now?' I asked.

'There are still four hours before the breakfast,' she said. 'We can't go home.'

And so instead, we drove. We drove up and down the streets around the water tower, past the old mansions built in a neighborhood where rich people no longer wanted to live, and we drove by the brick houses on Magnolia, past the Botanical Garden, south on Kingshighway, then north on Kingshighway, then west on Lindell, along the stately homes that had been built facing Forest Park for diplomats visiting the 1904 World's Fair – Tom had once told me that Chuck Berry lived in one of these houses, which I didn't learn until adulthood wasn't true – and then we drove by

Wash U, where I didn't know my one-day husband would work, up toward the Loop, down Delmar and past the Tivoli Theatre – we considered getting something to eat in the Loop, but then we'd driven by without stopping – and then we were on 170, up near the airport, out in St Charles and O'Fallon and Chesterfield, places that we never went, that would explode with housing subdivisions and schools and strip malls in the years to come. And then we were somehow all the way back on Kingshighway and this time, a little south of Barnes-Jewish Hospital, something blew across the dark pavement in front of our headlights, and Vi and I looked at each other with incredulity and delight. It was close to one A.M. by then, and we hadn't spoken for easily twenty minutes.

'Was that a Burger King crown?' I said, and Vi said, 'It's a miracle! A Burger King crown on Kingshighway? We should go back and get it!'

'We don't need to get it,' I said. 'We both saw it.'

Our windows were open, and the radio had been playing continuously – not one but two Billy Joel songs had come on during our drive – and the air was dense with the humidity of a midwestern summer, weather that even then made me homesick, though it was hard to say for what. Maybe my homesickness was a form of prescience because when I look back, it's the circumstances of this very car ride that I recognize as irretrievable: the experience of driving nowhere in particular with my sister, both of us seventeen years old, the open

130

windows causing our hair to blow wildly; that feeling of being unencumbered; that confidence that our futures would unfold the way we wanted them to and our real lives were just beginning.

'Now all our wishes will definitely come true,' Vi said. 'You can't beat a crown for a good omen.'

Four months later, on an overcast Tuesday morning six weeks into my freshman year at Mizzou, I awoke with a strong feeling that I needed to call Vi. It had been the dream I'd been having before my alarm clock went off, I realized, a dream of sitting in a lecture hall with my view of the stage blocked by a girl who had a pixie haircut. Then the girl turned around, and I saw that she was Vi. The expression on her face was unsmiling, as if she didn't know who I was.

Though it still sometimes surprised me not to find Vi next to me at a meal, or to return to my dorm room and realize that it wasn't Vi but a girl named Heather from Davenport, Iowa, reading in the other bed, the truth was that Vi and I hadn't been in close contact; we'd spoken on the phone infrequently since starting college. The two-hour time difference between Columbia, Missouri, and Portland, Oregon, made it always seem like not quite the right moment to talk, plus the busyness of college could consume me for days at a time: the cycle of classes and assignments and my work-study job (it was at an adult day-care center, but to my surprise, I kind of liked it), plus exercise and parties and post-party debriefings with girls I already felt closer to than the friends I'd had in high school.

All of this meant that Vi and I communicated primarily by email, which was new to both of us, and which we used to write four- or five-paragraph, correctly capitalized and punctuated missives every other day. Sitting in my dorm's computer lab, I'd start out *Dear Vi,* and I'd sign off *Love, Daisy.* I'd feel like I was starring in a wholesome movie about a well-adjusted coed as I wrote, *I just went with a bunch of people on my hall to a lecture by a man who's climbed the highest mountain on every continent.*

As it happened, I didn't get around to calling Vi that day. After returning from the adult day-care center, I met up with Lauren, a girl from Tampa who had during rush become my new best friend, and we went to the gym, climbed for forty minutes on adjacent StairMasters while listening to music on headphones, then stood outside the gym entrance for the same amount of time, drinking bottled water and discussing whether I should go for a freshman named Ben Murphy with whom I'd played ping-pong at a Delta Upsilon party the previous Saturday. (The second week of school, during one of our increasingly empty, stuttering phone conversations, I had worked up the nerve to say to Tom Mueller, 'I've been thinking maybe we should see other people,' and in a tone of great relief, he'd said, 'I've been thinking that, too.' We hadn't spoken since.)

Lauren and I lived on different floors of the same

dorm, Schurz Hall, and after we parted ways, I showered, read two chapters from Book IV of *The Wealth of Nations*, then met up again with Lauren and our friend Meredith to walk to dinner. In the cafeteria, some guys we knew invited us back to their room to watch *Animal House*, and it was after ten by the time I returned to my own room to make flash cards for an upcoming biology test.

My roommate and I got along but hadn't become friends. During the first week of school, our peer adviser had bought a birthday cake for a guy on the hall and that night, when I'd said to Heather, 'Are you going to Rick's room?' she'd said, 'I'm a Witness, and we don't celebrate birthdays.'

A witness to what? I'd thought before realizing she meant Jehovah's. I knew little about the religion, but after that, worried that she, too, would strongly disapprove if she ever caught wind of my senses, I kept a polite distance. It wasn't hard because she left every weekend. She either had family nearby or – I was never clear on which – was staying with people from her church whom she considered family.

On that night in October, I was at my desk copying phrases from my biology textbook onto index cards, and Heather was sitting on her bed, her legs tented and a notebook open across her thighs, when there was a knock on our door. Before either of us had a chance to stand or even to call 'Come in,' the door swung open and my sister appeared in the threshold. Vi wore a long-sleeved gray T-shirt, jeans, and Birkenstocks without socks, and over one shoulder she carried a green duffel bag. Unlike in my dream, her hair wasn't short; she'd parted it in the center and pulled it back into a low ponytail at the base of her neck, with the strands that weren't long enough to fit in the rubber band tucked behind her ears. She grinned and said, 'Look what the cat dragged in.'

In spite of the recent sense of her I'd had, I was stunned. 'What are you doing here?' I said. When I went to embrace her, I could smell her Vi-ishness – she had long ago stopped wearing cheap perfume in favor of patchouli oil, under which she always smelled in a good way like toast and over which, in this moment, she smelled like body odor.

'I was in the neighborhood,' she said. 'Also, Reed sucks.'

'Wait, did you just leave? You're not on a break?'

'I am on a break. A self-imposed one.' She entered the room, set her duffel on the floor, and sat on my bed. Then she said, 'You're Heather, right? I'm Vi, Daisy's original roommate.'

Heather looked between us, seeming confused, and I said, 'This is my sister.' *Daisy* wasn't how anyone at college knew me, and I felt a flare of annoyance. It wasn't that I didn't want to see Vi, but there were preparations I'd have made if I'd known she was coming.

'Do you have any food?' Vi asked.

Though Heather and I were co-renting a mini-refrigerator, it contained only yogurt, which belonged to her, and vodka, which belonged to me and which Lauren and I mixed with raspberry Crystal Light and drank before parties; I'd considered asking Heather if the vodka bothered her, but I was afraid of the answer. Looking down at my watch, I saw that it was just after eleven. 'We could go get pizza,' I said.

Vi set her palms against my mattress and pushed herself off. 'Sounds *magnifique.*' She walked over to a closet, the one that wasn't mine, and opened it.

'Here,' I said. From my own closet, I pulled out a fleece jacket and passed it to her. It was impossible not to notice that Vi's weight, which had stabilized in high school, had climbed again since we'd started college, and her face and body contained a new puffiness. Vi and I weren't beautiful – we had our father's long, narrow nose – but we could certainly be pretty, because we also had our mother's large blue eyes and light hair. And yet, with her dumpy ponytail and clothes, it almost seemed as if Vi were trying to look unattractive. It would have been mean to see her as a cautionary example, a warning of what would happen if I stopped climbing the StairMaster every day, but after our time apart, both our similarities and differences appeared more starkly to me than they ever had before. Her hand reaching for the doorknob as we left the room, cuffed by the red fleece of my jacket – it could have been my hand, there was a way in which it *was* my hand.

Outside, as we turned onto College Avenue, I said, 'What's going on?'

'I came here on the Greyhound, which did you know that's called riding the dog? A guy who got on in Salt Lake City asked if he could put his head on my shoulder to sleep, and a guy who got on in Denver asked if I'd pierce his ear.'

'You said no, right?'

'He even had a cup of ice. But yes – I said no.'

'You should have sat next to a woman.'

'For some of the time, I did. I've been on the bus since Sunday night.'

Which meant forty-eight hours before. I said, 'I still don't understand—'

'My roommate Lisa is totally anorexic. She goes running twice a day, for like six miles each time, and she talks about food constantly and hoards candy – Starbursts and Jolly Ranchers – but she doesn't *eat* it. And the other roommate, Wendy, she's supposedly some kind of engineering genius, but she has no sense of humor and uses this disgusting deodorant that she sprays on for so long every morning, I can taste it in my mouth. There's a lot of weirdos at Reed, but not cool weirdos. That's what I thought it would be.'

'But you're planning to go back, right? Did you tell your professors you'd be missing class?'

'The professors aren't friendly, either. It's just not my kind of place.'

'Vi, you've barely been there a month.'

'I want to take a gap year and travel, like everyone does in England.'

Vi also had a work-study job – hers was in food

service – but I knew without asking that she had no more money saved than I did, nor were our parents the kind to fund such activities.

As we passed Rosemary Lane, she said, 'So you're happy as a clam here, huh? Mizzou is a dream come true?'

Carefully, I said, 'I like it overall.' I decided then to come clean on the other piece of information I'd concealed in my emails, besides my name change. I said, 'I joined a sorority. I'm a Theta.'

To my surprise, she said, 'I thought I wanted to go somewhere without a Greek system, but now I can see the point of it, just for meeting people.'

Was it possible Vi hadn't made any friends at Reed? Perhaps her emails had been as selectively revealing as mine. *I went to an anti-apartheid rally,* she'd mentioned recently, which I'd interpreted as Vi having fun.

'So who's your boyfriend now that you and Tom are done?' she asked.

I thought of Ben Murphy, with whom I'd made out after our ping-pong match, but I said, 'Nobody.'

'Wait a second.' Vi actually stopped walking. '*You* don't have a boyfriend?'

'It's not that weird.'

'I feel like there should be dogs falling from the sky and statues crying blood. Are you still talking to Tom?'

'Not for a while.' We had reached University Avenue, and as we turned, I said, 'How long are you planning to stay? No offense.'

Vi laughed. 'No offense, but I've never liked you. No offense, but your personality sucks.'

'That's not what I meant.'

'I'm psyched to explore Columbia,' she said. 'I probably should have come here to begin with.'

Really? I thought. It was good to see Vi, but in the close quarters of college life, I wasn't sure I'd be able to contain her, or prevent her familiarity with my old self from spilling into my new life. But because it was the way I wished I felt, I said, '*Mi* dorm room *es su* dorm room.'

We ordered a twelve-inch pizza with sausage and green peppers, and while we waited for it, Vi said, 'I knew as soon as I got out there that I'd made a mistake. I should never have gone to Reed without visiting. The whole vibe was just off. But I was like, okay, I'll get through the semester, maybe even the first year, and then I'll transfer. And at first I tried to be a good little student. Really. I was all diligent. But in classes, everyone just loved hearing themselves talk. The place is overrun with pretentious windbags. And the bathrooms in my dorm were coed, did I tell you that? I was like, wait, I'm really expected to take a shit with some dude's hairy legs right next to me? I started walking over to this administrative building to poop.'

'I bet you'll get used to it,' I said.

She shook her head. 'That's not the point. This is the part I have to tell you. I'm in the library a few nights ago, sitting in this carrel, and all of a sudden, there's this crazy yellow light, this energy, and I'm inside it, and a voice is saying to me, "You're not meant to suffer." Over and over: "You're not meant to suffer, you're not meant to suffer, you're not meant to suffer."'

No, Vi, I thought. *No, no, no.* More than four years had passed since I'd felt the presence summoned by Marisa Mazarelli's Ouija board. I said, 'Had you done acid?'

Vi looked annoyed. 'This had nothing to do with drugs. It was a really beautiful experience. It was peaceful. I was inside the light, it was like being in a swimming pool except with light instead of water, and the voice says, "I am your guardian. You're not meant to suffer." And I'm like, okay, well, what *am* I meant to do? And the voice says, "You're on a journey of discovery." Then the light goes away, and I'm still sitting in the chair in the library, but I hadn't imagined it. It was definitely real.'

Across the booth, we looked at each other, and Vi's expression was eager. I said, 'Okay.' What I wouldn't have given to be someone who could dismiss her story as utter nonsense.

'I got on the bus the next day,' she said.

'That seems like a really literal interpretation of a journey.'

Seeming hurt, Vi said, 'I don't know why you can't be supportive. It wasn't scary at all, if that's what you're thinking. It was profound.'

'Reed is a great school,' I said. 'You were so excited to go there. Have you joined any groups?'

'I'm telling you I had a transcendent experience and you're saying I should try out for debate? I thought you would understand.'

Of course I understood; even at her most impossible, Vi had never said or done anything I could not imagine saying or doing myself, if I had less self-control and respect for convention. But her tone was rubbing me the wrong way, and I said, 'Sorry to disappoint you.'

That night, she started out on the carpet, but by two o'clock, which was half an hour after we'd turned out the light, she'd climbed into bed beside me; she said the floor was hard. By two-thirty, I'd insisted that she flip so her head was by my feet, though once she'd done so, it became clear that this setup was no better than being side by side. Around three-ten, she began scratching behind her knee, her nails scraping over the skin just a few inches from my face.

I pressed my hand to her leg and whispered, so as not to awaken Heather, 'Quit it.'

'I think I might have picked up something on the bus,' Vi whispered back.

'Great.' Before climbing into bed, she'd taken a shower, padding to and from the communal girls' bathroom in my white terry-cloth robe and flip-flops, though I wasn't sure if that meant Vi was clean or that my robe was now dirty.

'Not like an STD,' Vi said. 'Like a rash.'

'Then you'll only make it worse by scratching.'

Vi sighed loudly – was Heather really sleeping through all of this? – and I turned onto my side, away from my sister. I knew the exact second she fell asleep; I could hear the change in her breathing. Almost right away, our conversation at the pizza place asserted itself in my brain. Would the yellow light overtake me, too, in this moment or later? I didn't want it to. I wanted nothing to do with it. Vi had said the experience wasn't scary, but what if it *was* the same energy that had been there when Marisa and I had used the Ouija board? It wasn't that I necessarily believed in Satan, but I believed in the existence of darkness, which was perhaps the same thing. And back then, I also hadn't immediately recognized that presence as bad.

The next afternoon, when I returned from my economics lecture, Heather was away from the room and Vi was lying on my bed reading the *Missourian*, Mizzou's student newspaper. 'Someone named Ben Murphy called for someone named Kate.' Vi looked amused. 'Isn't Kate kind of bland?'

'It *is* my middle name.' This was what I'd planned to say if someone from high school asked about the change, though so far I hadn't ended up in a class with anybody from Kirkwood. That Vi was the first person for whom I needed to break out the excuse was deeply irritating.

'First of all, your middle name is Kathleen,' Vi said. 'But I just don't see you as a Kate. What about Maya? That's pretty.'

141

'Then you be Maya.'

'You don't have to get all grouchy.' She set down the newspaper. 'What do Mom and Dad think?'

'I haven't told them.' In fact, it surprised me that she assumed I had. Though St Louis was only two hours from Columbia, and many of my classmates who were from the area went home on weekends, it seemed understood that I wouldn't return to our house until Thanksgiving. 'Call after five on Sundays because the rates are cheaper,' my mother had said on the drive to Mizzou, and when I did call collect each Sunday, I spoke to her for five minutes, at which point, as precisely as if she'd set an egg timer, she passed off the phone to my father. After I'd spoken to him for five minutes, I'd hear her in the background, saying, 'Earl, that's enough. She'll call again next week.' During our conversations, my mother never asked questions. Instead, she told what might generously be called stories, many of which I already knew – that our neighbors the Pockneys had had to cut down the dogwood tree in their front yard because of a fungus, which would prompt her to recall the time their Jack Russell terrier, Eisenhower, had run away for three days, which would prompt her to say, as she often had in the past, that she didn't think it was right to give a dog the name of a president. When I spoke to my father, he did ask about my life at Mizzou, but in a general way, as if I were the daughter of a friend. How were my classes? Was I enjoying the bustle of campus life?

From week to week, he had no follow-up questions about the outcome of a particular paper I'd written or the craft project I'd planned at the adult day-care center; instead, in every conversation, we started anew with generalities. After my mother had given him notice, he'd always conclude by saying, in a rueful tone, 'It's awfully quiet here without you girls,' and I'd try to resist the downward pull of everything contained within the remark, the gravity of sadness in our house. Lightly, I'd say, 'Well, it's good to talk to you, Dad.' Often, when I placed the phone's receiver back in its cradle, I'd have to blink away tears.

But what I had said to Vi was true: While I'd been actively hiding my name change from her, it hadn't occurred to me to mention it to our parents. They were so confined to one particular part of my life that it didn't seem like it mattered if they knew. Maybe this was callous to think, but it just wasn't of much consequence what they called me.

Vi stretched her arms above her head. 'So, *Kate* – is Ben Murphy the guy who's not your boyfriend?'

'Did he leave a message?'

She shook her head. 'Just his number. Let's go get Chinese food. I'm starving.'

'I'm meeting my friend Ann for dinner at six so we can do problem sets.'

'Then eat two dinners. It's not even five yet.'

The truth was that I wasn't so sure I wanted Vi to accompany me to the cafeteria again anyway. That morning, when I'd taken her to breakfast, we'd sat with my friend Lauren and a couple other Theta girls I didn't know well, and after I got up to find an orange, I returned to discover everyone at the table with stricken expressions, listening to Vi deliver a speech about how women's armpit hair contained powerful sex pheromones. It could have been worse, though; she could have been talking about the yellow light. I said, 'I'll go with you to get Chinese food, and then I really do have to meet Ann.'

I ate strawberry frozen yogurt for my second dinner, and as Ann and I were leaving the cafeteria, we passed a group of guys, one of whom said, 'Kate?' When I looked over, Ben Murphy said, 'Hey, I don't know if you got my message.'

'Yeah, sorry . . .' I trailed off. In the not particularly flattering light of the cafeteria's entry hall, I noticed that Ben's wide nose turned up at the end, displaying his nostrils in a piglike way. He wore khaki pants and a tucked-in royal blue polo shirt, and he was okay-looking, but the fact that we'd made out at the frat party was clearly revealed in this moment to have been a result of drunkenness rather than any particular attraction between us.

He said, 'We're having a barbecue tomorrow at the DU house, and you should come if you can.' There was the smallest strain in his delivery, the effort he was making to sound casual.

'Oh. Well, I have a biology test, but I'll try to make it.'

'Yo, Murph, quit flirting,' said one of the guys

144

he'd entered the cafeteria with – they were lingering a few feet away – and Ben looked embarrassed.

'Come over anytime after five,' he said.

Heather was in the room but Vi wasn't when I returned from the adult day-care center the following afternoon. I changed into shorts and a T-shirt and walked to the gym to use the StairMaster. When I got back to Schurz Hall, Vi was sitting on the floor outside my room, which meant that Heather must have departed in my absence, locking the door behind her.

Vi had a book open on her lap, and as I approached, she held it up, cover out – it was *Their Eyes Were Watching God,* by Zora Neale Hurston – and said, 'Have you read this?'

I shook my head.

'I just went to an amazing African-American Lit class taught by this guy who's a major Hurston expert. Don't shorts that short give you a wedgie?'

I squinted at her. 'You went to a class?'

'When in Rome . . .'

'Vi, you're not a student here.'

'They weren't checking IDs at the door.'

'That's not the point.'

'What's it to you if I sit in on a class?'

I hadn't yet unlocked the door, nor had she stood. I folded my arms in front of my chest. 'You need to go back to Reed,' I said.

'Funny you should say that.' As if this were her ace in the hole, a triumph for her to lord over me, she said, 'Because actually I'm not enrolled. I stopped going to classes weeks ago, and the dean said I had to withdraw for the semester.'

I stared at her. 'What's wrong with you?'

'Nothing now that I'm gone from there.'

'Do you think you can just stay here forever? Because you can't. It's rude to Heather.'

'Oh, really?' Vi smirked. 'To Heather?'

'If you're not going back to Reed, then you need to go home.'

Vi did stand then, the book tucked under her arm. 'See, I can't do that, either,' she said, and again I could have sworn her tone contained a bragging note. 'Because if I'm in St Louis, I'll just keep fucking Mr Caldwell.' We looked at each other – I suppose I should have felt compassion, but I wanted to slap the smugness off her face – and she added, 'Don't even pretend you didn't know, because you knew.'

Had I known? People had said Vi was Mr Caldwell's favorite; junior year, she sat at the desk closest to his, and once my boyfriend, Tom, had jokingly told her that she'd sit on Caldwell's lap if she could. But there was an enormous difference between teasing Vi that she and Mr Caldwell were in love and her having real, actual sex with him. He was at least thirty-five, I was pretty sure, and he was handsome for a teacher, but the idea of him as someone you *touched* entirely changed the criteria for judgment. His womanly hips and butt, the paunch of his belly,

146

his blond beard and flushed cheeks – recalling them actively repelled me.

Finally, I said, 'Where? If you were hooking up with him, where'd you go?'

'It was mostly in his office during my free periods. I'd meet him about "a paper"' – Vi made air quotes – 'and he'd shut the door. And I'd be able to hear people in the hallway outside talking about the football game or whatever.'

'Weren't you scared of getting caught?'

'What, by a teacher?' She scoffed. 'I think he got off on the danger. Oh, he did once take me to a restaurant in Illinois, when his wife was out of town, but that actually stressed him out way more than banging me on school property.'

'Did you lose your virginity to him?'

'God, no.' Vi laughed. 'Patrick and I did it in ninth grade, and it's how he figured out for sure he's into dudes. Caldwell's not a pedophile, by the way. Pedophiles like children who haven't gone through puberty. Anyway, we were in touch when I was at Reed, but his wife just had a baby, and I'm thinking we should end it. It's a little gross now that he's a dad.'

'But it wasn't gross when he was your teacher?'

Vi shrugged.

Her nonchalance – it was infuriating. 'It's like you're trying as hard as you can to make a mess of your life,' I said. 'And you know what? I bet eventually, you'll succeed.'

'What the fuck is that supposed to mean?'

'Why can't you just be a normal person? Why do you have to have sex with teachers and talk to spirits and drop out of college?'

'Why do you have to be so narrow-minded and judgmental?'

'Judgmental?' My voice was raised in a way I'd regret later, not because I cared about offending Vi but because other people on the hall might have heard. Almost in a shout, I said, 'Judgmental is what you call letting you stay here after you show up with no warning? You're wearing my clothes, you're using my toothpaste, you're sleeping in my *bed*, for Christ's sake. So if that's judgmental, then I'd hate to see how you'd be treated by someone who doesn't feel as sorry for you as I do.'

As I stalked away, it wasn't that I forgot I was holding the room key – taking off with the room key accounted for the only satisfaction I felt. What I had forgotten was that I was wearing a sweaty T-shirt and shorts and that, as with my abrupt departure from my own high school graduation, I had no particular place to go. I'd find Lauren, I decided, but when I knocked on the door of her room, two floors below mine, her roommate said, 'I think she's at a barbecue.'

Ben's fraternity barbecue – I'd forgotten that, too. If I'd still been interested in Ben, I wouldn't then have decided to go; I wouldn't have wanted to appear before him unshowered. But my wish to tell Lauren what a terrible person my sister was exceeded my concern over Ben's opinion, and I walked down Rollins Street to the DU house. I had just turned onto Maryland Avenue when Ben himself appeared with another guy. Seeing me, Ben smiled so broadly that it was like I really had shown up for his benefit. 'We forgot the ketchup and mustard,' he said. 'Want to go on a Hy-Vee run?'

'Sure,' I said. (Sometimes when I look back, it feels as if what he said wasn't *Want to go on a Hy-Vee run?* but, rather, *Want to be my girlfriend for the next six years?* and with just as little thought, I still said sure.)

He drove a black BMW, which made me understand that he probably came from a rich family. The other guy, Nate, let me sit in front. Even on the ride, I could feel Ben's solicitousness, how his attention had shifted from his frat brother to me, a girl he barely knew.

By the time we got back to the DU house, my outrage at Vi had subsided; besides, it wasn't as if I'd have told Lauren or anyone else the whole story. Lauren was the one who approached me, saying, 'Why are you wearing workout clothes?' She had on a striped knee-length skirt and a cardigan sweater.

'My sister is driving me crazy,' I said. 'I look terrible, right?'

'You look cute,' Lauren said. 'Sporty.'

Ben had gotten me a plastic cup of beer and, when I finished the first, another; I ate a hot dog and some potato chips, and I joined a badminton game occurring on the lawn. U2 was playing on

149

speakers set in windows on the second floor, and it was a nice autumn evening that grew cool as darkness fell. 'Are you cold?' Ben asked. 'I could get you a jacket.'

Had Heather let Vi into the room, or was she out roaming the campus? I wasn't still furious, but I also wasn't ready to see her again. This barbecue, this was what I had come to Mizzou for. Not to be weighed down by Vi's weirdness, her bad choices and creepy spirituality. 'Maybe I will borrow a jacket,' I said.

What Ben had meant, of course, was from his own dorm room, which wasn't in the DU house and was in fact as far from it as my dorm, but I walked with him there, solidly buzzed, and when we got to his room – it was on the first floor of Hatch, a double he shared with a roommate who conveniently was elsewhere – he turned on the overhead light and we'd been inside no more than thirty seconds before he kissed me. Then he nudged me toward his bed, and he was on top of me, nibbling my left ear in a way that seemed ridiculous. He pushed up my T-shirt and stuck his hand under my sports bra, the base of which was still slightly damp from my time on the StairMaster hours before, but Ben seemed either not to notice or not to care. I kept tuning in and out of the moment – it was hard to decide if it was more alarming that Vi had slept with Mr Caldwell or been forced to withdraw from Reed – and I was half-aware of when Ben eased my shirt over my head. (Presumably Vi had done with Mr Caldwell the very things I was in the midst of doing with Ben.) I was the one who removed my bra, because it wasn't the kind that hooked in back, and then my shorts and underwear were off, too, but Ben was still dressed. At some point, he'd unfastened the dark brown leather belt he was wearing, then unbuttoned and unzipped his khaki pants, pulling them and his boxers down below his butt, but he didn't remove them, and the two sides of the unbuckled belt, the buckle and the leather tip, kept slapping my thighs as he thrust against me. No penetration had occurred when, without warning, he came. He froze immediately, and I said, 'Oh – okay.' I didn't want to offer reassurance if that would only embarrass him. But the fact that the hook-up had apparently concluded, that he didn't understand there was a way to make it up to me – it made me suspect he'd never had a girlfriend. Finally, I said, 'Do you have some Kleenex?'

What he handed me was a full-sized maroon bath towel, and I mopped up between my legs. He was standing by the bed, and he said in an almost mean tone, as if I were the one who'd done something I shouldn't have, 'Are you going to tell Lauren?'

'No.' I slid on my underwear and shorts and reached for my sports bra.

Again, accusingly, he said, 'I've had sex before.'

'Okay,' I said, and I pulled on my shirt. Remarkably, or not, I'd never removed my socks and running shoes. It seemed agreed upon that I

151

would leave, and I stood and stepped toward the door.

In a voice that was only incrementally less hostile, he said, 'We should hang out again.'

Back in Schurz Hall, Heather was sitting at her desk eating yogurt, and there was no sign of Vi. 'Have you seen my sister?' I asked.

Heather shook her head. 'Not since this afternoon.'

'I hope it's okay that she's still here,' I said.

'Oh, she's not bothering me.' Heather took a bite of yogurt. 'She can stay as long as she wants.' After a pause, she said, 'I apologize if this is weird to ask, but are you guys identical twins?'

Growing up, Vi and I had gotten the question endlessly, sometimes on a daily basis, but this was the first time it had come from someone who seemed to think the answer would be no rather than yes.

'Yeah, we are,' I said.

'Really?' I could tell she was surprised. 'I was wondering, but I didn't—' She smiled. 'I'm so jealous of you.'

Around eight in the morning, I became aware of someone lightly shaking my arms, saying my name. The room was still more dark than light because the shades were drawn, and I had two groggy realizations at the same time. The first was that the person waking me was Vi – the name she was saying

152

was Daisy – and the second was that she had never returned to the room the night before and I'd had my best night's sleep since Monday.

I propped myself up on my elbows, and Vi whispered, 'I need to talk to you in the hall.'

I climbed from bed and followed her out. Facing me, Vi looked wild and agitated: messy-haired and baggy-eyed and jittery, smelling like cigarettes.

'I got in trouble,' she said.

A window in the hall overlooked an oak tree, and even though the window wasn't open, I could feel what a pleasant fall morning it was; something about the sunny weather, the turning leaves, made me less alarmed by Vi's summoning than I should have been. It took her perhaps five minutes to explain what had happened: The night before, she'd had dinner in town and wandered around for a while before making her way back to Schurz Hall. Then she'd parked herself on a couch in the empty common room on the third floor and watched television for seven hours. Some students had come in and out during this time, but she hadn't spoken to them. Just before six in the morning, while Vi was watching the old movie *The Philadelphia Story*, a group of three girls had shown up in spandex shorts and tank tops, one of them toting a *Buns of Steel* tape. (Rising at the crack of dawn to exercise – I couldn't imagine.) The girl carrying the tape had told Vi that they worked out together at this time, in this place, every morning, and that it was their turn to use the TV and VCR. The movie was almost finished, Vi said. There were only a few minutes left, and then they could have the common room. But they'd reserved it starting at five-thirty, the girl said, and she retrieved a clipboard hanging from a hook outside the room to show Vi where she'd written her name in the time slot. Fine, Vi replied, but she just wanted to watch the end of the movie; surely the girls' buns could wait? No, the group's leader said. The room was theirs.

I had a hunch and said, 'Had you been smoking?'

'Just cigarettes,' Vi said, and I thought that this violation must have particularly galled the early morning exercisers.

The girl stood in front of the television screen, blocking Vi's view, and said again that it was their turn to use the common room, fair and square, and because the movie ended then and the credits started and the girl had made her miss the last part, Vi said, 'Are you happy now, you selfish cunt?' At that point she either tossed the remote control to the girl (Vi's version) or threw it at her head (the girl's version); in any case, the corner of the remote hit the girl in the jaw.

'And she started bleeding, but like, the tiniest, tiniest bit,' Vi said. 'From inside her mouth. She spit, and seriously, it was the amount of blood when you're flossing.'

As I listened, the leaves outside the window seemed considerably less cheerful, the day less promising. Really, what had Vi been thinking?

The girl freaked out, Vi said, claiming Vi had attacked her, and Vi insisted that it had been an accident, and the next thing she knew, two officers from campus security had appeared – one of the other girls had slipped away and called them – and Vi had been handcuffed.

'Are you kidding?' I said.

'Well, the handcuffs were plastic,' she said. 'Kind of like garbage ties.'

One officer had escorted her on foot to the university police station, which was on Virginia Avenue, and though she hadn't seen them while walking over, once there, Vi spotted the three *Buns of Steel* girls across the room. She was interviewed – not in an interrogation room, just sitting in a chair while the officer behind the desk took notes, and he'd already removed the cuffs during the walk from the dorm. He consulted with other officers, including the one who'd interviewed the girls, and after about forty-five minutes, by which point the girls had left, Vi's officer told her she was free to go but he was turning the matter over to the Office of Student Conduct, and she should expect to receive a letter from them shortly.

'Wait,' I said. 'You never told him you don't go here?'

'I know I fucked up,' Vi said. 'I know, okay? And I'm sorry, but I didn't know what else to do.' Then she said, 'They don't think I'm me. They think I'm you.'

Campus mail was, apparently, quite efficient, and I received the letter from the Office of Student

Conduct in my mailbox in the entry of Schurz Hall by noon that very day. It listed which of the Collected Rules and Regulations of the University of Missouri System might have been violated by Daisy Kathleen Shramm – 'Physical abuse,' which was further defined as 'conduct which threatens or endangers the health or safety of any person' – as well as the date and time of the incident of concern; the letter also provided instructions on scheduling my meeting with a Student Conduct officer and warned that if I failed to do so, a hold would be placed on my student account. I called the number and made an appointment for the following morning at eleven. Then I called campus information to get the number for Ben Murphy because I had no idea where the slip of paper was on which Vi had written it several days before. Vi was in the shower, after having slept for most of the morning.

When I identified myself, Ben sounded surprised as he said, 'Oh, hi.'

'I'm wondering if you can drive my sister and me to St Louis,' I said. 'She'll stay there, and I'll come back with you. I'll pay for gas.'

'When?'

'Now,' I said. 'It's sort of an emergency.'

'A medical emergency?'

'No, she just needs to go home, but if she gets on a bus, I'm afraid she'll go somewhere else.'

'I didn't know you have a sister who goes here.'

'I don't. She's been visiting. Can you take us?'

'I have class at two-fifteen, but I don't know – I guess I could skip it.'

'Come here at two-fifteen,' I said. 'I'm in Schurz, so you can pull up right in front.'

It wasn't that I'd changed my mind about dating him; it wasn't that I trusted him; it wasn't even that I felt he owed me after our botched hookup. It was that he was the only person I knew at Mizzou who had a car.

I told Vi after she returned from the shower, wearing my bathrobe, carrying my plastic bucket of shampoo and conditioner. Her hair was a wet rope that she'd twisted over her left shoulder – she'd squeezed it out after turning off the water, I knew the exact gesture – and it was then, observing her hair, that it first occurred to me to cut my own.

She looked at me with a wounded expression. 'You're kicking me out?'

'If you stay here, *I'll* probably get kicked out. There are rules against people who aren't students living in the dorm, and now I can't take any chances.' I hadn't gotten angry when she'd told me what she'd done in the common room; if she had proven that my wariness of her was warranted, she had simultaneously given me the reason I needed to send her away.

'Just let me have a few more days,' she said.

'What difference will that make?'

'I'm thinking I'll start taking classes in January.

And don't worry, I won't stay with you until then. I walked by a house on Bouchelle Avenue with a sign saying they have a room for rent.'

'Do you have any money?'

'I'm planning to get a job.' She was quiet. 'You could spot me.'

'Vi, I barely have money. Anyway, why do you want to live somewhere that you don't know anyone?'

In a quiet, defeated voice, she said, 'I know you.'

Oh, Vi, I think now. *Oh, Vi, forgive me.* I have no idea which house on Bouchelle she meant, but in my mind it's a co-op where they'd all smoke pot together while making tofu and kale for dinner; I never entered such a place, but Columbia was crawling with them. And in this alternate version of events, in the help wanted section of the *Missourian,* we find Vi a waitress position, and she remains in my dorm room until she's made enough for first and last month's rent, if the co-op hippies would even have required that much. She does indeed start taking classes at Mizzou in January, my second semester. She and I meet for coffee a couple times a week. She doesn't crowd or embarrass me; I don't exile her. We both have our own lives, and they overlap, but not excessively. After she catches up with a few summer classes, we graduate together in 1997. She enters the Peace Corps, or she enters law school, or she goes to work for a nonprofit, or she becomes a physical therapist or a vet.

Or maybe she never earns her degree in this

version of events, either, but at least I don't force her out. I let her stay a little longer, until she leaves on her own. What I did – making her go – was justified more than it was necessary; it was defensible more than it was right.

In the version of events that did occur, the real version, I didn't want the *Buns of Steel* girls to connect us, didn't want to risk them seeing us together, and so as Vi stood there in my bathrobe, her hair dripping, I said, 'I really think it's better if you leave.'

In Ben's car, I sat in the front seat and Vi sat in back, and Ben, looking at Vi in the rearview mirror, said, 'I talked to you on the phone, didn't I? You guys sound alike,' and Vi said, 'I assure you the similarity ends there.' And then she continued, embarking on a kind of monologue: 'But really, I only have myself to blame. No one knows *Kate* here better than I do, and that's why I should have realized she's not the person you turn to when you need a helping hand. If you behave yourself, if you're dressed up in your pretty clothes and acting all happy, then sure, Daisy will give you the time of day, but at the first sign of trouble, she's out of there. She doesn't like conflict, she doesn't like *weirdness*. And watch out, because according to her, I'm just getting weirder. I had this amazing spiritual experience, probably the most amazing experience of my life, and Daisy's like, "Yep, ignore it, pretend it didn't happen."'

In equal measures, I wanted to silence Vi and I felt hypnotized by the drone of her voice, the inappropriateness of her disclosures – the way that if I could have scripted her dialogue in this moment, everything she was saying was the opposite of what I'd have chosen. It was hard to gauge how much sense she was making to Ben, especially given that she'd switched back to calling me Daisy, but it seemed safe to assume that neither of us was coming off well.

'You know what, Daisy?' Vi said, but even then, when she was ostensibly addressing me, her words still had a distant, performative quality – they were more for Ben than for me, and more for some invisible, sympathetic audience than for either one of us. 'Just because that stuff in eighth grade with Marisa sucked for you, that doesn't mean all spiritual communication is bad. You can choose to cut yourself off, and hey, it's a free country, that's your choice. But that's not how I want to be. I want to open myself up, I want to experience other dimensions, I don't want to be bound by the rules of this world. Does that make me a freak? So be it. Now, what's your name again? Ben? Ben, don't worry that Daisy is like me. She's not *weird*. Yes, she has the senses. I cannot tell a lie. But she's going to hide them or die trying, so you're good to go with your vanilla romance. And you seem like a typical preppy guy, which I'm not saying to insult you, I'd assume most typical preppy guys are glad to be called typical and preppy. To each his or her own. What I'm trying to say is that I wish you and my sister a long and happy life together.'

The car was quiet – it was hard to believe Vi had truly stopped talking – and Ben said, 'Who's Marisa?'

'Nobody.' I turned around again, making eye contact with Vi, and said, 'Just stop, okay? He's doing us a favor by driving us.'

'He's doing *you* a favor.' But surprisingly, she didn't say anything else, and after a few minutes, Ben turned on the stereo; a Spin Doctors CD played, the one with 'Two Princes' and 'Little Miss Can't Be Wrong.' Even now, if I'm in a store and either of those songs comes on, I'll walk out.

An hour and a half passed, and dread collected in my stomach as I gave Ben directions for getting off 270. When we arrived at our strange familiar house on Gilbert Street, sitting there the same as always in our absence, Ben said, 'I'll go hang out in that McDonald's we just passed if you tell me how long you need.'

'No, I'm only going in for a second,' I said. 'Wait for me here.'

'Are you sure?' He looked perplexed, but I nodded and climbed from the car.

It was four-thirty P.M., and we had to ring the doorbell repeatedly because neither Vi nor I had a house key. After a minute, I could tell our mother was peering through the peephole, and then she opened the door and said in an alarmed voice, 'Why are you two here?' She was wearing a robe over her brown nylon nightgown, and white slippers.

I said, 'Vi wants to come home. Reed didn't work out.'

Our mother scowled. 'That was a waste of money. Does your father know?'

'Not yet.' I leaned in to kiss my mother's cheek; she and Vi didn't touch. I was carrying Vi's duffel bag, and I said to my sister, 'I'll put this upstairs, okay?'

Getting out of the car, Vi had seemed a little stunned, and she didn't reply to me. Then she said to our mother, in a normal voice, 'What's the difference between a screw and a staple?'

'I have no idea what you're talking about,' our mother said.

'I don't know,' Vi said. 'I've never been stapled.'

As I climbed the steps, I heard my mother say to her, 'You're just as snotty as you always were.'

The door to our old bedroom was closed, and the Sisterland sign that Vi had taped to it eight years before was still there; it had been there all along, but when I'd lived at home, I'd stopped seeing it. Surely, there was a kind of irony to it – the room had either a population of one or zero now, but definitely not of two – but there was nothing to be gained from pondering this incongruity. I pushed open the door, set down Vi's duffel, then walked out and used the bathroom before returning to the first floor. Vi and my mother had moved into the kitchen, Vi sitting at the table eating potato chips and drinking orange juice and my mother standing and watching her suspiciously. 'I have to go because the guy who gave us a ride is waiting,' I said. 'Tell Dad I'm sorry I missed him.'

'You're leaving?' My mother's expression was confused.

'This guy I know gave us a ride, but he has to get back.'

Vi wouldn't look at me; she got up, carried her glass of juice and bag of potato chips into the living room, and turned on the television. I leaned into my mother, and she was so insubstantial that it was like embracing a phantom. 'I'll be home at Thanksgiving,' I said. 'Which is only a month away.'

I stepped back, and my mother looked me up and down and said – really, her voice sounded more concerned than cruel – 'You should be careful, Daisy. You're starting to put on weight, too.'

Back in the car, I said to Ben, 'If you want to go to McDonald's, let's get on the highway first because the one here is really slow.'

As Ben started the engine, I felt an absurd fear that Vi would run out of the house, pull open my car door, yank me to the ground, and force me to stay while Ben drove away. Neither he nor I spoke as he navigated through downtown Kirkwood. Only when we were back on 40, headed west, did he say in a sincere tone, 'Does she have, like, a diagnosis?'

'A what?'

'Like if she's mentally ill, or—'

Icily, I said, 'She just has a lot going on right now.'

At the McDonald's where we did stop for an early dinner, we didn't talk much, but I didn't like Ben enough to find the silences awkward. If I felt grateful toward him, it was a resentful kind of gratitude; he seemed to be such a blandly ordinary person that I doubted he had a framework for understanding someone like Vi. Ben and I also spoke little once we were back in the car. But the next day, when he emailed and asked if I'd like to go to a movie on Saturday night, saying no would have been a rudeness more brazen than I had the courage for. We saw *The Fugitive* at the Hollywood Stadium, and afterward we had actual sex, in his dorm bed, with a condom. He didn't tell me until two months later that it had been his first time, but he didn't need to. It was just for a few weeks that I still saw his nose as piglike, and after that it only struck me when we were with his family, because his father and two older sisters had similar noses. Ben and I remained a couple all through college, and after graduation, we moved together to Chicago.

Vi no longer had an email account, or not one she had access to, but certainly I could have called her during the day, when our mother was in bed and our father was at work. I didn't. I heard, that Sunday, during the five minutes I spent talking to my father, that she'd been hired at a Lion's Choice,

164

a roast beef sandwich restaurant with franchises all over St Louis; the next week, my father said she'd moved into an apartment in Dogtown with Patrick, who was taking classes at Forest Park Community College. My father never seemed offended that I'd been home without staying long enough to see him, though he wouldn't have told me if he was. I assume that my parents asked Vi nothing about her return, that the questions they didn't pose were infinite.

On the night before Thanksgiving, after taking the bus from Columbia to St Louis and eating dinner at home, I borrowed my father's Buick and drove to Vi and Patrick's apartment. It was nine P.M., and they were having spaghetti with marinara sauce and watching TV with the volume turned way up while a haze of pot smoke hung in the air. Vi seemed heavier than ever and wholly upbeat. When she went to the bathroom, I said to Patrick, 'Are she and Mr Caldwell—'

'Unh-unh-uh.' Patrick wagged an index finger back and forth while shaking his head. 'In this abode, we do not speak that name.' Which wasn't a real answer, and one I gladly accepted. I learned later – three years later, after Mr Caldwell had been fired from Kirkwood High when four girls, none of whom were Vi, came forward to report their own sexual relationships with him – that he and Vi had continued to have sporadic contact that fall.

The following spring, Vi asked a patron at Lion's Choice how her french fries were, and the woman said, 'Them is disgusting.' This single grammatical

165

desecration prompted Vi to enroll at Webster University, which was just a few minutes from the house where we'd grown up. Though Vi eventually took classes from nearly every academic institution in St Louis, she never earned a bachelor's degree. In the almost two decades since I arranged for Ben to whisk us away from the campus of Mizzou, I've had ample time to consider my culpability in this fact.

The Student Conduct officer I met with in the fall of my freshman year was a warm, heavyset Latino man of about thirty. I'm not sure if it was because I expressed contrition (it never occurred to me that telling the truth might have solved more problems than it would have created) that I received a warning and one year of probation but no more severe sanctions. Under the Family Educational Rights and Privacy Act of 1974, my parents weren't notified; they would have been contacted only for an infraction involving drugs or alcohol. The conduct violation would remain on my record for five years, which was part of why I waited until a year and a half after graduation to apply to social work school. I wanted to be able to answer no to the question of whether I'd ever been subject to disciplinary action. I revealed to no one, not even Lauren or Ben, what Vi had done.

Right after my meeting in the Office of Student Conduct and before I was due at the adult day-care center, I hurried to a hair salon in town and asked the stylist to take off eight inches. This pixie was the most drastic haircut I'd ever had, and wrong for my face, but I didn't regret it because it was meant to prevent the *Buns of Steel* girls from recognizing me; it made me feel I'd taken every precaution. It wasn't until the stylist was finished and had removed the nylon smock that the dream I'd had the morning before Vi had arrived at Mizzou came back to me, that moment when she'd turned around in the lecture hall. But it had never been Vi I'd seen in the dream, I realized as I faced the mirror. Instead, I'd seen myself.

CHAPTER 8

It hadn't occurred to me that our dinner with the Wheelings – Amelia's first 'meat night' – would still happen, in light of the news Hank and Courtney had received the day before about Courtney's pregnancy, but on Saturday afternoon, Hank texted me: *5:30 for pizza yeah?* I texted back: *Sure if that works for u guys.*

The place our families liked had windows through which kids could watch a kitchen crew rolling the dough and topping it. Even though it was early, there were people waiting when we arrived, mostly other families, and I was glad to see that the Wheelings had already secured a table. As we approached, Courtney waved, and she and Hank looked like themselves, only more subdued.

In a voice of forced cheer, Courtney said, 'Rosie, Amelia and I have been waiting for you to go watch the pizza makers.'

'You want me to take her?' Jeremy said to me, and I said, 'Sure.'

Hank said to Courtney, 'You think pepperoni for Amelia or ham?'

Courtney rolled her eyes at me. 'Our bloodthirsty daughter.' To Hank, she said, 'You decide.'

When she and Amelia and Jeremy and Rosie were gone, I said to Hank, 'How are you doing?' at the same time he said, his voice low, 'Courtney still doesn't know I told you she's pregnant, so don't say anything about the whole—'

'No, of course not,' I said quickly.

'You didn't tell Jeremy, did you?' I'd been unbuckling Owen from the car seat, not exactly making eye contact with Hank, and when I looked across the table, Hank had a particular kind of uneasy expression on his face, an expression that I was pretty sure was a request for me to lie to him.

Which I did. 'No, no,' I said as I lifted Owen out. I wasn't even sure if Hank was asking if I'd told Jeremy about the pregnancy or the CVS results, but since I'd told Jeremy both, the distinction was moot.

'She's just private about stuff like this,' Hank said, and I thought that he had to know I'd told Jeremy. In that case, Hank was really asking if I'd make sure Jeremy didn't mention anything to Courtney. Without much conviction, Hank added, 'I should have kept my big mouth shut.'

'You didn't know.' I dug around in the diaper bag at my feet for a toy for Owen and came up with a translucent rattle that had little orange stars inside. The truth was that Owen's presence seemed almost in bad taste, as if I were gloating over my healthy baby.

Hank said, 'Remember that stuff I was saying about not wanting to get up early with a newborn? I feel like such an asshole now.' He seemed to be on the cusp of tears, and if he was crying when our spouses and daughters returned to the table, surely it would, among other things, reveal to Courtney that I knew exactly what was going on. The only previous time I'd seen Hank cry had been the night Barack Obama was elected.

'Hank, don't beat yourself up,' I said. 'You can't. No matter what, you guys will figure things out.'

Hank was silent, blinking a few times. 'In Courtney's mind, she already has.'

'You mean—'

He sniffed once – the moment of almost tears seemed to have passed – and when he spoke again, he sounded more sarcastic than weepy. 'I mean, the winner of the Macelwane Medal can't have a retarded kid.'

A college-aged waiter appeared then, and I said, 'Sorry, but we need another minute.' Yet by the time Jeremy and Courtney had returned with the girls, Hank and I still had neither ordered nor even discussed what we were ordering, a fact that clearly annoyed Courtney. She turned to Jeremy. 'You guys like pepperoni, right?'

'We do.'

'Okay then, a thirteen-inch pepperoni for your family that Amelia can sample, and the mushroom one for us. Which one is our waiter?' She was scanning the restaurant.

'If Amelia's eating their pizza, they should get a seventeen-inch,' Hank said, which I'd also been thinking, but Courtney scowled and said, 'Amelia will have one piece.' She stood, menu in hand, and strode toward the bar to place our order, even though this wasn't a restaurant where you placed your order at the bar. When she returned, she was carrying four pints of beer, and not for the first time, I understood why Courtney Wheeling was a tenured professor and I wasn't. I hadn't seen Courtney drink for a while, and I felt Hank take note of it, too, as she distributed the glasses. She sat down and lifted hers. 'To efficiency,' she said.

Briefly, for about thirty seconds, I thought that harmony had been restored to the table; Courtney's bad mood, which I couldn't exactly fault her for, even if I'd also witnessed this same mood under ordinary circumstances, seemed to have subsided. Then she looked at me – I was sitting directly across the table from her – and said, 'Kate, has your sister spent much time in Central Asia?'

'Central Asia?' I wasn't certain I'd heard her correctly.

'I was wondering because of the prayer flags.'

'Oh,' I said. 'No. No, she hasn't been there.' I had a strong suspicion of what the answer would be as I asked, 'Have you?'

'I have.' Courtney took a sip of beer.

'For your research?' I knew Courtney had spent time collecting data in Chile and Indonesia.

She shook her head. 'Just for fun. Hiking in

Nepal after college. So I was thinking today, how *does* someone become a psychic? Do you get certified? Is there a test you have to pass?'

I looked at her, and for a few seconds we held each other's gaze – *I'm sorry your baby has Down's,* I thought, *and I'm sorry Channel 5 interviewed Vi, but neither of those things is my fault* – and I said, 'Not that I'm aware of.'

'What'd Vi major in in college?'

Did she already know? But I didn't see how she could. 'Vi started at Reed, but she left before she finished,' I said.

'She doesn't have a college degree?'

Hank said, 'Courtney, if you're trying to prove Vi's not a scientist, I don't think anyone at this table will dispute that.'

Courtney turned to face him, smiling an enormous smile that I could tell, even from the side, was false. 'What?' she said. 'Kate would tell me if my questions bothered her.' She turned back to me. 'Are my questions bothering you?'

I shook my head, and under the table, on my leg Owen wasn't balanced on, Jeremy patted my knee.

Courtney said, 'You don't actually believe your sister's prediction, do you?'

It wasn't realistic to expect Hank to say, as he had during our walk to Kaldi's, that he didn't see why being psychic was impossible. Still, I felt myself waiting hopefully. When he said nothing, I said, 'It's kind of complicated.'

In a genial voice, Jeremy said, 'Show me one family that isn't. Hey, Amelia, I hear you'll be trying meat for the first time tonight.'

Courtney gave Jeremy an unimpressed look. 'Are we really not allowed to have an adult conversation? If we're just hiding behind our children and making boring small talk, I could grab any random mom off the playground for that.'

Still genially, Jeremy said, 'We can talk about whatever you want to talk about, but for you to hold Kate accountable for her sister's actions is silly, as you pointed out the other night.'

Courtney glanced first at Hank then back at Jeremy before saying, 'Both of you are acting like Kate is a delicate flower who can't stand up for herself. Are you a delicate flower, Kate? Am I making you' – she switched to a tone of faux sympathy – '*uncomfortable?*'

I was pretty sure I was flushed as I said, 'Actually, there is something you should know about Vi. She's been invited to be on the *Today* show next week.' I already knew Jeremy would ask later what had made me tell Courtney. Because she'd find out anyway, I'd say, though if Jeremy had been the one to divulge the information, I'd have wondered why he had. I added, 'So I guess they don't have a problem with her not having a college degree.'

Courtney's expression was contemptuous. 'People go on *Today* because they've had hiccups for two weeks, or because a shark bit their leg off. It's not like it means you've achieved anything.'

'Courtney, come on,' Hank said. 'Vi's her sister.'

'Vi's a public health threat,' Courtney said, and the conversation might have escalated from there, but our waiter appeared with the pizza, and as we dealt with the logistics of the food, it seemed that Jeremy, Hank, and I mutually decided to pretend we hadn't heard Courtney's last remark.

'I don't want this,' Amelia said then. She was pointing to the pepperoni on the pizza slice Hank had just set on her plate.

'That's the pepperoni,' Courtney said.

'I don't want it. It's brown.'

'Pepperoni *is* brown,' Courtney said.

'I don't like brown pepperoni.'

'You don't even want to try it?'

As Amelia shook her head, Courtney exchanged a look with Hank. 'I don't like brown pepperoni,' Amelia said again.

Courtney picked off the pieces, and when she was finished, Amelia lifted her slice and bit the tip. With her mouth full, she said, 'This is yummy!'

Maybe Amelia's change of heart about trying meat would be enough of a victory for Courtney, I thought; maybe she wouldn't need to be victorious over me, too. And we did, tentatively, begin talking about other things – another pizza place in the Loop we wanted to try, a new restaurant downtown by Citygarden – but when we finished and were standing and gathering our jackets and bags, Courtney approached me as I was buckling Owen back into his car seat. She said, 'Your sister is really for real going to be on *Today*? You weren't just saying that to depress me?'

Surprisingly, I felt less cowed by Courtney one-on-one than I had with our husbands listening, even if they'd been on my side. I said, 'Courtney, whether or not you believe it, and whether or not I believe it, Vi believes what she's saying. She's not just pretending she thinks there'll be an earthquake.'

'Have you considered having Jeremy explain basic geology to her?'

We were standing only a foot apart, and the restaurant around us was loud. I could see Courtney's pores, the tiniest clump of mascara on her lower right eyelashes, and I felt, beneath her toughness, her essential vulnerability; hers was no different from anyone else's. I said, 'What do you want me to say?'

She was looking at me appraisingly but also dispassionately. She said, 'There's always been something so evasive about you.'

In the car, I said, 'I know Courtney's really stressed out, but I was kind of shocked by how aggressive she was.'

Mildly, Jeremy said, 'Yeah, we probably should have rescheduled dinner. I don't think it was personal – you just happened to be caught in her crosshairs.'

'It's not that I don't feel bad for her.'

'I know it's not. There's a lot going on in both

175

your lives.' As Jeremy turned onto Forsyth Boulevard, he said, 'I won't defend her behavior tonight, but I'd cut her a lot of slack if I were you.'

'Do you think I'm being too hard on her?'

Jeremy wasn't looking at me as he said, 'I think no matter what, she's already grieving.'

After I put Rosie down for bed, my phone dinged with a text from Hank: *Don't give up on us yet. Still friends?*

Of course, I texted back.

In studio not painting, Hank texted.

Have a beer, I wrote.

I fell asleep after Owen's two A.M. nursing but awakened well before the next one. I thought it was almost morning, but when I pressed the little glow button on my watch, it wasn't yet four. I closed my eyes, and as soon as I did, I opened them again. *October 16,* I thought. That would be the day of Vi's earthquake.

I waited until ten A.M. on Sunday to call my sister and tell her. 'You think that sounds right?' I asked.

She was quiet before saying, 'It doesn't sound wrong.'

'But it doesn't sound right?'

'I haven't gotten anything that specific, but sure. It could be the sixteenth. Why not? Speaking of you not being wrong, it pains me to admit this, but I have nothing to wear on the *Today* show. I should have bought something at the Galleria when we were there for Dad's birthday present.'

Subtle, I thought.

'If you could take me, I promise I'm not just using you as a taxi service,' she said. 'I need your fashion advice.'

'Then you must really be desperate.'

'Oh, come on – you're stylish.'

In fact, I had spent so much of the last three years in a forest green fleece vest that first Jeremy had started calling the vest Greenie, then he'd started calling *me* Greenie, then, at Christmas a month before Rosie's first birthday, he'd given me two more, both in the same shade of green, so that I wouldn't have to either be apart from the vest during the time it took to wash or, as was more often the case, continue wearing it after it was covered with a crust of spit-up and food.

'Well, you're stylish compared to me,' Vi was saying, and I could sense then her impulse to say, *In the land of the blind, the one-eyed man is king,* which was an expression she hadn't used around me ever since we'd gotten in a fight about it a few years before.

'Just say it,' I said.

'I don't know what you're talking about.'

'I'm over it,' I said.

'How about if I put it like this? In this scenario, you're royalty. That's flattering, right?'

I said, 'I can't go now, but I might be able to take you to the mall this afternoon.'

'Are you going to bring Owen?' By which, of course, she meant, *Don't bring him.* 'You have the kids all week,' she added. 'Make Jeremy pull his weight.'

'Let's talk again in a few hours,' I said.

At Macy's, Vi tried on an orange peasant smock (her choice), a tan scoop-neck jersey (my choice), and a lavender V-neck, also picked out by me, though as soon as she was wearing it, I saw that the neckline didn't do her any favors. Standing in front of the three-way mirror in the dressing room, she said, 'When did my tits get so saggy?'

'You just need a better bra,' I said. 'Don't be offended, but what if we go look for clothes in Lane Bryant?'

'The big-girl store?'

'I think they'll have a wider selection.'

Vi grinned. 'No pun intended?'

I'd left Owen home, which did make it easier to get around. Inside Lane Bryant, I pulled a bunch of tops off various racks and passed the hangers to Vi. 'Start with these, and I'll meet you in the dressing room.'

I ended up finding five more possible shirts – none that were white or patterned because my brief online research had advised against those for TV – and on my way to join Vi, I saw a pale pink blouse I liked for myself. I took it in the smallest size.

When I opened Vi's door, she was wearing a

black tunic, her underwear, and nothing else, even though I hadn't given her any pants to try on.

'You know that's not a dress, right?' I said.

'I'm not retarded.' She said it good-naturedly, and I tried not to wince. 'My pants were making it bunch up.'

'Will they be filming you from the waist up or full-body?'

She shrugged.

'Then we should assume full-body. Do you have black dress pants?'

She furrowed her brow. 'Possibly.'

'Let's get a pair just in case. They're useful in general.'

'Today's woman can *never* have too many pairs of black dress pants.' She was using her pseudo-British accent. 'They're *so* posh and versatile.' I'd hung the new batch of shirts on a hook, and she pointed to the pink one in front. 'I don't like that.'

'It's for me.' I took off my vest, then crossed my arms, pulling my T-shirt over my head and tossing it in the corner of the bench. When I removed the pink blouse from its hanger, I saw that it had easily two dozen tiny buttons up the back, and as I stood there in my nursing bra – a beige, pilly item from Rosie's infancy that was just as unsupportive as the bra Vi had on – I knew already that the quantity of buttons meant I wouldn't buy the shirt. 'Keep trying stuff,' I said to Vi. I gave her a navy short-sleeved sweater. 'This is my new favorite.'

I was still unfastening buttons by the time she

had it on. Our eyes met in the mirror, and I said, 'I like that.'

She shook her head. 'This is so not me.'

'You actually look very elegant.'

'I look like a lesbian running for president.'

'At least one of those things is true, huh?'

She smirked. 'You think I have any chance of getting elected?'

I passed her a maroon top with three-quarter-length sleeves. 'This could work.' Then I looked down at the half-unbuttoned shirt in my own hands and decided just to try it on; at the rate I was going, Vi would be ready to leave before I was.

'By the way,' Vi said when my head was inside the shirt, 'I might start driving again.'

I was glad that my face was hidden so my surprise didn't show; I made an effort to sound low-key as I said, 'Oh, yeah?'

'The woman I'm seeing – Stephanie – I haven't told her about not driving, and I don't know if she'd understand. I think she might be one of those really normal people. Like Jeremy.'

'Did you guys go out again?'

'We went to a movie last night.'

If Stephanie were a man, surely I'd have asked if they kissed. And certainly I was in favor of Vi finding her Jeremy, even if her Jeremy was female. But the idea of Vi making out with another woman – it was just weird. After a beat, still from inside the shirt, I said, 'And you had fun?'

'It was okay. I mean, it wasn't the greatest night of my life or anything.'

'Well, it was a second date. You might want to keep your expectations in check.' I added, 'If you want to drive back to your house from here, you're welcome to.'

'Oh, God, no,' she said. 'It's been so long I need to practice first, like in an empty parking lot.'

'We could go out to the country next weekend.' The shirt was still over my face, my right arm raised straight above my head because the right sleeve was caught around my elbow; when I used my left hand to try to pull down the neck, I heard the delicate splitting of seams. I froze. 'Vi,' I said, 'I think I'm stuck.'

'For real?' Her voice was already thick with amusement.

'Can you help me?'

'How can you be stuck in a Lane Bryant shirt? You're not that fat.'

'Will you undo the buttons?'

'I wish my phone had a camera. Wait, yours does, doesn't it?' She was laughing, and though I was starting to feel overheated, and though I had an increasingly urgent wish not to be trapped inside this prison of pink satin, I began laughing, too.

'If you take a picture of me,' I said, 'I'll kill you. Just unbutton the buttons.'

She was behind me then, fiddling, and I could tell she was shaking with silent mirth.

'I hate you,' I said.

'Hold still.' I tried to, and she said, 'Your hair—' but she couldn't get the sentence out. She gave it a second try. 'Your hair is tangled in the buttons. I think we need the Jaws of Life.'

In equal measures, I found the situation funny and unendurable; I moved my right arm, and there was another sound of ripping fabric.

'Oh my God,' Vi said. 'What a cheap piece of crap. Okay, it's all unbuttoned.'

I raised my left arm so it was parallel to my still-raised right one. 'Pull it off,' I said. 'But be careful.'

When the shirt was finally above my head, I felt as if I were emerging from a cave; in the mirror, I saw that my cheeks were flushed. As we looked at our semi-matching reflections, Vi snorted with laughter. 'Sorry.' She set the back of her hand against her nose. 'But you should have seen yourself.'

'Thanks for saying I'm not *that* fat.'

'Well, you're not the thinnest you've ever been.' She was holding the pink blouse, which was inside out, and she reversed it. 'But you're a baby-making machine. It's not your fault.'

I pulled on my T-shirt, which was roomy and forgiving and cotton, then my green fleece vest, and then I held out my hand so Vi could give me the pink blouse. 'I'm not a baby-making machine anymore,' I said. 'We're done.'

'So you say now.' Vi was still in the maroon top, which had ruffly cuffs that were, I thought, reminiscent of a clown at a child's birthday party.

'I totally just realized what you should wear,' I said. 'I have a silver shirt from a wedding a few years ago.'

'Nothing of yours will fit me.'

'No, it will. It's a maternity shirt.'

'And you give me shit for saying you're not thin.'

'I was only about five months pregnant when I wore it. It's sheer and you wear a camisole under, which I also have. Are they sending someone to do your hair and makeup?'

'They didn't say.'

'Then I'll come do it. What time are the camera people coming over?'

'Five-thirty.'

'Jesus.'

'I know, but that's six-thirty in New York, and they think my interview will air in the seven o'clock hour.'

'Live?' I asked.

'Live on the East Coast and delayed an hour here.'

'I'll come at five.' We hadn't previously discussed whether I'd be present for the taping, and I'd have imagined that I couldn't stand to be, whether Vi wanted me there or not, but now I felt relief; I'd be able to help create a positive outcome. Later, I wondered when I'd decided not to try dissuading Vi from appearing on the show at all. When had I decided it was too late? It wasn't too late until the cameras started rolling.

I said, 'Take a shower before I get there. And if

183

they do send a makeup person, they'll just improve what I've done.'

'Don't make me look like a hooker.' She was changing out of the maroon shirt, and I was returning the others, including the pink one, to their hangers; I briefly wondered if I ought to confess the damage I'd wrought to a saleswoman, but the pink shirt wasn't visibly altered.

'Vi,' I said, and she looked at me. 'I know it's a big thing to go on TV, but you definitely still think there's going to be an earthquake, right?'

She didn't hesitate. 'Yes,' she said. 'I definitely do.'

It was dark and cool when I stepped outside and pulled the front door shut behind me at four forty-five on Wednesday morning. From the car, I texted Vi – *You're up?* – and she texted back: *Haven't gone to bed yet.* Great, I thought.

Between Big Bend and Manchester, there were few cars on the road. When Rihanna's 'Umbrella' came on the radio, I turned it up in a way I never did when Rosie and Owen were in the car, even with kids' music. As early as it was, and as squeamish as I felt about the reason Vi would be appearing on national television, the morning contained an undeniable charge of excitement. Because, hell, Vi would be appearing on national television!

Was my mood driving in the dark what Jeremy experienced on the days he flew to a conference in another city or to give a talk at a different university? He could have us – a family – and he could have another life, too, whereas I had figured out only how to have us.

All the lights were on in Vi's house, and all the curtains were open, and she was standing on the front stoop smoking a cigarette. I hadn't yet set foot on the walkway when she called, 'I haven't had one for three months, but this is just way too stressful. I'm canceling.'

There was a shift in my chest – my ambivalence, stretching like a cat. I'd be thrilled for her to back out of the interview, because she'd be sparing both of us humiliation, but if she backed out, our glamorous morning would cease to exist. The momentum of my drive through the dark would sputter; I'd have gotten up at four-fifteen and pumped a bottle for Owen for no reason. 'Do you want to cancel?' I said.

'Nah.' With unnecessary vigor, Vi smashed out the cigarette in a red porcelain bowl that contained at least twenty other butts. 'Honestly, business hasn't been great lately, and if nothing else, this ought to get me some new clients. People just don't value their spiritual life. When it's time to start cutting back, they still spend five bucks on a latte but not a penny nourishing their own energy.'

I hated this kind of talk, which Vi knew, which had to mean, since she didn't seem to be trying to irritate me, that she was already practicing for television – that when she'd suggested she might not go through with the interview, she was bluffing.

Or this was what I subsequently told myself, when I didn't want to believe I could have stopped her. But I am almost sure that I could have. The more vehemence I'd shown, the likelier she'd have been to defy me; of this I am certain. But couldn't I have gently swayed her, letting her reach her own conclusion? My sister was the kind of person who'd enjoy giving the finger to the *Today* show. I didn't nudge her toward this outcome, though, because what if her prediction was right?

I did her makeup in the living room, while she held a round two-sided mirror that had once been mine. Vi smelled like an ashtray, but at least no one watching her on TV would have any idea. Through the large living room window, as I was applying eyeliner, we could see the van with its satellite pole pull up on the dark street, and I felt my heartbeat quicken. This was actually going to happen. She went to change into the silver shirt, which she'd tried on previously and which did look good, while I opened the front door.

'Violet Shramm?' said a guy in a baseball cap. 'Bill Sichko, producer.' He stuck out his hand and gave mine a forceful shake.

'I'm Violet's sister,' I said. 'But she'll be right out.'

'You got a name, Violet's sister?'

'Kate,' I said.

He pointed his thumb over his shoulder toward two other men holding equipment. 'This is Tim with the camera, and Sully's our sound guy. We gonna do this thing?'

'I guess so,' I said, and I'm pretty sure that it was because I sounded so hesitant that he laughed.

By the time Vi emerged from her bedroom, Bill Sichko had walked around the house, decided to film the interview in the living room, and was conferring with the cameraman.

'You look great,' I said to Vi. 'Really.'

She smirked. 'Maternity clothes suit me.'

They wanted her to sit not in the lounger where she held court during her sessions but in one of the cheap folding chairs her clients sat on. 'No one will notice,' Bill said.

'Do you guys work full-time for *Today*?' I asked.

He shook his head. 'We're based up in St Charles.'

The sound guy wanted the fountain in the corner of the living room moved, and Vi, who was by then perched on the folding chair, having the cord of a microphone snaked inside her – my – shirt, said to me, 'Put it in the tub.' While I was in the bathroom, the doorbell rang, and when I answered it, a woman wearing a black pantsuit was standing there, holding a cardboard tray containing three coffees. 'You must be Kate,' she said. 'I'm Stephanie. I'd shake your hand, but I'd probably spill on you.'

In the instant of seeing her, I'd decided she was a local NBC liaison, and I had to correct my misimpression even as I was saying aloud how nice it was to meet her. She appeared to be about five years older than Vi and me, with gray threaded through her otherwise brown bob, and she was attractive and (perhaps this was unfair to note) not at all

187

overweight. She said, 'Not sure how you take yours, but I'm trusting Vi's got some milk and sugar.'

What I thought then – besides that if I used up my one allotted coffee so early in the morning, which of course I was about to, it was going to be an awfully long day – was that instead of being wary of Stephanie on my sister's behalf, I was wondering precisely what Stephanie saw in Vi. Stephanie seemed like someone who had her act together; she seemed like a grown-up. The coffee smelled warmly nutty as I lifted off the plastic lid and took a sip. 'Black is perfect,' I said. 'Thanks.'

Stephanie followed me into the living room, where Vi was sitting with atypically erect posture on the folding chair and the sound guy was inserting an earpiece into her left ear. I could feel Vi and Stephanie's confusion over how to greet each other, which surely had as much to do with the newness of their relationship as with the presence of the television crew. Then, decisively, Stephanie leaned in, kissed the top of Vi's head – much as I had kissed Jeremy before leaving the house that morning, and the right choice given Vi's makeup, I thought – and stepped back. 'I got you a coffee,' Stephanie said. 'Don't worry, it's not cinnamon-flavored. But I'll just hold on to it for now.'

'Vi, you don't want to smudge your lipstick,' I said.

'Smudged lipstick is the least of it,' Vi said. 'I'm about to have a heart attack.' She gave me an accusatory look and said, 'Matt Lauer is interviewing me, but did you know I won't be able to see him? I'm supposed to be looking at that thing' – she gestured toward the video camera, set on a tripod – 'and I'll just hear his voice.'

'Take deep breaths,' Stephanie said. 'In through the nose, out through the mouth. You're going to do awesome.'

'Violet, you're on in thirty seconds,' Bill said, and my own heart began hammering.

Then Bill was saying, 'Five, four, three, two' – so they really did that – and even though I was standing still, next to Stephanie in the doorway of the living room, I was breathless. Without a doubt, Vi looked the prettiest she had in years. Was it too much to hope this wouldn't be a trainwreck? And soon I heard Matt Lauer, his voice weirdly familiar, saying, 'We turn now to St Louis, Missouri, where a local psychic has made a prediction that has, no pun intended, unsettled many residents. Last week, Violet Shramm went public with her belief that a major earthquake will rock the region in the near future. Critics say she's a fearmonger, but Shramm claims she just wants to save lives. Violet Shramm, welcome to the program.'

There was a slight delay, and Vi said, 'Thanks for having me.'

'You've put a lot of people on edge with your prediction,' Matt Lauer said, and the first thing I thought was *That's not a question.* The second thing was *Why didn't I offer to practice with Vi?* I could have acted like the interviewer.

But in a tone of chummy assurance, Vi said, 'Matt, it absolutely wasn't my intention to scare people,' and I knew then that she'd be okay. Using his name like that – I loved her presumptuousness. 'But a piece of information was available to me,' she said, 'and I thought it was important to make it available to other people.'

'What's your response to the scientists who say that predicting an earthquake is impossible?'

'We're all entitled to our opinion.' There was still the delay after Matt Lauer's questions, but it was obviously due to something technological and not hesitation on Vi's part, because she was smiling warmly. Good for her for not being defensive, I thought. 'I received a message, though, and frankly, it was an urgent message. Now, Matt, your viewers might not know that one of the biggest earthquakes ever in this country happened in Missouri back in the nineteenth century.'

'Right, the New Madrid earthquake. Still, some might argue that what you've done is a bit like yelling fire in a crowded theater.'

'I'm yelling fire because I think there's about to be one.'

'When you said a quake would happen soon, can you be more specific?'

The expression on Vi's face was still calm and open as she said, nodding, 'The date I'm getting is October sixteenth.'

'Wow, that is specific,' Matt Lauer said. 'And just a little more than two weeks away. Now, when you say you received a message, can you explain what you mean? Do you hear voices? Do you commune with the dead?'

'Those are all good questions, Matt. It's different for different people in my line of work, and for me it's always been a combination of things – sometimes dreams, sometimes a conscious visualization, other times just a gut feeling. I'm privileged to have a spiritual guide I call Guardian, and in this case, he's the one who warned me.'

'Interesting.' Though of course I couldn't see Matt Lauer's face, his voice was both disbelieving and respectful – not an easy feat but perhaps the explanation for why he'd succeeded in his field. 'And how are you personally preparing for an earthquake? Where will you be on October sixteenth?'

'I'm not fleeing the state, if that's what you're asking. I'll probably pick up some bottled water and that kind of thing.' Vi would never pick up emergency supplies; the only way she'd acquire them was if I carried them into her house, which I made a mental note to do. She said, 'You know how if you live in Florida, there's hurricane season, or here in the Midwest, the spring is tornado season? Well, the advice I'm giving people is to consider this earthquake season. Just be smart about it. But the biggest point I want to convey to your viewers is that I don't stand to benefit from this. I don't sell earthquake insurance. What I always say to my clients is, okay, here's what I'm getting from Guardian. Make of this information what you will. I'm just the vessel.'

'All food for thought,' Matt Lauer said. 'Very provocative food for thought. That's Violet Shramm, a St Louis psychic warning people in the area that a major earthquake is going to hit just over two weeks from now. Thanks for being on the program, Violet.'

'Thank *you*, Matt.'

Then I heard Matt Lauer say, 'Coming up: A mouse who lives up to the name of "mighty," and a controversial new trend in tattoos. That's after the break,' and then there was music, and Bill was walking out from behind the camera, and Vi was saying, 'Oh my God, I completely just sweated through my shirt. My pits are literally waterfalls right now.'

'She's off-mike, right?' I said.

'You're still miked, but you're not being broadcast.'

'Vi, you were cool as a cucumber,' Stephanie said. 'You were fabulous.'

'You were great,' I said. 'You really were.'

'I wish we could have heard the questions,' Stephanie said. 'I can't wait to watch the whole thing online.'

I squinted at her in confusion. She wished we could have heard the questions? And then I had the queasy realization that Matt Lauer's part of the interview had, presumably, not been audible except in Vi's earpiece. Which meant – I didn't even want to think about it – that I had somehow been in her head. If I'd done so on purpose, it would have been a violation of the pact I'd made with myself, but given that it had been involuntary, was I responsible? It was like breaking a diet while sleepwalking.

As the sound guy unhooked Vi's mike, he said, 'You really believe we're gonna get a big one?' He sounded skeptical but affably so.

'Sorry,' Vi said. 'But yes.'

The three men packed up their equipment and moved the furniture back to how it had been before, and by the time they left, it still wasn't yet six-thirty. Vi gestured toward her face. 'I'm going to scrub off my makeup. If I'm not out in an hour, send reinforcements.'

When she was gone, Stephanie chuckled. 'I have to say that your sister might be the most fascinating person I've ever met.'

'I take it you haven't spent a lot of time around New Age types?' I didn't know if she'd be able to tell that I considered this a point in her favor.

She laughed again. 'I guess it doesn't take much to seem interesting compared to us folks in IT. Speaking of which, I have a meeting in the Central West End at nine, but I thought we could take Violet out to breakfast. Are you free awhile longer?'

The way she seemed to see Vi's profession – it was as low-key, as unfraught, as if Vi conducted research in Antarctica or was the personal assistant to a movie star. Vi's psychicness was intriguing to Stephanie but not repellent, not laughable.

I felt an impulse to decline the breakfast invitation – away from both children, I was always on borrowed time – but surely Vi's appearance on national television granted me an exemption from our household's morning routine. 'Where were you thinking?' I asked.

'The restaurant at the Four Seasons has quite a view. Or if you know somewhere else Violet would prefer—'

'That sounds great.' I'd envisioned a place like Denny's, and a chance to go to the Four Seasons, child-free, sounded like a delightful novelty. The hotel had opened next to the river a few years earlier, and I'd never set foot in it; in fact, I couldn't remember when I'd last been downtown. I said, 'I won't be a third wheel, will I?'

'Kate, if anyone's a third wheel, it's not you. But how can I really get to know Violet unless I know her twin?'

No man I'd dated, including Jeremy, had ever expressed a comparable sentiment.

Then she said, as if catching herself, 'Not that you're the same person, I realize. But that's why I want to get to know you, too.'

'Just to warn you, compared to Vi, I'm very boring.'

'Ah, but Kate,' Stephanie said, 'aren't we all?'

A moment of logistical indecision occurred just before we departed for downtown, when we were standing on the sidewalk outside Vi's house and it became apparent that Stephanie thought we should take three separate cars, which was a sensible enough idea if we were each headed in a different direction after breakfast and if we were each in the habit of driving. But Vi was looking at me beseechingly, and I said, 'Stephanie, if you want to take Vi, I can drop her off back here, and that way, we both get to ride with the celebrity.' If Stephanie had no problem with Vi being a professional psychic, I doubted Vi's not driving would be a deterrent, either, but the announcement wasn't mine to make.

And of course, if I dropped Vi back at her house after breakfast, I'd be even later getting home, but as she climbed into the passenger seat of Stephanie's Volvo, Vi widened her eyes and raised her eyebrows; she was thanking me.

As I arrived downtown, Jeremy called my cellphone, and when I answered I said, 'Is it airing here?'

'It just finished. She was good.'

I could hear a withholding in his voice. 'What did you really think?'

'She looked great. You may have missed your calling as a makeup artist. Rosie said, "That lady looks like Aunt Vi."' I wasn't thrilled to hear that he'd let Rosie see the segment, which Jeremy must have guessed, because a second later he said, 'Don't worry – she didn't understand it. She was barely paying attention.' Then he said, 'Vi set herself up for even more of a media storm by saying it'll be on the sixteenth. Now it's like an end-of-the-world prediction.'

'You think?' I needed to tell him, didn't I, about my complicity in this date?

He continued, 'But maybe it's for the best, because then the sixteenth comes and goes, and it's over instead of the prediction lingering indefinitely.' Then he said, 'We can talk more about this when you get home, but you remember that October sixteenth is the weekend of my conference in Denver, right? It's that Friday.'

'Is it really?' Now I couldn't tell him; if I did, it would look like I'd picked the sixteenth on purpose.

'Don't answer this now, but what if you guys come with me?' Jeremy said. 'I checked, and the hotel has an indoor pool. We could have a little Colorado vacation.'

It was, in some ways, a tempting idea. But the one plane trip we'd taken so far with both Rosie and Owen, to visit Jeremy's family in Virginia, hadn't gone smoothly, and the prospect of getting through the flight to Denver, convincing the children to sleep in unfamiliar cribs, all of us in the same hotel room, and looking out for them by myself for three days while Jeremy attended panels – it actually would be the opposite of a vacation. In fact, I wouldn't even be able to take Rosie swimming without Jeremy because I couldn't watch her and Owen in the water at the same time. Plus, I'd be worried about leaving my father and Vi behind in St Louis; I was sure that neither of them would consider leaving town.

'Just think on it,' Jeremy said. 'So I've already gotten emails from people who saw Vi.'

'Who?'

'Let's see – from Sally, from Cockroach's wife, and from Xiaojian Marcus.' These people were, respectively, the wife of Jeremy's cousin, the wife of his best friend from college, and the wife of Jeremy's department head, a professor herself at Wash U's medical school, who had no children and who had told me when Jeremy and I were engaged that being a good mother and a good employee were mutually exclusive. That Xiaojian had emailed Jeremy meant, presumably, that she'd told her husband – that Jeremy's boss now knew for sure that the earthquake psychic was his sister-in-law. But if Jeremy wasn't going to point out this fact, neither was I. 'Do only women watch the *Today* show?' he was asking. 'By the way, Owen had a blowout.'

'Which pants?'

'The gray ones.'

'Put them in a plastic bag and leave it at the top of the basement stairs.'

'Done and done.'

'I'm actually not on my way home yet,' I said. 'Stephanie – Vi's girlfriend – or whatever – she also came for the taping and she wants us to take Vi out for breakfast at the Four Seasons. Is that okay? You don't teach until eleven today, right?'

'The Four Seasons? This woman must really like your sister.'

'So what did the email say from Xiaojian? Something snotty?'

'It was one line. I think all it said was "I just saw your sister-in-law on television."'

I said, '"And P.S. I'm still gloating that I turned out to be right about your wife not being able to handle motherhood and a job."'

'I guarantee you've spent more time thinking about that conversation than she has.' I could tell Jeremy had turned his mouth away from the phone receiver as he said, 'Let him play with it, too, Rosie.' To me, he said, 'Go have fun at your fancy lesbian breakfast.'

The silverware was big and heavy and the table-cloths were thick and white and there were fresh roses in a vase. The person who approached us as we were finishing our food was someone I had never seen before: a woman in her fifties wearing running shorts and a red mesh T-shirt that seemed so inappropriate for the restaurant that she had to be someone who found herself in elegant settings frequently enough to have become indifferent to them. Looking right at Vi, she said in a scolding tone, 'Didn't I just see you on TV?'

'Oh—' This was probably the last time being recognized surprised Vi. 'Yeah, I guess you did.'

'I don't usually watch those morning programs, but I was on the treadmill upstairs.' The woman pointed vaguely above her head, then said, 'I'm so glad I don't live in St Louis! I'm here for a meeting, and thank God I'm flying out this afternoon.'

Stephanie said to the woman, 'Do you want Vi's autograph?' Was Stephanie being sarcastic? It appeared not.

The woman made an expression of distaste. 'No,' she said. 'I need to go shower.' She looked again at Vi and said with self-satisfaction, 'I knew I recognized you.'

After she was gone, Vi said, 'That was kind of weird.' She didn't seem entirely displeased, but I could feel the way she didn't yet have a framework for thinking about such encounters.

'Get used to it, sweetie,' Stephanie said, and the surprise wasn't the *sweetie;* it was that Stephanie sounded proud. At what point had Vi revealed her occupation – at the same time as or prior to mentioning her upcoming appearance on the *Today* show? How did a conversation like that unfold? I recalled telling Jeremy about having senses in the car on a drive back from an overnight trip we'd taken to see a concert in Kansas City, but we'd been together for six weeks at that point, not a few days, and even that amount of time had later seemed to me inadequate to have supported the weight of the disclosure. And besides, when I'd told Jeremy, I'd presented the senses as involuntary and private – not as my calling or vocation, certainly not as anything I'd be chatting about on TV.

When the bill came, Stephanie picked it up immediately, and I said to her, 'Let's split it.'

Stephanie was sticking her credit card in the leather folder. She shook her head. 'Definitely my treat. It's not every day I get to have breakfast with a gorgeous set of twins.'

'Although you did once date the winner of a beauty pageant,' Vi said. Nodding toward me, she said to Stephanie, 'Tell her.'

Stephanie laughed. 'This was in another lifetime, and I'm not sure *dating* is the right word. I grew up in the sticks, in a tiny town in Arkansas called Cave City, and back in high school, I had a fling with our town's Miss Watermelon.'

'Whose official title was Queen Melon.' Vi was beaming.

'She now has three children,' Stephanie said. 'And a plumber husband.'

'She's become Mrs Melon,' Vi said.

'I guess we all have our claim to fame,' Stephanie said.

After Vi and I were inside my car, I said, 'I like her.'

'We'll see.'

'What's the problem? I thought that was a totally fun breakfast.'

'What's the problem besides that she's female?' From the passenger seat, Vi smirked at me. Then she said, 'Have you ever heard the joke about how a lesbian takes a U-Haul on a second date? Well, I think she's ready for us to move in together.'

'Literally?'

Vi leaned forward and changed the radio station from pop to classic rock. 'When you went to the bathroom, she mentioned getting together tonight. For like the sixth time in less than a week!'

By my own calculation, it would be the fourth time. I said, 'She's into you.'

'Do you think she's pretty?' Vi's voice was surprisingly vulnerable, and I thought how I had forgotten this part – how when you got together with someone new, you had to adjust to the ways in which they implicitly represented you. First you had to figure out what those ways were; then you had to determine whether you could put up with them.

'Yes,' I said. 'I do.'

'She looks kind of like Mrs Kebach,' Vi said, and I began laughing. Mrs Kebach had been our elementary school music teacher, a woman who led us in rounds of 'Row, row, row your boat' and group sessions on the xylophones.

'She does!' I said. 'But Mrs Kebach was pretty, too. I mean—' I paused. 'I never imagined you'd end up going out with her, but she was pretty. So what did you tell Stephanie about tonight?'

'I said I'd look at my schedule.'

'Don't game her, Vi.' I switched into the left lane, passing a van, and glanced over at my sister. 'She seems like a straightforward person.'

'You know what a wise woman once told me?' Vi said. 'She told me the homosexual lifestyle is

201

complicated, and all things being equal, I should date a man.'

I said, 'But all things are never equal.'

I knew that Hank and Courtney were meeting with the genetics counselor that day, but I wasn't sure what time; I waited until Rosie and Owen were up from their naps and texted Hank, keeping it vague in case he was in Courtney's presence: *U guys around? Hope things going well* . . . Thirty seconds later, Hank texted back, *Come on over, in yard.*

Rosie helped me push Owen in the double stroller down the sidewalk and up the Wheelings' driveway to the backyard, where Hank and Amelia were kicking a soccer ball back and forth; to my relief, I didn't see Courtney. As we approached, I heard Hank saying, 'Only the goalie uses hands.' He turned toward us, and though his appearance and demeanor were entirely normal, I knew.

'Rosie, want to play soccer with Amelia?' I said.

'Rosie wants chalk,' Rosie said.

'Don't feel obligated,' I said, but Hank was already opening the plastic bin where they stored their outdoor toys. (That even the Prius-driving, organic-cotton-wearing, non-meat-consuming Wheelings owned things made of plastic – it made me feel better.)

'Draw a octopus, Daddy!' Amelia shouted as I set Owen on a blanket in the grass and placed toys around him. Hank was squatting in the driveway, the chalk scraping across the pavement, and the girls were hunched beside him. I walked over and watched as he finished the octopus – I often forgot about his artistic abilities – and then he began the outline of a cat. When he was finished with the whiskers, he passed his piece of chalk to Amelia and said, 'Now you color the octopus, and Rosie, you color the cat.' He dusted off his palms and came to stand next to me. 'Courtney definitely wants to terminate.'

'Hank, I'm so sorry.'

'Daddy, she's messing it up!' Amelia cried as Rosie scribbled over the cat's face.

'Chill out, Amelia,' Hank said. 'Let her do it her own way.' To me, he said, 'I once went to a pro-choice march in college. You know, up on Beacon Hill in Boston, holding my sign, sporting my dreads. I definitely think it should be legal. But somehow the idea of it and then, like, my own wife—' He stopped talking, and I wondered again if he was about to cry.

After a minute, in a relatively composed voice, he added, 'She says she doesn't want to try again, that the pregnancy was all a big mistake. We knew we only wanted one kid, we changed our mind, and ever since then, things have sucked – the infertility, the morning sickness when she finally did get pregnant, and now this. Her attitude is, put it behind us and enjoy life again.'

'I'm sure that everything is overwhelming right now.'

'Sure, but Courtney rarely changes her mind.'

Owen had backed into a sitting position from his knees, and I said, 'Good job, O. Good sitting up.' He flashed me a proud, gummy smile.

'I usually admire her stubbornness,' Hank said. 'Whether it's not accepting excuses from an undergrad who tries to turn a paper in late or standing up to some crusty-old-man scientist who's condescending to her. But being stubborn doesn't work for this. You can't just erase a pregnancy.'

'Do you not want her to terminate?' I felt conscious of using the same language he did, not saying *abortion*.

'I want us to consider our options.'

'Maybe she'll feel different in a few days.'

Hank shook his head. 'The procedure is scheduled for next Tuesday. She'd have had them do it today if they were willing.'

My cellphone, which was in the pocket of my fleece vest, rang then, and I said, 'Sorry. Let me just see if it's Jeremy.'

It was. 'Are you at the Wheelings'?' he asked, and his voice contained a weird ridge of hardness that put me on alert.

'Yeah, why?'

'I just tried you at home, and the voice mail is full. So I listened to it, and it's all calls about Vi's prediction. Have you checked your email today?'

'Not yet. Are the phone messages from strangers or people we know? Because how would a stranger find me? Especially when my name was completely different from Vi's. And in this moment, I arrived at a belated understanding that *this* was what I'd been preparing for. For more than half my life, I'd been laying the groundwork for my own invisibility – for far longer, in fact, than Vi had been laying the groundwork for her exposure. But as a fluttery sensation passed through my stomach, I thought how unsurprising it would be if her preparation, her power, trumped mine.

'St. Louis isn't that big,' Jeremy said. 'In the age of the Internet, the world isn't that big.'

'So who called?'

'For starters, my mom, my dad, my brother, and your Mizzou friend Meredith. Also someone from the *Riverfront Times*, a reporter who says her editor went to high school with you.' The *Riverfront Times* was the free alternative weekly that cheekily covered bands and restaurants and local political scandals and featured advertisements for trans-sexual escorts; I had read it when I'd first moved back to St Louis but not since I'd had children. 'And there was a message from Janet,' Jeremy was saying, 'and someone named Elise, who said she's Travis's mom—'

Janet was my old friend and co-worker, and dimly, I had a recollection of a boy named Travis from Rosie's music class, but how would his mother know I was Vi's twin – how could she connect Violet Shramm to Kate Tucker?

'She wanted to know if you're planning to leave town. And one from the mom in that family you babysat for growing up. Melissa Barrett?'

'Melissa Garrett,' I said.

'And also there were some – I don't want to upset you. I don't see this as a big deal.'

Again, my stomach fluttered. 'What?' I said.

'Some anonymous calls. Just two. One was a person saying, "Tell your sister she's irresponsible," and the other was someone who yelled, "Fire!" and hung up. I think as in—'

'Yeah.' I swallowed. 'I get it.'

'The person who yelled fire just sounded like they were playing a prank. Is your refrigerator running, that kind of thing. And the other one sounded kind of schoolmarmy, like a self-righteous little old lady. I deleted them, but now I wish I hadn't, because describing them makes them sound weirder than just hearing them.' And yet there was that hardness in Jeremy's voice; he didn't like this, either.

I said, 'So what are we supposed to do?'

'Have you checked on your dad today? I bet reporters are calling him, too. But tonight let's get takeout and just relax. Maybe Thai?'

That was all Jeremy had to offer? Thai food?

'We can't let this be about us, Kate,' he said. 'It's about Vi.'

But that morning I had done her makeup for the *Today* show; from the end of sixth grade through to our high school graduation, we had cooked dinner together so as to pretend our mother hadn't failed us; and thirty-four years earlier, we'd been one person. Of course it was about me.

As I hung up, Hank was regarding me with unabashed curiosity. I said, 'Apparently, our phone is ringing off the hook because of Vi being on the *Today* show this morning.'

'Wait, that was today? And you waited until now to tell me?' He seemed not just interested but downright titillated; for the first time since we'd arrived in their backyard, there was about him no haze of grimness.

'They interviewed her from here, not in New York. At her house. Matt Lauer did it.'

'Let's go watch it right now.' 'You think just because my life is in shambles I wouldn't want to see Vi shooting the breeze with Matt Lauer? You know what your sister needs?'

'A muzzle?' I said.

'A publicist.'

'Vi doesn't need a publicist.'

'It's not like only drug-addled starlets have them. It's someone who knows how to handle the media, and if Vi's been on *Today*, she'll get more requests. Courtney and I went to college with a woman who does PR in L.A. Why don't I shoot her an email?'

The offer seemed very Harvard-like to me, that Hank not only understood what a publicist did but happened to know one. I said, 'Won't Courtney be annoyed if the woman helps Vi? And wouldn't someone like that charge an arm and a leg?'

'A good publicist ought to be able to make some money for Vi out of all this. I think some TV shows pay not for the interview exactly, but they pay a licensing fee for personal photos or whatever, which amounts to the same thing. Or Vi could get a book deal. Or her own TV show.'

'Oh, Jesus.'

Hank smiled. 'Not what you were hoping for? Look, why don't I email Emma, and if she can't help, I'm sure she knows lots of other people. She could at least get us a ballpark estimate of how expensive it is.'

'Thank you,' I said. He had not, I noticed, answered my question about Courtney.

'Hey.' Hank made a sheepish expression. 'Glad I'm good for something right now.'

CHAPTER 9

One Sunday evening during my junior year in college, my father answered the phone and there came a point when I was pretty sure we'd been talking for more than our allotted five minutes; I looked at my watch and saw that it had, astonishingly, been twelve. Then my father said, 'Your mother's gone to bed. The doctor has her on a new medicine for the fibromyalgia, and it's making her tired.' He said this matter-of-factly, as if we'd discussed a diagnosis of fibromyalgia before – at the time, I had never heard of it, and I woefully misspelled it when I looked it up online – but out of some combination of surprise, politeness, and cowardice, I asked him nothing. A few days later, I emailed Vi and wrote, *Have you heard Mom or Dad talk about her having fibromyalgia?* Vi wrote back, *What the fuck is that?*

Since starting Mizzou, I'd gone home infrequently. To be alone in the house on Gilbert Street with my parents, without Vi, was almost unbearable, and though she'd drop by, it was never for long. I'd suggest that we see a movie or meet up in the afternoon to have lunch, but she worked most nights at one restaurant or another and slept half the day. Was this, I wondered, what it had felt like for her when she'd stayed with me in the dorm and I'd barely had time for her in my schedule?

I'd learned that taking Ben with me, seeing my parents' house through his eyes, was worse than going home by myself. This mausoleum of unhappiness was where I'd grown up? I'd try to explain that it hadn't been as bad when I was younger, that the plates in the kitchen and the television set in the living room and the hand towels in the bathroom hadn't looked as old and outdated because they hadn't *been* as old and outdated.

Ben would sleep in the ludicrous guest room, the expectation that he would do so conveyed by the folded towels on the bed, though I never knew if it was my mother or father who'd set them there. Initially, I assumed that from visit to visit he was the last person to have used the bed, until I realized the guest room was where my father now slept; I discovered an empty bottle of his blood pressure medication under the nightstand. But even before I knew this, I'd have Ben sneak into my room instead of joining him in the bigger guest bed, and he would try to initiate sex, and I would start crying. Not because of the sex – that had gotten better for us after our first dismal hook-up – but because of everything else, the grip of family and the past.

If I hadn't previously thought of my mother as making much effort, after the fibromyalgia diagnosis she either stopped trying entirely or didn't have the ability. Where once she'd run errands, she now remained in bed until five P.M. Prior to five, she was up only for doctors' appointments, which my father left work to drive her to. If I arrived home in the middle of the day, the single indication that I was expected would be a key beneath the mat outside the front door. My father ate frozen dinners every night – I did the same during my visits – and my mother subsisted on orange juice, Triscuits, and spreadable cheddar cheese. She didn't have the energy to attend my college graduation, and my father didn't want to leave her by herself, so neither of them came. At the last minute, Vi and Patrick drove out, surprising me, and though I'd probably have told them not to if they'd offered in advance, I was glad to see them. Ben's parents took all of us, plus Ben's two sisters and grandfather, out for dinner at the fanciest restaurant in Columbia; Vi ordered lobster, and she and Patrick drank four cocktails each.

Vi had vacated our parents' house in a way I never had. She had cleared her belongings out of our childhood bedroom – even the Sisterland sign was gone – while my old clothes still hung in the closet, my Nipher and Kirkwood High yearbooks rested on the shelf, and a googly-eyed turtle sticker I'd arbitrarily stuck on my desk lamp in 1986 was still there eleven years later.

In the summers during college, I stayed in Columbia and worked full-time at the adult day-care center; after graduation Ben and I rented a one-bedroom apartment in Lincoln Park. Our first year out of college, we hosted Thanksgiving in Chicago for our friends, who were mostly other Mizzou graduates, and I felt a particular kind of twenty-two-year-old's pride in the fact that, unlike at Thanksgivings of my youth, we used fresh rather than frozen spinach for the casserole and real whipped cream instead of cans of Reddi-wip. (Also around this time, one ordinary weeknight after making dinner, I heard myself say to Ben, 'I'm going to compost the rest of the bok choy' – there was a little yard with a compost bin behind our building – and pretty much everything I was smug about then was encapsulated in that single sentence. I thought – foolishly, obnoxiously – that I'd left my former self behind.) At Christmas, Ben and I went to see his family in Indianapolis, and these patterns held the following year, too: Thanksgiving in Chicago, Christmas in Indianapolis. 'I don't suppose you'd be able to come home just for a day or two,' my father said in early December, and I said I couldn't. Ben and I had recently gone to look at engagement rings, and I definitely didn't want his proposal to occur in St Louis.

Vi was working Christmas Eve but was supposed to go over to the house on Christmas Day, when my father would make steak for dinner. On Christmas Eve, my mother went to bed without eating, which wasn't unusual; her door, the door to the room she no longer shared with my father, was closed by eight P.M. Because she regularly awakened so late in the day, twenty hours passed before my father knocked on the door shortly before Vi's arrival to see if my mother needed help getting up. When she didn't answer, he knocked again, then a third time. After he entered the room and found her unresponsive in bed, he called 911; the EMTs who came to the house declared her dead. Vi pulled up outside my parents' house to find not just an ambulance but a fire truck and a squad car, all their lights flashing.

For a full day, I didn't know. I hadn't been home for seven months, and that afternoon – this is only one of my regrets – I'd called to wish my parents a Merry Christmas when I knew my mother would still be asleep. This was after the big meal at Ben's family's house in Indianapolis; I'd been using the phone in the kitchen, and when I'd hung up I'd experienced a gut-wrenching sadness that I had mistaken for run-of-the-mill holiday sorrow. On the other side of the kitchen's swinging door was Ben's extended family: little kids hopped up on sweets playing with new toys while the adults watched football and lamented having overeaten.

I sat by myself in the kitchen for perhaps ten minutes, scanning the photographs on the refrigerator door, waiting to be interrupted by someone and to have to rearrange my features so I wouldn't seem like I was in an unfestive mood. Ben's family was sporty and boisterous, his parents much younger-seeming than mine, and among the refrigerator photos was one of them looking at each other and smiling, his father in a tuxedo and his mother in a strapless red dress, at their thirtieth-anniversary party. There were also photos of one of Ben's sisters grinning broadly, wrapped in a foil sheet, having just completed a marathon; of both sisters in hiking boots and shorts and fleece sweat-shirts, standing on a mountain, the older one holding her fingers in a V behind the head of the younger one; of the whole family on a beach somewhere. Looking at this display, I knew suddenly that I couldn't marry Ben, or anyone whose family was this normal and happy. Ben's mother, whom I actually liked a lot, had once said to me that her goal in life was for each of her children to find someone who loved them as much as she and Ben's dad did, and I had felt at the time like I was auditioning for a part I was very close to getting, but in this moment I realized I didn't want it. The differences between our families would always be too painful.

And so when at last I returned to the living room, I murmured to Ben that I had a headache and was going to bed early. The dismay on his face confirmed to me that he had planned to propose that night. Maybe we'd have taken a walk down the cold, dark street of brick houses, or it would have been by the fireplace, after the cousins had left and his sisters and parents had gone to sleep. I felt a churning in my stomach as I brushed my teeth and climbed into the double bed that

Ben's parents didn't care if we shared. (In contrast to the mother of my high school boyfriend Tom Mueller, Ben's mother adored me – she would send fruit-scented soaps and packets of fancy powdered hot chocolate to our apartment in Chicago and sign the cards 'Mom Sylvia.' I think she had never quite gotten over the fact that my parents hadn't attended my college graduation.)

I would still have to stave off a proposal for the two days before Ben and I returned to Chicago, I thought, and then I'd have to stave off whatever new plan he came up with after proposing at his parents' house hadn't worked, and it all made me feel tired. It wasn't that I wanted to break up with him, just that I wanted to halt further progress – I wanted to enter a holding pattern. These were the thoughts I went to sleep thinking the night after my mother died. Then I dreamed not of her but of Vi yelling my name from across a grassy field; in the dream, I pretended I couldn't hear her.

I didn't have a cellphone then, and because Ben's last name was Murphy and neither Vi nor my father knew the first name of Ben's father, it was useless for them to call information in Indianapolis; they had no way of reaching me. Vi sent an email – *Call me ASAP* – which I got while sitting in front of a computer at the desk in Ben's father's home office on the evening of December 26. Immediately, my pulse began to race. Normally, I'd have gone to find Ben's mother and asked if I could make a long-distance call, but instead I simply lifted the receiver of the office phone and dialed Vi's apartment. Patrick answered on the fifth ring, and when he realized it was me, he said, 'I'm so sorry, Daze.'

'What happened?' I said.

'Oh, shit, I thought Vi reached you,' he said. 'Your mom died.' I almost thought he was kidding, but then he began to sob.

I swallowed and said, 'But how?'

'The EMT told your dad he thought it was a reaction to her medications. It was in her sleep.'

I had known my mother took several prescription medicines, I'd seen the forest of bottles on her nightstand, but I couldn't have said exactly what they were for.

'Vi's at your parents' house now,' Patrick said.

Ben drove me to St Louis that night; it took us four hours, and there was the threat of a snowstorm, but the flakes didn't start to fall until we'd arrived. My father greeted us at the door and said, 'I'm glad you've come home,' and his voice cracked. Behind him, I caught sight of Vi in an old University of Nebraska sweatshirt with the hood up, her eyes puffy and rimmed with red.

My mother's was the first funeral I'd ever attended. There was a service at the funeral home, a large white house on Manchester Road that I'd passed many times without taking note of it, then the burial at Oak Hill Cemetery. My Mizzou friend Lauren had wanted to come, but she was a

216

paralegal in her hometown of Tampa and had to work over the holidays. My father's brother and his wife flew in from Omaha, and Patrick and his mother were there, along with a handful of Vi's restaurant co-workers, some of my father's colleagues, a few of our neighbors, and all four members of the Spriggs family. I didn't realize I'd been waiting for Pete Spriggs, who'd become a rotund man in his late twenties, to announce to Vi and me, 'You're twins because there's two of you' until the burial was finished, everyone had dispersed, and he hadn't said it.

During the service, I'd had trouble remembering what my mother had looked like. I could remember certain photos of her but not her moving around, talking to me. What came to mind instead was something Vi had once said when we'd studied the civil rights movement in high school, which was that if our mother had lived in Little Rock, Arkansas, during desegregation, she was the kind of person who'd have spit at the black students as they tried to get inside the high school. I attempted to chase the comment from my brain.

Patrick, his mother, and our aunt and uncle came back to our house for lunch, which was a tray of cold cuts Ben had picked up that morning from Schnucks. From the moment Patrick had told me my mother had died, I'd felt both clingy and jumpy around Ben – glad that he hadn't given me the opportunity to turn down his proposal, that I hadn't made things officially bad between us and he was willing to drive with me to St Louis and stand next to me at the funeral, but aware that I still couldn't marry him, even though my mother had died. I just couldn't.

There had been, as Ben and I had talked increasingly seriously about marriage, two points of tension between us, and we'd looked at engagement rings without resolving either one. The first was that he didn't want to adopt Chinese girls. After several conversations about it, he'd finally said, 'I know how this sounds, but I can't picture having squinty-eyed kids.'

If the statement was shocking, it would have been disingenuous for me to act shocked by it. I said, 'What if we adopted from another country, like in South America?'

'It's all kind of the same.' Then he said, 'I like my family. I think the Murphy genes are worth passing on.'

The second point of tension between Ben and me, which we never discussed, was Vi. He at least had the wisdom not to say so, and maybe I shouldn't have held it against him, given the way they'd met, but he didn't like her. And Vi either could tell, and amped up her Vi-ishness with him, or else I was just more aware of her Vi-ishness when Ben was around to disapprove of it: She'd bring up the old story of Patrick's cousin and the Naughty Biscotti, or she'd talk about how her friend Nancy had bought a huge purple dildo with lifelike veins in it, or she'd fart loudly, look at Ben, and say, 'Pardon my French.'

The afternoon of my mother's funeral, my father drove his brother and sister-in-law to the hotel where they were staying and returned home for a nap; he took it, I noticed, in the guest room. In the living room, Vi lit a joint and passed it to Patrick, who passed it to Ben, who shook his head. I had seen Ben smoke pot countless times in college, if not much since, and his demurral irritated me. It was mostly for this reason that I took a hit myself.

When the joint reached her again, Vi inhaled before saying, 'The EMTs took Mom's body to the medical examiner's office to do an autopsy.'

'What are you talking about?' I said. Ben sat in an armchair watching bowling on TV, and though neither his head nor his eyes moved, I could tell his attention had shifted to Vi.

'Because of how young she was,' Vi said. 'I had a sense before she died, you know. Jocelyn was doing my tarot cards, and the Ten of Swords kept coming up.'

In the last five years, I had never mentioned senses to Ben. Whatever it was that Vi had divulged during the ride in his car from Mizzou – I hadn't expanded on or tried to explain that.

'Now I think, well, why didn't I just ask Guardian who the card was for?' Vi said. *Guardian* was how she'd been referring to the entity who had spoken to her in the library at Reed, whom she'd continued to communicate with. 'But maybe it was her time.'

'She was forty-six,' I said. If I didn't acknowledge

Vi's reference to Guardian, perhaps Ben wouldn't notice it, I thought; it didn't seem to occur to Vi that Ben wouldn't be well-acquainted with our senses.

'What a tragedy,' Patrick said. 'Poor Rita.' He and Vi were both on the couch, her feet on his lap.

As Vi passed the joint to him again, she said, 'I wonder if Mom will contact us from the other side.'

'Ben.' I stood. 'Let's go for a walk.'

Six weeks later, on a Sunday evening after he returned to our apartment from playing touch football, I told Ben that I was moving back to St Louis. 'Is this because of what I said about squinty eyes?' he asked.

For a few seconds, I was genuinely confused, and then I said, 'It has nothing to do with that.'

'I'm not an asshole,' he said.

'I didn't say you are.' After my mother's death, I'd been unable to re-enter the once-enchanted-seeming life Ben and I led together in Chicago, shopping at the farmers' market on weekends and seeing independent movies at the Music Box. (The truth was, because we were only twenty-three, neither of us was in a hurry to have or adopt children anyway, and even in our disagreements, there was a self-congratulatory note about how responsible we were to discuss these important issues in advance.) It had been the acceptance letter I'd received from the social work school at the University of Illinois at Chicago that had made me decide for certain: I wasn't enrolling. And not only that, I was leaving Chicago. I'd been working for a year and a half as the activities director at a nursing home, and I'd given notice there before I told Ben, partly so that I couldn't back out.

He said, 'And I'm supposed to just be cool with a long-distance relationship?'

I said nothing, and an expression of dawning comprehension formed on his face. 'What the hell is wrong with you?' he said. '*This* is how you tell me you want to break up?' I wondered if he was wishing he could undo all our time together, starting with that game of ping-pong in the basement of the Delta Upsilon house in 1993, if he thought I'd turned out to be someone other than the person I'd presented myself as. He said, 'I'm sorry your mom committed suicide. I really am. But that's no reason to destroy your own life.'

In a small, tight voice, I said, 'My mother didn't commit suicide.'

He blinked in surprise, and his lips parted, as if he was about to speak. But he was quiet for more than thirty seconds before saying, 'Wow. Okay. Okay then, Kate.'

I rented a car to drive myself home; there wasn't much I wanted to take from the apartment in Lincoln Park, but there was more than I could carry on the bus. Because I wasn't yet twenty-five, the rental company imposed a surcharge, in addition to the exorbitant fee for dropping off the car in a different city from the one where I'd picked it up, but I wasn't going to ask my father or Vi to come get me. And so on February 12, 1999 – it seemed like a good idea to leave town before Valentine's Day – in a maroon Chevy Malibu, I drove south on Interstate 55, through Bloomington and Springfield, and as I crossed the Pine Street Bridge, the Arch on my right, I thought how strange it was that my belief that I'd never again live in St Louis had not only been wrong but had been wrong so quickly.

I hadn't told my father to expect me, but he didn't appear particularly surprised to see me. In fact, I was the one in for a surprise: As I pulled up in front of the house on Gilbert Street, I saw a FOR SALE sign in the yard, and beneath the name and number of the real estate agency, a rectangular metal attachment that read UNDER CONTRACT. I knew right away, with a gasping kind of fury, that my father had already gotten rid of the only things I'd have wanted from the house, which were my mother's Christmas records. And though I quickly confirmed this suspicion, there was no point in confronting my father; the records would still be gone. He'd be moving into a rental apartment in Des Peres, my father told me, then said, 'Ben's not with you?'

I shook my head. 'But I'm here for good.'

I suppose I'd expected him to express pleasure

or even gratitude, but he looked stern as he said, 'Are you? I hope that's what you want.'

My father was sixty-three then, and what I had thought in the days after my mother's death was that if he – or, for that matter, she – had lived in the nursing home where I worked in Chicago, I would have been attentive to them in a way I'd never been as their own daughter. I wasn't under the illusion that I could solve all the problems of the nursing home residents, or even any of their problems, but I could lead them through chair exercises and bingo, I could hold spa sessions in which I painted the women's toenails and applied face masks. The previous summer, we'd planted a vegetable garden and had succeeded in deterring squirrels from the tomato plants with a mixture of hot pepper juice and water that two of the men and I made in the kitchen. I liked these old people, even when they were disagreeable – to cajole them into participating in activities was a satisfying challenge – yet it hadn't occurred to me to demonstrate to my mother or father the patience I reserved for my job. Now it was too late to do so for my mother.

As it happened, however, it wasn't clear that my father wanted me around. He was cordial in those early days following my return home, but in the way of one tenant of a boarding-house to another; he didn't change his habits on my behalf. He read the newspaper as he ate toast in the morning, though I was at the table, and he watched television at night. When the weather rose to fifty degrees, he declined my invitation to go for a walk, and he didn't want to see a movie or try a tapas restaurant. After a week, I was unable to suppress the suspicion that I'd made a huge mistake.

But having returned the rental car, I was trapped in the house with no way of getting anywhere other than downtown Kirkwood when my father was at work; I had to wait until after dinner to go to Kinko's to print résumés and cover letters. One morning, I tried to go running, but it had gotten cold again, and my chest hurt. I took to reading the *Post-Dispatch* cover to cover, which made me paranoid about all the crime occurring in the city and county; besides that, I mostly watched TV.

Another two weeks passed before I called Ben. It was late at night, around the time he'd be going to bed, and after we'd exchanged greetings, his none too warm, he said, 'Why are you calling?'

I was startled. 'I guess because I miss you.'

'I should probably tell you that Lauren and I are seeing each other.'

'Lauren who?'

'*Lauren* Lauren. Lauren Mitchell.'

'But she's in Florida.' Though I had never consciously thought that Ben and my friend Lauren might be attracted to each other – wasn't this shockingly disloyal on both their parts? – I immediately remembered the very first night he and I had hooked up, when he'd ejaculated all over me. He hadn't said, *Are you going to tell your friends?* He'd said, 'Are you going to tell Lauren?'

On the phone, I said, 'I thought you were opposed to long-distance relationships.'

'There's such a thing as airplanes,' Ben said. 'Kate, you broke up with me. Unless I'm mistaken.'

'What would happen if I wanted to get back together?' I said.

'Do you?'

'I don't know.'

'Then quit fucking with me,' he said.

They were going to get married. Not right away, but eventually, Ben would become Lauren's husband, not mine, and I sensed this. Nevertheless, the next day, I called him at work and said, 'What if I take the bus up there this weekend?'

After a pause, he said, 'Lauren's coming here on Friday.' Lauren, who hadn't been able to get away from her paralegal job to attend my mother's funeral? I had last seen her when she'd visited Ben and me in the late summer, when we'd gotten along the way we always had, but now it was impossible not to second-guess our entire friendship.

'You could tell her not to come,' I said.

'I could.' Ben was quiet, and I heard some of his co-workers talking in the background. 'But I don't think I want to.'

I'd been in St Louis for five weeks when I got hired, through an agency, as a home health aide for a rich old woman who lived in a huge house in Clayton. As soon as I shared the news with my father, he managed to convey his preference that I not move into his apartment by saying, 'I bet you'll be glad to live on your own again.'

By chance, Patrick was moving in then with his boyfriend, a lawyer who was ten years older than us and owned a condo in the Central West End, and Vi suggested that I take Patrick's room.

'I'll think about it,' I said, and she looked at me with amusement.

'You have a better plan?'

Twenty-four hours later, I told her, 'I'll live with you if you don't communicate with Guardian in the apartment.' I had no idea if she talked to him out loud, but I didn't want to ask.

Vi seemed more baffled than offended. 'It bothers you that much?'

'Even when I'm not there, you can't,' I said. 'Not at all.'

'Guardian is a totally peaceful entity,' Vi said, and I said, 'Maybe we shouldn't live together. We'll probably just fight.'

Vi held up one hand. 'No, no, I can meditate at the bookstore.' She meant at the New Age one in Maplewood where she went a few nights a week, when she wasn't working. 'And we can do a sage cleansing in the apartment if you're worried about spiritual detritus.' Then she said, 'You know what? Let's find a different place. It's not like this one is that great.'

The day that Vi and I were to take occupancy

of the second floor of a duplex in Richmond Heights, I ate toast for breakfast at the kitchen table while my father read the *Post-Dispatch*. All my things were packed – repacked – into suitcases and boxes waiting by the front door, and Vi and her friend Seth, who owned a van, were coming over to help me move them. The closing for the house on Gilbert Street would happen in less than a week. This breakfast was, presumably, the last meal I'd eat in the house where I'd grown up, but it didn't feel momentous. My father set down the business section of the paper and said, 'I wonder if you might show me sometime how you do your grocery shopping.'

While home, I hadn't reverted to making my mother's old recipes, but, not wanting to live on frozen dinners, I did borrow my father's credit card and drive to Schnucks a few nights a week. That purchasing bananas and cottage cheese and deli ham was a skill had never occurred to me, nor had it occurred to me that it was one my father didn't possess. I even wondered if he might be humoring me, trying to make me feel useful in the way I'd persuaded myself I would be before I'd left Chicago, but it appeared his request was sincere. This was how it happened that I began taking him grocery shopping. Certainly after a time or two, he knew what he was doing – a little ridiculously, I'd drawn a chart on a sheet of paper with each day of the week and a space beside it, so he could plan his dinners in advance – but we kept going to the store together. Back then, we did it on Sundays, after I moved in with Jeremy we went on Thursday nights, and when my father was retired and I had children, we switched to weekdays.

Part of the reason Vi and I had chosen to live in the neighborhood we did was its proximity to the job I'd gotten. I could walk there in fifteen minutes, and because I didn't need a car to drive to work, Vi said I could use hers for errands if I chipped in on insurance and gas. That I hated the home health aide job pretty much from the moment I took it should, perhaps, have made me question the wisdom of letting it determine where I lived.

The woman was named Mrs Abbott, and she was a ninety-six-year-old widow who was mostly lucid, though also mostly asleep during the hours I was there. Every Tuesday, Saturday, and Sunday, I arrived at her house at seven P.M. and left at seven A.M., when my replacement showed up. Mrs Abbott's son, who was himself in his seventies and lived out in Ladue, had hired attendants to be with her twenty-four hours a day, and there were five other versions of me, though I never met all of them and some didn't last more than a few weeks.

At seven-thirty P.M., I gave Mrs Abbott a bath, rubbed Vaseline on her skin, helped her into an adult diaper and a nightgown, and got her settled in bed. (I didn't realize at the time what good training this would be for motherhood.) I'd line up three Ritz crackers and a plastic cup of milk with a straw so she could take her medications, then I'd check off the meds I'd administered on a clipboard kept on the mantel above the bedroom's fireplace. Then I'd turn out the light but remain in the room until I left in the morning, which was sometimes before Mrs Abbott woke. Occasionally, she needed to be changed during the night, or would just wake up disoriented, but mostly she slept, snoring gently.

In spite of there being plenty of space in her bedroom for a twin bed or cot for the aides, there wasn't one; I sat in a large armchair upholstered with a blue-and-white pattern of fox-hunting aristocrats. Yet because no one at the agency had told me I couldn't sleep, I assumed it was understood that I would. Though there was a small television set I was allowed to watch propped on a nearby bureau, I never did – first, because Mrs Abbott listened to the radio when she slept, and I didn't like the competing sounds; and second, because I feared that if I did have the TV on, she'd die and I'd fail to notice. I was warned never to use Mrs Abbott's phone to make long-distance calls, never to help her with anything financial – managing her checkbook, for instance – and never to allow my family members into her house. On my own, I don't think it would have occurred to me to do any of these things.

It wasn't because of Mrs Abbott that I hated the

job; if I'd worked for her during the day, I might even have liked it. I hated it because the first week I was there, an idea lodged itself in my head, an idea that was somewhat ludicrous during daylight hours, even to me, but less so at night, when Mrs Abbott and I were alone in her vast, dark house. The idea, which occurred to me during my second night on the job, was that the Ouija presence from all those years earlier with Marisa was going to find me. It was going to find me in Mrs Abbott's bedroom, perhaps appearing before me physically, and then – well, I didn't have a clear idea of what it would do, but surely it would mock me for thinking that by telling Vi not to communicate with Guardian in our duplex, I could prevent my own contact with the spirit world.

Every night after Mrs Abbott was asleep, I'd pull out a book or magazine and wait to feel tired enough to fall asleep myself. I'd have drunk as little as possible in the hours prior to my arrival at Mrs Abbott's because I didn't like using the master bathroom – it had a raised toilet seat with arms – but I also didn't want to leave her room to use the one down the hall. When I did manage to fall asleep, I'd often startle awake.

I'd been stunned to learn that Mrs Abbott had no security alarm. She lived on one of those semi-private streets St Louis is full of, a loop without sidewalks, and though there was a wrought iron gate at the loop's entrance, it was open day and night and served the purpose of merely seeming unwelcoming rather than preventing access. A few years later, I told Jeremy that Mrs Abbott's house had been at least ten thousand square feet and he was skeptical, so we went online – by then, such information was easy to find – and it turned out it was twelve thousand.

On the first floor were large, shadowy rooms, and an enormous front hall with nothing in it but the stairs and a two-story mullioned window. The kitchen, which I found particularly creepy, had a black-and-red checkerboard floor and, except for the dishwasher, appliances that were decades old.

I worked for Mrs Abbott for fourteen months, a period that in retrospect is vague, though I also feel, because my unhappiness and anxiety made time pass slowly, that I spent more like ten years as her employee. Though I could have stayed with the same agency but asked to be transferred so I was working with a different client or with multiple clients, and working during the day – it's clear now that I should have done exactly this – I didn't because then I'd have needed to buy a car.

It's also clear, of course, that the presence I feared was less the Ouija one than my mother's. The medical examiner's report that had come in the mail to Gilbert Street shortly before I moved out had stated that her death was a result of combined drug intoxication; she'd been taking nine medications, including (this mystified me) sleeping pills. On the evening I found the envelope open on the kitchen counter, I read the enclosure, replaced it, and discussed none of its contents with my father.

I myself was perpetually sleep-deprived, and on the nights I didn't work at Mrs Abbott's house, if Vi wasn't around, I'd drink a smoothie for dinner and go to bed as early as seven P.M. Due to our schedules, Vi and I saw each other erratically. She spent four nights a week, including either a Friday or Saturday, as a hostess at an Italian restaurant on the Hill. Her shifts ran from four to midnight, meaning we were rarely both home for dinner, and unlike me, she was good at sleeping during the day. On Sundays, we had lunch with our father, and afterward, Vi drove off alone, and my father and I went to the Schnucks on Manchester Road.

Because Vi had lived in St Louis since dropping out of Reed – it was strange to realize that she'd only ever been away for six weeks – she had an extended group of friends who weren't people we'd known growing up. There were the ones she meditated with at the bookstore, an activity I never asked about. There was also a group with whom she played bar trivia on Mondays, an event I did attend once, only to discover that I could answer almost no questions and that the few I could answer could also be answered by several other people on our team; I left reeking of cigarette smoke, much of it directed at me by my sister.

Vi's friends Patrick and Nancy regularly came over to get stoned and make catty comments about the contestants on reality television shows; Nancy was a frizzy-haired yoga devotee who'd been at our mother's funeral and who was the owner of the purple dildo with lifelike veins. Sometimes I'd join them in the living room, but I couldn't summon the energy to contribute to their commentary.

One afternoon in November, by which point Vi and I had been living together for eight months, she entered the apartment just after five P.M. to find me sitting in the living room with the TV on and the lights off; I was watching an old *Star Trek*, wearing my bathrobe from college with a sweater that had belonged to Ben's father over it, drinking red wine from a coffee mug and eating Doritos from a family-sized bag. I'd been under the impression that Vi would be working that night, but apparently, when she'd shown up at the restaurant, the other woman who hostessed was there already, and the manager sent Vi home.

'Wow,' she said as she threw her keys into the basket where we kept mail. She walked into the living room, flipping the switch that turned on the ceiling light, and I blinked. I could have feigned confusion and said, *Wow what?*, but there didn't seem to be a point. Vi said, 'You know you're depressed, right?'

'I didn't realize Doritos were against the law.'

'Don't be defensive. I'm not criticizing you. But you should see a shrink.'

I didn't have health insurance – for that matter,

233

neither did Vi – but I just said, 'That's not going to happen.'

She settled into the papasan chair and yawned, not covering her mouth. 'I've always wanted to be in therapy. Like the old-school kind where you lie on a couch not looking at the person.'

I took another chip from the bag.

'So this is your plan?' She set one foot on the coffee table and crossed the other over it. '*Star Trek* and jammies on by five o'clock every night?'

'Excuse me if I haven't taken St Louis by storm.'

'I think it's because you don't have a boyfriend right now.' Vi's tone was musing. 'It's like you aren't yourself without one.'

I said, 'Have you ever considered having a thought but not expressing it?'

'I come in peace, Daze.' This was what Vi called me long after almost everybody else except our parents called me Kate – *Daze,* short for Daisy. Patrick was the one other person who called me *Daze,* and I let him because he'd cried when he'd told me my mother had died. Vi said, 'You're in a bad place, and I want to help.'

I stood and dropped the Doritos bag on the table. Before I stalked off to my bedroom, I said, 'If I wanted your help, I'd ask for it.'

One morning, as I was returning home from a night at Mrs Abbott's, I had just crossed Clayton Road when I became aware of a person behind me. I turned and made quick, unfriendly eye contact with a black man wearing navy blue scrubs under an open winter coat. He was less than ten feet back – the sun had just risen, and we were the only ones outside – and when I made a left onto Brookline Terrace, I thought he'd go straight. But he went left, too. As we passed Edward Terrace and then Ralph Terrace, I waited for him to turn, but he still was behind me. Those weren't scrubs he was wearing, I suddenly realized. I myself had on scrubs, so I had foolishly assumed he did, too, but it occurred to me then that he was an escaped convict wearing a prison uniform and that he was planning to rob, rape, or kill me. (If it is tempting, after the fact, to try to defend or excuse my thinking in this moment, it also would be dishonest. And it wasn't even that no black people lived in the neighborhood, but not many did.)

The duplex Vi and I rented was on the next street, Moorlands Drive, and my mind raced: Instead of turning right, in the direction of our apartment, would it be smarter to turn left and go back to Clayton Road, where I could wave down a passing car? Or should I start running toward the duplex with the idea of unlocking the door and hurling myself inside as quickly as possible or, if I couldn't manage that before the man grabbed me, just start screaming for Vi?

But when we reached Moorlands, I didn't turn left, and I didn't start running. I went right, still walking, and so did the man, and then I crossed the street, and so did the man, and there were only two houses remaining before our duplex, one house remaining, and then I turned onto the walkway, and when I was no more than ten feet from our front door, I couldn't stop myself from glancing back, and he'd turned onto the walkway, too. This was when two things happened very quickly: I knew, with a sickening kind of terror, that I was really and truly about to be assaulted; and as I stood there frozen, he passed me, went left toward the door of the duplex that wasn't ours, pulled a key from his pocket, opened the door, and walked inside. Which meant, it appeared, that he was the new tenant who'd just moved into the rental unit below Vi's and mine. And while this didn't exclude his being a murderer or rapist, it indicated that being a murderer or rapist wasn't the reason he'd followed me from Clayton Road.

I waited until I was inside our apartment and had locked the door before I started crying, and though the tears were the result of my humiliating, offensive fear, they soon came to feel, as all tears I cried then did, like a lament for what a mess I'd made of my life by breaking up with Ben and leaving Chicago. Still bawling, I went and woke up Vi, and after I'd described to her what had just happened, she laughed, which actually did make me feel better; also, she didn't say that if I'd lived in Little Rock during desegregation, I was the kind of person who'd have spit at the black students as they tried to enter the high school.

★　　★　　★

The next week, while I was standing in front of the bathroom mirror blow-drying my hair, Vi pushed open the door and sat on the edge of the tub. She'd hostessed the night before, and she usually went out with her co-workers after the restaurant closed. Even this late, around noon, her face retained the pale, doughy look of having just awakened, and I could smell smoke coming off her.

'I decided what we should do,' she said. 'We should take belly dancing.'

I had turned off the blow-dryer when she entered the bathroom, but I turned it back on.

'There's this place in the Loop that has classes.' She was yelling cheerfully over the roar of air. 'We'll get out of the apartment, *and* I heard it burns a lot of calories. Which is counterintuitive, isn't it, because what if your belly goes away?' I bent my head forward and turned it to the side, still blow-drying, and she said, 'Just promise you'll think about it.'

She walked away, but when I'd finished and was putting the blow-dryer in the drawer under the sink, she returned and stood in the threshold of the door. 'By the way,' she said, and she was smirking, 'I met your scary black man. He's a resident in radiology at Barnes.'

We never took belly-dancing lessons, but that New Year's Eve, Vi convinced me to go with her to a dinner party Nancy was hosting to welcome the new millennium, or to welcome it prematurely, depending on your viewpoint – Vi and Patrick bickered over this, and I found the debate too boring to form an opinion. I was more interested in whether the Y2K problem would make utilities fail and planes crash, but when I was reading an article about it one evening, Vi said, 'That Y2K stuff is bullshit. My meditation group was talking about it, and we've all gotten messages that the transition will be peaceful.'

On Christmas Eve, the day before the anniversary of my mother's death, I had worked at Mrs Abbott's, and for Christmas, my father had come over to our apartment. I'd bought a precooked ham from Schnucks that I served with mashed potatoes, green beans, and crescent rolls – Vi had said she'd help me make the sides, then hadn't – and for dessert we ate pumpkin pie, also from Schnucks. My father gave us Starbucks gift cards for twenty-five dollars each, and the modesty of the present – it was what you'd give your mailman, I thought – made me feel embarrassed for him, even though there was nothing else I'd hoped for. Then, thank God, Christmas was finished.

Nancy lived in Tower Grove, and on New Year's Eve, there were about fifteen of us at two tables set up in her dining room and living room. She turned out to be a great cook, and it was the best meal I'd had since moving back to St Louis: figs wrapped in bacon, olives with blue cheese, rosemary garlic lamb, warm spinach salad, popovers, and a chocolate torte. Nancy had set out place cards, and Vi and I were at different tables; I was next to a guy named Maxwell who looked to be in his late thirties. He was pudgy, with a dark, full mustache and beard, and he wore a burgundy guayabera shirt embroidered with white birds, which I heard myself compliment him on when I took my seat, less because I actually liked the shirt than because I'd noticed it. Also, I'd already had three glasses of wine. After we finished the main course, by which time I'd had a fourth glass, he reached out, pressed his fingertips to my cheeks, and said, 'You have an amazingly symmetrical face.' I was drunk enough that this didn't entirely put me off. I said, 'You should see my sister.' He laughed and said, 'I have.'

This was when Nancy tapped a fork against her wineglass and said, 'Attention, everyone. It's time for the Burning Bowl Ceremony.' On small pieces of paper that were being passed around, Nancy explained, we would all write something negative in our life that we wanted to leave behind in the old millennium. Then we'd put the pieces of paper in a large tan ceramic bowl, which she held up, and we'd light them on fire. The spirit of the universe would receive our requests, release us from the forces that had been holding us back, and allow us to have new beginnings. As Nancy spoke, I tried to catch Vi's eye, but my sister wouldn't look at me.

I waited for a slip of paper to make its way to me; then, because there were fewer pens than guests, I waited for Maxwell to finish using his. I saw him write *SEXUALLY INSATIABLE* in all caps, and I couldn't help wondering if this was for my benefit.

And yet, after he'd given me the pen, I felt what I'd felt almost seven years before, making wishes under the Arch with Vi on our high school graduation night: that to be sincere in this moment was a bit silly, but to be insincere was to waste an opportunity. For a full minute, I wrote nothing. When Nancy came by, collecting everyone's scraps, I scribbled, in tiny letters, *Mom guilt.* Then I folded the paper in half and handed it off.

A discussion started about whether to burn the paper inside, where it might set off the smoke alarm, or outside, where it was ten degrees. I went to stand with Vi, Patrick, and Patrick's lawyer boyfriend and murmured to Vi, 'I thought Nancy was one of your restaurant friends, not one of your meditation friends.'

'She's both.' Vi was reading my face, trying to gauge my mood, and she said, 'They're not going to howl at the moon. After this, Nancy wants people to play Charades.'

'I wrote something,' I said.

'Good. You get a gold star.'

'Is Nancy trying to set me up with that guy Maxwell?'

Vi grinned. 'No comment.'

'Are *you* trying to set me up with him?'

'Supposedly, he has a Prince Albert. You know what that is?' When I shook my head, she said, 'Of course you don't. It means his dick is pierced.'

'Who told you that?'

She shrugged, and I said, 'Maybe you should hook up with him.'

'I'm having a drink tonight with Scary Black Man.'

'Our neighbor?'

'We've hung out a few times.'

'When?'

'You don't know everything about me.' Then she added, 'When you were at Mrs Abbott's.' Another guest, a guy, wolf-whistled so we'd quiet down and listen to Nancy again. It had been decided that we'd go outside for the ceremony, she said. In the small square of frozen grass between Nancy's apartment building and the sidewalk, we all gathered in a circle, and she held the bowl, in the center of which stood a fat white lit candle.

'Energies of this and other universes, we are grateful for everything you've provided to us,' she said. 'As we continue on our journey, we ask that you receive our humble prayers and help clear our hearts of that which has been holding us back. Enlighten us on our path into the future.' She looked around the circle. 'Let's be quiet for this part so it'll be easier for the energies to hear our prayers.'

A woman named Jocelyn was standing to Nancy's right, holding a smaller bowl, and she lifted the little folded pieces of paper out of it and passed them one by one to Nancy; one by one, Nancy held them to the flame and let them burn. I was standing across the circle, but I could tell, I could sense, when she got to mine. In spite of the fact that it was by then after eleven on New Year's Eve, there was little noise outside except for the sound of cars on Grand Boulevard. It was very cold, and I felt my heart bulging a little, perhaps with hope.

That night, somewhat to my own surprise, I did end up sleeping with Maxwell; he lived a block from Nancy, and I'm not sure I'd have gone home with him if I'd had to get into a car, but as it was, not much effort was required. And he did have a Prince Albert – he wore a curved silver barbell, which I encountered first with my fingers but truthfully couldn't feel when we were having sex, perhaps because he had on a condom. Afterward, he slept spooning me the entire night, his arms crossed in front of my chest in a way that was both sweet and a little entrapping. Early in the morning, he got up to pee, then released a fart so thunderous that I started laughing; when he returned to bed, I faked still being asleep and he spooned me again. A few hours later, after I really had fallen back to sleep, then awakened, and he had, too, he suggested we get brunch and I declined in what I hoped was a friendly way; when he called our apartment a few times in the next week, having procured the number from Nancy, I didn't call him back.

Vi didn't actually hook up with our neighbor on New Year's Eve, but she did two nights later, and it went on for a few weeks before fizzling. The part I wish I could undo is that we kept calling him Scary Black Man. Not to his face, obviously, but whenever we discussed him. His real name was Jeff Parker, but all this time later, if Vi told me she'd run into Jeff Parker on the street, I don't think I'd know who she was talking about. If she said Scary Black Man, I'd know immediately.

In February, I started looking for jobs again and quit working for Mrs Abbott when I was offered a position at an elder-care services agency; although no apparition of any sort had ever appeared to me at Mrs Abbott's, on my final night at her house, Mrs Abbott greatly unsettled me by calling me by my mother's name. 'Rita, dear,' she said as I tucked her in, 'be sure to take sixty dollars from my pocketbook.' Briefly, I was speechless, but then I concluded it was just a coincidence; for all I knew, another of the aides was named Rita. 'I'm not supposed to do that,' I said. 'But thank you.'

In my new job, I helped clients figure out if they qualified for Medicaid or meal deliveries at home, and I served as a liaison between their families or doctors. Even then, when I did have health insurance, I didn't see a shrink, but I bought a Jetta

243

with forty thousand miles on it, which I suspect did more for my sense of well-being than years of therapy could have. In the fall, a woman in my office named Janet asked if I wanted to do a 5K run with her, a fund-raising race, and I said yes. We started running together in Forest Park before or after work, and at a brunch held by Janet after the race, I met a guy named David Frankel who was a manager at a big rental-car company head-quartered in St Louis. Almost immediately, we were dating seriously. If it never felt as if David and I were infatuated with each other (he frequently corrected my driving, and he told me that I talked too loudly when I was on the phone with Vi), he was someone to go to movies and restaurants with on the weekend, and Vi had not been entirely wrong when she'd said that I was more myself when I had a boyfriend. I might have disagreed with her about the reason why – I'd always felt that boyfriends were a distraction from the exis-tential abyss Vi chose to hover closer to than I did – but the sentiment did have some basis. The night before I went out with David for the second time, while I was applying makeup, Vi burst into the bathroom and said, 'You can't marry him! You can have a roll in the hay, but you're not supposed to marry him!'

'I think you're getting ahead of yourself,' I said.

'No.' Vi's face was serious. 'You're supposed to marry someone else.'

Two years later, the day Vi and I turned

twenty-seven, we had dinner at Hacienda with our father, Patrick, and David, and afterward our father went home to his apartment, and Vi and I drove to a bar in the Loop with the guys. While they played pool, I said to Vi, 'I just want to tell you that David and I are getting engaged soon, and I hope you'll be happy for us.'

Vi looked unimpressed.

'He's up for adopting from China, which not all guys are,' I said. 'And he can afford it, too, and it's expensive.'

'Why don't you adopt on your own?' Vi said. 'I'll help you raise your wee little lotus flowers.'

'Did you not hear what I just said? The adoption alone costs like twenty thousand dollars.' Vi and I had both been in debt for years.

She said, 'You know what you should do is, you should secretly get knocked up by him and then break up. That'd be free, and you'd still get to be a mom.'

'That's a terrible idea. I don't want to be a single mother, and I don't want biological children.'

'The Chinese adoption thing is noble, but it's not who you are.' After taking a sip of beer, Vi wiped her mouth with the back of her hand. She said, 'Your destiny is to breed.'

'Luckily, it's not up to you.'

'How about this?' Vi said. 'Just promise me you won't get engaged before Christmas.'

Christmas was four months away. 'What difference does it make?' I said.

Vi's smile was ludicrously confident. 'Because by then you'll have met the guy you should marry.'

On that New Year's Eve of the new millennium, after all the pieces of paper were burned, Nancy said in a somber tone, 'Thank you, energies, for letting us make this offering to you.' Then she looked around the circle and said, 'Who needs another drink before midnight?'

Inside, Vi and I ended up squeezed together on Nancy's low couch. I said, 'Should I ask what you wrote on your paper or will that make it not come true?'

'What do you think I wrote?' I looked at her, and she added, 'I'm sure it was the same thing you did.'

I looked away then, toward the TV, which had at some point been turned on. It was so pleasant to be drunk in a warm, crowded apartment, to have eaten a delicious meal, to know that there was a guy hovering nearby who wanted to have sex with me (even a guy who was odd and, by his own admission, insatiable) that I was reluctant to let my mother into the night, or to let her in any more than I already had by invoking her on my own scrap of paper. Vi patted my knee, and I felt – this had to do with being drunk, though it also wasn't untrue – that no other person would ever understand me as my sister did.

And then everyone was moving, we had arrived at the last ten seconds before midnight, and Vi stood, then stuck out her hand to pull me to my feet. 'Ten, nine, eight,' people shouted, 'seven, six, five, four' – and Vi, who was bellowing, nodded her chin once at me, meaning, *You do it, too!* and so I joined in – 'three, two, one!' and everyone was cheering and flowing noisemakers, and from somewhere 'Auld Lang Syne' was audible.

'Happy 2000,' I said, and Vi stepped forward – to this day, it's the only time in our lives she has done this – and kissed me on the mouth.

CHAPTER 10

These were the topics of some of the articles that ran in local and national publications in the weeks after Vi's prediction:

A bride whose wedding was scheduled for Saturday, October 17, at the Chase Park Plaza heard from several out-of-town guests who'd changed their minds about attending.

For the Blues' first home game of the season, which was supposed to be on October 16 against the Buffalo Sabres, there was a glut of tickets.

Religious groups in the area were condemning the prediction, and a large evangelical church in Arnold had raised money to pay for a billboard along I-55 featuring a quote from Leviticus: DO NOT TURN TO MEDIUMS OR SEEK OUT SPIRITISTS, FOR YOU WILL BE DEFILED BY THEM. I AM THE LORD YOUR GOD.

Local frozen-custard shops were selling so-called quake shakes, and a sports bar was selling a quake burger, and two community college students were selling bumpers stickers that said I BRAKE FOR QUAKES.

Across St Louis, Targets and Walmarts kept selling out of bottled water and batteries.

The city and county superintendents had agreed that school would not be canceled on October 16, though emergency drills were being staged so students would know what to do if an earthquake occurred.

Professors at both the Saint Louis University Earthquake Center and Washington University's Department of Earth and Planetary Sciences – that is, Jeremy's department – were adamant in stating that no one could predict earthquakes; that anyone who claimed otherwise was a fraud; and that it was irresponsible of the media to devote so much attention to such an outlandish story. In the *Post-Dispatch*, Leland Marcus, the chair of Jeremy's department, was quoted as saying, 'I would stake my career on it. There's absolutely no such thing as earthquake season.'

Hank had been right: By the afternoon following her appearance on the *Today* show, Vi, whose phone number was listed, had been called by dozens and dozens of reporters and producers throughout the United States and even by a columnist at a tabloid in Sydney, Australia, where it was already the next morning; by the next morning in St Louis, she'd received requests for interviews from a producer of a radio show in Amsterdam and from reporters at *Haaretz*, in Israel, and the *Sun*, in England. After I'd dropped her off following our breakfast at the Four Seasons, she'd gone to sleep, and while she'd slept, her phone had rung and rung, her prediction spreading across the Internet. Also while she'd slept, reporters from the *St. Louis Beacon* and the *Riverfront Times* had slipped notes and business cards through the mail slot in her front door, a reporter from the *Post-Dispatch* had set up a camping chair on the sidewalk outside her house, simply waiting for her, and a dog had taken an enormous shit on her lawn, though she said she wasn't sure if the shit was connected to the prediction, and when she asked the *Post-Dispatch* reporter, he said he hadn't seen it happen. (Of course it was connected, I thought.) But until Vi woke, just after five that afternoon, she was unaware of the building frenzy; everyone else knew about it before she did. And when I reached her, around six, she sounded stunned as she said, 'You won't believe what's happening.'

'No,' I said. 'I think I will.'

'So I get off the phone with some dude at a newspaper in Longview, Washington, and I'm thinking, how weird is it that someone from the state of Washington even cares about an earthquake in St Louis? And then I check my messages, and the state of Washington is the least of it. And while I'm listening to all these voice mails, I hear a knock on my door, and it's a guy from the *Post-Dispatch,* and while I'm talking to him, a van shows up from Fox. I already can't remember what I said to which person.'

'Maybe you shouldn't talk to any more reporters.' I didn't tell her there had been one at our house, too, also from the *Post-Dispatch,* a girl lurking by the driveway when we returned from the Wheelings' whom I didn't recognize as a reporter because she looked about sixteen. After she introduced herself, when I did understand, I pushed past her and brusquely said, 'No comment.' I'd been surprised, though, when I peeked outside a few minutes later, that she was gone.

'It's not like I'm hawking salad choppers,' Vi was saying. 'I'm trying to warn people so they can protect themselves.'

'What if you come over here tonight?' I didn't want her in my house; I didn't want her to infect my children with the germs of public exposure, the antipathy of strangers. And it wasn't entirely true that she wasn't selling anything – as she'd mentioned to me before her *Today* interview, she'd be happy to generate new business. But nothing good could come of Vi hanging out by herself at home, accessible to anyone. I said, 'Hank knows a publicist he thinks could help you, a woman he went to college with. How about if we get in touch with her before you talk to anyone else in the media?'

'And I just don't call back the *Washington Post* or the L.A. *Times*?'

'Yeah,' I said. 'For now.'

'A publicist probably charges a million bucks.'

'Hank said there might be ways for you to make money off this.' I couldn't bring myself to specify what the ways were. I said, 'If Jeremy drives over right now, will you just promise me you won't talk to more reporters before he gets there? I'm not saying you shouldn't at all, but we need to come up with a plan. I'll call Hank and get the publicist's number. She's in L.A., so she might still be at work.'

'Hold on,' Vi said. 'My doorbell is ringing.'

'Don't answer it!'

She laughed. 'What are you so scared of?'

Besides the potential for mass hysteria? The professional humiliation for Jeremy? The official destruction of our friendship with the Wheelings? 'What's to be gained by doing all these interviews?' I said. 'Your prediction is out there. It's all over the Internet, too, in case you don't know. But you've said what you have to say, and aren't you just repeating yourself now?'

She was silent for a few seconds, long enough that it didn't seem unreasonable to hope I'd persuaded her, but when she spoke, she sounded peevish. 'Guardian told me to warn people.'

I said nothing – wasn't the deal we had that if she invoked Guardian around me very infrequently, I would be respectful when she did? – and she added, 'I know you think I want attention. And maybe compared to you, I do. It's not my goal to be invisible. But that isn't what this is about.'

'Just stay where you are,' I said. 'Jeremy will be there in ten minutes.'

While I'd been on the phone, Jeremy had begun giving dinner to Rosie and Owen, and as I returned the receiver to its cradle in the kitchen, I said, 'How about if we switch and you go get Vi and bring her back here?'

He looked less than thrilled.

'Otherwise, she'll keep talking to reporters,' I said. 'They're knocking on her door and calling nonstop.'

'Are you thinking she'd spend the night here?'

'Maybe.' Our eyes met.

'I'll go get her,' Jeremy said. 'But it's not your job to save her from herself. She's her own person.'

Not really, I thought. *Not entirely.*

And he could tell this was what I was thinking, evidently, because he said, 'I'm not talking about when you were embryos. I'm talking about now.' He passed me the spoon he was using to feed Owen sweet potatoes, and as he walked out of the kitchen, I called, 'Thank you.'

I texted Hank then, to ask if he'd had a chance to contact the publicist, and he called and said, 'I'm forwarding her email to you right now, and she said she's happy to help however she can.'

'Did she say how much she charges?'

'You can read her email, but it would be about fifteen thousand to have her on retainer for the next few weeks.'

'Fifteen *thousand*?' I knew I sounded like a rube, but it was hard to conceal my shock.

'She's good, Kate. I trust her completely. And I think that's the going rate for people at her level.'

I had two thoughts then, and the first was that one or both of the Wheelings had to have family money. Because they never seemed worried about it, but even when he'd been an art teacher, before Amelia was born, Hank couldn't have made much more than I had at the elder-care agency. My second thought was that I wished Hank would come over to our house because I was pretty sure he'd be better than I would at persuading both Vi and Jeremy that Emma would be worth the expense. But even if things weren't tense between Courtney and me, this would be an inappropriate favor to ask in light of her pregnancy. I needed to let Hank stay home.

When Jeremy returned with Vi, it emerged that in addition to the various reporters I already knew she'd granted post-nap interviews to, she'd spoken to people at newspapers in Naples, Florida; Richmond, Virginia; and Wellington, New Zealand. She mentioned this with what I felt was increasingly disingenuous surprise that all these journalists were interested in *her*, and she did not acknowledge the request I'd made for her to stop; it was possible, however, that she'd talked to the reporters before our conversation. 'Oh, and good news.' She grinned. 'Patrick says he'll be my publicist for free.' Given that Patrick was a manager at Crate & Barrel, this was not encouraging. 'Can I have a beer?' Vi asked. As she headed toward the kitchen, she called over her shoulder, 'Either of you want one?'

In the living room, Rosie had just yanked a dump

truck out of Owen's hands. I whispered to Jeremy, 'We're about to call this publicist Hank gave me the name of, but she costs fifteen thousand dollars. Can we pay for it?'

Jeremy looked faintly amused, as if I were joking.

'I know it's a lot,' I said, 'but things are getting out of control.'

His expression changed – he was registering my desperation, which was not the same as agreeing to my request – and then Vi was back in the living room. 'Let's call the publicist,' I said. 'Her name's Emma, and Hank said she's really great. And' – my face was burning even before I said it; surely this was the worst act of manipulation I'd committed in my marriage – 'she's kind of expensive, you were right about that, but Jeremy and I want to pay for her because it just seems worth it.' Feeling Jeremy's angry surprise (it did not billow from him, as with smoke, but rather was laserlike in its precise focus on me), I added, 'After you're flooded with new clients, you can pay us back.' She would never pay us back, I knew, and I would never try to get her to, but perhaps the suggestion would assuage Jeremy.

I didn't dare make eye contact with him as I retrieved the phone from the kitchen and pressed the number from Hank's email. 'Emma Hall PR,' said a female voice, and I said, 'It's Kate Tucker, Hank Wheeling's friend. I think he told you my sister and I – ?'

'Emma's out of the office, but let me check if I can find her,' the voice said – of course she wasn't

Emma Hall; of course a publicist in L.A. had an assistant – and after a silence, she said, 'Putting you through to Emma Hall.'

Emma Hall was driving, possibly with her windows down, and she was also British, which Hank hadn't mentioned, and the combination of the rushing air, the fact that I'd put her on speakerphone, and her accent made her hard to understand; I needed to hear an entire sentence before I could decipher it. Also, one of the first things she said was 'Isn't Hank the best? And Courtney, too, I love them both. I've always fancied the idea of a trip out to Kansas City to see them.' But I liked everything else about her: She was friendly and confident and not condescending, she had already watched the clip of Vi on *Today*, she complimented the shirt Vi had worn, meaning she complimented my shirt, and when I said, 'We just want to make sure we know what it is a publicist does,' Emma laughed and said, 'Right, what a great question.'

All media queries would go through her, she said; if journalists contacted Vi directly, Vi would forward their number or their email to Emma, and Emma would be the one to respond. She said she'd decline most requests, which alone made me want to hire her. 'Once you've done the *Today* show, there's no reason to talk to the *Bumblefuck Gazette*,' she said, and as I confirmed to myself that yes, in her elegant voice, she had indeed just said *Bumblefuck*, she was already moving on. 'And we can think about what your goals are, Violet,

256

what image you want to project, so you're not simply being reactive.'

'I want to get the word out so people can take precautions.'

'Absolutely, absolutely,' Emma said, and I had the distinct impression that she'd encountered people like Vi before – sincerely altruistic, but not completely so.

'And I don't want to seem like a nut job,' Vi added. 'I want people to know I don't stand to gain from this.'

Emma asked if Vi had a website, and when Vi said no, Emma said, 'Then that's the first order of business. I'll have my assistant get cracking on this the minute we hang up, on securing the URL and setting up something rudimentary for now. What I'd like you to do, tonight even, is write a personal statement. Something brief, one paragraph or so, about who you are and how your prediction came to you. Just very plain language. Nothing fancy.'

'Would you come to St Louis or handle things from there?' I asked, and Emma said, 'Well, that depends.' Then she said laughingly, 'And I said Kansas City before, didn't I, when you don't live in Kansas City at all? And you were too polite to correct me. Shame on me!'

There was never a moment when we officially agreed to work together; by the time I told her that I'd be handling payment and that I was taking her off speakerphone so she and I could square it away, it seemed we'd all already decided. Vi was still right next to me, and because I didn't want her to hear me say the number, I said to Emma, 'The fee you mentioned in your email to Hank—'

'Fifteen thousand for thirty days.' Emma did not seem at all embarrassed. 'Plus travel expenses and accommodations in the event of my visiting St Louis.'

I felt a swirl of nausea in my stomach. 'And we'd pay that up front or in installments?'

'Half now and the second half after two weeks.'

'So for the first part, I'd wire it to you, or write a check – ?'

'As you prefer,' she said. 'I trust you, of course, Kate. Any friend of Hank and Courtney's . . .'

I was aware that at some point, Jeremy had collected Rosie and Owen and taken them upstairs, though until I hung up the phone, I didn't entirely attend to this fact.

'I thought you were just trying to censor me, but she sounds awesome,' Vi said. 'You really won't tell me how much she costs?'

'Don't look a gift horse in the mouth.' Was Jeremy merely annoyed or outright furious? Either way, it wouldn't improve matters if Vi knew that I hadn't gotten his blessing.

'More or less than a thousand?'

'We're finished talking about this,' I said.

'More, huh?' Vi raised her eyebrows. 'Thanks, Daze. What does Courtney Wheeling think of their friend helping me spread my witchy message?'

As if I hadn't wondered the same thing, I said, 'She's preoccupied with other stuff right now.'

Vi looked at me intently. 'She didn't miscarry, did she?'

If Courtney planned to terminate, it probably was better for my sister to believe Courtney had miscarried. But it also felt wrong to say she had while she was still pregnant. 'Don't ask me that,' I said.

'Yikes,' Vi said. 'You think it was because she wasn't eating enough?'

'Courtney eats. She's just thin.'

'You know, I still haven't watched myself on *Today*,' Vi said. 'Have you?'

Didn't I need to go upstairs and nurse Owen before he went to sleep? And I always put him down for bed, too. But maybe I'd let Jeremy handle tonight, I thought. Owen had polished off an unprecedented two jars of sweet potatoes at dinner, and anyway, it wasn't like he wouldn't wake up to eat again in three hours. 'I've watched it, but I'll watch again,' I said. To my surprise, it had calmed me to watch online with Hank; the knowledge of Vi having been on *Today* was the opposite of calming, but seeing the segment itself, I'd been reminded of how well she'd come off.

Vi and I sat next to each other on the couch, Jeremy's laptop resting half on my left thigh and half on Vi's right one. 'My hair looks awesome,' Vi said. 'Good job. But holy shit, do I really have three chins?'

'You don't have three chins.'

After the segment finished, she said, 'That wasn't bad.'

'Didn't you believe me?' Then I said, 'You haven't changed your mind about October sixteenth?'

Vi was looking into the distance, in the direction of our dining room but not at the dining room itself, and simultaneously I didn't want her to visualize a natural disaster from inside my house and I felt her separateness from me, her mysteriousness, in a way that was almost impressive. She did have an ability, one I'd never been impressed by back when I'd shared it; but now mine was mostly gone and hers was sharper than ever.

'No,' she said. 'I haven't changed my mind.'

I'd said she was welcome to stay over – although this prospect had seemed unappealing a few hours earlier, it had proven pleasant to spend the evening with Vi – but her cellphone had rung a few times, and around nine, her friend Nancy, hostess of the millennium New Year's Eve party, had picked her up to go meet people for drinks. Though Vi and Nancy remained close, Vi had grown apart from some of her other meditation friends; she'd told me they were jealous that after the Brady Ogden case, she'd been able to make a living as a psychic while they still had to hold down day jobs.

Nancy didn't come inside, and I waved to her from our porch as Vi headed out. 'If there are any reporters, or just any weirdos, waiting at your house, come back over here,' I said. 'When Nancy drops you off, don't let her leave until you're inside.'

'You're being paranoid.' Vi grinned. 'It's kind of flattering.'

As she reached Nancy's car, I called, 'Don't forget about writing the statement for your website.'

'Aye, aye,' she replied.

I locked the front door, organized the diaper bag, went around turning off the lights on the first floor, and set the security alarm; normally Jeremy closed up the house while I was nursing Owen. Had Jeremy eaten dinner? I hadn't, except for some stale pretzels I'd brought out to the living room after we'd watched Vi's interview.

It was definitely unusual that he hadn't returned downstairs, though it was also clear why. And I'd never before dreaded walking up to bed, but on this night I did; the door to our bedroom was closed. I went into the bathroom, and when I was finished, I paused in front of our bedroom – I wondered if I should knock, but that would be downright bizarre – and when I pushed the door open, I saw that the light on Jeremy's nightstand was on, and he was sitting up in bed, wearing his glasses and an old Wesleyan T-shirt, the sheet and comforter pulled to the middle of his chest. He held his phone in front of him with one hand, the glow from the screen reflected in the lenses of his glasses, and I heard what sounded like a bus driving and then a man saying, 'That's for sure,' from which I inferred that Jeremy was watching a

TV show or movie, and for some reason the small-ness of the screen and him up here alone, in his college T-shirt, made me sad.

'Hi,' I said, and in a tone that was tight but not gratuitously mean – he wasn't trying to show that he was pissed, he just *was* pissed – he said 'Hi' back.

I took a step forward. 'Are you mad because I said we'd pay for the publicist or because I said it without you agreeing to it?'

'Both.' There was no humor in his voice, despite a joke's easy proximity, and it was only then that he paused whatever he was watching and really looked at me. He said, 'I'm curious how much you think we have in the savings account.'

I swallowed. 'Twenty thousand?'

'Well, I got paid today, and that put us just over eleven.'

'Eleven thousand?'

'Yes,' Jeremy said. 'Eleven thousand.'

Would Emma accept payment by credit card? 'I'm sorry,' I said. 'I'm sorry we didn't have a conversation about it, but I really want Vi to work with this woman, and I was afraid that if she knew how much it costs, she'd say no. She wouldn't even listen. And instead she really liked her, and she said – Vi, I mean – she said she wouldn't talk to more reporters without having them go through Emma. That's exactly, exactly what I was hoping.'

'You need to realize that you can't control Vi's behavior. I'm serious, Kate. She's a grown woman, a willful grown woman. And even if you've temporarily got a leash on her, this idea that you can keep her in line is going to end badly in the long run.'

I folded my arms. 'Okay.'

'I'm not saying this to be a jerk. I'm saying it because I'm worried that you're setting yourself up for something really ugly.'

'I get your larger point,' I said. 'And I'm sure you're right. But to have a professional handling the media – I don't see how that can be bad. Vi is in over her head. You're the one who listened to those messages on our voicemail. Well, multiply that by a hundred and that's what she's going through. Every time she turns around, another reporter wants to talk to her, and she can't say no. She loves the spotlight, *and* she believes she's helping people.'

'So let her talk to the reporters. They'll go away eventually.'

This was such a radical notion, so contrary to the frantic way I was expending my energy, that there was in it something enticing, something liberating. What if I simply stepped back and did nothing at all? But I couldn't. I said, 'Let's just give Emma a chance.'

'And our savings.'

Would our disagreement have had a different tenor if I were still generating an income? But then he said, 'If you were going to impulsively spend fifteen grand that we don't have, I wish it had been on a really awesome flat-screen TV.'

So he was going to forgive me; I was lucky.

'I know.' I gestured toward his phone. 'What are you watching?'

'A comedy that's completely not funny, which is a feat.'

I took another step forward. 'You feel like doing something else?'

For the first time since I'd entered the room, he smiled, or at least he half-smiled. 'It depends what you have in mind.'

I climbed onto the bed, over him, so that my knees were on either side of his waist. 'I have a few ideas,' I said. I took his phone out of his hand and set it on the nightstand, and when I leaned in and kissed his mouth, he kissed me back right away. Jeremy and I were like everyone else with young children – we went weeks without having sex. We were always too tired, or a baby was crying. We joked about not having it, while listening to our children on the monitors. 'We could schedule it,' I'd once said, and he'd said, 'I never wanted to become those people,' and I said, 'But you can see why it happens, right?'

As he pulled his shirt over his head, then raised my arms to pull off mine – I kept my bra on during sex, so I wouldn't leak milk – I thought that maybe this was what we ought to do every night: forgo ice cream and TV downstairs and just come up to bed. I could've done without the fight, though as we kept kissing, as he rubbed his hands over me, I thought that what people said about make-up sex was true.

I was still on top, and he had been inside me maybe four minutes when I felt that surge, my body shuddering against his. I was usually first, though he didn't take much longer; we were compatible in this way. (And maybe, given our efficiency, there was no reason we didn't do it far more often.) As he was coming, Jeremy said in a kind of heaving whisper, 'I love you so much, Katie,' and I kissed his neck. I don't know if he realized that the only time he called me Katie was when we were having sex.

We'd fallen asleep with the light on, and were both still naked except for my bra, when Owen started crying. I scrambled out of bed and gathered my clothes from the floor on Jeremy's side, hastily pulling them on as I walked.

Owen's room was dark except for the starfish night-light. As soon as he saw me, he stopped crying, and I scooped him up and sat us both in the glider, him sideways on my lap.

Earlier, with Vi, as we'd talked to Emma and watched the *Today* interview, a scheming sort of air had developed between us, a mood like the one twenty years earlier on all those afternoons when we'd practiced our dance routine for 'You May Be Right.' Other people receded until it was only us and our project. Or so it had felt, but as I nursed Owen, it no longer felt this way at all. Vi's prediction wasn't fun; it was scary. And the people I'd allowed to recede were my children, who were so small, who needed me so completely. Owen weighed sixteen pounds; he could do nothing

265

for himself, couldn't speak, couldn't even reliably sit up; he slept in pale blue pajamas and a sleep sack with a brown teddy bear on the front. There was nothing that mattered besides protecting him and Rosie. Maybe we *should* leave town, I thought. Or, at the least, I needed to convince Jeremy not to go to Denver.

Owen was mostly asleep as I changed his diaper and brought him back to the glider to burp him. He breathed deeply, curled into me with his left cheek pressed over my heart, and for a long time I kept on patting his back, holding him in my arms.

Vi had writer's block, she explained when we spoke around ten o'clock the next morning, which was why she hadn't yet finished the statement for her new website. I was pretty sure that writer's block was code for being hungover, but scolding her wouldn't help. 'Emma wants this as soon as possible,' I said. 'I'll hammer something out and call you back.'

I'd just put Owen down for his first nap, and I set Rosie up in front of an episode of *Dora the Explorer* and opened Jeremy's laptop on the dining room table. I probably had about ten minutes before Rosie started wandering around, and so in seven, I finished a paragraph, which was all Emma had requested.

Hello, my name is Violet Shramm, I wrote. *Thank you for visiting my website. Since childhood, I have experienced premonitions, also known as extrasensory perceptions. I was born and raised in St Louis, Missouri.*

I enjoy cooking, watching reality TV (my guilty pleasure), and spending time with my family. As you may have heard, I recently had a premonition that an earthquake will happen in the St Louis area. It was not my intent to scare people. Instead, I wanted to help them make preparations to stay safe. We could link here to FEMA's recommendations, I thought. I concluded with a variation on what Vi had said to the Brookstone cashier when she'd bought the slippers for our father: *I sincerely hope that my prediction turns out to be wrong. I am not a scientist, and I'm capable of making mistakes like anyone else, but it is only in good faith that I share my views and ideas.*

When I called to read Vi what I'd written, she wanted me to insert references to her having helped the police find Brady Ogden, as well as to her having publicly predicted Michael Jackson's death, both of which had been mentioned on Channel 5. (The latter had occurred during a session with clients at her house, which I wasn't sure counted as public – in June, two days before Michael Jackson died, she'd told clients she was worried about his health.) After I'd reluctantly taken her suggestions, she also wanted me to cut the last line; I convinced her to keep it, and she convinced me, even though it made me cringe, to add *To anyone reading this, I wish you a day full of positive energy.* Emma subsequently excised the first two sentences; the rest of the paragraph appeared on Vi's website, which was up later that afternoon. Next to the statement was a picture of Vi I'd taken the previous Thanksgiving; she was wearing a red cape, but it looked like a normal sweater if you didn't know, and she was smiling prettily. In the original photo, Rosie had been sitting next to Vi, so I'd emailed the photo to Jeremy, had him cut Rosie out – I didn't want Rosie on Vi's website but didn't have the technological skills, modest though I knew they were, to remove her myself – and then emailed the photo to Emma.

While sending this email, I saw dozens of notifications of Facebook messages from people I hadn't been in touch with in years, and I realized that I couldn't go back on Facebook itself until after October 16, or perhaps I could never go on again. I closed my email and found the website of a large national sporting goods chain, from which I ordered a crank radio, a first-aid kit, three LED waterproof flashlights (we currently owned one flashlight that wasn't waterproof), and a propane stove. If Jeremy asked, I wasn't going to lie about what I'd bought. Still, I couldn't help hoping that the packages would arrive while he was at work.

In those first days following Vi's appearance on the *Today* show, I would read the comments that appeared online after articles about the prediction. *This woman is an idiot and anyone who trusts her is an idiot, too.* Or: *She should quit trying to scare people, take a good look in the mirror, and go on a diet!!* And of course: *If she can predict the future, why doesn't she win the lottery and buy a nicer house? Hers looks like a shithole from what I saw on TV.* There was always, always that lottery one.

Vi was reading the comments, too; she'd call me when Rosie and I were building a tower out of blocks or I was changing Owen's diaper, and I'd answer because what if it was urgent? In the past, I'd sometimes not pick up if I was in the middle of something, but this was one of the ways of quantifying her celebrity, that now I didn't dare. 'Okay, listen to this,' she'd say, and begin reading: '"Like other end-of-the-world prophets, Ms. Shramm obviously has not only delusions of grandeur but outright delusions." But I never said the end of the world is coming! When did I say that?'

'Ignore it,' I'd say. 'Quit reading.' It was in advising Vi not to read the comments that I was able to convince myself, which is to say that I persuaded one of us.

'I never realized how mean people are,' she said another time, after an article in an online magazine – not even the comments but the article itself – compared her to an agent of Satan.

'Really?' I said. 'You didn't?'

During one of our calls with Emma – again, Vi was at my house, Jeremy was watching the children upstairs, Emma was on speakerphone – Vi said, 'How do we get websites to take down the stuff people are writing about me? Because it's not true, and they don't even have to put their real names.'

'Oh, you mustn't read that rubbish,' Emma said, as if she were surprised to learn Vi had been; it seemed this was another of our novice mistakes. 'It's absolutely awful what people write, isn't it? But trust me – the sort of person posting comments, it's a forty-year-old man who lives in his parents' basement and works at some shit job and he's furious, just furious at the world, and you mustn't let him get under your skin, but instead you should feel pity for him.'

During this same conversation, Emma reiterated her earlier instructions to Vi not to grant additional interviews to the reporters loitering outside her house, which was now normal; there'd be one or two on the sidewalk almost all the time during the day, and some would wait into the evening. And they were no longer just from local publications. One had come from a Japanese newspaper, a trim man in khaki pants and a white short-sleeved button-down shirt. So incredible was this fact to me that I yearned to ask him: Had he *really* boarded a sixteen-hour flight just to talk to Vi? Of course, I didn't say a word to him, and after picking Vi up that day around noon, with Rosie and Owen in the backseat, I decided that I wouldn't return to her house again with them in the car. Ideally, I wouldn't return to her house, period, until this was all over.

Reporters were occasionally outside our house, too – I always checked to make sure the street was empty before going somewhere with Owen and Rosie in the stroller or putting them in the car, though once a guy had tricked me by waiting across the street – and for several days, a reporter from the *Post-Dispatch* had rung the bell in the late morning and again at six o'clock. It wasn't the girl from before but a middle-aged man who left notes and business cards – his name was Phil Krech, and he was the one Vi had spoken to the afternoon following her *Today* appearance – but when I told Emma about Phil Krech, he stopped coming by; I think he stopped because Emma had Vi agree to another interview with him. That Vi was a twin had been mentioned in an article in the *Post-Dispatch* and repeated elsewhere, and photos of Vi and me from our Kirkwood High senior yearbook had run in the *Riverfront Times* and also, rather shockingly, in *People* magazine. In both these articles, I'd been referred to as Daisy Tucker – I'd never legally changed my first name – and Jeremy's name and job had also been disclosed. And we'd gotten plenty of phone calls from journalists; I no longer checked messages, and we agreed that Jeremy would delete them without my listening to them. I wondered if, as October 16 drew closer, Vi's house would turn into one of those circuses of cameras and lights and satellites, as when the media staked out the home of a woman who'd had sex with a famous politician, or the campus of a school where a shooting had just occurred.

On the phone, Emma was telling Vi, 'You say, "I'm so sorry, but all requests have to go through my publicist." You make me the villain.' Hearing Emma say this, I again felt an immense gratitude, until she said, 'Meanwhile, my negotiations with *Today* continue, and I should have more information in the next day or so.' She pronounced the *t*'s in *negotiations* like soft *c*'s.

'Wait, is Vi going back on the *Today* show?' I asked.

'Did I not tell you?' Vi said.

Was Vi talking to Emma without me? Apparently so. 'Why would they want you again?' I asked Vi.

'They feel that they own the story,' Emma said. 'They have a relationship with Vi now, having introduced her to the country. Obviously, if they want her a second time, it would be only appropriate for them to pay licensing fees for family photos and such.'

'Family photos?' I repeated.

'Chillax,' Vi said. 'Nothing is definite.'

I said, 'Emma, I really appreciate everything you're doing and I know this isn't about me, but I don't want to be in any photos on *Today*.'

'Duly noted,' Emma said. 'On a different topic, how would the two of you feel about an interloper from Los Angeles popping in for a visit?'

'We'd feel fabulous,' Vi said.

Emma flew out for twenty-four hours. She stayed at the Ritz-Carlton in Clayton, at our expense, though she spent most of the time on a tour of what she referred to as 'Vi's St Louis,' as in 'What I really yearn to do is see Vi's St Louis.' In a town car also subsidized by us (and truly, I had never

272

heard of anyone in St Louis hiring a town car), Vi and Emma and Patrick, who'd invited himself along, drove by Nipher Middle School and Kirkwood High School and the house on Gilbert Street; they had lunch on the Hill, at the restaurant where Vi had worked the longest.

'You should come on the tour,' Vi had said the day before Emma's arrival. 'Hire your babysitter.'

She meant Kendra, a Wash U undergrad who helped me one morning a week. 'I doubt she can do it on such late notice,' I said.

Vi said, 'Well, Emma definitely wants to meet you.'

After an absurdly long discussion, we agreed that Emma and Vi would come to our house for a pizza dinner to which we'd also invite the Wheelings, since they were the reason we knew Emma. Having Courtney into my home wasn't my first choice at this point, but trying to avoid doing so would only draw more attention to the awkwardness between us; besides, I didn't want to give Vi the satisfaction of knowing that Courtney and I weren't getting along. 'And you're welcome to bring Stephanie,' I said.

'She can drive over in her U-Haul,' Vi replied.

Stephanie didn't end up coming for dinner, though Patrick did. And Emma turned out to be stunning, with pale skin, a dark bob, and four-inch heels. Upon meeting, she kissed me on both cheeks and remarked on how darling Rosie and Owen were. She'd brought to our house a bottle of red wine and an enormous bouquet of Stargazer lilies – I couldn't help wondering if we had paid for these as well – and there was a sort of amusement accompanying her good manners that made me suspect she found it a great lark to eat dinner at six P.M. in the suburbs. It wasn't that I didn't like her, but rather that I wasn't sure I trusted this version of her – in-person, high-heeled, gorgeous Emma – quite as much as I trusted her voice on the phone. Also, she flirted with Hank.

Hank and Amelia came without Courtney – 'She's laid up with a sinus infection,' he announced as they walked in – and as I went to the kitchen to get drinks for people, I heard Emma saying, 'Hank, how is it that I've become an old crone and you're just as young and handsome as the day we graduated?'

Jeremy returned then from picking up the pizza and salad, and I passed him glasses of wine to distribute. I was still in the kitchen, dumping the salad into a wooden bowl, when Hank came to get a beer, and I said in a low voice, 'Courtney's not mad that you're here, is she?'

From the drawer next to the oven, he pulled out our dinosaur-shaped bottle opener. 'Honestly,' he said, 'she just wants to lie low before tomorrow.'

'Oh.' He meant before her abortion, and I felt clumsy. 'How is she?'

Hank shrugged, and at that moment Rosie clattered into the kitchen wearing pink pants, no shirt, and my clogs on the wrong feet.

'You ever feel like something's missing, Rosie?' Hank said.

'Pumpkin, I think you'll be more comfortable with your shirt back on,' I said.

The Wheelings left first, a little after eight – I'd already put Owen and Rosie to bed – and when Owen woke to nurse at ten, Emma, Patrick, and Vi were still there; and then, to my surprise, when I returned downstairs, they had just opened a new bottle of wine, though at least they appeared to be making quick work of it. Given that the town car had disappeared after dropping them off hours earlier, it was unclear to me how they'd be departing from our house. Jeremy shot me a look that I understood to mean *Make them leave.*

I turned to Emma. 'Are you worn out, or are Vi and Patrick going to show you the St Louis nightlife?'

'There are some decent bars a few blocks from here,' Jeremy said. 'Within walking distance, in fact.'

'No, no, no.' Vi shook her head. 'Those are boring yuppie bars. I'm thinking Arsenal Street.'

'Want me to call you a cab?' I asked.

'Or downtown,' Vi said. 'Because we never ended up seeing the Arch today.'

'Which almost means I haven't really been to St Louis, doesn't it?' Emma said. 'Not officially.'

I was so tired that I had to raise my eyebrows so my eyes would stay open. I tried to make my voice festive as I said, 'You should definitely go downtown, in that case.'

'You won't be joining us, Daze?' Patrick curled his lower lip toward his chin.

'I wish.'

When they finally, finally were gone – Emma kissed me again on both cheeks before they took off – I walked into the kitchen, where Jeremy was washing dishes. I patted his butt. 'Sorry.'

'I was about to get my sleeping bag and unroll it on the living room floor.'

'They just don't have children.' I passed him a plate from the table and said, 'Besides that, what did you think of Emma?'

'She was fine.' Had I expected that he'd say she seemed worth all our money? Jeremy wouldn't have thought this of anyone. He added, 'Patrick seemed wasted.'

'He told me the salad dressing was divine. I said I couldn't take credit.'

Jeremy forced a smile. The truth was that there was a certain fizzy excitement they'd taken with them, the luster of California, and in their absence, there were only our dirty dishes, our tiredness, and the fear I felt for all of us.

The next morning, at the office of her ob/gyn, Courtney terminated her pregnancy. Amelia was at school, but I didn't – I couldn't – offer to take her for the afternoon (they hired a sitter), or to drop off food for them, because Courtney still didn't know that Jeremy and I knew. I waited to get a text from Hank afterward, but I didn't, not that day or the next.

'I hope there weren't complications,' I said to Jeremy, and he said, 'I'm sure they're just resting.'

Hank called on Thursday morning. 'So she's back at work.'

'That's a good sign, right? It sounds like a good sign.'

'I should have tried harder to talk her out of going through with it. I didn't try very hard.'

'You can't beat yourself up.' Rosie and Owen and I were in our living room; Rosie was balancing the baloney on Owen's head like a cap, and he looked over at me in a tearful way, as if surprised and disappointed that I wasn't intervening. 'Don't do that, Rosie,' I said. 'Leave him alone.'

'Don't *do* that, Rosie,' Rosie repeated, then tossed the baloney toward the ceiling and said, 'The baloney wants to fly.'

'You're a great husband and a great father,' I said to Hank. 'I hope you know that.' And I thought then, though I hadn't clearly thought it before this moment, that if I learned I was pregnant with a baby who had Down's, I wouldn't have an abortion; I wouldn't have made the choice Courtney had.

'So I took Amelia to Oak Knoll yesterday, just to get her out of the house,' Hank was saying. 'And she's on that bird toy, you know the thing that rocks? And a girl who's maybe five comes up to us, she points to Amelia, and she says to me, "Where's her sister?"'

'Oh, God.'

'I almost lost it. I did lose it, truthfully, but not till we got home.'

As I watched Rosie and Owen – Rosie was sending the baloney airborne again, and Owen was trying to rip an ad for antacids out of an issue of *Time* magazine that was three months old – my heart clenched. 'I'm so sorry,' I said.

I heard Hank swallow. 'I always thought it was a girl,' he said.

CHAPTER 11

It was in October 2002, on an evening shortly before Halloween, that Jeremy and I almost collided in the pasta aisle of Schnucks. He was holding a grocery basket, and I was pushing a cart, which came within an inch or two of him as I rounded the corner before I abruptly pulled it back. 'I'm so sorry!' I said, and he said, 'No, no, it's my fault,' and then he looked at me and exclaimed, 'You're the smoothie girl!'

I said, 'I am?'

Jeremy felt very silly for having blurted this out, he told me later, and at the time I knew he was embarrassed, but I thought he was cute. He was shorter than any guy I'd dated, and he had close-cut dark hair and small glasses with metal frames, and though he seemed solemn, his cheeks were flushed in a way that was endearingly boyish. I knew then, before he'd asked me out, before he'd even said his name, that we would get married. Next to the boxes of spaghetti and rigatoni, I had just met my husband.

He said, 'I think I've seen you at that place—' He gestured toward the western side of Schnucks,

279

beyond which was a row of smaller stores and restaurants, including a wrap and smoothie take-out place, and I said, 'Oh, I go there all the time,' and he said, 'I've always thought it's weird that they're so organic and natural, but they're next door to a tanning salon,' and I said, 'I always think the same thing!' There was a silence, and I added, 'And they sell those diodes to protect you from your cellphone, but you have to wonder about the ultraviolet rays beaming onto their food from the other side of the wall.' Then I said, 'I don't even know what a diode is.'

He smiled. 'They must be powerful.'

Another silence arose; surely this was the turning point of the interaction, when we'd either extend our conversation in a way that would be explicitly unnecessary or we'd head off in opposite directions. But I wasn't anxious. If we didn't extend our conversation, we'd have another one later. We needed to, in order to get married. Also, I was at this time still going out with David.

Then Jeremy said, 'I'm guessing you live in the neighborhood?'

I nodded. 'On the other side of Big Bend.'

'I'm off DeMun.'

'Are you a grad student at Wash U?' I asked.

The flush of his cheeks deepened. 'A professor in Earth and Planetary Sciences.'

'You don't look old enough to be a professor,' I said – I said it teasingly – and he said, 'Believe me, that's why I always wear a tie on the days I

280

teach.' In the ensuing lull, he added, 'Well, maybe I'll see you when we're next getting smoothies,' and I said, 'Yeah, definitely,' and he said, 'We could even meet there on purpose,' and I said, 'That'd be fun,' and he said, 'Or we could, you know, go somewhere and have a real drink,' and I said, 'Why don't I give you my email?' The guilt I felt as I wrote it on a scrap of paper from my grocery list was overridden by my sense of optimism, the chemical shift I experienced in Jeremy's presence. I said, 'I'm Kate, by the way.'

'Jeremy.' There was a moment in which we both tried to discern if the other person wanted to shake hands, and then it didn't happen – it would have seemed too formal or dorky, I thought, to shake the hand of the man I was going to marry – and instead I lifted my right arm and waved. 'See you soon,' I said.

He emailed the next day and asked if I'd like to get dinner at a restaurant in South City the following week. And though I'd planned to break up with David well in advance of my date with Jeremy, I didn't do it until an hour before Jeremy was to pick me up. We were at David's apartment, and after I said I felt like we had grown apart, he said, 'I guess you don't care that everyone we know assumes we're getting married.'

'I just think we both might be happier with other people.'

Sarcastically, he said, 'Isn't that what people say when they've met someone else?'

I hesitated then said, 'I'm saying it because it's true.'

He squinted at me. 'So you are or aren't planning to go with me to my nephew's bar mitzvah?'

'Why don't I email you?'

As I drove home, took a shower, and waited for Jeremy, I felt growing awareness that I'd handled this sequence very badly. When I opened the door and saw Jeremy standing outside the duplex, his dark hair and metal glasses, the distance between not really knowing him and marrying him seemed unbridgeable; it seemed to require an effort I suddenly doubted I had in me. I suspect now that I wouldn't have had these doubts if I hadn't already felt sure Jeremy would become my husband.

As I learned in the car, he'd been born in 1970 – five years before I had – and had grown up in Arlington, Virginia. He had an older brother who was married and had children. He'd attended Wesleyan University in Connecticut for his undergraduate degree and Cornell for his master's and PhD. He'd been at Wash U for just two months, having never visited St Louis before his job interview on campus; prior to this position, he'd done a postdoc at Berkeley. But these were mere facts. There remained the accretion of our respective pasts, the tiny and numerous experiences that didn't exactly matter individually but in the aggregate defined us.

At the restaurant, there were many silences, presumably because I was trying less than I had at Schnucks and making him work more, and then because he could tell that I was trying less and was wondering why. My plan was that after we finished eating, I would tell him I had enjoyed getting to know him but that it wasn't the right time for me to be dating. Then I thought, was it necessary to say anything at all? If it was, maybe it ought to be just before he dropped me off for the night, or maybe not even in person. An email could suffice and would be far less awkward.

He was so nice, though. I pictured his calm disappointment on opening this email, his confusion and I thought that I didn't want to hurt his feelings. On the drive back, as he pulled onto the ramp for 40, he said tentatively, 'There's a bar around the corner from my apartment if you'd be interested in getting a drink.' I could tell he thought I was going to say no. He didn't know why, but he knew the date had gone badly. I imagined he'd decided ahead of time to suggest the bar after dinner and he'd still suggested it even though the evening hadn't been much fun.

I said, 'Okay.'

He glanced across the front seat. 'Okay?'

With more enthusiasm, I said, 'Sure.'

After he parallel parked on Southwood Avenue, we emerged from the car, and when we met up on the sidewalk, he briefly set his hand on my back; there seemed to be something generous in the gesture, a willingness to forgive my bad behavior.

We had split a bottle of wine over dinner, and

at the bar – it was a nice bar, one I'd been to a few times – he ordered whiskey on the rocks and I ordered a vodka tonic. As we talked about nothing in particular, I felt a relaxed warmth spreading through my body; this warmth increased as we downed two more cocktails each. At some point he made a fleeting reference to his parents' divorce, and I was drunk enough that I didn't conceal my surprise.

'Your parents are divorced?'

He blinked, as if surprised that I was surprised, then nodded. He had mentioned both his parents before but not in ways that I'd guessed this fact.

'How old were you?' I asked.

'Seven,' he said. 'In second grade. My brother was nine.'

'Which I would think is the worst possible time because you'd be old enough to understand that things have changed but too young to really get why.'

Again, he regarded me seriously. 'That's about accurate.'

'Were you traumatized?' My tone didn't sound quite right, I could tell; it sounded eager.

'My parents made an effort to be civil to each other,' he said. 'But, yeah, it was hard.'

So he hadn't, like all my previous boyfriends, led an improbably painless existence; perhaps we could get married after all. Had I really had the foolish intent, just hours before, to tell him I didn't want to see him anymore? He had such intelligent eyes, and he had hands that were quietly beautiful, straight fingers with clean, short nails, and I could imagine them on me. At close to midnight, he said, 'You want to get out of here?' and I nodded, and we stumbled up the block to his apartment, which turned out to be exactly the apartment I would have wanted him to have: a tidy, comfortable one-bedroom with furniture that was grown-up – a tan living room couch, a teak bed frame that I saw as I walked past the open bedroom door – but not macho or glitzy. Plus, as I peed at length, the sound was concealed by a fan in the bathroom. What more could I hope for on a first hook-up?

He'd put on music – Van Morrison – while I was in the bathroom, and pretty much immediately we were making out on his tan couch, and then we moved with little discussion to the bedroom, and we never even got under the covers; within ten minutes, we were both completely naked, and he was pulling out a condom from a drawer in a table beside the bed, and though I had had enough boyfriends that I'd learned how to be a girlfriend who conveyed what felt good, I had never before encountered a guy who, the very first time, just seemed to know. He was alert to every way I moved, every sound I made – and it wasn't that I was particularly noisy – and he adjusted the way he touched me accordingly, doing more or less of whatever it was he'd already been doing. I was very drunk, of course, and delirious with lust, but I had a fleeting moment in which I thought, with total clarity, *I cannot believe I found this guy*. Then I felt, in the happiest possible way, like I was exploding.

Afterward, he shifted off me, holding me from the side, and we were quiet, and finally he said, 'Do you want a blanket or some water?' There was something plainly courteous or decent about him that I found far preferable, in such a moment, to excessive emotion.

I said, 'We could get under the covers.'

So we did; we'd never turned on any lights in his bedroom, but a wide yellow bar came in from the hall. Again, he slipped his arm behind my neck and clasped my shoulder, curling into me.

I said, 'About earlier tonight, I'm sorry if I—'

'It's okay.'

'But you don't know what I was about to say.' I wondered if he thought that I was going to apologize for my intrusiveness about his parents' divorce; in fact, I had been planning to apologize for being withdrawn at dinner.

He said, 'Whatever it is, it's okay. There's nothing you need to be sorry for.'

Surely this wasn't true. But it was so generous, so unsentimentally kind, that it silenced me.

After that night, I didn't question whether we ought to be a couple, whether getting to know him was worth the effort (and it really wasn't an effort anyway). Sometimes, of course, I questioned why he wanted to be my boyfriend or my husband. But even that night at his apartment, and certainly as time passed, the feeling that being with Jeremy gave me was like the one I'd had listening to my mother's old Christmas records during childhood. Especially with the lyrics that went 'Oh the weather outside is frightful, but the fire is so delightful . . .,' I'd wish I could climb inside the song, that I could be festive and protected among sleighs and snow. With Jeremy, it was as if I had actually succeeded in breaching the song; to my own astonishment, I had gotten what I wanted.

On the first anniversary of our first date, I said to him – I was conveying this information humorously, to illustrate my own earlier stupidity – 'I was planning to tell you that night that I couldn't go out with you again.'

He was serious as he said, 'I know.'

'You do?'

'Of course,' he said, and he didn't seem to find the memory at all amusing.

Already, long before then, I'd told him about having premonitions; I'd told him after we'd been together just six or eight weeks, which seems shocking in retrospect, especially since I'd never told Ben or David at all, but once Jeremy and I were on stable ground as a couple, there wasn't much that changed between us. We'd gone to a Wilco concert in Kansas City – as much for the novelty of traveling somewhere together, staying a night in a hotel, as for the concert itself – and it was halfway through the four-hour return drive that I said, 'There's something I want to tell you.'

Jeremy glanced across the front seat of his car and said, 'As long as it's not that you're married.'

'I'm not married. Or pregnant.'

'Good.' Then he said, 'I mean, if you were pregnant—' and he reached for my hand. What he meant, clearly, was *we'd figure it out; it'd be fine.*

I said, 'I'm kind of psychic.'

We looked at each other, and he was smiling, but when he saw my expression, he tried to bite back the smile. 'I'm sorry, but that's not what I thought you were about to say. Keep going.'

'I know how it sounds. And especially with you being a scientist. But I just – I feel like I should tell you.' Was this what it was like to disclose to a romantic partner that you had an STD? Though presumably you had to do that even sooner.

'So did you know we'd meet before we did?' Jeremy asked.

I thought of the glimpse I'd gotten of him the night Vi and I had graduated from high school, but if I tried to describe it, it would sound like a bigger deal than it had been. I said, 'I've never been that good with stuff in my own life.' I looked at the license plate of a truck in front of us – Tennessee – just before Jeremy pulled into the left lane to pass it. I said, 'It's like with an instrument. If I'd learned to play the violin early on, and if I'd also had some innate ability, maybe eventually I'd have gotten really good. But if I never took lessons, or I took lessons for a few years and then quit, the ability would barely be part of my life.' I was quiet before adding, 'My sister has kept up with it. She sees it as a positive thing.'

'But you don't?' Jeremy's tone had become serious, matching mine. When I'd told Vi that I'd met a guy named Jeremy Tucker, she'd chortled and said, 'That sounds like the name of a boy explorer.' But I was pretty sure she liked him, because when we all went out for Mexican food, he'd ordered a strawberry margarita after we both did – I think she'd found this endearingly unmasculine – and following dinner, he'd accepted her invitation to join her for bar trivia. And then at the bar, he'd known so many answers that Vi's team came in first, unseating the usual winners, whom Vi and her friends loathed. Patrick leaned over and whispered, 'Where did he learn all this random shit about European history?' The next evening, when I returned to our apartment after work, Vi grinned and said, 'He even *looks* like a boy explorer. He's perfect for you to marry.'

In the car returning from Kansas City, I said to Jeremy, 'It's a long story, but in middle school, I started using a Ouija board a lot with another girl. The girl turned against me and exposed me and Vi for having this creepy ability, but the girl was right – it *was* creepy.'

'So your premonitions now are like what? Who'll win the Super Bowl? Where you left your wallet?'

I hesitated. 'Neither, exactly. With a wallet, that would be remembering more than sensing. With the Super Bowl, if I was at a party, it's possible that I'd have a feeling about which team would win. But the senses are usually darker than a football game. Back in middle school, I had a premonition about a girl in my class dying. It didn't happen until years later, but it did happen – she fell while she was hiking. Or I can tell when I meet a woman if she has an eating disorder, or other things that are messed up about a person. In college, I signed up for a sociology class, and the first day, I got a gross feeling from the professor. I dropped the class, but later that semester he was arrested for having a huge collection of child pornography.'

'But you didn't have a hunch about him being into child porn specifically, did you? So maybe he just seemed generally off. Or with the eating disorder stuff, you'd never know if you were wrong, would you?'

I was quiet. I had thought in advance that I wouldn't try to convince Jeremy.

'It's not that I think you're making this up,' he added.

When our eyes met, I said, 'I'm not.'

'Just bear with me,' Jeremy said. 'No one's ever told me something like this.'

'I've never gotten a speeding ticket,' I said. 'That might be a less depressing example. And I've definitely sped. But at certain times, I'll just know I should slow down, and right after I do, I'll pass a cop car.'

'So why am I the one driving right now?'

'Or another time in college, I was on the steering committee for a big Greek Week party, and at the last minute, I had a really strong feeling I shouldn't go. It was very weird for me to skip it, but I pretended to have the flu. I was worried something bad would happen to everyone at the party, like the roof collapsing, but what did happen was that the police came and arrested a bunch of people for drinking.' If I had been among them, I might have been expelled, given the infraction already on my record at Mizzou, but I thought I'd hold off on sharing that saga for another time; there was no need to inundate Jeremy.

'So basically being psychic allows you to get away with a life of crime.' He glanced at me. 'You know I'm teasing, right?' Then he said, 'I have a premonition about us.'

Immediately, I knew where this was headed, and it wasn't because I was psychic. But I tried to form a good-natured expression.

'I think we're a great couple,' he said. 'And we'll make each other really happy.'

If he was underestimating what I was trying to convey, he was also being sweet. It was time to let the conversation end.

After a silence, he said, 'That's not the kind of premonition you mean, is it?'

It was true that he had disappointed me, possibly for the first time. But the fact that he knew it had the strange effect of negating the disappointment. I said, 'I realize this is really weird.'

'Well, I probably wouldn't use the word *psychic*, but I'm sure we all subconsciously pick up on cues about situations.'

'Right,' I said. 'But that's not what I'm talking about. I have dreams about things, and a lot of the time I don't understand what they mean, but then the things I dreamed about happen. It's like I saw a scene from a movie, and only later do I watch the movie from start to finish.'

'I'm still confused about how ongoing this is for you.'

'It's as much in the past as I can put it,' I said.

'Because of middle school?'

'Having senses just isn't necessary,' I said. 'It's not even practical.' I was looking out the window at the farmland on our right. 'It's okay if you don't believe that people can be psychic.'

'Whether I believe it is immaterial,' Jeremy said. 'What you're telling me is part of who you are, and I believe you.' The distinction he was making in this moment – it didn't seem like it would come to matter as much as it did. 'Anyway,' he continued, 'as personal confessions go, you have to admit this is of a different order than "I'm not a natural blonde."'

'I *am* a natural blonde.'

'Phew.' Jeremy grinned. 'Because that might really have been a shock to my system.' Then he said, 'So the stuff that happened in middle school – when you said it's a long story, did you mean one you do or don't want to tell? Because no pressure, but we are on a long drive.'

For several seconds, I considered the question. From the vantage point of Jeremy's passenger seat, beside this man who had grown up in a different state from me, who was five years older and a science professor and absurdly kind, middle school finally seemed like a long time ago. I said, 'I could tell you.'

It was around the time of the trip to Kansas City that we started talking about marriage – fleeting references at first. Once, as I flipped channels on his TV while he made dinner, he came into the living room when I was stopped on a program about animals on the islands of Fiji. 'Look how pretty that is,' I said, and he said, 'Should we go there on our honeymoon?'

On an evening during which we'd eaten next to a large family at a pizza restaurant and were in the car driving back to Jeremy's, I asked, 'Can you picture adopting kids from another country?'

'Sure,' he said.

'Can you picture adopting them from China?'

Again, as easily as if I'd asked if he could turn up the radio, he said, 'Sure.'

In a rush, I said, 'In high school, I used to babysit for these people who lived on my street, and they had really cute daughters from China, and ever since then, I've wanted to do that. And that way, they wouldn't be psychic, because I think it comes from my mom's family.'

'Wow.' But Jeremy said it calmly. 'I do want

biological kids, but I don't see why we couldn't do both. You're sure having senses is hereditary?' It was weirdly endearing to hear the phrase 'having senses' come out of Jeremy's mouth – it had been such an intrafamily reference that it was as if he'd prepared Wonder bread toast with cinnamon sugar for me while we watched Rob Lowe in *Class*.

I said, 'I've always thought so. Do you feel like in order to be happy in life, you have to have biological children?'

'I don't know,' Jeremy said.

The subject came up again from time to time – if we were out somewhere and saw white parents with a little Asian girl, I'd nudge him and murmur, 'Look.' One Sunday morning after we'd slept in and then had sex, he said, 'Here's the thing. I just think you and I would have really great kids. They'd be part Kate-ish and part Jeremy-ish and part just themselves, and it'd be fun to watch them grow up.'

This was not so different from the argument Ben had once made, minus the part about squinty eyes. I said, 'But what if they have senses?'

'What if they're nearsighted? What if they can't carry a tune?'

'Those aren't the same.'

'What if we adopt kids with serious behavioral problems?'

'That's more common in children from Eastern European countries than China. Anyway, even if we're imperfect parents and our kids are messed up, their lives will still be better with us than if they were in an orphanage. But if we have kids and they're messed up, it's our fault.'

'Of course we'll be imperfect parents. But do you really believe if we provide biological children with anything less than ideal lives, then it's better for them not to exist?'

'Sort of.'

'Do you wish *you* didn't exist?'

'At times.'

Jeremy laughed. 'You usually do a good job of hiding your bleak world-view.'

'Thanks.'

'Can I just make one point? I know having senses has been a burden to you. But from my perspective, it doesn't define who you are. If I were describing you to someone, it wouldn't be in the top ten of your personality traits. It might not even make the top fifty.'

The following week, Jeremy flew to Vancouver to present a paper on biogeochemical iron cycling, and while he was gone, I spent the nights at the apartment I still, technically, shared with Vi. On the third morning of Jeremy's absence, I woke up and thought, *I'll have two white babies.*

It was still true that I didn't see how having children was anything other than a roll of the dice; what was different was that being with Jeremy made me feel like perhaps luck was on my side.

I waited until it was seven A.M. in British Columbia, called his cellphone – I had no idea if the call would cost either or both of us a small fortune – and when he answered, I said, 'I'll have two white babies.'

He laughed. 'With anyone in particular?'

'I'm serious. But we shouldn't wait too long, because I don't want to be trying to get pregnant when I'm, like, thirty-nine.'

At the time of this conversation, I was twenty-seven, and Jeremy laughed again. He said, 'Is that an invitation to leave Vancouver early and come knock you up?'

'You don't seem very surprised. Did you think all along I'd give in?'

'I'm happy,' he said. 'This is exciting news. It's just that I woke up about three seconds before you called.'

As it turned out, Rosie was born when I was thirty-one, and Owen when I was thirty-three. And really, it wasn't that Jeremy had convinced me. It was that he'd been smart enough to let me convince myself.

CHAPTER 12

On Friday, October 9, a week before the day of Vi's predicted earthquake, a man in O'Fallon waited until his wife and children were sleeping, shot them in their beds, then turned his gun on himself. He'd done it because he'd wanted to save them from the impending destruction, according to the initial news reports, and I thought, *No, no, no, no, no.* It wasn't in the morning paper, but there was an article on the *Post-Dispatch*'s website that I read on the small screen of Jeremy's phone as soon as I came downstairs in the morning, while my stomach churned.

My impression was that Vi's prediction was considered mostly ridiculous and not credible; certainly it was seen as such by people outside St Louis. Within St Louis, as far as I could tell, people who'd admit to being nervous would then express embarrassment at their nervousness. St Louisans weren't evacuating the city. And yet, as with the warnings of doomsday cults, even if you didn't buy the claims, you'd still breathe a sigh of relief when the day in question passed without event.

I took Owen for a walk in the stroller, and when

we returned home, Jeremy waved his phone at me. 'There's all this stuff coming out about how the guy had lost his job months ago, he was mentally unbalanced, et cetera, et cetera.'

'Obviously, he was mentally unbalanced,' I said.

When Vi called that afternoon, she said, 'People are so fucking nuts,' and I could feel her refusal of culpability.

'And you still think the earthquake will happen?'

She sounded impatient as she said, 'If I get word to the contrary, you'll be the first to know.'

The next evening, Jeremy and I were sitting on the couch in our living room, watching the episode of *Saturday Night Live* we hadn't stayed up for the night before, when we heard a whimper from one of the two monitors set on the coffee table. I said, 'Is that him or her?' Jeremy paused the TV, and there was a silence and then another whimper – a whimper of bereftness, it seemed to me, of desolation even – and I said, 'It's her. Should I go up?'

'She's probably not even awake.' Jeremy hit the Play button on the remote control, and I set my hand on his arm.

'Hold on.'

'You'll hear her.' But he'd frozen the screen again; he was indulging me.

We were quiet for a minute – Jeremy pulled his phone from his pocket, presumably to check either his email or football scores – and I sat there listening. After another minute, I said, 'I might go sit upstairs in the hall.'

He looked up from his phone. 'Seriously? For how long?'

I gestured toward the television. 'You can keep watching.'

'If she needs us, she'll let us know.'

'I won't go in her room unless she makes more noise,' I said. 'But I just want to be up there if she does.' It wasn't that I thought I was being rational; it was that something about hearing that whimper had triggered anxious heart, and I knew I couldn't sit and chortle at sketches featuring men dressed as women. This was a difference between Jeremy and me, that he probably thought men dressed as women were the perfect cure for what ailed me.

Upstairs, I took a seat on the bare wooden hall floor; I could have gotten a magazine, but I didn't. It would in my life then have been impossible for me to feel bored by doing nothing. To do nothing was a rare treat, almost like taking a nap.

Rosie didn't make more noise, and after five minutes, contrary to what I'd promised Jeremy, I opened her door and crept into her room. She was lying on her stomach, her palms and knees beneath her and her little butt bunched up in the air. Her face was turned away from me, toward the wall, but I could hear her rhythmic breathing. This wasn't, I was fairly sure, a night on which she'd get a fever, though I knew those nights well:

After we gave her medicine, as she rolled around and mumbled, I'd keep getting up to check on her, and at some point, I'd just give in and lie down on the floor next to her crib.

But no, I had to remind myself. Not tonight. Just because I knew how to slip into these nervous patterns, just because the idea of her having a fever was in my head, it didn't mean she had a fever. I was barely psychic anymore, and moments like this were the reason why.

When I went downstairs, the television was still paused at the same sketch, and Jeremy was reading an issue of *Journal of Geophysical Research*. As I re-entered the living room, I said, 'Sorry. You could have kept watching.'

'I was waiting for you.'

'I want to try getting the stain out of Rosie's pink sweatshirt. I'm not in the mood for TV anymore.' What I really wanted to do – I kept meaning to do it while Jeremy was at work – was to remove everything hanging on our walls. But I didn't have the nerve to do it in front of him.

He nodded in the direction of Rosie's monitor. 'She's been totally quiet.' Had he heard me go into her room?

We looked at each other, and I said, 'I think everything will be better when we're on the other side of Vi's prediction.'

'When Kendra comes this week, you should go get a manicure and try to relax. Call tomorrow and schedule one.'

'Maybe,' I said. Apart from the fact that I no longer had manicures from one year to the next, there was a secret I kept from Jeremy, a stupid secret, which was that when Kendra babysat, I left only Rosie with her. Running errands was far easier with just Owen than they'd have been with both children, which meant that Kendra's hours were in fact a break for me, if not exactly the one Jeremy believed I was getting. But so greatly did Rosie relish Kendra's company, and so rare was it these days for Rosie to receive the undivided attention of any adult, that it didn't seem like such a sacrifice on my part to permit her this treat. I didn't tell Jeremy because, in the abstract, I always planned to leave both Owen and Rosie with Kendra the following week, and it was only when Kendra showed up and Rosie went berserk with excitement that I reconsidered.

Jeremy was still watching me, and he said, 'I know we haven't talked about this for a while, but you remember I'm leaving Thursday for the conference, right?'

Did I remember he was leaving Thursday for his conference? I remembered that that had once been the plan, but I had convinced myself that he would stay – that he'd canceled his reservation already, because surely he wouldn't get on a plane to Denver with everything that was going on.

'I realize this conference is big for you,' I said. 'But since it's annual, if you miss one in your whole career, it probably doesn't make a difference.'

'I thought our deal was that if I postponed my

Cornell talk, you were okay with me going to Denver. Does that ring a bell?'

'A lot has happened since then,' I said. 'Anyway, now that you have tenure, don't you not have to do as much stuff like this?'

'Kate, I'm delivering a paper on Sunday morning. And I have meals and coffee scheduled with literally twelve different people.'

'Other professors have families, too. If you say an emergency came up, I'm sure they'll understand.'

Jeremy sighed. 'Let me put this in perspective. Courtney is still going to the conference, even after last week.' He meant after her abortion, but if he thought this was a persuasive point, he was mistaken.

I said, 'What Courtney does has nothing to do with us.'

'Have you given more thought to going out there with me? I'm sure the tickets are insanely expensive now, but at least we don't have to pay for Owen's. And hey, we're big spenders.'

The remark was clearly a reference to Emma Hall, and I didn't acknowledge it. I said, 'Meaning we'd just ditch Vi and my dad? Besides that Owen and Rosie are hell to travel with.'

'For the sake of discussion,' Jeremy said, 'if I skipped the conference, what do you picture me doing here? I've already canceled my classes.'

This was when I felt the first flare of true anger. 'Really?' I said. 'Because if you're not teaching, there's no other reason for you to be here?'

'You want the moral support. I understand that. But I question the point of staying in town for something that won't happen.'

I snorted – an unintentionally Vi-like snort. 'It must be nice to be so certain.'

'I want to float an idea,' Jeremy said. 'I'm not saying it's right. But I want you to consider it. What if neither you nor Vi is psychic?'

I glared at him. 'What if you're not really American? Maybe you're French – has that ever occurred to you? Or maybe you're not even a human being. What if you're a giraffe? I'm not saying you are, but I just want you to consider the idea.'

'Come here.' He patted the couch next to him, and I didn't move. 'Or don't,' he said. 'Suit yourself. For one thing, I'm not that tall.' I didn't laugh, and he said, 'That's how I know I'm not a giraffe.'

'I got it,' I said.

'We have these articles of faith about ourselves, but sometimes they're wrong. And for you, the senses – it doesn't bring you pleasure anyway, so why not just let it go?'

I sometimes forgot this, that not leaving Owen with the babysitter wasn't the only secret I kept from Jeremy; there was the much larger secret of how two years earlier I'd discarded my own ESP. Which made Jeremy at least partly right. And his rightness, his unearned knowledge of me – it was infuriating. Looking at his boyishly handsome face, his intelligent countenance, his easygoing confidence that I was a solid wife and a good mother and that he knew more than I did about every subject in the world, including the subject of psychicness and the subject of myself, I felt indignant.

'It's not just Vi who has a proven track record,' I said, and at some level I was conscious of the peculiar relief of my concern about Rosie having been replaced with anger. 'Have you forgotten that I was involved with finding Brady Ogden's kidnapper, too? Or at her *Today* show taping, I could hear the questions Matt Lauer was asking even though no one else in the room could besides Vi? I don't want to be like this. I just am. And for you to be so sure you're right and everyone else is wrong, especially when her prediction affects the safety of our children – it's arrogant, and it's really fucking insulting.'

He still wasn't mad; Jeremy was never mad. He said, 'I was just thinking about Brady Ogden. Remember how you wanted to call off our wedding so you could devote yourself to worrying about him full-time? That seemed like a good idea to you.'

'Why is it bad to have compassion for other people? Vi and I were totally right.'

'All I'm saying is you let your worry get the best of you. You were doing it at our wedding, you were doing it a few minutes ago when Rosie made a noise, and you're doing it now. I know the last few weeks have been hard, but the solution isn't to put your life on hold.'

'There's never going to be a situation like this in our lives again!' I said. 'This is huge, and it's directly connected to us. And let's say Vi is right, there's a big earthquake, and we lose power on our street, people all over the city lose it. Or what if, I don't know, a shelf falls on me and I break my leg and have to go to the hospital and can't take care of Owen and Rosie? I would need you. Or what if Vi is wrong and you're right, and nothing at all happens? This Friday is the same as any other day. In that case, Vi is humiliated and who knows what she'll decide to do, or who will be hounding her from the media? And then *she'll* need me. And if she needs me, I also need you. I can't take care of Owen and Rosie and her all at the same—'

He held up his hand, palm toward me. 'You're imagining worst-case scenarios. Those things could happen, sure. But I just don't think they're likely.' He was quiet, and then he said, 'If you're psychic, why don't you answer the question yourself and we can plan accordingly. Is there going to be an earthquake?'

How strange it was to be put on the spot by my own husband. And clearly this was the moment to tell Jeremy that I had destroyed my senses. But was it possible that all I had to do to get him to skip his conference was to agree with Vi, even if I wasn't sure? The truth was that in recent weeks I had sometimes felt the dread of certainty and sometimes felt the opposite – the shame of Vi being laughably wrong. But being unsure wouldn't keep Jeremy in St Louis, and I heard myself say, 'Yes. Yes, I do think there'll be an earthquake on October sixteenth. I think Vi's right.'

The expression that crossed Jeremy's face then – it was as if I'd said something sweet but ridiculous, like that I'd seen a unicorn.

'And you think there's no chance,' I said.

'Not no chance. There's always a chance. But it's infinitesimal.'

I said, 'So all along, for the last seven years, you've thought having senses is bullshit?'

'There are these probability experiments,' Jeremy said. 'In a room full of people, statisticians figured out how many had the same birthday. The number was always much higher than non-mathematicians would guess. But the telling part was that the people who thought the coincidence was the most meaningful were the ones who actually shared birthdays. They thought it meant something because it was personal to them.'

'In other words, all the times I've dreamed of something that's come true, it's just been a coincidence?'

'It's called confirmation bias – attributing greater meaning to so-called evidence that supports your existing belief while ignoring information that contradicts it.'

I wanted to be calm as I spoke next, as calm as Jeremy. 'Why do you get to decide what's true about me and what isn't? And why have you acted all this time like you were open-minded when you weren't? Remember when you told me about that exploding church?' A few weeks after I'd disclosed to Jeremy that I was psychic, he'd referred in passing to the 1950 church choir practice in Beatrice, Nebraska, which was supposed to be a famous example of group ESP, and I'd had no idea what he was talking about. Apparently, it was when a gas leak caused a Baptist church to explode during what should have been a weekly choir practice, but nobody was injured because – the chances of this were something like one in a million – not a single one of the choir members had shown up on time. I didn't know about this incident because I didn't know about psychicness from the outside, as a topic I'd researched, but I had found it strangely touching to learn that Jeremy had checked out a book on paranormal phenomena from the Wash U library. I said, 'Was all of that just to humor me? You pretended to take it seriously while you were laughing behind my back?'

'I was never laughing behind your back.' After a pause, he said, 'In grad school, there was this woman in my program who had blue hair. I don't know what her real hair color was, and she didn't have a particularly unusual personality. When I first met her, I assumed she was a punk, whatever that means, but she was a regular person. She just had blue hair. And that's how I've seen your senses. They're your blue hair, but they're not that big a deal.'

Perhaps there had been a time when the analogy he was drawing would have seemed sweet. But having called his bluff, having forced my loving, thoughtful husband to admit that he'd always believed I was full of shit – harmlessly full of shit, but full of shit nonetheless – it was apparent that the accord in our marriage was overly reliant on a fundamental lack of specificity or resolution. We didn't fight because we usually stopped short of acknowledging any reason to.

There was a wail then, a high wail, from one of the monitors, but this time I recognized it immediately as Owen, wanting to nurse. I turned to go back upstairs – *Saturday Night Live* still unwatched, Rosie's sweatshirt still unclean, the question of Jeremy's trip still undecided. Or perhaps just not decided to my satisfaction. Because in a conciliatory tone, when I was halfway up the steps, Jeremy said, 'A shelf won't fall on you. I'll secure them all with brackets before I leave.'

On the mornings Amelia Wheeling was in preschool, I took Rosie and Owen either to story hour at the Richmond Heights library or for a long walk to a park on Wydown, but not to our usual parks on DeMun or at Oak Knoll. So Rosie wouldn't be bored without Amelia, I told myself, though maybe it was so I wouldn't be bored without Hank.

On Monday, October 12, which was sunny and cool, we skipped the library because I couldn't face hearing the other mothers discuss Vi's prediction. We had just arrived at Wydown Park – Rosie and I called it the acorn park because it had a huge stone acorn statue set in a little garden above a low brick wall – when my cellphone rang. I saw that it was Vi.

'I'm at your house.' She sounded cheerful. 'But where are you?'

'Why are you at our house? Wait – did you drive?'

'I took a taxi. I have a question for you.'

'That you have to ask in person?'

'It's nothing bad,' she said. 'Don't start freaking out.'

'We're at a park, the one on Wydown across from the deli.'

'That's kind of far.' I said nothing, and she added, 'But I'll be there as fast as my little feet can carry me.'

After I hung up, I sprang Rosie from the stroller, and she took off toward the acorn statue. There were only four other people in the park on this morning, two of whom were an old man and a boy, a little younger than Rosie, who I assumed was his grandson; we'd seen them here before, and Rosie and the boy usually sniffed each other out without exactly playing together, while the grandfather and I nodded in greeting (I was pretty sure he didn't speak English). Also, at a table near the fence between the park and the street, a man and a woman dressed in business clothes drank from paper coffee cups; she was skinny, wearing a pin-striped silk suit and stylish, uncomfortable-looking black heels.

I pulled Owen from his stroller seat and inserted him into the baby carrier I'd put on before leaving the house (it had long ago stopped seeming strange to me to walk around wearing an empty baby carrier). When he was secure, I squatted to get a ball from the undercarriage of the stroller and followed Rosie across the grass. As I got close, she looked over her shoulder, smiled mischievously, and took off running again, this time toward the man and woman at the table. Owen and I stayed close behind. Rosie slowed down a few feet from the couple and said loudly, 'That man's not Daddy.'

The man and woman both laughed, but an unhappy energy hovered around them, as if Rosie had interrupted a serious conversation. And then, with a start, I realized that the woman was Marisa Mazarelli. I hadn't seen her for nearly seventeen years, since our high school graduation, and she looked simultaneously the same and much older. Patrick had run into her a few years earlier and had described her to Vi and me as 'hagged out,' and while this was definitely an overstatement and she was still pretty, she did appear diminished. She was brown-eyed and brown-haired and pert-nosed, but there was nothing exceptional about her beauty, about her presence. Was that only because middle school and high school, the era of her power, was long past? Or was it that her power had always hinged on an audience and here in this park, on this sunny October morning, she no longer had one? Surely she knew about Vi's prediction, and probably found it risible. But even if she chose at this moment to make a ruthless comment about my sister and me, who'd witness it except the grandfather and grandson and Marisa's boyfriend, or whoever he was? Then I thought he had to be her boyfriend, because once you were married, you didn't hang out in parks on weekday mornings without kids.

Warmly, the boyfriend said to Rosie, 'How old are you?'

I was reluctant to speak; I suspected my voice would give me away, if Marisa didn't already know who I was. But after a few seconds of silence, it felt weird for me not to prompt Rosie. 'Do you know how old you are, sweetheart?' I said. 'How many years old?' I avoided Marisa's gaze and looked instead at the back of my daughter's head, her wavy dark brown hair.

'Seven!' Rosie shouted.

'You're two and a half,' I said. 'You're not seven.'

'You're seven!' Rosie yelled, and she started running away from them. I turned, too, saying in a tone of light regret, as if I'd hoped to stay and visit, 'Onward.'

I could feel Marisa's eyes on my back. She definitely knew who I was, and she probably knew that I knew who she was, but we'd silently decided not to acknowledge each other. And as I chased Rosie, I was fairly sure that I'd come out ahead in our exchange, or non-exchange. Because here

I was with my two cute children, and I'd noticed that the ring finger of Marisa's left hand was bare. This was the nastiest, most elemental math, made no less ugly for its undeniability: *I ended up with a husband and you didn't.* Or at least she hadn't so far, or if she had, she'd gotten divorced.

Rosie made her way to the little boy and his grandfather, who were standing near a bench on which the boy had set a bunch of plastic action figures. The grandfather and I smiled at each other. By the time Vi arrived, Rosie was busy repeatedly burying a plastic soldier under mulch, then yanking him up and flinging mulch everywhere.

'That was at least two miles,' Vi said from a few yards away. Her cheeks were flushed, her forehead sweaty. She waved at the grandfather. 'Hi there,' she said. 'Violet. Kate's sister.'

With a thick accent, he said, 'A pleasure to meet you.' So he did speak English. In any case, it felt as if Vi had violated park etiquette by introducing herself. Then she said to me, 'See that woman over there? I swear it's Marisa Mazarelli.'

I hesitated before saying, 'It is.'

'What, and you weren't planning to tell me? Are you afraid I'll go punch her?'

It was within the realm of possibility. But all I said was 'What's the question you want to ask?' Was it weird to be having this conversation in front of the grandfather, knowing now that he did speak English?

Vi was still gazing across the grass. 'You think Marisa's having an affair with that guy?'

I'd had the same thought, that he could be married – I hadn't taken note of his ring finger, only hers – but I shrugged. Owen had started fussing, and I reached into my pocket for a pacifier. I stuck it into his mouth and he immediately spit it onto the grass. When I retrieved it, I had to bend at the knees and hold my palm against his chest so he didn't topple out of the carrier.

'Should I ask if Marisa caught me on the *Today* show?' Vi's voice had turned proud, and I thought of what Courtney Wheeling had said about people appearing on *Today* because they had extended cases of the hiccups or had been attacked by a shark – that it didn't mean you'd succeeded in life.

And then the grandfather said, with the same thick accent as before, 'You are on the television program for earthquakes. You are famous lady!' He was smiling broadly.

Vi seemed pleased and not particularly surprised. 'Oh, did you see it?' she said. 'Yeah, that was me.'

'I come from Turkey, where there is terrible earthquake in Izmir. Buildings there not strong like here.'

'Right,' Vi said. 'No retrofitting.'

'Here the buildings are strong.'

'Let's hope,' Vi said.

'It is honor to meet such a famous lady.' The grandfather was looking at me as he spoke, as if I would verify that he was having this encounter.

Owen spit his pacifier onto the grass again, and I glanced at my watch and realized that it was time for him to eat and that – I could see it in my mind – instead of packing the jar of squash, the little spoon, and the bib for him in the diaper bag, I'd left them all on the kitchen table. Which meant that unless I wanted him to become frantic, even though I preferred to nurse only at home, I had to do it here.

'Vi,' I said. 'I'm going over to that bench to feed Owen. Will you make sure Rosie doesn't put mulch in her mouth?'

Vi rolled her eyes at me.

I went two benches away, where I'd left our stroller. As I eased Owen from the carrier, I thought maybe I could get away with feeding him on only one side. Back across the grass, I saw that the boy and his grandfather were leaving, and I hoped Rosie wouldn't have a fit when they took the action figures. Then I saw Vi get on all fours and let Rosie climb onto her back, which made Rosie squeal with happiness. Vi crawled forward, her hair flopping into her face, and then she flung her head backward and let loose with an enormous neigh. 'The horsey likes to eat carrots,' I heard Rosie say. Maybe I'd underestimated my sister, I thought; maybe I was always underestimating her. At some point, Rosie slid off Vi, and Vi remained on her hands and knees while Rosie frolicked around her. 'The horsey takes a nap!' she shouted, and Vi rolled onto her side.

And then I heard Vi say, 'Oh, Rosie, watch out! Oh, no. Oh, yuck.' But she was laughing as she said, 'Your mom will *not* be happy.'

'What is it?' I called.

'She stepped in dog poop. Whoops.' Vi was still laughing.

'Weren't you watching her?'

'I didn't think there'd be poop in the middle of the grass.' I hadn't either, or else I wouldn't have kept popping Owen's pacifier back into his mouth after it fell out. Still, it felt like it wasn't a coincidence that this had happened under Vi's supervision.

Rosie was wearing pink sneakers, and as she and Vi walked toward us, I saw that the poop was of the fresh, moistly glistening variety; it clung to the upper part of her left sneaker. 'Can you take her shoe off?' I said.

'I'm not touching it,' Vi said.

'Vi, my hands are kind of tied right now.' The clock was ticking; I was sure of it. 'Come on,' I said. 'There are wipes in the diaper bag.'

'Sorry,' Vi said, and she didn't sound sorry at all. 'But there's a reason I don't have kids.'

And then, exactly as I'd known she would, Rosie reached down, swiped her hand against her left shoe, raised her brown-streaked palm victoriously, and said, 'Rosie makes a mess.' She sprinted away from us, back toward the acorn statue.

'Rosie, stop!' I yelled. I pulled Owen off my boob – he wailed, of course – and passed him to Vi so I could run after Rosie. When Rosie sensed me behind her, she shrieked with joy. I was only a few feet from her – I probably could have reached out and grabbed the back of her jacket – and then, just as she got to the sidewalk in front of the low wall, she tripped and fell face-first onto the pavement. Immediately, she was hysterical, and as I lifted her from behind, I felt that dread, not yet knowing how bloody she'd be. The answer was very: The blood was surging from her nose and lips, and her upper lip was already swelling. My heart pounded against my chest.

'It's all right, Rosie,' I said. 'You're okay.'

She was screaming so loudly that I don't think she could hear me; tears cascaded down her face. Carefully, I carried her in my arms – it seemed safe to assume that by this point there was shit on both of us – and we walked toward Vi and Owen. He was still crying, too; both my children were sobbing desperately.

Vi's brow was furrowed, and in a tone of concern, as if it hadn't been mostly her fault, she said, 'Is she okay?' Then Rosie turned her face toward Vi and Vi said, 'Oh my God.'

'I need to wash off the blood,' I said. 'Put Owen in the stroller, and get the wipes out of the diaper bag, and I'll clean her hands and face the best I can now and do the rest at home.'

Vi did as I said, and her obedience was disturbing. I kept Rosie on my lap while I wiped my own hands, then her hands, then brought a wipe toward her mouth, at which point she howled and backed her head away from me. 'I'll be very careful,' I said. 'I know it hurts. I know.'

'Daisy,' someone said – not Vi, but someone whose voice was simultaneously familiar and unfamiliar. I looked up, and Marisa Mazarelli was standing in front of the bench in her pin-striped suit, dangling car keys from her fingers. 'Does she need to go to the hospital?' Marisa said. 'I'm not sure how far away you guys live, but it looks like you walked—' She sounded tentative in a way that was utterly unlike the Marisa from before, as if she were not offering a favor but requesting one.

I hesitated for less than a second before saying, 'We'll take a ride to our house. Vi, can you push Owen home in the stroller?' Marisa and Vi said nothing to each other.

She drove an enormous white SUV, and I sat in front, holding Rosie on my lap, not bothering with the seat belt; I was simultaneously breaking about three different laws. Also – did Marisa realize this? – Rosie smelled like dog shit. Maybe I did, too.

As Marisa pulled out of the space where she was parked, she said, 'I saw her fall, and I thought, *Poor thing!*'

'She'll be okay,' I said. 'Right, Rosie? We'll make you feel better.' I didn't think the cuts were that deep, though it was hard to tell with all the blood.

Sorrowfully, Rosie said, 'Rosie fell.'

I was almost but not quite too distracted to take note of the clutter piled on the floor under my feet – running shoes and home furnishings catalogs and half-full bottles of water and more than one Steak 'n Shake bag (surely, as skinny as she was, there was nothing Marisa could get from Steak 'n Shake besides Diet Coke). When Marisa had started the car, a loud Kenny Chesney song had burst out of her stereo speakers, which she lowered in volume without turning off. (Marisa listened to country music?) But mostly I just wanted us to get home. I said, 'We live on San Bonita Avenue, which is off DeMun, but you should take Big Bend to Clayton because you can't cut through from this side.'

There was minimal traffic, and we drove without speaking, listening to a very faint Kenny Chesney. Rosie was insubstantial in my arms; given how much bigger she was than Owen, I often forgot how little she herself still was.

In front of our house, I opened the car door before Marisa had turned off the engine. 'Thanks,' I said.

'I hope she's okay,' Marisa said.

I started up the walk, Rosie in my arms, and behind me, I heard the passenger side window opening and Marisa calling, 'Daisy—'

I turned.

'There's something I want to ask you,' she said. 'Can I call you?'

'Yeah, fine,' I said, and I turned again.

The way I got Rosie to hold still while I cleaned her wounds was by parking her in front of the TV and letting her watch *Curious George*. I dabbed at her lips and nose with a soapy washcloth, then with a wet washcloth, then with Neosporin (which made me think, as I suppose it always will, of Brynn Zansmyer); every time I made contact, Rosie whimpered and her eyes welled. Both her upper lip and her right nostril had been scraped and were oozing pink fluid – also, her upper lip was twice as big as normal – but she was no longer crying, and the cut was soon clean. To reduce the swelling, I gave her a Popsicle. I considered taking a picture with my phone and sending it to Jeremy, but it seemed like that would be alarming without serving a purpose; I'd call him later. Through the living room window, I saw Vi and Owen approach, then Vi heaved the stroller up the four steps leading to our front porch, Owen still strapped in. I wondered, did I appear as unsteady as she did when I carried the stroller? I opened the front door, and Owen smiled at me and said, 'Da-da.'

'Ha,' Vi said. 'Almost. How's the patient?' Looking at Rosie, she said, 'What's that snot-looking stuff?'

'I think just drainage.'

'First dog poop, now facial leaking. What a morning, huh?' She sat down in the armchair, eased off her clogs, and propped her socked feet on the coffee table. 'I could go for one of those Popsicles.'

Holding Owen, I sat on the couch next to Rosie, pulled up my shirt – I had, apparently, never refastened the front of my bra after nursing Owen in the park – and let him latch on again. To Vi, I said, 'Help yourself.'

When she returned from the kitchen, Vi said, 'Did the Bitch of Christmas Past say anything interesting in the car?'

'We didn't talk. I was pretty focused on getting home.'

'Did she mention my prediction?'

'I'm telling you we barely talked,' I said. 'You have to admit it was nice of her to give us a ride.'

Vi snorted. 'I don't have to admit jack shit.' Then she said, 'Aren't you curious what I want to ask you?'

I had forgotten she wanted to ask me anything.

She said, 'I'm going back on the *Today* show on Friday morning, and this time, the producer wants you to come on with me.'

'Why?'

She laughed. 'You should see your face right now. It looks like you licked a lemon.'

'I just don't know why they'd be interested in me when I have nothing to do with your prediction.'

'You know how people are about twins, though. They want us all to have ESP, and here we are, the ones who really do.'

'You didn't tell the producer I'm psychic, did you?'

'I described you like you are – total suburban mom, white picket fence – and the guy was like, "Even better!" Because as Emma put it – you'll love this – you give me credibility. You're a stand-in for Mrs Normal American Viewer who's skeptical about'

– here, inexplicably, Vi adopted her awful British accent, which I thought she might have put to rest during her contact with the authentically British Emma – 'these very, very strange predictions.'

'So you did tell the producer I'm psychic,' I said. Like Jeremy, Vi was unaware that I'd done my best to kill my senses.

'It's time to get over your hang-ups,' Vi said. 'Because guess what? The thing you always thought was so embarrassing turns out to be the thing that makes us cool. Plus, when will you next get invited on the *Today* show?'

'I'm definitely not going on TV with you,' I said. 'There's no possible way.'

'What if no one says anything about you having senses? Then will you?'

'There's no possible way,' I repeated.

'Even if you could help save lives – even then, you won't?'

'This isn't *Show Me St Louis* on KSDK, Daisy. This is the *Today* show!'

'Vi, what man, woman, or child in America doesn't know about your prediction at this point?' Owen finished nursing, and I lifted him into a sitting position.

'Emma said Matt Lauer, or whoever interviews us, will be more respectful this time because they realize we have plenty of other options for Friday. I'm a "get" now.' Vi made air quotes, and it looked like the remaining chunk of Popsicle was about to fall off the stick.

Owen burped as I patted his back, and I said, 'Good boy.'

Vi took a last, oversized bite of Popsicle and said, with her mouth full, 'If you don't do it, I bet in a few years, you'll regret it.'

'Then that'll be my problem,' I said.

'You're being really selfish.'

It was not news to me that Vi was, on a regular basis, hypocritical and irrational and contradictory. Still – still, there was a line I just couldn't let her cross. I said, 'You won't wipe poop off Rosie's shoe, but I'm the selfish one?'

'Oh, so if I had, then you would have done this for me?'

'If you knew I wouldn't do it, why did you even ask?'

When she spoke next, I could tell she was being sincere, not glib, which only made what she said more insulting. She said, 'I thought maybe for once your loyalty to me would trump your fear of what other people think.'

'Just because I'm not an exhibitionist doesn't mean I'm afraid.'

She removed her feet from the table, leaned forward, and set her Popsicle stick on the wood where her feet had been, with nothing underneath it. 'When you decided to tell everyone about us having senses, I stood by you,' she said. 'Did you ask me first? No. But did I say, "Oh, I'd rather not be exposed"?'

'You mean in eighth grade?'

'You can't deny that you're the one who first spilled the beans.'

'That was twenty years ago,' I said. 'We were thirteen.'

Vi shrugged. 'So?'

'That's completely—' For a few seconds, I couldn't speak because I couldn't decide which of her ludicrous accusations to address first. Finally, I said, 'First of all, you love attention. You always have. You like being a big fucking weirdo—' Had I really just said *fucking* in front of Rosie and Owen? Yes. I had. 'There's nothing I could ever do to embarrass you that compares to how you choose to embarrass yourself on a daily basis. I'm sure the last few weeks have been the highlight of your life, and you don't even care how much your prediction scares people, or whether it's wrong. You're just excited that you get to be on TV. And the reason you stood by me, as you put it, in eighth grade, is that you didn't give a shit. It made no difference to you, so don't pretend it was about loyalty. I've been plenty loyal to you, Vi, and plenty generous, too—'

'Like when you pay for my eight-dollar fajitas with the income you earn from your exhausting job?' she interrupted. 'Is that what you're talking about?' And really, Vi and I argued often, but what I felt at this moment was an anger whose purity and heat were unlike any I'd previously experienced.

'Fajitas are the least of it, you sociopath! You want to know how much Emma's charging? You really want to know? Fifteen thousand dollars. Now get out of my house!'

'With pleasure.' Vi was standing, shoving her feet into her clogs, picking up her bag, and it was gratifying to see that she herself was shaking with rage. Maybe if she'd been a little more efficient, I wouldn't have had the chance to say what I said next.

But she still hadn't reached the front door when I said, 'You know nothing about being an adult – nothing about marriage or having kids or holding a real job. So the way that you constantly pass judgment on me is absurd. That's why I bite my tongue when you do it, because it's laughable that you have the nerve. It's like having my manners corrected by a caveman.'

'Maybe if you keep telling yourself how perfect your life is, eventually you'll believe it.'

'I never said—'

But she was talking over me. 'You just can't imagine that not everyone wants to spend their days changing diapers. Some of us think the world has more to offer. Can you believe it? And it's hilarious that you see yourself as such a great mother because from my perspective, you're turning your children into clingy little wimps. You cut Rosie's blueberries in half, for Christ's sake! Yeah, Mom was fucked up, but at least she gave us room to breathe.' With her hand on the front door, Vi glared at me. 'So I guess you haven't been the only one biting your tongue.'

CHAPTER 13

Less than two weeks before I was to marry Jeremy, Vi called me at work and said, 'There's something I need to talk to you about.'

She was going to announce that she wasn't coming to the wedding, I thought immediately, or that she was coming but was no longer willing to be the maid of honor, or that she was willing to be the maid of honor but didn't want to wear the dress we'd picked out together. I had prepared myself for all these possibilities and decided that I wouldn't fight her – that I couldn't let her spoil the celebration. Then she said, 'It's not about your wedding.'

'So what is it?'

'Can we meet up tonight? Without Jeremy?'

'His department head is taking us out for dinner, but you can come over before. I should be home by five-thirty. Is it something serious?'

'Yes,' Vi said, 'but it doesn't have to do with us.'

Jeremy and I had decided on a destination wedding in Mendocino, California, a plan that had once seemed perfect. The ceremony would occur at the same bed-and-breakfast where he'd proposed a year earlier; he'd had a conference in San Francisco, I'd flown to join him afterward, and we'd driven up the coast to stay at an inn. Holding the wedding in Mendocino would, we thought, make it fun even though it would be small, with the inconvenient location a justification for not inviting our distant relatives or any co-workers except my friend Janet.

The deeper we got into the planning, however, the more obvious it became that even a small wedding in Mendocino would be prohibitively expensive. In fact, I had the impression that it was our very attempts at being understated that would cost so much. Shortly before Jeremy and I had moved in together, we had been mutually discomfited to learn opposite pieces of information about each other: He'd been surprised to find out that I had debt, and I'd been surprised that he didn't. At that point, I owed nine thousand dollars in student loans and four thousand in credit card bills, neither of which seemed to me disgraceful – I had a decent credit rating, especially compared to Vi – but I could tell that Jeremy didn't like these facts about me. He didn't say so, but he might even have considered my debt low-class, to borrow a term from my mother. Meanwhile, it hadn't occurred to me that he *wouldn't* still be paying off student loans; I didn't understand until meeting Jeremy that most people with doctoral degrees received funding during their years of graduate work. And his parents had paid for the entirety of his undergraduate education, which at a private university had cost far more than mine.

The week I was to stop being Vi's roommate, Jeremy said that he'd been thinking about it and suggested the following: that as a gift, he wanted to pay off my student loans; that after I moved in with him, I didn't need to pay rent at first but should instead put what would have been rent money toward paying off my credit card bills; that when I had, we'd both pay rent proportional to our salaries (he earned twice what I did); and that we'd take turns covering daily living expenses such as dinners out. Growing up, I'd regularly had the feeling that my mother hadn't taught Vi and me the things a mother was supposed to teach you – to put toilet paper on the seat in public bathrooms or to straighten my leg when shaving my knee – and there were lessons I'd had to glean from observation or just from the hunch that I'd done something wrong. The evening when Jeremy laid out his financial proposition was the first time it occurred to me that perhaps my father had failed to impart certain lessons, too. I was also, of course, dumbstruck by Jeremy's generosity.

And yet, as the wedding expenses added up – deposits for the inn where the rehearsal dinner, ceremony, and reception would take place; the invitations; the photographer and the cake and the flowers – Jeremy was the one who was prepared to splurge, and I was the one who balked. 'You only get married once,' he'd say with a smile. 'Hopefully.' (As it happened, even though Jeremy's parents were long divorced, they were that civilized brand of divorced people who, with their respective second spouses, would all good-naturedly socialize; his father and stepmother had attended the engagement party that Jeremy's mother and stepfather had held for us the previous winter in Virginia.)

Eventually, I convinced Jeremy that we needed neither a band nor a DJ – Patrick said he'd download songs for us on his iPod – and I bought two used dresses online for a hundred and fifty dollars each, kept the one that fit better and resold the other. My friend Janet would do my hair and makeup, we'd have no wedding attendants except Jeremy's brother and my sister, and we'd cap the guest list at twenty-six people, including us. The two areas where Jeremy was inflexible were that he wouldn't consider a cash bar – it wasn't that I was hell-bent on it, but this was another instance in which he might have considered me low-class for even floating the idea – and he also for some reason really wanted to give out matchbooks with our names and the date on them, though these turned out to be relatively cheap, as wedding favors went. Even so, when all was said and done, the weekend would cost over twenty thousand dollars, which meant, after his parents told us they'd cover the rehearsal dinner, we'd still deplete Jeremy's savings. (He'd have to sell off stocks, though to me the notable fact was that he owned stocks – really, unlike me, Jeremy was a bona fide grown-up before we met.) I had wondered if my father might pay for at least some of the wedding, but no offer had been forthcoming. My father had retired the previous summer, and I had little idea of the state of his finances, though his rental apartment was a modest one.

If I was being honest, the cost wasn't the only reason for my ambivalence about my own wedding. The closer the date drew, and the more I found myself fielding friendly questions about it from co-workers and acquaintances, the more self-conscious I grew about the fact that it would be in northern California. It seemed the choice of a woman who fancied herself free-spirited – who wore a toe ring, say, and who baked bread from scratch and whose name was Daisy.

On a hot Sunday morning in August about a month before the wedding was supposed to happen, Jeremy and I went for a walk in Forest Park. 'I want to marry you,' I said. 'But I wish we were just doing it at the courthouse.'

'That's so dreary.' A second later, when Jeremy apparently remembered that my parents had done exactly that, he added, 'Sorry. Listen – I don't care what we're wearing. I don't care if we have a first dance or place cards or any of that shit. But weddings are one of the only times in life that people come together for happy

329

reasons, and I want that – I want to be in a nice setting, surrounded by people who love us. Anyway, if we cancel, we won't get the deposit money back.'

'And you think *I'm* unromantic. Did you find out if Cockroach is bringing his new girlfriend?' Cockroach, whose real name was Nick Chandler, was Jeremy's Wesleyan roommate.

'I'll email him today.'

'Try to be a little discouraging. Subtly discouraging.'

'"I know you're into her, but are you hundreds of dollars" worth of our money into her?' That kind of thing?' We were passing the boathouse, and Jeremy took my hand. He said, 'Have a little faith, okay? Not everything can be quantified.'

When I'd moved into Jeremy's apartment, Vi had found a stranger named Sheila to take my room in the duplex on Moorlands Drive. Within two months, Jeremy and I were engaged while Vi and Sheila had had a series of explosive arguments, broken the lease, and gone their separate ways. Vi, who'd recently been promoted from hostess to assistant manager at Trattoria Marcella, found a place in Rock Hill, where she lived alone for the first time. When she enthusiastically recommended it, I said, 'It's not that I don't believe you, but it's kind of too late for me.'

As I let Vi in the evening of her unsettling phone call, she immediately spotted an unlit pale green candle on the table just inside the front door, lifted it, and sniffed. 'Cedar?'

'Pine.'

'Where's it from?'

'Some store at the Galleria. Want it?' Offering Vi my possessions was a slightly weird impulse I'd developed during my relationship with Jeremy. It was hard to say if it arose from my proximity to Jeremy's money, or from vague guilt over the fact that Vi was still, eternally, single, or perhaps from something less insidious, something as simple as affection.

'Really? Thanks.' She tossed the candle into the oversized straw bag she was carrying and walked into the living room, where she took a seat on the couch, set down her bag, kicked off her Birkenstocks, and put her bare feet on the coffee table. She was wearing a thin-strapped sundress that exposed her back, shoulders, and ample cleavage; her chest and cheeks were flushed, and her hairline was sweaty. 'It's hotter than fucking bananas out there,' she said.

I'd gone to the refrigerator to get us both Diet Cokes, and from the kitchen I asked, 'Are you working tonight?'

'No, thank God.'

Back in the living room, I said, 'What's going on?'

'You know Brady Ogden?'

'The kidnapped boy?'

'I had a sense about him.'

331

'Oh God, Vi.'

'I think it's a postal worker who did it. That's what they're called, right? Postal workers?'

'Like a mailman?'

'Maybe. Or just someone who works at a branch office. A male.'

'And Brady's—' I almost couldn't bring myself to say it. 'Is he alive?' Brady Ogden was a nine-year-old who'd lived fifteen miles away, in Florissant. On a warm May night three months earlier, when he'd heard the music of the ice cream truck, he'd asked his parents if he could go buy a Bomb Pop and had never returned home. After police questioning, the ice cream truck's driver – a recent high school dropout – had been cleared of suspicion. He'd been stoned, apparently, but he hadn't kidnapped anyone. The disappearance of Brady Ogden had repeatedly appeared on the front page of the *Post-Dispatch*, as well as being a frequent topic of discussion on all the local news programs; more briefly, it had made national news.

Vi's expression was one I knew well, as if she were trying hard to remember something, though remembering wasn't what she was doing. 'He is alive,' she said. 'I'm pretty sure. But I think the guy might be – you know—'

'Torturing him?' I could barely stand to have this conversation.

'Well, molesting. If there's a difference between that and torture – I don't know, I guess there is. But what I wanted to ask you is, I think I'd recognize where the guy lives if I saw it, so what if we drive around together?'

Because this was years before Vi stopped driving, so the request seemed particularly odd. I said, 'You think we should just get in the car and go up and down every street in Florissant?'

'I don't think he's still in Florissant. He's in one of those suburbs that people barely lived in when we were growing up. Maybe Chesterfield?'

'Maybe?'

Vi seemed preoccupied, and also uneasy. After a pause, she said, 'Yeah. Maybe.'

'You should go to the police.'

'You think?' She looked at me with surprise.

'Let's say you and I are driving around Chesterfield. In a best-case scenario, we pass some house and you're really having a sense, and then what? I'm sure as hell not getting out to knock on the door.'

'It's not a house,' she said, and her voice was more confident. 'It's an apartment building.' Then she said, 'I didn't think you would tell me to contact the police because what if I'm wrong and I seem like a big nut job?'

'But if this kid is being—' We looked at each other, and I said, 'If I was having a sense, I'd go to the police.'

On her face was an expression of great skepticism.

'I'm sure they have a system for dealing with this,' I said. 'There's a tip line just for Brady

Ogden, right? And I bet a lot of the tips are wrong, and they're not fazed by that. And who knows – if you go to them and say, "I'm having this hunch he's been kidnapped by a mailman who lives in an apartment building in Chesterfield," maybe they have a list of suspects and one of them fits that description and they can go back and investigate that person more.'

Vi bit at a hangnail on her thumb. 'With your wedding, I thought you'd tell me to forget it.'

'Because heaven forbid that a kidnapped boy take attention from me? Thank you.' I took a sip of Diet Coke and steeled myself. 'Have you been getting messages from Guardian?'

She pulled her thumb away from her mouth. 'Not about this. I've been waking up in the morning with visuals.' Unexpectedly, she grinned. 'And men think it's bad when they wake up with boners.'

'I'm not sure most men think it's bad,' I said.

She leered. 'That's more than I need to know about you and Jeremy.' I started to protest, and she said, 'You aren't planning to take his name, are you?'

When I hesitated, she said, 'Really, Daze?'

'I think it's nice when a couple has the same last name.'

She removed her bare feet from the coffee table and sat up straighter. 'So putting aside the patriarchal brainwashing, do you realize your name will now be a hundred percent different from the name you were given at birth? Daisy Shramm to Kate Tucker?'

Of course I realized this. 'So?'

'Kate Tucker is the name of a pilgrim. You'll be a pilgrim married to a boy explorer.'

'Thank you for sharing your opinion. Have you gotten shoes for the wedding?'

Vi and I had found her maid of honor dress at T. J. Maxx, a deep pink cowl-neck sheath that looked great on her. My only reservations were that, because it was unusual for Vi to wear something so fitted, she'd have a change of heart after it was too late to get anything else or that she'd decide it was humorously subversive to wear, say, Doc Martens on her feet.

'I bought some flats that will totally pass your smell test,' Vi said. 'And they were on sale for nine dollars. You have nothing to worry about.'

'What color?'

'Black.'

I definitely wanted to see them before the ceremony. I said, 'Tomorrow after work I'll drive you around.'

We ended up leaving the apartment together, and when we were outside, before we turned in opposite directions to walk to our cars – I was about to go pick up Jeremy for dinner – I said, 'Call the police and just see what they say.'

When Jeremy's department head, Leland Marcus, had said he and his wife, Xiaojian, who was an oncology professor at Wash U's medical school, wanted to take us out to celebrate our engagement, it had felt awkward given that we hadn't invited them to the wedding; we hadn't considered it. They were both about fifty and didn't have children, and I hardly knew either of them. Xiaojian had been born in Shanghai and had recently led a high-profile study on hormone therapy and breast cancer; Leland had started his career at NASA. The previous winter, at a department holiday party, I'd had a twenty-five-minute conversation with Leland about fishing in Minnesota's Boundary Waters that was basically a monologue on his part, and on the car ride home, Jeremy said, 'That's the longest any human being has ever spent talking to Leland.' (Later, it was odd to think that this party was where I'd met Hank and Courtney, speaking to them first by the buffet table and later when we happened to leave at the same time, heading out into the cold night and exchanging pleasantly distant farewells, with no idea of the friendship that would eventually develop among us.)

At the restaurant with Leland and Xiaojian, we somehow got through the selection of wine and food, our appetizers and entrées – I could hear myself prattling on about the view from the grassy cliff where Jeremy and I would exchange our vows, and I was conscious, though less than I once would have been, of being the only person present without a PhD – and then the waiter brought out cappuccinos for Xiaojian and me and a raspberry tart for Leland.

Xiaojian turned to me. 'After the wedding, you will have babies.' It was hard to tell if it was a question or a comment.

'Probably,' I said.

'It is babies or job. You know this, yes? Women pretend they can do it all, but it is a lie. Babies or job. Never both. You work with elderly?'

I nodded, unsure if it was more surprising that she knew what field I was in or that she was, without apparent hesitation, delivering this diatribe.

She said, 'If you have babies, say bye-bye to elderly.'

'A lot of the women I work with have children.'

'Small children?'

'Some of them.'

'Then they are bad mothers or bad workers. On this, trust me.'

Was Jeremy listening? I hoped so, because I doubted I'd be able to do justice later to Xiaojian's remarks.

'I guess everyone has to figure out their own path,' I said, and Xiaojian replied, with a mirthful expression, 'I see you do not believe me, but you will soon find out.'

And then someone had approached our table and was standing at the corner between Xiaojian and me. At first, I thought it was the waiter, but the person leaned in and touched my elbow. 'Daisy Shramm?'

Even before I looked up, my body tensed. It wasn't that this never happened. I lived in St Louis, after all, where your next-door neighbor would turn out to be your co-worker's cousin, where you'd run into your bank teller at the gym and your gynecologist at the farmers' market. The suburbs were crawling with people with whom I'd gone to elementary school, middle school, high school, and college. But out in public I often noticed these people before they noticed me; the truth was, I could usually sense them. And then I could lower my head or walk away or, in particularly dire cases, hide in a bathroom stall. Once, in the parking lot of Ted Drewes, Jeremy and I had been sitting on the hood of his car, eating our concretes, when I'd said to him, 'Give me the keys.' And I'd hit the Unlock button, jumped into the front passenger seat, and slumped there with my frozen custard until Alex Cooke – the first guy I'd ever kissed, while watching TV at Marisa Mazarelli's house, who now appeared to be a father of four – had walked by with his large family. Afterward, when I tried to explain, Jeremy said, 'For a minute there, I wondered if you're in the Witness Protection Program.'

In the restaurant, this person from my past had come upon me without my noticing; I had been distracted by Xiaojian Marcus's rant. The person was male, about my age, and I knew that I knew him, but I didn't know who he was. He had a cheerful face, and he held one hand to his chest and said, 'It's Laird. Laird Mueller. Tom's brother.'

'How are you?' I said. I didn't stand because it seemed like if I did, we might have to hug. The last time I'd seen Laird, which was when his brother had been my high school boyfriend, he hadn't yet entered puberty.

'So the weirdest thing is, your name came up last week,' Laird said, and I was aware that Leland and Jeremy had gone quiet and were, like Xiaojian, observing this interaction. 'What are the chances, right? I'm at the Cards game with a couple buddies from work – I'm at Selvin and Associates in Clayton – and one of my co-workers is another fellow from Kirkwood, Kevin Chansky. Don't know if you'd remember him, but he was my year. He says to me, "Didn't your brother go out with Daisy Shramm?" and I say, "Did he ever!"' Laird cupped one hand around the side of his mouth, as if he were conveying confidential information rather than performing for a table of four. 'Between you and I, I had a mondo crush on you back in the day. Anyway, Chansky says, "Daisy was a witch." And I'm like, "Huh? No way!" And he's like, "Yep, her and her twin sister both. They had crazy psychic powers." And I'm like, okay, so *that's* why Mom always hated Daisy. Good old ultra-conservative Peg Mueller.' Laird laughed then with warmth and sincerity, and the moment was so unendurable that a part of me couldn't believe we were all still in the middle of it.

'So, Laird,' Jeremy said. 'It's Laird, right?' Jeremy's tone was mild; it might even have seemed friendly, if you didn't know him. 'We're just finishing up dinner here. But thanks for coming over.'

There was a little delay, while Laird absorbed Jeremy's diplomatic snub, and then with great enthusiasm, Laird said, 'Likewise! Awesome to see you, Daisy, and nice to meet the rest of you.' As he wandered off, returning to a stool at the bar near the front of the restaurant, it was hard to feel true relief; it was like when you find yourself on a street where a menacing dog comes toward you, then walks away but without your having any assurance that he won't turn back with renewed, unwholesome interest.

And lest I should have comforted myself by imagining that Laird's babbling had been too convoluted for my fiancé, his boss, and his boss's wife to follow, Xiaojian said brightly, 'So you are a—' Truly, I thought she was about to say *witch,* but instead she finished with 'twin.' Again, it was unclear whether she was asking or observing; however, the follow-up was definitely a question. She said, 'You are the good twin or bad twin?'

If Xiaojian hadn't rubbed me the wrong way before Laird's appearance, I would have offered her my twin boilerplate (identical, really fun, didn't try to trick people much growing up, still close, almost every day); I'd have felt that it was only polite. Instead, without smiling, I said, 'I'm the bad one.'

In the car, I said to Jeremy, 'I'm so sorry.'
'For what?'
'We don't have to pretend that wasn't excruciating when Laird came over.'
'Do you seriously think I hold you accountable for what some doofus you went to school with twenty years ago does?'
I was quiet and then I said, 'Are you nervous about marrying a witch?'
Jeremy laughed, which I hadn't expected. 'I'm just hoping you'll twitch your nose and get me tenure.'
'Do you think it's weird that I don't want to leave St Louis even though I hate running into people?'
'You don't want to leave because of your dad and Vi.' Jeremy was driving my car, and he made a left onto the ramp for 40 East.
I could have told him then about Vi and Brady Ogden, but instead I said, 'I'm afraid Vi's going to wear Doc Martens to our wedding.'
'Whatever floats her boat,' Jeremy said.

The next afternoon, I picked Vi up, and we got on the highway at McKnight; normally, it would have taken about twenty minutes to drive to

Chesterfield, but because it was rush hour, it was more like forty.

We passed the hospitals, several big new office parks, and as we closed in on Chesterfield, I said, 'Which exit?'

'Oh, God. Your guess is as good as mine.'

'Clarkson Road? Chesterfield Parkway?' Later, I would go to the Chesterfield Babies 'R' Us on a regular basis, but on this late afternoon in September 2004, I had an idea of where I was going only from having looked at a map I kept on my backseat.

'Either one,' Vi said, and I wondered how long she envisioned us driving. I'd told Jeremy only that I was meeting up with Vi about her wedding outfit and that if he got hungry, he should go ahead and eat dinner without me.

Vi and I circled Chesterfield Parkway and then I went north, somewhat arbitrarily, on Olive Boulevard, past the Butterfly House – another place I never went until I had children – before pulling off in the parking lot of a gas station and reversing direction. I could feel Vi's alertness, her head angled toward the window, but she was quiet. 'Anything seeming familiar?' I said, and she didn't answer. Because there wasn't much reason not to, I turned onto a residential street, but it was lined with new-looking, nice houses, and I knew it wasn't right even before Vi said, 'It's an apartment building.'

We ended up in Ellisville, then Ballwin – St.

Louis County was divided into dozens of towns and cities with no centers, some with only houses and populations of just a few hundred – and I said, 'You know we've left Chesterfield, don't you?' and Vi said, 'Maybe we should go back. Sorry.'

I turned, and we found ourselves back on Clarkson Road, which led us to Baxter Road, Wild Horse Creek Road, Eatherton Road, Olive Street – we were passing the small Chesterfield airport – and near the mall again, there were a few clusters of townhouses, but Vi repeated that we were looking for an apartment, and then there was a cluster of apartment buildings, but they weren't the right ones. We'd been in the car for an hour and a half, and the sun was setting. Without consulting Vi, I got back on the highway and began driving toward St Louis. Twenty-five yards from the exit for Woods Mill Road, she said, 'Get off here.'

I wasn't even in the right-hand lane; I glanced in the side mirror, swerved over, and got on the exit ramp. 'Go right,' Vi said. Though I still wasn't expecting much, we'd already passed Woods Mill Road on our way west, we'd been driving for no more than two minutes when she said, 'Turn into that parking lot,' and she was gesturing just up ahead, where a wooden sign said TERRACE VIEW APARTMENTS, and beyond it was a paved driveway that dipped down then rose up. In the parking lot proper, where I pulled into a space but didn't turn off the engine, Vi and I both craned our necks back. In front of us were three enormous, identical buildings covered in cream-colored stucco; they were five stories high and contained perhaps fifty units each. Though it was a fuzzily golden late summer evening, I felt their ominousness right away, their containment of something bad. I wanted to leave, even as I believed Vi with a new certainty.

'It'd be like finding a needle in a haystack,' Vi said. 'Jesus.'

'Why don't you sleep on it?' I still hadn't turned off the car or even set the gearshift in Park, and I added, 'You don't want to get out, do you?'

Vi looked up through the windshield at each building, one after the other, but to my relief she said, 'No.' On the ride back, neither of us spoke, and in front of the four-unit brick building where she lived – it seemed so little after the Terrace View Apartments – I didn't have the energy to ask if I could see her wedding shoes.

At home, Jeremy said, 'Did she feed you?' It was almost eight, and he was scrambling eggs.

'Actually, no,' I said. 'Did you make enough for both of us?'

'I'm about to,' he said.

That night I awakened just before twelve o'clock, which was less than an hour after Jeremy and I had gone to bed; I felt that old sense of menace from my childhood, and I wondered at first if there'd been a noise in the apartment, an intruder even, but as I continued to listen, I heard nothing irregular. Jeremy was next to me, sleeping on his side, and I considered waking him but resisted; usually, it was enough just to know I could. I smoothed out my T-shirt, which had ridden up, and tucked my hair behind my ears, and I thought to myself, *Everything is fine,* and in the next instant, I thought, *He doesn't work in a post office, he works in a copy shop on New Ballas Road.* Though I could see why Vi had been confused, because his uniform, his button-down shirt, was pale blue. He was a clean-shaven guy in his forties, with a blond, almost military crew cut, and the name tag over the left pocket of his shirt said DEREK.

I got up and went into the living room; I dialed Vi's cell number and sat down on the couch. (I sometimes had to stop and think, when I called Vi, which was her phone number and which was mine. Once, shortly after moving in with Jeremy, I'd meant to call Vi from my cellphone but called my own home phone, had heard but not really paid attention to my voice on the outgoing greeting, and had proceeded to leave a message for Vi. Later, I was briefly bewildered listening to it.)

'What are you doing up?' Vi said when she answered. In the background, I could hear music and the rise and fall of multiple voices.

'Where are you?' I asked.

'A few of us are at this guy Maxwell's house, but I'm leaving in a sec.' Then she laughed. 'Wait, *you* know Maxwell.' She lowered her voice to a whisper and said, 'Should I tell him you're about to get married, or you think that'd break his big, bearded heart?'

'Vi, I saw the kidnapper,' I said. 'In a dream, I mean. I think he works at a copy shop.'

'A coffee shop?'

'*Copy*. Like Kinko's but not a chain. I think you're right, though – I think he lives in one of those buildings. So what do we do now?'

'He has really short hair, right? And he's almost handsome in this cheesy way, like he should be on a reality show except that he's so creepy?'

'His name is Derek. I could see it on his badge.'

She was quiet for so long that I might have thought, if I hadn't still been able to hear the background noise, that we'd been disconnected. At last, she said, 'I'll make you a deal. If you call the police, then you can say you're me.'

If I'd looked on the Internet to find the number for the Florissant Police Department, surely I'd have seen that the tip line was anonymous, but I didn't look on the Internet. Instead, I pulled down the White Pages that Jeremy and I still kept, back in 2004, on top of our refrigerator, and I called the main number, and the person who answered connected me to the tip line, and I said the following: 'I hope this doesn't sound too weird, but I'm a person who sometimes has premonitions or I guess you could say ESP, and I've had one about Brady Ogden and what I think is maybe the person who kidnapped him – well, who was involved in kidnapping him, or could have been – I think it's a man named Derek – that's his first name – and he works in a copy shop, like a Kinko's but not Kinko's, and he lives in a complex called Terrace View Apartments, which is on Woods Mill Road. I don't know any of this for sure, but I think maybe. And my name is Violet Shramm, Violet like the flower and Shramm is S-H-R-A-M-M.' I left Vi's cellphone number; she didn't have a home phone. Then, as ordinarily as if I'd called to cancel a dentist's appointment, I said, 'Okay. That's all. Thanks so much.'

When I returned to bed, Jeremy said, 'Who were you talking to?' But he seemed barely awake.

'I was watching TV,' I said. 'I couldn't sleep.'

On Thursday nights, Jeremy played what he called nerd poker – all the players were professors from either his department or the physics department, and the only woman who participated was Courtney Wheeling – and I took my father to the grocery store. We still returned to the Schnucks on the corner of Manchester and Woodlawn; from year to year, it was the closest I got to our old house on Gilbert Street. In the cereal aisle, my father said, 'Your sister has liked living on her own.'

'I'm trying not to take that too personally.' I had last spoken to Vi the night before, about forty-eight hours after I'd left the message on the tip line, and she hadn't heard from the Florissant police, which made me unsure whether to be relieved or disappointed. Either way, I couldn't imagine she'd have mentioned the Brady Ogden business to our father.

Then he said, 'I know the bride's family usually pays for the wedding,' and for about a second, I felt a surge of hope – I hadn't even been sure that he was aware that this convention existed – but my hope began to wither when he said, 'My dilemma is that I question if Vi will ever marry.'

Though I questioned the same thing, it was still a bit shocking to hear him state it so baldly. 'We're barely twenty-nine, Dad. People get married later now.'

'Well, don't forget I was a good deal older than you girls when I married your mother. But I'm referring less to your sister's age than what you might call her temperament. I don't know that she's the marrying kind.' Again, I felt a little shocked, even a little defensive on Vi's behalf, while essentially agreeing.

'I'd like her to have some stability like you have with Jeremy,' my father said. 'Just something to fall back on over the long term, after I'm not around, and I wonder if you wouldn't be disappointed if instead of helping out with your wedding, I made a down payment on a house for your sister. I'm awfully sorry I can't do both. As your mother knew all too well, I've never been a financial whiz kid.'

I blinked and said, 'That's fine.' My voice was

uneven, but not so hideously that it required his acknowledgment.

'I know it isn't fair to you—'

'Dad.' I held up my hand. 'It's fine. We don't need to talk about it.'

But he wasn't finished. 'I'm sure they must pay the professors handsomely at Wash U,' he said. 'If you weren't marrying someone responsible, I wouldn't—'

'It's completely fine,' I said. 'Really.'

'There *is* something I want you to have.' He was the one pushing the grocery cart, and he looked at me then, my tall, thin, old, sad father, wearing a short-sleeved poly-blend plaid shirt and gray slacks. 'It's in the car.'

We finished shopping and loaded the plastic bags into my trunk. I wasn't planning to remind him of whatever it was he intended to give me – I feared another twenty-five-dollar Starbucks gift card – but when we were seated, he passed me a small royal blue velvet pouch cinched at the neck. I knew immediately what was in it; to open it would be like opening the past. But he was waiting, and I had no choice. I was then holding my mother's charm bracelet, the charms dangling like false promises: the little gold baseball bat and the malachite shamrock, the windmill, the poodle with eyes of tiny turquoise, the miniature beer stein. 'How does the saying go?' my father said. 'Something old, something new . . . I thought this could be your something old.'

There had been certain things I'd wanted badly in my childhood, and instead of getting them, I'd grown up; I did not want them any longer. But I said, 'Thank you, Dad.'

'Would you like me to put it on you?'

I forced a smile. 'I think it'll be more special if I save it.'

Jeremy was usually out until after eleven on poker nights, and back in our apartment, I turned on the TV. I would have called Vi to tell her about the bracelet, but I thought she was working, which was why I was surprised when my cellphone rang shortly before nine and her name came up. 'I just got back from meeting with a police detective,' she said. 'I think they believe us.'

'You're not at the restaurant tonight?'

'I called in sick. The detective was a woman, but her name is Tyler.'

'When did you hear from them?'

'Just this afternoon. Come over and I'll tell you about it.'

'I'm in my pajamas already.'

'So?'

After a second, I said, 'Okay. I'll come over.'

When the detective – Tyler McGillivary – had called Vi that afternoon, she'd wanted to see Vi as soon as possible; twenty minutes later, she was in Vi's living room. Detective McGillivary had asked her questions for close to an hour: about Vi's life and her job, about her previous premonitions, about the specific senses Vi was having with regard to Brady Ogden. Detective McGillivary wanted to know how closely Vi had followed the case, which wasn't all that closely, or if she'd ever had contact with the Ogden family. 'Did you know Brady has two brothers?' Vi said, and I said, 'Did you not know that?'

Detective McGillivary used Vi's bathroom – Vi wondered if she was snooping – and when she emerged, she asked if Vi had time to come in to the station. Detective McGillivary gave her a ride (it wasn't a police car she drove, and it didn't even look like an unmarked police car; it seemed like it was her personal car, partly because Vi saw the stub to a movie ticket on the dashboard), and at the station, Detective McGillivary took her to a private room. The detective went to get them coffee and returned accompanied by two other people, both men, who obviously were also on the police force, though Vi forgot their names and titles immediately upon being introduced. With these men present, Detective McGillivary asked many of the same questions she'd asked at Vi's apartment, especially the ones about the guy Vi thought was the kidnapper and the ones about being psychic. 'You didn't say anything about me, did you?' I said.

'It came up that I have a twin.'

'Did they ask if I have senses, too?' They had; I knew they had.

'I said you don't like talking about it. Which, I know, Daze, I promised you and everything, but what would you have done? And I swear I didn't say you were the one who came up with the name Derek. They really weren't that interested in you.'

They all were respectful toward her, Vi continued, much more than she'd expected. The way they talked to her, it was as if she'd been a witness to a crime and they appreciated her help. Even when she described how Guardian had first spoken to her at Reed – here she looked at me meaningfully – they didn't seem to be rolling their eyes.

Detective McGillivary suggested they go for a drive, and one of the men went, too; Detective McGillivary drove, the guy sat in front, and Vi sat in back. This time, on the backseat, Vi saw a pair of swimming goggles.

They took her past the Ogden family's house and around their neighborhood, past the elementary school Brady Ogden had attended, and then they drove to the apartment complex where I hadn't turned my car off, and they sat there for a long time, maybe forty-five minutes, and talked about different things. They were relaxed with her, Vi said; it was like they were just hanging out, but as they were leaving, Vi abruptly felt short of breath and heard Guardian say, 'He needs your help.'

'Did the detective say she'd be in touch?' I asked.

'Yeah, or that I should call her if more stuff comes to me.'

'Will they tell you if they find him?'

Vi gave me a peculiar look. 'They won't have to,' she said. 'It'll be national news.'

Again, as when I'd called and left the message on the tip line, I thought something would or should happen immediately; Brady Ogden should be found, and the man who had abducted him should be arrested. But the weekend passed, the last weekend before my wedding, and Vi had neither called nor been called by Detective McGillivary. I had had no further senses about Brady Ogden, though I'd had plenty of thoughts about him during the hours I couldn't sleep at night – a nine-year-old boy inside an apartment in one of those big awful buildings, with a predatory, blond-haired man.

Jeremy and I were to leave for Mendocino on Wednesday. On Monday, I called Vi and said, 'Will you ask the detective if there's any news?'

'You ask her. Just say you're me again.'

'Our deal was that you'd talk to the police.'

'But I have nothing to *say* to her.' Didn't Vi always have something to say? She added, 'You just want this to be resolved before your wedding.' But she didn't sound mean or judgmental as she said, 'Daze, there's nothing you can do right now for Brady Ogden.'

That night, Jeremy had just dumped spaghetti into a pot of boiling water when I said, 'I want us to still get married, but I think we should cancel our wedding. I'm sorry.'

353

He looked at me with an unfriendly expression. 'Didn't we already have this conversation?'

'Vi's been having senses about Brady Ogden, and I drove around with her last week and she thinks she knows which building his kidnapper lives in, which means it could be where Brady Ogden is, too, if he's still alive, and I had a dream that the kidnapper's name is Derek, and then Vi met with the police.'

'And that changes our wedding plans how?' If I'd thought Jeremy's jaw would drop in astonishment, it would have meant I didn't know my fiancé. I hadn't thought this, but it still surprised me just how unruffled he was.

And his question was, in a way, a good one. But in another way, its answer seemed self-evident. I said, 'You don't think it's gross for us to have a fancy party celebrating ourselves when a little nine-year-old boy is still missing?'

I could see Jeremy's irritation around his mouth. We virtually never fought, which Vi had once told me meant we weren't honest with each other, so my familiarity with his displeasure was as its observer rather than its inciter. Every few months, someone would royally piss him off – a drunk guy at a Cards game who threw a cup that hit Jeremy in the head or a mechanic at a garage who he felt had overcharged me – and in a clipped way Jeremy would make two or three comments about what a bottom-dwelling waste of humanity the person was, and then his ill humor would pass.

But this was different; this time, Jeremy's displeasure was directed at me. He said, 'Brady Ogden has been missing for, what, two months?'

'Almost four.'

'Okay. Almost four. He's been missing for almost four months, and during that time, we've been debating steak versus chicken, and stuffed mushrooms versus spanakopita, and what color flowers . . . So help me out here in understanding—'

'I said that I'm sorry. I know how annoying this must be.'

'Annoying?' Again, those almost pursed, almost amused lips, and the strangeness of his not being my ally. 'Kate, the world is a big place, and there are always good and bad things happening at the same time. Should we cancel our wedding because of the Iraq War? Or violence in Kosovo?'

'My sister's not directly involved in that.' Then I said, 'Remember when J.F.K. Jr.'s plane went down? He was on his way to his cousin's wedding, and the cousin called it off, but she and the guy still got married later. They just knew that weekend wasn't the right time.' The plane accident had preoccupied me the summer it happened not only because of how young and good-looking Kennedy had been but also because the other passengers on his little plane had been his wife and the wife's older sister, who was a twin. For months – even still sometimes – I'd wonder, what was the other twin, the living twin, supposed to do after the accident? She'd had two sisters and lost them both at the same time.

'Don't take this the wrong way,' Jeremy said, 'but you're not a Kennedy. And Brady Ogden isn't your cousin. Would you know him if you saw him on the street?'

'I definitely would.'

'Maybe I'm a jerk, but I wouldn't.' Jeremy folded his arms. 'Here's the thing. If we don't get married in Mendocino, I don't want to get married.'

Without a doubt, this was the most shocking thing Jeremy had ever said to me. I hadn't imagined that he'd be pleased about my decision, but I had thought he'd let me persuade him. He'd be disappointed but he'd understand, and perhaps even be touched by my sensitivity.

I said, 'So *you're* willing to call off the wedding?'

'I don't want to.'

'Are you afraid that people will be mad about having to cancel their plane tickets? Even if they're not refundable, they can put the amount toward a different ticket.'

Jeremy was shaking his head. 'That's not what this is about. It's about a precedent for our life together that I don't want to set.'

'Meaning what?'

'This idea you have that you'll be punished for enjoying yourself – it's a huge bummer, Kate. You're allowed to experience ordinary pleasures, even if you didn't get to when you were younger. You're even allowed to have children.'

'Having children and not getting married in California have nothing to do with each other.' But I felt two opposing emotions: flattery that Jeremy had observed me so closely and betrayal that he had observed me so closely.

'I'm just afraid that if we get married' – he paused, possibly having jarred himself, as he'd jarred me, with that *if* – 'that when anything bad happens, you'll let yourself be consumed by it. You'll shelve the rest of your life.'

Was this what he believed I'd done in the past? During the witches episode in eighth grade or after my mother's death? I said, 'If you think that, I'm not sure why you'd want to marry me in the first place.'

'Besides that I love you?' We watched each other over the kitchen's high wooden table, and he said, 'The wedding is all planned. There's hardly anything left for us to do but get on the plane.'

'What if my feeling that we shouldn't get married out there isn't just about Brady Ogden? What if we get in a car accident driving up the coast?'

Prior to this, Jeremy's anger had been dimming; it flared up again as I spoke. He was almost clenching his teeth as he said, 'Do you think that will happen?'

'It could.'

He took a step backward. 'I can't let you drag us both to crazyville, Kate. Okay? I just can't.'

In a small voice, I said, 'I don't think our car will crash. I just – sometimes it's like my mind is this echo chamber.'

He stepped toward me again, around the table, and set his hand on my shoulder. 'We're going to have a really nice, fun, relaxed wedding. That's not something you need to feel guilty about.'

We took a cab to the airport because we'd be gone long enough that it was cheaper than paying to park. Sitting together in the backseat, passing the Dr Pepper syrup plant and the billboards for radio stations and car dealerships, Jeremy and I didn't speak; an observer could have been forgiven for imagining we were on our way to a funeral rather than a wedding, and certainly it wouldn't have seemed that the wedding we were on the way to was our own. In the airport, after we'd made it through security, we bought lunch at separate places and ate together at our gate, still barely talking. As the plane lifted off, I closed my eyes, and Jeremy took my hand.

I felt a strange weightlessness, a kind of absolution. I had tried to cancel the wedding; Jeremy had countered by saying he wouldn't marry me; not marrying Jeremy would, clearly, be an enormous mistake. This sequence felt neat in the way of a syllogism – it seemed to mean there was no alternative and I was not responsible for whatever had befallen Brady Ogden, whatever was befalling him still.

And so if I could put one foot in front of the other, if I could merely not deviate from the path I was on, that would be enough. Though if I managed to fake a little bridal joy, that wouldn't hurt. With my eyes still closed, I wondered if I ought to let Jeremy off the hook, if it was unfair to go through with marrying him. But surely I had given him an out, and he hadn't taken it.

Now, when I look back on that plane flight, besides remembering the pall over what should have been a festive time, what I'm most struck by is how unencumbered we were – physically unencumbered, I mean. We were two adults sitting in our seats, dozing, reading, sipping soda. Did we have any idea how soon there would be little bodies squirming against our chests, grabbing our hands, bleating and whining, wanting to eat or be entertained? I'd thought back then that I needed to be vigilant, but what was my vigilance for? It was only practice.

Or maybe I am being disingenuous – if I borrowed problems then, maybe I am borrowing them still. Maybe I have always been, as Vi would subsequently accuse me, someone who creates obstacles for myself then looks around in surprise, wondering where they came from.

It was better in California: the change of scenery and the fact that the scenery was so pretty, the deep blue sky and green hills, the glittering water and crashing waves. We arrived in Mendocino around dinnertime and walked to town from the inn, ate at a restaurant that seated us on a patio with little white lights woven into the trellis beside our table, and split a bottle of wine. We spoke more, but still solemnly – mostly about the logistics of the next few days. Jeremy ordered an after-dinner cognac, and we were both already buzzed as we returned to the room, where we found champagne in an ice bucket and two flutes awaiting us, compliments of the inn's staff. Without consulting me, Jeremy opened the champagne – the cork hit the ceiling, the liquid foamed out in a way he did nothing to stop, instead letting it spill onto the carpet – and poured us both a glass. He passed one to me and said, 'To us,' and we clinked.

'This is good,' I said, and he said, 'It's amazing what they throw in when you spend a mere twenty thousand.'

We got halfway through the bottle, sitting up side by side on the thick white comforter of the king-sized bed with our backs against the pillows, and then he took my glass out of my hand, set it on the floor, and rolled onto me. His mouth was over mine, and he was pulling at my clothes, and when I was naked, his teeth were on my nipples, his fingers inside me, and after a few minutes, he withdrew his fingers and slid into me, rocking his hips against mine; I gripped his arms above the elbows. We finished at the same time, and instead of pulling out, he just lay there, still inside me, and I could feel the trickle of liquid between us. After a minute, I said, 'I'm glad you're making me marry you.'

Our families arrived the following day – Jeremy's two sets of parents, his brother and brother's wife and their two children, plus Vi and my father and Patrick. 'I seriously almost puked on the drive in,' Vi said as we stood outside the main entrance of the inn in the cooling late afternoon. 'You didn't tell me the roads were so twisty.'

'Have you heard from the detective?'

She shook her head.

Jeremy had made a reservation at a Chinese restaurant, which seated us at a big round table with a lazy Susan in the middle, and it was seeing people interact from such separate parts of my life, of the life Jeremy and I now had together, that made me understand for the first time that a wedding was more than a party where you got married – that I had indeed been too literal in gauging whether it was worth the expense. Jeremy's sister-in-law, Meg, was laughing uproariously with Patrick, and Vi and Jeremy's mother were talking intently about something, and my father was very earnestly drawing a picture of a tractor for Eddie, Jeremy's three-year-old nephew.

This feeling of enlargement, of random and merry reconstitutions of our friends and family, continued as people kept arriving the next day: Meg and my friend Janet in the pool together with their children, Jeremy's friend Cockroach tossing a Frisbee with Patrick and Jeremy's grad school adviser on the lawn in front of the inn. All the guests, which was still only twenty people because a handful wouldn't arrive until Saturday, were invited to the rehearsal dinner on a terrace behind the inn. Jeremy's divorced mother and father gave a joint toast about how wonderful Jeremy was and how thrilled they were that he was marrying me, and after they sat down, my father rose, and embarrassment clutched me; was it some breach of protocol for him to speak when he wasn't paying for any of the wedding? But no one besides Jeremy and me knew, I reminded myself. 'I've never been terrific at expressing my feelings,' my father said. 'But Daisy and her sister used to like to sing and dance, and this is a song I want to sing in their honor.' It was 'The Way You Look Tonight,' and he sang without musical accompaniment, and for several seconds I was horrified. Plus, he'd just called me Daisy. But his voice, which had been a little thin to start, thickened – my father had always had a good voice – and at some point the song transformed from unbearable to charming. For the rest of the weekend and long after, my father's toast was often mentioned by our guests as the wedding's highlight.

Following dinner, the older generation and the parents of young children returned to their rooms and the rest of us sat around on big outdoor couches – Vi and Patrick were intertwined in a

362

nearby hammock in a way that I was glad my father wasn't awake to see, because it could only have confused him – and someone from the inn turned on two patio heaters, and I had that feeling, with the cool, sweet-smelling night air and the warmth of the heaters, of being inside a Christmas carol. This was the moment when I decided that instead of giving my father an excuse later on, I would wear my mother's charm bracelet after all. I had packed it at the last minute, and really, there was no reason not to.

It was one o'clock when Jeremy and I returned to our room; we weren't avoiding each other the night before our wedding, and he'd already seen my dress, hanging in a clear plastic bag in our coat closet in St Louis for the last five months. He was in the bathroom brushing his teeth, and I was already in bed, when there was a knock on the door. I startled – after wanting so badly for Brady Ogden to be found, I now just wanted not to think of him, for his existence to be suspended until we got through the ceremony the next after-noon – and when I looked through the peephole, my fears were not allayed; it was Vi in the hall.

But when I opened the door, she was grinning. 'I'm here to kidnap you.' An expression of alarm crossed my face, I knew, because she said, 'Sorry, bad word choice. I'm here to squire you away.'

'Why?'

'It's a surprise.'

'That can't wait until tomorrow?'

'If you must know, I'm throwing you a bachelorette party. It's only going to last five minutes, but it'll be the best bachelorette party ever. You thought I didn't know the maid of honor's supposed to do that, didn't you?' She was clearly pleased with herself.

I called, 'Jeremy, I'm going with Vi for a second.'

He opened the bathroom door, his toothbrush in his mouth. 'Now?'

'Hi, Jeremy,' Vi said. 'She'll be back before you know it, so don't worry your pretty little head.'

I let her lead me down the hall and around the corner to her own room, and she did the shave-and-a-haircut knock on the door, then followed it herself with the two bits. Then she turned the knob, and when we walked in, a gaggle of women whisper-shouted, 'Surprise!' I saw that they were my almost-sister-in-law, Meg; my almost-mother-in-law, Carol; my friend Janet; and Patrick, who apparently was an honorary woman, or maybe he was just there because he and Vi were sharing the room. Along the dresser, Vi had lined up six shot glasses of something pink, and she began passing them out as Patrick set a plastic tiara on my head; I was still, of course, wearing pajamas. 'What is this?' asked Carol, and Vi said, 'Bridal ambrosia. Everyone on the count of three?' She counted down, and, somewhat to my astonishment, all six of us threw back the liquid. It was vodka, I was pretty sure, mixed with lemonade. 'That wasn't nearly as disgusting as I anticipated,' Carol said.

Vi was holding an ice bucket against her hip, and she said, 'So I have an announcement. I couldn't find a male stripper to come to the hotel, which I know will really disappoint Kate.'

Meg said, 'You're telling me I woke up in the middle of the night for no stripper? I feel cheated!'

'Here's the good news.' Vi dug one hand into the ice bucket. 'Look what I did find – penis confetti!' She flung a fistful at me, she began flinging it at the other women, and sure enough, when I glanced down at a piece that had landed on my upper arm, I saw that it was a tiny, glittering yellow penis. At one end was the rounded tip, and at the other end were heart-shaped balls; the other penises were pink and blue and green, and they all glittered, too. 'Kate, on behalf of the female species, congratulations on getting married. May Jeremy's penis always appear as sparkly to you in the years to come as it does right now.' She looked around, grinning lewdly. 'Okay, everyone, the party's over. Go back to your rooms.'

An hour and a half before the ceremony, Janet was doing my makeup – I was sitting in a chair we'd pulled into the bathroom, facing the sink, and she was standing – when Vi burst in and shouted, 'They found him! This morning, they found him, and the dude who took him is in police custody.'

I was barefoot but already wearing my wedding dress, with an old T-shirt over it. (When my makeup and hair were finished, Janet would cut the shirt off me with scissors, which was a trick the professional makeup artist she'd hired for her own wedding had taught her.) I leapt up, and Vi and I embraced, and I said, 'I can't believe it,' and Vi said, 'I know! Holy shit, right?'

'Found who?' Janet said.

Vi and I both were quiet – Vi was deferring to me, if only because it was my wedding day – and then I said, 'Brady Ogden.'

Janet appeared confused. 'Do you guys know him?'

After a pause, I said, 'No, but we've followed the case really closely.'

'I couldn't.' Janet was shaking her head. 'Too depressing.'

I sat back down in the chair, and Vi hoisted herself onto the marble counter by the sink. I could feel the energy coming off her, the excitement, and I desperately wanted to ask what else the detective had told her. I settled on saying, 'Do they know how he is?'

'Well, alive,' Vi said. 'So that's a start. The guy, the kidnapper' – she was speaking slowly, choosing carefully what to say and eyeing me – 'he works in a copy store. It's on New Ballas Road.'

'Ew, a grown man kidnapped him?' Janet said. 'That's so sick. The poor kid will be messed up forever.'

'No,' Vi said quickly. 'People recover.'

Before Vi had entered the bathroom, Janet had

been applying foundation to my face with a triangular white sponge, and she resumed rubbing it across my cheeks. I could tell she was offended, that she believed she'd been scolded by Vi. I said, 'Vi, you remember the photographer is expecting family members outside by the flagpole at four o'clock, don't you? Maybe you should go take a shower.' But then – because Janet was only my friend while Vi was my sister – I added, 'But I agree. People do recover.'

How naïve I was to imagine, that afternoon in the bathroom, that if I could conceal Vi's involvement in the discovery of Brady Ogden, I could conceal her senses altogether; how naïve to merely imagine I could conceal her involvement. It wasn't Detective McGillivary who had called Vi the day of my wedding to tell her Brady had been found. It was Vi's friend Jocelyn, with whom Vi was in the meditation group, and the news was apparently all over St Louis. When she spoke to reporters, Detective McGillivary never said the break in the case was a tip from a local psychic. But Vi told her New Age friends about having talked to the police, and they told their friends, and soon she began to get calls from people she didn't know who wanted her to perform readings. The first few times, she did it for free, and Jeremy was the one who told her she ought to charge, which is to say perhaps he's complicit, too, in everything that eventually happened.

Intermittently – when Derek Smith was indicted, then went on trial, then was convicted of kidnapping and child molestation and began serving a life sentence – there would be flare-ups, recapitulations of the story of what Brady Ogden had been through, and Vi would complain that she'd missed her due. Yet within less than a year after Brady had been found, Vi was able to support herself just by holding readings. Increasingly, she held group sessions; there was, it turned out, more of a market for the lower-priced ones and, on occasion, she hosted them for bachelorette parties. What really surprised me was that she had a few corporate clients, including a regional burger chain and a real estate firm; she had to sign confidentiality agreements before she started working with them, but of course she told me anyway.

She once said to me, 'So it never bothers you at all that the cops gave us no credit for finding Brady?'

This is one of the most confusing parts of life: that even when confronted with an amplitude of evidence, we find it impossible to believe that others want what we don't or don't want what we do. The expression on my face must have been one of incredulity, because Vi said, 'Right, right. I forgot who I was talking to.'

I don't remember my wedding that well, which I think isn't particularly unusual; all I really recall is the sensation of time unspooling more happily and also more quickly than ever before or since.

I hadn't put much stock in the idea of a wedding being the best day of one's life, but I would say that for me, it was. The days on which my children were born have been more consequential and, certainly, joyous in their ways, but delivering a baby hurts, whereas a wedding can just be fun.

During the brief ceremony, the ocean sparkled below the cliff; exchanging our vows, with their familiar cadences, was like joining the club of adulthood. For the reception, the inn had decorated the tables with pale blue cloths and dark blue napkins and shiny wineglasses, with vases of delphiniums and cornflowers, and after a first dance with Jeremy and a second dance with my father, I danced third with Vi. We danced to 'You May Be Right,' and I could feel the guests being reminded of, being tickled by, our twinness. There was a moment when Billy Joel, via Patrick's iPod, was singing, and Vi and I found our faces close together, both of us flushed, me in my white strapless dress and her in her pink sheath (she was already barefoot, though she had indeed worn flats for the ceremony), and she said, 'Did you know Dad wants to give me the down payment to buy a house? He must feel guilty for spending so much on your wedding.' And then we'd danced apart, so maybe she didn't hear what I said next, though I actually meant it. I said, 'That's great.'

This is the part of my wedding I remember clearly: that after the photographer took family pictures before the ceremony, Jeremy and his brother went to stand beside the cliff where the justice of the peace had taken his place; that Vi walked down the short aisle formed between white folding chairs; and that then, on my father's arm, accompanied by no music except the wind, wearing no jewelry except my mother's charm bracelet, I followed her. And there Jeremy was with the sky behind him, in khaki pants and a navy blazer and a green tie, and I thought with amazement that he was a surprise again, though I'd seen him less than five minutes before: the man who was about to become my husband, waiting for me to become his wife.

CHAPTER 14

Rosie and Owen had just one framed print each hanging in their rooms – Owen's featured the alphabet with animals clinging to various letters, and Rosie's was a drawing of a little girl walking on a beach – and I had removed them and stored them in their closets the day after Vi made her prediction. It wasn't until the morning of Tuesday, October 13, that I waited until Jeremy had left for work, inserted Owen into the baby carrier, started *Dora the Explorer* for Rosie to watch in the living room, and walked around the house taking everything else down from the walls: the large black-and-white photo of mountains over the fireplace, and the mirror close to the front door; the painting in the dining room that we'd bought at an art fair; the three pictures from our wedding hung in a row by the staircase.

After I'd carried the wall hangings to the basement, I took the standing lamp next to the living room couch down there, too, and the smaller lamp on the end table. I didn't touch the chandelier in the dining room or the track lighting in the kitchen, not because they didn't pose a threat but because

371

they were too much trouble; also it seemed a little extreme, even for me, to sit around in darkness for the next three days. As if preparing to move, I pulled the glasses and dishes from the kitchen cabinets, wrapped them in newspaper, and stacked them in cardboard boxes. Our TV wasn't flat-screen so my plan was to just lift it off the table and set it on the floor on the night of the fifteenth.

When Kendra arrived to babysit, I was making a list for Target. Rosie jumped into Kendra's arms and said with great excitement, 'Kendra wants to play with Play-Doh.'

'I would *love* to play with Play-Doh,' Kendra said as she carried Rosie from the front door into the living room.

I'd considered texting Kendra to warn her about Rosie's split lip but neglected to do it. Jeremy, upon arriving home from work the previous after-noon, had looked at Rosie and said, 'Yeesh.' Then he'd lifted her up, spun her around, and said, 'I hope you showed the other guy what's what.' He'd glanced at me. 'Don't beat yourself up. This stuff happens.'

In the morning, the once-bloody area between Rosie's upper lip and nose was a dark yellow gooey patch, and I murmured to Jeremy, 'She has a Hitler mustache.'

Jeremy murmured back, 'I think the comparison you want is Charlie Chaplin.'

Yet again, in advance of Kendra's arrival, I'd pretended to myself that I'd leave both Rosie and

Owen with her, and yet again, seeing Rosie's delight in Kendra's presence, I decided to let my daughter have the sitter all to herself. This was how I ended up driving to Target with Owen, and at the checkout I realized I'd forgotten our reusable bags in the trunk of the car, which was what I usually did. The cashier was a middle-aged black woman who said to Owen, 'Hi there, Mr Man. You're a good-looking Mr Man, aren't you?'

As I laid our purchases on the conveyor belt, she said to me, 'I bet you were looking for the bottled water, but soon as we get a new shipment, we sell out again.'

'I got some before today,' I said, though in fact I had planned to buy more and had uneasily taken note of the empty shelves. But I'd been most intent on stocking up on paper plates and cups, now that all of ours were boxed, and I'd succeeded in finding these.

'You know what?' The woman leaned toward me, as if confiding. 'I figure when my time is up, my time is up. It's not for me to question the good Lord's plan. Now, I live alone, so I've got no one but myself to worry about. My youngest baby is twenty-eight years old. If I had a little one under my roof, sure, I'd buy some bottled water. Sure I would.'

I had to pass her my credit card after I'd run it through the machine, and she looked at the front of it, then at me; this might have been the first time she was really taking in my face. And then she made that whistling noise people make when they're impressed, though not necessarily by something good. She said, 'Girl, if you aren't the spitting image of that psychic!'

After Target, we stopped by the Galleria, where I bought sneakers – even if the earthquake didn't occur, and I didn't need to walk across a broken city while pushing a stroller, my old pair had gotten worn out – and the fountain on the Galleria's first floor delighted Owen. By the time we left, it was a few minutes after noon and I was craving a hamburger. In the parking lot, I looked at Owen in the rearview mirror; he'd pulled a sock-clad foot up to his mouth and was sucking away. I leaned into the backseat and removed his sock – if he was going to suck his toes, he might as well enjoy them without a barrier – and I said, 'Should we go out for a lunch date, then home for a nap? Is that a good plan for Mommy and Owen?'

I decided we'd head to Blueberry Hill, a St Louis landmark where an eighty-something-year-old Chuck Berry still performed regularly, though I'd never been to see him until Jeremy bought tickets for us shortly after we started dating. I carried Owen inside in his car seat; he still wasn't quite big enough for a restaurant high chair. 'Seat yourself,' a bartender in the front told me, and I turned right, into a large room with booths, tables and chairs, arcade video games, a pinball machine, and lots of music paraphernalia – framed concert posters and albums and covers of *Rolling Stone* – plus random knickknacks like *Simpsons* figurines and lava lamps. I slid Owen's car seat across the bench in an empty booth and sat down next to him. When the waiter brought water, I said, 'I already know what I want: a hamburger cooked medium.' I paused. 'And fries.' After a second pause, I said, 'And what kind of beer do you have on tap?'

'We've got an Oktoberfest that's kind of malty and—'

'Perfect,' I said.

'Lettuce, tomato, or onions?'

'Yes,' I said. 'All of them.'

When the waiter was gone, I groped under the table, where I'd set the diaper bag, and found Owen's orange star rattle. I had just given it to him when I felt a hand on my back, and I turned and discovered that Jeremy was standing next to the booth and that Courtney Wheeling was standing beside him.

'Kate?' Jeremy seemed surprised but genuinely pleased to see me. He leaned in to kiss my forehead, then kissed Owen's as well. 'When we walked in, I thought, Wow, that baby looks like Owen,' he said. 'And then I was like, And that woman is wearing Kate's vest.' Jeremy and Courtney were dressed professionally: Jeremy in a jacket and tie and Courtney in a pantsuit. 'Can we join you?' He gestured to the bench opposite Owen and me, and then, just before Jeremy slid in, he exchanged a look with Courtney in which I could have sworn he was apologizing to her. *Are you fucking kidding me?* I thought. Was the apology because I was Vi's sister or because of the tension during our pizza dinner? Or was it because now, with me present, they wouldn't be able to talk about, say, lunar radar altimetry and instead would have to discuss potty training?

'Don't tell me Hank's about to walk in with Rosie and Amelia,' Courtney said. Her tone was warm, as if this possibility would delight her, but I didn't trust her. In fact, although this wasn't fair of me, just a week after her abortion, I found her normalness, even cheerfulness, jarring.

I said, 'Not that I know of. Rosie's actually with a sitter.'

Jeremy nodded toward Owen. 'Why isn't he?'

A lie presented itself, and I seized it. 'He was fussing when I was about to leave, but I knew he'd calm down in the car.'

'You decided not to get a manicure?' Jeremy seemed disappointed.

'I needed to run errands,' I said.

Jeremy made a mock-scolding face at Owen, waving his index finger. 'This is supposed to be Mama's downtime, O. This isn't *your* time with her.' With the handle of the rattle jammed in his mouth, Owen beamed. 'Pass him over here,' Jeremy said. Though I'd been considering saying that I was finished eating – if I'd thought I could get away with changing my order to takeout and secretly waiting for it up at the bar, I would have – I went ahead and unbuckled Owen, pulled him from the car seat, and handed him across the table.

This was when the waiter materialized, carrying my rather large glass of beer. An expression of alarm flashed across Jeremy's face, an expression he took care to eliminate before saying in a neutral tone, 'What kind is that?'

I hadn't yet taken a sip, but I nudged the glass toward him. 'An Oktoberfest special. Want to try it?'

As Jeremy took a sip, Courtney said, 'God, that looks good,' and he passed it on to her, an act that somehow contained the intimacy of their sharing a glass rather than her drinking from mine. After she'd swallowed, she said to the waiter, 'I'll take one, too.'

'Then make it three,' Jeremy said. 'I can't be outdrunk by two girls, can I?'

The waiter took their food order – a chicken sandwich for Jeremy and red beans and rice for Courtney, the virtuous vegetarian – and after he had left again, Courtney said good-naturedly to Jeremy, 'Did you really just call Kate and me girls? I think that was the most sexist thing I've ever heard you say.'

Jeremy laughed, and I felt a strong desire for him not to apologize to Courtney. Not that he necessarily was going to, but before he could, I said, 'So do you guys come here a lot?'

They both laughed before looking at each

other – I then felt an antipathy for Courtney so intense that it was hard not to believe it hadn't been there all along – and Jeremy said, 'That sounded like the classic pick-up line. You come here often? I guess I've been a couple times with Schwartz and Marcus, but we've never been together, have we?' He glanced at Courtney, lowering his eyebrows as if trying to recall information, and I thought, *Stop looking at each other!*

My plea worked, or at least Jeremy turned back toward me. He said, 'So what errands were you running?'

I'd once read an article about a study showing that the stereotype of men not liking to date or marry smart women was false; men were fine dating and marrying smart women, just as long as the men were smarter. *She can have her master's,* the article had said, *as long as he has his PhD.* And maybe I was flattering myself that I was, by anyone's definition, smart – after all, I'd never earned a master's – but the article had made me uncomfortable. Because was this what I was in Jeremy's eyes: his sweet, tedious wife, with whom he had conversations about what had been on sale at Target? And then I wondered, was part of the reason Jeremy was insisting on going to Denver so that he could spend time there with Courtney?

I had never been gripped by such insecurity. I said, 'Well, we just came from the mall, but I'll spare you the boring details. Owen was really into the fountain.'

'I hope not literally,' Jeremy said.

'Wait, you think it was irresponsible of me to let him go swimming?'

Jeremy laughed politely, and Courtney said, 'Speaking of which, I think I've convinced Hank that we should go to Hawaii for Thanksgiving.' Looking at me, she said, 'To a resort where Julia Roberts supposedly stayed with her family. Ooh la la.'

The salient piece of information here seemed to be that the Wheelings wouldn't be celebrating Thanksgiving at our house, though they had for the last two years. And it wasn't that I'd have hoped they would, if I'd thought about it, but there was a kind of double snub from Courtney in not acknowledging that we'd shared the holiday in the past.

'You get your own cottage with a kitchen, so you don't have to eat every meal out,' she was saying. 'And they give surf lessons right on the hotel beach. Fun, right?'

'I guess if you go for that kind of thing,' Jeremy said. 'We prefer the glamour of November in Missouri, right, Kate?' At that moment, my exciting and embarrassing burger and fries arrived.

'Go ahead and start,' Jeremy said. 'I'll give O back to you when mine comes.'

The waiter brought their meals a few minutes later, but Jeremy kept holding Owen, even when I offered to put him in the car seat; Jeremy took me up on the offer only after I'd finished. Somehow, the food made things normal, or normal-ish, among us. Yes, I no longer liked Courtney, and yes, she and Jeremy were sitting on the same side of the booth together, even though I was married to Jeremy and Courtney wasn't, but our conversation stopped seeming quite as fraught and off-kilter. By unspoken agreement, none of us mentioned Vi or her prediction – not that I was in the mood to defend Vi anyway, given how she'd stormed out of our house the day before.

Eventually, Owen, bless his heart, really did begin to fuss, and I was able to leave without it seeming weird. I didn't pay first, because Jeremy would cover my portion. 'Tell Hank I say hi,' Courtney called as I carried Owen's car seat out.

At home, I took Owen right up to his room, nursed him, and put him down, then returned to the living room to pay Kendra before she left. Rosie walked with us to the front door and grabbed at Kendra's hand. 'Kendra wants to stay,' she said.

'Kendra *does* want to stay,' Kendra said. 'But I have to go to class, and I think it's time for you to take a nap. Will you let me come back next week?'

By which point an earthquake would or wouldn't have happened, I thought. By which point was it unrealistic to hope that regular life might have returned? As a child, when Christmas or my birthday – our birthday – was approaching, I'd note the expiration dates on cottage cheese containers or cartons of orange juice and feel excitement if the date fell after the one I was anticipating. I experienced a darker version of this urgency as I closed the door behind Kendra: *Let these days pass quickly. Please, please, just let them pass.*

After I'd wrestled Rosie into letting me apply Neosporin, then put her down for her nap, our home phone rang, and when I saw that it was Jeremy, I simultaneously felt relief and a gamey, adolescent temptation not to pick up. But then what? I'd want to talk to him in an hour, and he'd be teaching.

'I know that was weird,' he said when I answered. 'But it wasn't weird for the reason you think it was.'

'What's the reason I think?'

'Well, Courtney and I aren't having an affair,' he said, and honestly, tears pooled in my eyes – idiotic tears, because Jeremy was so nice and I was so ridiculous – and he added, 'Kate, if I ever cheat on you, I won't be sneaking away to Blueberry Hill for my adulterous lunches.' In a more serious tone, he said, 'When we ran into you, Courtney had just told me about her abortion. As in, about a second before I saw you. She even asked me if I knew, if Hank had told you, and I lied and said no, which felt really fucked up. And then we see you and Owen and – well, you know the rest. It was awkward all around, but it had nothing to do with you.'

I did feel assuaged; in fact, I felt humiliated by

my lack of trust in Jeremy. 'How did she seem about the whole thing?' I asked.

'We barely ended up talking about it. She brought it up a little after you left, just saying it's been a rough few weeks, but she didn't say much.'

'I'm starting to think Courtney's more like a man than a woman,' I said. 'The way she keeps her feelings to herself.'

Jeremy didn't reply immediately, and I wondered if he was checking his email, but when he spoke again, I knew he wasn't. He said, 'I don't like it that she doesn't know Hank told you. If he eventually does tell her, she'll realize I was lying today. But more than that, what's he doing confiding in you and withholding information from his own wife?'

Was Jeremy subject to the same spasms of jealousy about my friendship with Hank that I was to his friendship with Courtney? This dynamic had always seemed so obvious and expected – so retro, even – that I think we'd all imagined it was beneath us. But now that it turned out it wasn't, was it pathetic that I found Jeremy's jealousy, if that's what it was, reassuring and flattering?

'Maybe he's scared of her,' I said.

'Of Courtney?' Jeremy's tone implied that the suggestion was silly.

'I'm kind of scared of her,' I said, and he laughed.

'No, you're not. How's Rosie?'

'They're both sleeping.'

There was a pause, and I knew Jeremy was about

to turn back to his work. Beyond the general sense I had of him teaching, meeting with students and colleagues, and dipping into his own research when he could, his days were mysterious to me, though in some ways my own days were mysterious to me, too; in the late afternoon or evening, I often struggled to recall how it was I'd spent the time. I said, 'In case you're wondering, I don't usually drink beer for lunch.'

'I was a little surprised.' His voice was mild; he wouldn't have asked if I hadn't brought it up.

'It was an impulse order. I think the last time I had beer before five P.M. was tailgating in college.'

'Kate, the hard-partying sorority sister – it kills me I never got to meet her.'

'I wasn't that hard-partying,' I said. 'You didn't miss much.' Then I said, 'See you when you get home.'

'I love you, Greenie,' Jeremy said, and I said, 'I love you, too.'

The knock on the door came around eight forty-five, when Jeremy and I were finished with our ice cream but still watching TV. We looked at each other quizzically, and I said, 'If it's a reporter, maybe we should call the police.' I'd have preferred for Jeremy not even to check who it was, but we were right there in the living room, with the lights and television on.

He got up, opened the door just a little, and said, 'Can I help you?' I could tell that he didn't know who it was but also didn't consider the person threatening.

'Sorry to bother you,' a female voice said. 'I'm here to see Daisy. I didn't know – I know you have kids, so I thought maybe after they went to bed was a better time—'

'Does my wife know you?' Jeremy asked. This – *my wife* – was his way of handling the Daisy-Kate confusion. He never called me Daisy.

I went to the door myself and said, 'Hi, Marisa.'

'Sorry,' she said. 'I just – I couldn't find your phone number, and I didn't know when you'd be around, and who knows what will happen Friday, so I thought it would be better if I came before. How's your little girl?'

'She's fine.' I was incapable of sounding as distant, as coolly neutral, as Jeremy, though of course Marisa was a stranger to him. She'd never held power over him, not in middle school or at any other time. And it was so clear that Marisa wanted to enter our house, that she wanted *something,* which gave her an air of neediness. 'Would you like to come in?' I heard myself say. To Jeremy, I said, 'This is Marisa Mazarelli. We went to school together.' To Marisa, I said, 'My husband, Jeremy.'

She sat in the armchair, and Jeremy and I returned to sitting side by side on the couch. She was wearing another professional outfit: shiny brown pants, a sheer white blouse, and a brown jacket. She took the jacket off, folding it in her lap, and I saw that her blouse was sleeveless and her upper arms were very skinny. She gestured toward our frozen TV screen and said, 'I won't keep you. It's just, yesterday, seeing you in the park, it was like fate. Because you know that guy I was with?'

I nodded.

'That's Ryan. And it's on-again, off-again, on-again, off-again – it's been seven years. We've been this close to getting engaged—' She held her thumb and index finger a few centimeters apart. 'I mean, he has the ring. He keeps it in his sock drawer, which is basically an invitation for me to find it. Hello, I'm not an idiot! And there was this time we'd more or less decided to get engaged, we were going on vacation to Miami, but we got in a big fight there, and the whole trip was a disaster. And that was two years ago.'

Was she waiting for me to speak, or was there more? Next to me, I could feel in Jeremy a vague amusement.

'We don't live together,' Marisa added. 'Our places are around the corner from each other, but a long time ago, I was like, I'm not taking it to the next level unless there's a ring on my finger. Why would he pay for the cow and all that, but look where it's gotten me.'

This time, she was obviously expecting me to speak. I said, 'That sounds hard.'

'I'm just wondering, *is* he going to propose? Ever? Or is he stringing me along?'

I felt foolish that it had taken me until this

moment to understand where she was headed. 'Oh, I don't do that anymore,' I said. 'I can't. I haven't been able to for – a while.' The quality of Jeremy's attention was shifting; he was watching me with an interest he'd been unable to muster for Marisa, and he must have assumed I was lying.

'I'm not saying, like, how many children will we have or will they be boys or girls.' Marisa laughed in a bitter way. 'Just, do I stick it out with him or do I give up? Because after seven years – I was twenty-eight when we started going out, and I'll be thirty-five in April. And for a woman, thirty-five's a major cutoff.'

'It's not that I don't want to help you,' I said. 'I really can't. Vi is the one who still does this, but I don't.' Would it be karmic justice for Marisa to have to pay Vi for her insights, or was it unfair to inflict Marisa on Vi even when I was mad at my sister? It was possible, I thought, that Vi would find it more gratifying than I did to encounter this pleading, needy version of Marisa. I added, 'But if you get in touch with her, you should wait until after this Friday.'

'Are you kidding?' Marisa said. 'We're getting the hell out of town tomorrow. Aren't you?'

She was actually the first person I knew who was leaving St Louis because of Vi's prediction, and although it felt like her plans ought to have been proof of something to Jeremy, he wouldn't see it that way. 'No,' I said. 'I don't think we are.'

'But what if you and your kids get trapped under rubble? Aren't you scared?'

'We're taking precautions,' I said.

'Why don't you ask Ryan about getting married?' Jeremy said then. 'Ask him what you're asking us.' Even if he was only trying to change the subject, there was something decidedly surreal about my kind, sensible, good-looking husband giving romantic advice to my adolescent nemesis. Jeremy added, 'Be clear about what you want, and if Ryan doesn't want the same thing, dump him. Plenty of people get married after the age of thirty-five.' He patted my thigh. 'I was thirty-four, and look how lucky I got.'

Marisa squinted at Jeremy. Was she noticing that my husband was good-looking, or was she too mired in her own self-absorption? She said, 'I bet you're not from St Louis.'

'Northern Virginia,' Jeremy said.

'Yeah, see, if you're from somewhere else, that's why you think thirty-five isn't old. But for here, it is. Trust me.' She turned back to me. 'I don't understand how you can just not be psychic anymore. Isn't that like losing your sense of smell?'

I shook my head. 'Yeah, I'm not sure why.' If she thought I was going to explain, let alone apologize, she was mistaken.

She glanced around the living room, and I could feel her energy adjusting itself. She hadn't gotten what she wanted, and we weren't being solicitous enough that she'd feel welcome just to settle in and chat, or at least I hoped she wouldn't. 'You took stuff off your walls, huh?' she said. 'I'm really surprised that you're not leaving town.' And it was only then, after it became apparent that it wouldn't happen, that I realized I'd been expecting an apology from her. I would have accepted it graciously, unfussily; I wouldn't have made her grovel. *I'm sorry I was such an awful person when we were growing up,* she'd have said, and I'd have said, *Don't worry. It was a long time ago.*

'We'll be fine,' Jeremy said.

Marisa was standing, pulling on her jacket over her skinny arms, lifting her hair around the jacket's collar. She looked at me. 'You should move back to Kirkwood. It's such a good place to raise kids.' Then she withdrew a phone from her black leather purse and said, 'Tell me your number and I'll text you mine, so if anything pops into your head, you can reach me.'

She was loathsome; she was just as unrepentant, just as much of a user, as she'd always been. And of course I gave her my number – the number for my cellphone, which somehow seemed like it would limit her ability to infiltrate my family's life more than giving her our home number would. I never wanted her to come back. If she did, I would think of a way to prevent her from walking inside.

After I closed the door behind her, Jeremy said, 'Wow.'

'Wow that she's leaving town or wow about the boyfriend?'

'The smartest thing poor Ryan can do is run really far and really fast in the other direction.'

So Jeremy preferred not to discuss the fact that Marisa was heeding Vi's warning; he would have if I'd forced the subject, but I wasn't going to. I wasn't leaving it alone because it didn't bother me, however. I was leaving it alone because hearing about what a rotten couple Marisa and Ryan were, I wanted us to be better. At the least, I wanted us not to be experiencing discord currently. And so I said, 'In her defense, two years of the ring in the sock drawer has to be a mindfuck.'

'That's what she gets for being a snoop,' Jeremy said. I had walked from the door back to the couch, where he was still sitting, and he pulled me onto his lap. 'You know what her punishment is for tormenting you way back when?' he said.

I looked at him.

He said, 'Her punishment is being her.'

But then things unraveled between Jeremy and me; they unraveled the next morning. Rosie refused to eat the oatmeal Jeremy had fixed, and she was still at the table when I came downstairs. When I entered the kitchen, she said, 'Rosie gets up with Mama.'

'She's had about two bites,' Jeremy said. Owen was on the kitchen floor banging a spatula against the linoleum squares.

I took a seat beside Rosie and, after much wheedling, got her to eat half the bowl; I was the one

389

holding the spoon, which I was fairly sure I shouldn't still have been doing for an almost-three-year-old. Then I wolfed down a banana, washed my hands, and when I reached for the Neosporin, which I'd been keeping on top of the refrigerator, Rosie screamed, 'No medicine! No Rosie medicine!'

'It helps keep your boo-boo clean. Mama will just put on a little.'

'No medicine!'

She was twisting away, pushing at me when I tried to get closer, and I said to Jeremy, 'Can you hold her arms?' This was how we'd done it the night before.

He did, and I gripped her chin with one hand and dabbed on the antibiotic while she continued to flail her head. When I finished, she was sobbing. I lifted her from her booster seat, and she clung to me as I carried her into the living room. Jeremy followed us with Owen, and after he'd set Owen on the floor by the shelf, Jeremy said, 'Okay if I go pack?'

'Hold on.' I hadn't planned to say it; I just did. 'I don't want you to go to Denver.'

Jeremy's expression was sympathetic. 'I know you don't.'

'No,' I said. 'I mean, please don't go. Fine if you never believed I'm psychic, but' – here my words turned into sobs – 'but I need you to stay. I need you here.'

'What's Mama saying?' Rosie said, and I sniffed and blinked, trying to straighten out my crumpled face.

'We're talking about Daddy's job,' I said.

Jeremy perched on the arm of the chair and said, 'Let's break this down. What are your specific concerns? Because I think we can work around them.'

'My concern is that we have two young children, and I'm worried about their safety.'

'No, I know you are. And let's face it, it's challenging enough to take care of them on a good day with both of us here. But what if we get your dad to come in for a couple hours each morning, Kendra comes in a couple hours at night – or you could have your dad sleep here, give him our bed, and you sleep downstairs, if you just want another adult in the house.'

'Jeremy, I want *you* here! You're my husband.' I was probably terrifying Rosie, and possibly Owen, too. I said, 'My dad would be a burden as much as a help, and you know it. He'll give Owen pennies to play with.'

Jeremy looked genuinely pained. 'This whole situation sucks,' he said. 'Don't think that I don't realize how hard it's been for you.' At some point in graduate school or as a new professor, had Jeremy been required to take a seminar on negotiating? Because that's what it felt like, like he was very diplomatically preparing me not to get what I wanted from him. And sure enough, he added, 'But I can't skip this conference just because we have young kids.'

'I don't see why not,' I said. 'I did quit my job to take care of them.'

His expression became incrementally less sympathetic. 'Voluntarily,' he said.

'Because I thought it was in the best interest of our family.'

'Well, I guarantee that putting my job at risk isn't in our family's best interest.'

'Give me a break, Jeremy. Even if you didn't have tenure, skipping one conference would *not* be putting your job at risk. And everyone knows conferences are mostly schmoozing in the hotel bar.'

Jeremy's jaw had tightened. 'Which can have a direct effect on things like what journals you get published in. It's all interconnected.'

At this moment, I became aware of the smell of shit – actual shit, not conversational bullshit – and I said to Rosie, whom I was still holding, 'Is that you?' I pulled back the waistbands of her pants and diaper, and it was her. I said to Jeremy, 'I know you think I don't understand the intricacies of academia, but either you'll fly to Denver today or you won't. What I'm telling you is that I really, really, really don't want you to.'

'Will the locks be changed when I come back?' He smiled a little.

'I'm glad you find this funny.' And yet I was starkly aware that I had nothing with which to threaten him. How and when had I arrived at this point of powerlessness in my marriage? Short of invoking divorce, which even in my current mood I recognized as insane, what leverage did I have?

There was my anger, yes, but Jeremy was making it clear that he could tolerate that just fine.

Rosie and I were halfway up the stairs when he said, in a voice that contained no humor at all, 'You know what, Kate? A part of me doesn't want to go, either. And you know what else? If I cancel at the last minute, and if there's any hint that I did it because of your sister's prediction, then I might as well leave Wash U. I'll lose all credibility in the scientific community.'

I stopped on a step, shifting Rosie against my hip. 'Is that what this is about? Your professional pride?' Wasn't part of Jeremy being Jeremy that petty gossip didn't bother him? It bothered me, but not him.

He said, 'Remember when you asked if people know that Vi is my sister-in-law? Well, they do. And I've tried to protect you from this, but, yeah, it *is* awkward. Because as much as the media treats this as a complex issue with two viewpoints – maybe it's possible to predict earthquakes, maybe it's not – there's nobody, *nobody,* who's a scientist who thinks anything other than that Vi's premonition is a total sham. If I don't go to Denver, everyone I know will be talking about me. I need to show that I'm still myself, nothing has changed, and the coincidence of me being related to Vi is just that – a coincidence.'

So I did, in the end, embarrass Jeremy; instead of him lifting me toward a happier, more financially secure, less freakish existence, I'd pulled him down with me. This was heartbreaking; it elicited my sympathy in a way no other argument he'd made for traveling to Denver had. But I still didn't want him to go.

'So how about this?' he said. 'I'll have my phone on me all the time, and when I see that it's you, I'll stop whatever I'm doing to answer, even if I'm in the middle of delivering my own paper.'

'Jeremy, it doesn't matter if you take your phone with you,' I said. 'What will you be able to do from a thousand miles away?'

He didn't go to campus that day but left for the airport when the children went down for their afternoon naps; as if to rub salt in my wounds, he gave a ride to Courtney, who was on the same flight out he was, though she was returning to St Louis a day earlier than Jeremy. I'd been sorting laundry on the dining room table when he came to say goodbye after setting his wheeled suitcase by the front door. (A suitcase filled with only the belongings of an adult; because I'd never, since their births, traveled without our children, such a prospect was unthinkable. No diapers or tubes of Desitin, no tiny shirts with butterflies or trucks on them, no copies of *Goodnight Moon*.)

Jeremy stood next to me, and I couldn't look at him.

'I'm sorry that everything is so screwed up right now,' he said.

I folded a pair of Rosie's polka-dotted pants and said nothing.

'Sweetheart,' Jeremy said.

I finally looked up.

'It'll all be fine,' he said. 'Call whenever you want, I'll be home Sunday, and we'll put this behind us. Think of what we have to look forward to, like Owen dressed as a carrot.' This was what Rosie had decreed Owen should be for Halloween, though we didn't yet have costumes for either of them.

Jeremy hugged me, and I put my arms around him in return, but loosely. Maybe this wasn't really the reason why, but it seemed like if I held him tight, it would just make it harder to let him go.

CHAPTER 15

My sister came to the hospital a few hours after Rosie was born, and the first thing Vi said was 'She doesn't look very Chinese.' Then she grinned. 'No, she's adorable. She's perfect. Did you poop on the table?'

Jeremy had gone downstairs to the cafeteria, and I was sitting up in bed in a gown, holding Rosie, who was wearing a diaper, a little cap, and a duck-covered blanket that kept slipping off her. At seven pounds even, she was unimaginably tiny – her nose was tiny and her ears were tiny and her arms and legs were tiny and her fingers were tiny and her fingernails were shockingly tiny; her butt had been tiny when I'd watched Jeremy change her diaper as she lay in the plastic bassinette. She had inter-mittent swirls of hair that was dark like Jeremy's, and dark blue eyes with creases under them, as if emerging into the world had exhausted her, and there was some sort of womb crust on her fore-head that the nurses hadn't cleaned completely. And also – Vi was right – she was perfect.

'I pooped, but it's true what everyone says. I was too out of my mind to care.'

'I totally knew you were having a baby last night. I was playing pool with Patrick and all of a sudden, I was like, yep, it's started. I almost called, but I didn't want to interrupt a contraction.'

'Well, my water broke at midnight,' I said. 'And we came to the hospital around three A.M., and she was born right before eleven.'

'Wow, you had an easy delivery. Jack's wife was in labor for thirty-three hours.' Jack was the manager at the Italian restaurant where Vi no longer worked. 'Can I hold her?'

'Will you wash your hands?' I said. 'Or use that dispenser on the wall?'

Vi squirted out some antibacterial gel, rubbed her hands together – for a not entirely satisfying length of time – and extended her arms. 'Come to Auntie Vi,' she said.

'Be careful of her neck,' I said as I eased Rosie toward her.

'You think I've never held a baby before?' Vi scrunched up her nose. 'Wait. *Have* I ever held a baby?' She stood there with Rosie's head against the inside of her elbow and swayed. 'I have the touch,' Vi said. 'She just closed her eyes. So did you get an epidural?'

I shook my head.

Vi held up her free hand. 'High five, girlfriend. I was sure you'd cave and ask for drugs.'

'You know those golf shoes with spikes on them? I felt like someone was wearing those and jumping on top of my vagina.'

She laughed. 'At least you only had one baby, huh?'

Her 'easy delivery' remark had rubbed me the wrong way, and then the high five had mollified me slightly, and then her remark about expecting me to cave had rubbed me the wrong way again, and then the opportunity to say how painful the delivery had been had mollified me again. The allusion to our own birth was neutral – on the one hand, Vi was minimizing what I'd just been through, but on the other hand, I, too, had been thinking about our mother. Her experience giving birth to us had been a major factor in my wish not to have an epidural.

I said, 'Is it weird we're giving the baby a flower name? She was going to be Sophie, but I was holding her right after she was born, and I had a change of heart.' Jeremy had been surprised but amenable; he'd actually suggested the name Rosie months earlier and I'd nixed it *because* it was a flower name.

Vi looked down at Rosie. 'It fits her. And *Rosie* isn't as – whatever it is you thought *Daisy* was. As hippie chick–ish.'

'You don't think we should name her Rita, do you?'

'Because all it would take to undo everything that was messed up about Mom would be to name your child after her? No. You shouldn't.' Vi was still looking at Rosie as she said, 'How weird is it that you have a kid? I always knew you would, but—'

'I know. It's surreal.'

'She didn't even used to exist and someday she'll have a favorite color. She'll eat pancakes. Did Jeremy cut the cord?'

'He decided to leave it to the professionals.'

'But he's a doctor.' Vi said this in the mocking way she sometimes invoked Jeremy's PhD, though he never identified himself as Dr Tucker; he had his students call him Professor Tucker. She'd say, *Jeremy, feel my pulse. Take my temperature. Oh, wait.*

'I have to show you something,' I said. 'Give me Rosie, and go in the bathroom and look in that plastic bag by the sink.'

After my daughter (my daughter!) was back in my arms, I heard Vi whoop with delight from the bathroom. She reentered my room holding up with both hands a pair of the white mesh underwear a nurse had given me a pack of after the delivery; they were so enormous that they resembled shorts. 'These are awesome,' Vi said.

'I knew you'd appreciate them.'

'Are you wearing some right now?'

'And a maxi pad that's about a foot long.'

'Can I keep this pair?' Vi was dangling the underwear off the tip of her index finger and twirling them. 'Patrick will fucking freak when he sees these.'

There was a knock on the door, and the nurse who'd started at three o'clock walked into the room. 'Baby last nursed at two-thirty, right?' she said to me. 'So let's give it another go. You need any ibuprofen?'

'Not right now.' They had me breast-feeding every hour, even though my milk hadn't yet come in and even though no matter what position I maneuvered myself or Rosie into, it didn't seem like the right one.

'Will you wait in the hall?' I said to Vi.

'Wow,' Vi said. 'Still a prude, even after childbirth.' She gathered up her purse and the cape she now wore instead of a coat, a fashion choice that had coincided with the ascent of her new career. 'I'm going to go find Jeremy so we can smoke cigars. Oh, I almost forgot Rosie's present.' From the purse, Vi withdrew a small cardboard box. Rosie was nestled against my chest, and I said, 'You open it.'

After Vi had pulled off the tape, she lifted out a layer of white tissue paper and then a small pale blue pear-shaped bottle with a clear crystal stopper. Holding it up, she said proudly, 'It's an antique perfume holder.'

Of course it was an antique perfume holder; I had to bite my lip to keep from smiling. Two months before, my friend Janet had thrown me a baby shower, for which Jeremy's mother and sister-in-law had flown to St Louis and at which I'd had bestowed on me onesies and bibs and stuffed animals, a baby carrier and a mobile and a special trash can just for diapers. Vi had forgotten to show up. It had crossed my mind that she either consciously or subconsciously wasn't pleased that I was pregnant, but I was fairly sure the shower had just slipped her mind; it was on a Saturday at eleven in the morning, when she wasn't necessarily awake. Afterward, she'd been determined to make it up to me. A few nights later, Jeremy worked late and she brought over pickles and ice cream, neither of which I was craving, as well as a DVD about natural childbirth that a friend had loaned her. After the first birth, Vi said, 'I'm sorry, but that's the grossest thing I've ever seen. Can we watch *Project Runway*?'

In the hospital room, the perfume holder caught the dim January light coming in the window.

'It's really pretty,' I said. 'Thank you.'

'But wait for the best part.' She turned the bottle around, and I saw that across its widest surface was painted a white-and-pink rose. To the nurse, Vi said, 'And I didn't even know what my sister was naming her baby.'

'How about that?' said the nurse. 'You're psychic.'

There was, of course, that blur of early days and nights after we'd brought Rosie home, a tiredness deeper than any I'd ever known, the endless cycle of nursing her and burping her and changing her, of all three of us slipping into a desperate kind of sleep before resuming the cycle. But slowly, a kind of schedule asserted itself; the exhausted confusion cleared. Rosie ate every three hours. Each morning, an hour after nursing her, I sat at the dining room table and pumped milk that I'd then transfer into freezer bags in preparation for when I'd return to my job at the elder-care agency and Rosie would enter day care. I hated the pump, the whirring nipple-yanking tugs that made me not simply feel like a cow but gave me new sympathy for cows themselves, and I forbade Jeremy to enter the room while I used it.

Rosie began to look back at us when we looked at her, began to smile, began to sleep for longer stretches; she developed a particular affinity for a little stuffed cat and would suck joyfully on its left ear. At twelve weeks, we moved her from a bassinet in our room to her own room, which made me uneasy, but Jeremy reminded me that all the books said moving her would only get harder as she grew older. 'For me or for her?' I said and he said, 'Aren't you guys still kind of the same?' Which he meant as a joke, but it was how I felt – that once Vi and I had been a single person split apart, and now my daughter and I were. With her in the stroller, Rosie and I took long walks north on DeMun and west on Wydown, up and down the fancy streets with the old, big houses and tall trees, and though I purposely didn't go onto the street where Mrs Abbott had lived, passing the entrance to it always filled me with gratitude that I was no longer in my twenties and miserable. (In the summer of 2001, I had awakened one morning and known Mrs Abbott was dead; I waited a week, then found her obituary online. She had been born in Bristol, Connecticut, I learned, and her maiden name had been Spaeth.)

When Rosie and I drove to Schnucks, in the parking lot I carefully lifted her from her car seat and inserted her into the baby carrier, her chest facing mine because she was still so little. Inside, she'd turn her head to see the apples or cereal boxes. When the other customers or the checkout woman would remark on her cuteness, I'd smile modestly, as if I didn't secretly consider their compliments insufficient. If she fell asleep on the ride home, I would sit in our driveway with the car in Park and the engine on and the air conditioner running, the ozone layer be damned – this was in April or May – and as I waited for her to awaken, I'd do absolutely nothing because I didn't yet have a cellphone with Internet access, didn't want to disturb her by talking on the phone, and usually wouldn't have remembered to bring along a book in her diaper bag. I'd look in the rearview mirror at the street behind me, the green leaves on a ginkgo tree and the cars passing, and I'd feel not bored or impatient but rather, as I observed her (her car seat faced backward, with her own mirror reflecting her closed eyes and tilted head into my mirror), as if, in watching her sleep, I was making a deposit in the bank account of her well-being. This was how I felt when she nursed, too, when I also wasn't bored despite the fact that, unlike other mothers I knew, I never read or watched television while doing it. But perhaps it was not the magic of motherhood that I was experiencing in these moments; perhaps I just had a greater capacity for inertia than I'd ever realized.

I had prepared myself for the tedium of life with a baby, warned about it by co-workers and friends and countless movies and sitcoms, but I'd experienced much in my adult life that was more tedious: office meetings and office paperwork and wedding toasts and the wait at the mechanic's while my oil was changed. Rosie was not tedious to me; rather, she was my own tiny and charming companion. It wasn't that I endlessly tried to amuse or edify her. I just brought her along when I did things, in and out of the house, and her skin was very soft and her expressions were sweet and she was a real person, a miniature person who clearly adored me, and I adored her in return.

And then she was sixteen weeks old, and it was time for me to return to work at the elder-care agency and for Rosie to go to the day care Jeremy and I had picked out when I was still pregnant. Rosie would be entering the Zucchini Room of a medium-sized place on Hanley Road, and I accompanied her for a half day on the Friday before she started. This time, I noticed things I hadn't when Jeremy and I had visited months before: how runny the other babies' noses were and how chewed-on the toys looked, plus could two teachers really look after eight babies when it took all my energy and attention to look after one? But the kids seemed mostly happy, and the adults were warm. Jeremy would take Rosie on Monday, we decided, so that I wouldn't bawl.

After going to sleep on Sunday night, I awoke around three from a dream in which Rosie was in a prison cell; she was crying, reaching for me, from behind bars. I got out of bed and hurried to her room, where I found her asleep on her back, breathing evenly. My heartbeat slowed as I watched her in the dark. Eventually, I went back to bed.

In the morning, when I tried to describe the dream to Jeremy, he smiled. I was changing Rosie's diaper while Jeremy stood nearby. 'Are you a baby bandit, Rosie?' he said. He touched my shoulder. 'It's natural that you're feeling nervous.'

But in some ways, it was easier being back at work than I'd expected: The schedule and the rooms were familiar; talking to other adults, having conversations, consumed my attention. There was a routine I could slip into, that could carry me along, and there was the shocking weightlessness of being responsible only for myself. Except when I closed the door of my office and taped paper over the rectangular window to pump, my body belonged to me. But when Rosie came into my mind, I'd feel a lurching worry. What if one of the teachers dropped her?

Meeting with a diabetic eighty-six-year-old and his sixty-five-year-old daughter, I kept looking at the clock above my bulletin board, waiting for the minutes to pass until I could walk out to the parking lot, get into my car, and drive to pick up Rosie.

As the weeks passed, my uneasiness waxed and waned. 'She had a good day,' Miss Helen would often say when I picked Rosie up. Rosie's clothes smelled like the teachers, which wasn't to say the teachers smelled bad – just that there was no denying Rosie had been elsewhere.

I started putting her in leather booties with a smiling teddy bear over the toes. She didn't need shoes, in that she was many months away from walking. But her socks always fell off, and then she was barefoot, and how could I endure my tiny daughter being out in the world without me, barefoot? Every morning, I'd pull the shoes over her feet before securing her in the car seat so Jeremy could carry her away.

On Jeremy's side, Rosie wasn't the first grandchild, and while Jeremy's parents and stepparents were pleased for us, they weren't that brand of grandparent who can't get enough of the new baby or who while visiting does laundry and cleans the kitchen; even if they hadn't lived several states away, I don't think they'd have been that kind of grandparent. They were happy to come see us, to hold Rosie and eat a few meals, and then to fly out again.

Carol and Ned, Jeremy's mother and stepfather, visited the week after Rosie's birth, and when Rosie was five months old, Carol had a meeting in

Chicago and decided to add an overnight trip to St Louis. My mother-in-law was a petite woman with salt-and-pepper hair; when dressed formally, as for her job as an attorney, she wore black and beige and maroon, classically tailored slacks and jackets and turtleneck sweaters that, I'd realized over time, were quite expensive. When dressed informally, she wore jeans and suede driving shoes. Every morning, she swam two miles at a gym, and once a year, she and Jeremy's stepfather, who was also a lawyer, took a ten-day vacation to somewhere sporty and international: Australia, say, or Kenya. I liked Carol, and I knew I could do much worse in the mother-in-law department. At the same time, we weren't close. She had a brisk, sometimes preoccupied energy – she was always checking her smartphone years before everyone was always checking their smartphone – and she was fond of games I wasn't good at, like Scrabble and Trivial Pursuit. Also, she had asked me four separate times if I ever regretted not getting my master's in social work.

Carol arrived on a Friday afternoon about a month after Rosie had started day care. Jeremy met her at the airport, I picked up Rosie an hour early, and we converged at home, sitting in the living room, Jeremy and his mother drinking red wine while I drank a beer and we all made faces at Rosie. Rosie had had a cold earlier in the week and was still fussier than usual but sat happily on Carol's lap, turning the pages of a board book.

Around seven, I took Rosie up for bed. It was while changing her diaper that I noticed that her left eye seemed watery. 'Are you okay, little pumpkin?' I said. 'Are you sad?'

She looked at me somberly, but she wasn't crying. I zipped the pajamas up the front. In the glider, Rosie nursed for perhaps a minute before pulling off, and then she did begin to cry.

'What's wrong?' I said. 'Should we try again later?' I held her against me, rocking, and she calmed down, but twice in a row, when I set her in her crib, she howled. Only on the third try, after I'd held her for over ten minutes following her descent into sleep, was I able to successfully deposit her in the crib and creep away.

Jeremy and Carol had gone to pick up a pizza, and I'd been upstairs so long that they were back and already eating in the kitchen when I returned to the first floor. 'Everything okay?' Jeremy asked.

'Forgive our bad manners in starting without you,' Carol said, 'but I have exciting plans tonight that I can't be late for.'

'Plans here?' Jeremy said. 'In St Louis?'

Carol beamed as if about to divulge a juicy piece of gossip. 'I'm going to a séance.'

I understood immediately, but I could tell Jeremy didn't.

'Violet invited me, and she said her house isn't far from yours,' Carol said. 'So, Jer, if I can borrow your car—'

I tried to sound undistressed as I asked, 'When did you and Vi schedule this?'

'You never even told me what your sister does, Kate!' Carol wagged her finger at me in a mock scolding. 'And truly, my entire life, I've wanted to see a psychic. When I walk by one of those places with the neon hand in the window, I'm always dying to go in.'

Jeremy said, 'You're going to one of Vi's sessions?' *Sessions* was what Vi herself called them; she would never have said *séance*.

'I told her I absolutely want to pay the full amount, no family discounts.' Carol looked at me. 'So she doesn't undercharge me, what's her usual fee?'

'I think thirty,' I said.

'She doesn't make you pay?' Carol winked, and in the wink, I understood that she saw Vi's psychicness as unconnected to me – that she didn't assume I shared Vi's abilities, or her pretense of them. Whether Carol believed that Vi was genuinely psychic was a separate matter from whether Carol was titillated by the idea of it; for many people, I knew, the titillation lay in the unlikeliness.

Carol said, 'When I was here after Rosie was born, I said, "Violet, how's the restaurant?" Well, she told me she's been doing this for the last two years, and my jaw about dropped to the floor. I said, "Next time I'm in St Louis, you *must* let me come." She offered to do a private séance, but I think the group sounds like much more fun.'

After a silence, Jeremy said, 'I hadn't pegged you as a fan of the supernatural, Mom.'

Carol laughed lightly, catching my eye. She said, 'Our children never give us credit for being interesting, do they?'

After Carol had gone to use the bathroom Jeremy whispered, 'Sorry.' In a non-whisper that was still quiet, he added, 'I think she just sees it as a lark.'

'I'm going with her.'

He squinted at me. 'Why?' When I didn't answer, he said, 'They'll be fine. They're both grown-ups.'

'Think how easily Vi could say, "Yeah, Kate's psychic, too. Oh, she hasn't told you?" It'll change the way your mother sees me forever.'

'But not necessarily for the worse. Little did I know that my mom was so fascinated by this stuff.'

'She thinks she's fascinated, until it weirds her out.'

'So call Vi and ask her not to mention you.'

'Then she definitely will. She'll pretend it was a mistake, but I'm sure she's getting off on having been in contact with your mom without us knowing.' I heard Carol open the bathroom door, and then she was entering the kitchen, saying, 'Now, don't wait up for me because I have no idea how late I'll be.'

'Carol, if you don't mind, I'd love to go with you,' I said.

Without hesitating, Carol said, 'Fabulous. Do you think it's all right if I'm wearing jeans?'

'I'm sure it's fine.'

I went upstairs to check on Rosie, and inside her darkened room, listening to her baby snores, I thought maybe I *should* skip Vi's. The session was called for eight, and it was already a quarter to; I could feel Carol's antsiness emanating from the first floor. There was no way Vi would start on time, but Carol, who was herself unfailingly punctual, didn't know this. I really didn't want to go, I thought. I wanted to stay at home, to be in the same place as my daughter. But after a few more seconds of standing over Rosie's crib, I tiptoed out.

In the car, Carol was talkative, asking how many people would be at Vi's and who they were, and I tried to answer her questions in a way that didn't reveal that I had never attended one of the sessions. As I parked on the street, I could see, past Vi's small yard and through the lit-up front window, the living room of the house she'd bought with the down payment from our father. Beyond the candelabra on her windowsill, a dozen people stood in clusters of two or three, and hanging on the wall behind them were Vi's Tibetan prayer flags.

As Carol and I entered, the volume of voices was high, and I felt a jolting reminder of how the rest of the world carried on in the evenings while

Jeremy and I were cocooned away with Rosie. (Apparently, people still left their houses.) The folding chairs were set up in a circle in the living room, with Vi's lounger at the top of the circle, beneath the prayer flags.

Vi was uncorking a bottle of wine when she caught sight of me. She made a theatrical expression of astonishment, opening her mouth wide and holding her fingers in front of it. Approaching us, still holding the wine bottle with the opener embedded in the cork – I'd wondered if she'd be outfitted in flowing robes, but she wore denim shorts and a Mizzou T-shirt – she said, 'I feel like I'm being visited by the queen of England.'

'Oh, I wouldn't have missed this for the world,' Carol said, and neither Vi nor I corrected her misunderstanding.

There was no one else there that I knew, which was weirdly impressive: Total strangers paid my sister to attend her sessions. Vi had gone to get plastic cups from the kitchen, and Carol was helping, when someone tapped me on the arm, and when I turned, a woman my age or a little younger stood a few inches from me, beaming. She was very pretty, with long red hair that she wore in two braids, and she seemed kind and warm and open in a way that put me on edge. 'You're Violet's twin, aren't you?' she said. 'I've heard amazing things about you.'

I summoned a smile. 'Thanks.'

'You two must have an incredible connection.

I've always wished I had a twin.' She leaned in, though we already were standing close together. 'I even wonder if I *did* have a twin who, you know—' She waved one hand in a circle, by which I understood that she meant *died in the womb*. This wasn't the first time someone had made a comment like this to me. As I took a step back, she said, 'Or maybe it was in a previous life.' A man was passing us, and the woman reached out and pulled him toward her – he was one of only two men present, and he looked about sixty, with a silver beard and small gold-rimmed glasses – and said, 'Bob, this is Violet's twin sister.'

Bob brought his hands together in a yoga pose, bowing his head. 'A privilege.'

I held up one of my own hands and waved.

Vi and Carol reappeared in the living room, distributing wine, and after one more trip to the kitchen and back, Vi called out, 'Does everyone who wants a drink have one?' She scanned the living room. 'Then let's get cracking.'

We all took seats, and she said, 'Some of us here are old friends, but for those who are new, let's everyone go around and say our names. And I want to mention two special guests tonight – my twin sister, Kate, and her mother-in-law, Carol.'

There was applause, and I smiled sheepishly. Vi's clients – they weren't my kind of people, but it was undeniable that they were nice. When we introduced ourselves, Carol said she was a séance virgin, and I cringed, wondering if in anticipating

413

that Vi would embarrass me in front of Carol, I'd had it backward.

Following introductions, Vi delivered a kind of prayer, invoking our sacred energy and our open hearts and our gratitude for the gifts around us. Then she began a monologue – perhaps it was a sermon – about how she'd been out for a walk in Tilles Park the other night and had seen a toddler and a puppy playing hide-and-seek, approaching and retreating from each other, and it had reminded her that even in our hectic, twenty-four/seven world, we need to take the time to be playful, and while I was wondering whether Vi had really taken this walk and whether the toddler and puppy actually existed, I realized that everyone else was nodding their heads. Even though what she was saying seemed neither interesting nor original, she spoke with an authority I hadn't previously observed in her. She expected the group to buy what she said, and they did. I probably would have, too, if she weren't my sister.

'Is someone here tonight having conflict with a co-worker?' she asked then, and a woman in a purple tank top raised her hand.

Vi said, 'I'm picking up on that, Penny. Tell me a little more.'

'My supervisor never gives me credit,' Penny said. 'I busted my ass to get this project done, and at a department meeting yesterday, she kept saying, "We did this, we did that." "We" nothing!'

'That's hard, isn't it?' Vi said. 'She's not being honest.'

'It's just really frustrating,' Penny said.

'You know what?' Vi said. 'She's not being honest with you and your colleagues, but the part that'll come back to bite her is she's not being honest with herself. And when you get to the point where you can't face your own reflection in the mirror' – Vi chortled but not unsympathetically; it was a we've-all-been-there chortle – 'well, that's a place none of us want to be. Penny, this woman is struggling. She's having a rough ride, and I want you to meet her with compassion. I want you to dialogue with her, but I want you to remember that she wouldn't be acting this way if she wasn't in a dark place.' Vi looked around the circle. 'Someone's worried about health. Don't be shy. You're safe here.'

Silver-bearded Bob said, 'As most of you know, I lost a hundred pounds two years ago. My wife and I started out dieting together, but she had trouble sticking with it. She's still very heavy, and I want to support her, but it's hard when I'm trying to eat celery and carrots and go for runs and she's ripping open another bag of chips in front of the TV.'

Bob's quandary seemed to me only loosely health-related, but Vi didn't hesitate. 'Bob, first, I want to acknowledge your incredible courage and tenacity.' My sister brought a hand to her forehead in a military salute. 'From someone who knows how hard dieting is, really, hats off. You're an inspiration to all of us. Now, here's what I want you to do. I want you to be totally and completely on your wife's team. Not like, "Honey, quit pigging out on chips," but like, "I am *there* for you. One hundred percent, I am there for you, and together we're going to beat this." Start small. You're running, yeah, but how about going for a walk around the block with her? Let me ask you this: Who makes dinner?'

'Usually, she does.'

'Uh-huh, uh-huh. How did I know that?' There was group laughter. 'Bob, I want you to take over the cooking a couple nights a week. Make salad, grill some fish. No discussion of calories, just a healthy, delicious meal prepared with love. Can you do that?'

'You're right,' Bob said. 'I know you're right.' He and the woman with red braids, whose name I couldn't remember, were sleeping together, I thought suddenly. Or about to, or hoping to. And I doubted grilled fish would stop it.

A middle-aged woman whom I guessed to be of East Indian descent talked about her daughter's divorce (ultimately, it would be for the best, Vi said), and a white woman with short black hair and bushy black eyebrows wanted to know whether she should take a job in Seattle (absolutely, Vi said, though the group would miss her), and the other man, who was maybe forty and balding, said that his wife wanted to put an addition on the back of their house even though they already had plenty of space and never used their living room and also he had begun to wonder if she was a compulsive shopper. Vi was quiet for longer after he spoke than she had been after anyone else's disclosure. She even shut her eyes, and queasily, I understood that she was communicating with Guardian – that this would represent the first time in the evening she'd acted as a medium rather than relying on some combination of presumptuousness and common sense. When she opened her eyes, she said, 'It's Tiffany, right? That's your wife's name?'

The man nodded.

'I hate to tell you this, but I'm wondering if Tiffany has a problem with prescription drugs. Is that possible?'

He grimaced, and in the grimace was recognition. He said, 'She's been having back pain again, so I thought—'

'I'm sorry, Jay,' Vi said. 'We can talk more after if you'd like.'

Carol wanted to know if she ought to let a case she was working on go to trial. She said, 'I can't go into the specifics, but my co-counsel thinks we'd be making a mistake, whereas I just have this feeling that we'll win.'

What I'd been thinking was that surely, the more Carol had listened, the more unimpressive Vi must have seemed to her. I wouldn't have disputed that this gathering served a purpose for its participants; that it illustrated my sister's psychic talents would have been a harder proposition for me to defend. And yet Carol seemed as earnest and believing as anyone else present. Was I exceptionally cynical? Well, yes, I thought, compared to the group assembled, because the group had attended voluntarily, whereas I had come along only to prevent my sister from telling my mother-in-law embarrassing secrets about me.

Vi looked around. 'What do I always say?' No one responded, though the room was filled with a communal affability; allowing Vi to answer her own question was, I guessed, part of the ritual.

'Trust yourself,' Vi said. 'Trust yourself, trust yourself, trust yourself. Carol, I can't emphasize this enough. If *you* think you should take the case to trial, then I want you to listen to that inner voice. Our intuition is the most powerful tool we have in our kit.'

The formal part of the session had lasted for close to an hour, and it went on for another fifteen minutes, but I could feel that the emotional high point had occurred with the revelation about Jay's wife and the segue into Vi's more general exhortation. When it was clear that the discussion was winding down, Vi said, 'Any final concerns?' She was looking at me, and I looked back, widening my eyes, which I intended to mean, *There's no way.* She had not, thus far, embarrassed me; she hadn't even explicitly mentioned Guardian. I had felt squirmy and skeptical, but it hadn't been nearly as bad as I'd feared. 'All right then,' Vi said. 'Shall we join hands?'

On my left, my mother-in-law's hand was small and cool; on my right, Jay's was warm and limp, and I felt that Vi was right about his wife and prescription drugs. 'May the energies offer us their guidance and wisdom,' Vi said, 'and may we take time amid the hustle and bustle to listen to them, and to inhabit the refuge they offer.'

Three or four people said amen, and then everyone was standing and talking, checking their cellphones, throwing away their plastic cups. While Vi collected money and asked who'd be bringing the wine next time, I went to use the bathroom; unlike Carol, I had no problem accepting a family discount. During the session, I had been away from Rosie, but when I looked in the mirror above the sink, she came back to me. I missed her, and I wanted to get home.

Vi was waiting for me outside the bathroom door. 'It was a little lame tonight,' she whispered, making a face. 'It's usually juicier.'

'You were good,' I said.

'You expected me to be wearing a turban and speaking in a Jamaican accent, didn't you?'

'Just say thank you,' I said. 'I gave you a compliment.'

On the drive home, Carol was as talkative as she'd been on the way over, eager to discuss the other clients – 'Wasn't that girl with the braids darling?'

she said – and I waited for her to remark on how the event had more closely resembled group therapy than legitimate clairvoyance. Instead she said, 'What a gift your sister has.'

Really? I thought. *That's really what you think?*

'But the thing I kept wondering,' Carol added, 'is who she's communing with. If she can access information that the rest of us can't, who's telling it to her?'

'Well, I don't think it's ghosts in white sheets.' I'd been trying for a joke, but Carol didn't laugh. I said, 'I mean, I guess she's just attuned to the energy of the world. What's all around us.' Carol still didn't respond. We were on Manchester, about to hit the light for Big Bend, and tentatively – it was somehow unsurprising to me that I was about to reveal what Vi herself hadn't, it made me feel that all along my defeat had been inevitable – I said, 'There's, like, an entity she talks to. Like someone in the spirit world, and she calls him Guardian, and she thinks he first visited her maybe fifteen years ago. He's the one who tells her things.' Still Carol said nothing – was her silence some lawyerly technique designed to make people blurt out things they hadn't intended to? – and I continued, 'I think, technically, that makes Vi a medium, but sometimes she picks up on stuff in other ways. And not everyone who's psychic is a medium. You could get information that came to you in a dream, or you could be walking down the street, or sitting in a room, and all of a sudden you have a sense.' It seemed I'd just revealed more about myself to Carol in the last minute than in all the years since I'd met her, that now, only by ignoring the most obvious signals could she not know that Vi and I were the same. But she accused me of nothing. 'At least I think you could,' I said.

At home, as soon as Carol had excused herself to go to bed – she had an early flight out in the morning and had insisted on calling a cab – Jeremy said, 'I finally got Rosie to sleep again, but she wasn't a happy camper tonight.'

I frowned. 'You should have called me.'

'I wanted you to have a night out.' He sighed. 'Anyway, she's asleep now.'

'How much was she up?'

'A lot. It sounds like my mom had a ball, though.' We looked at each other, and he said, 'Don't go into Rosie's room. You'll wake her up.'

But around three, it was Rosie who awakened us, and she felt hot. When I took her temperature – it said 101.6 – Jeremy and I then held a whispered conference in Rosie's room about whether or not to give her acetaminophen. She was just five months old, and we hadn't yet given her medicine of any kind. 'Let's wait and call the doctor in the morning,' Jeremy said. 'Her fever's not that high.'

But after I'd nursed Rosie, I couldn't bring myself to put her back in bed. I sat in the glider holding her, and she fussed at first until eventually she settled down and fell asleep, and after a while, so did I.

It wasn't yet six when the sun rose, white light showing in around the sides of Rosie's curtains, and for the first time since I'd put her to bed the night before, I had a clear view of her face. This was when I saw that her left eye was extremely swollen. Both the eyelid and the area beneath the eye were puffy and pink, two discrete half-moons. I ran my fingertip over the pouch below her eye, and she woke and looked at me with an agitated expression. Her left eye opened only about a third as much as usual.

Trying to sound calm, I said, 'Hi, little pumpkin. How are you?'

She began to cry, and my heart clenched like a fist; this was the first time I experienced anxious heart, when it came into existence for me. Had a spider bitten her, or had she had an allergic reaction to something that had passed through my milk, or was it connected to her cold from a few days before? I tried to think of what the next sequence of events should be. I hoped Carol had left for the airport but was pretty sure she hadn't. I stood and carried Rosie into our bedroom and said, 'Jeremy, her eye looks horrible. I don't know why, but it's almost swollen shut.'

There was a stern expression on Jeremy's face as he sat up, reaching for the wire glasses on his nightstand, and then he looked at Rosie and said, 'Whoa.' I began to cry, and Rosie, who had stopped crying, did, too. 'No, no,' Jeremy said. 'Let's not panic. Let's figure out what to do. What time is it?'

'Six.' I sniffed. 'I think your mom's in the shower. Do we take Rosie to the ER now or wait till the doctor's office opens?'

'Have you taken her temperature again?'

I shook my head.

'I'll get the thermometer.' He pushed back the sheet.

This time, her temperature was 103.2. 'Here's what I think we should do,' Jeremy said. 'Give her medicine now, and call the pediatrician the minute the office opens. If we go to the ER, we could end up waiting so long that it wouldn't be any faster. Have you nursed her?'

'Not yet.'

'Nurse her,' he said. 'I'll see my mom off.'

It was good, it was reassuring, to have a plan. After I heard the front door close, Jeremy came back upstairs, checked on us, then showered; I lay in our bed cradling Rosie, wanting to stay on the same floor as Jeremy. When he went downstairs for breakfast, we followed him, though my own stomach was churning and I was afraid to consume anything other than a glass of water. Simultaneously, I was getting used to Rosie's swollen eye and it still retained its power to shock me. When, I kept wondering, had this happened? And if I hadn't gone to Vi's with Carol, would I have noticed it before it got so bad?

Jeremy called the pediatrician's office, and when they said someone could see us immediately, I passed him Rosie and raced upstairs to change out of my pajamas. In the car, Jeremy drove and I sat in the back, next to Rosie.

The nurse who opened the waiting room door to usher us back looked at Rosie and said, 'Oh my goodness!' Which I didn't like, though being at the doctor's office did decrease my fear slightly.

It wasn't our regular pediatrician we saw but another doctor, who kept trying to figure out if Rosie's eye was moving, but she couldn't tell because the eye was now open only a sliver. She said that she thought Rosie had cellulitis – a bacterial skin infection – which was probably from having had a cold, and that while normally she'd have given us a prescription for antibiotics and sent us home, because she couldn't tell if Rosie's eye was moving, she wanted us to take Rosie to the ER after all.

Rosie was still on the exam table at this point, with me propping her up, and she was so subdued that I wondered if she was about to fall asleep. When the doctor said we needed to go to the ER, there was a moment of Jeremy and me not making eye contact, of him knowing I was surprised and telling me – he wasn't speaking, of course – *There's no reason to panic. She's just being careful.*

So we drove from the pediatrician's office to Children's Hospital – this time, on seeing Rosie, the woman we checked in with said, 'Yikes!' – and after we'd waited forty-five minutes, we were admitted to a little room, where a nurse took Rosie's vitals and then a man named Dr Mittra came in and examined her. Her eye was by this point swollen shut. He, too, said he thought she had cellulitis but that he couldn't confirm the diagnosis without seeing if the eye was moving – he couldn't know if the infection was preseptal, which meant in front of the eye's septum, or orbital, which meant within it.

'If the infection's in the eye, then what?' I asked.

Dr Mittra was calm but not warm; he was not reassuring. He said, 'Because the optic nerve leads to the brain, there are risks of meningitis and cavernous sinus thrombosis.' When I asked what cavernous sinus thrombosis was, he said, 'A blood clot.'

Again, I could feel Jeremy telling me, *He's not saying the infection is orbital. He's saying he thinks it isn't.*

After Dr Mittra was gone, two nurses inserted an IV into Rosie's hand, and over the hollow needle, they attached a plastic shield, like half a cup, so that Rosie wouldn't pull the IV out. (Later, a doctor told me that when you asked children what they'd been in the hospital for, those old enough to talk would say it was because they'd hurt their hand.) The nurses started Rosie's antibiotics immediately, while I sat with her on my lap, and she fell asleep. With the administration of the antibiotics, I thought, her recovery had officially begun; we had reversed directions. Hadn't we?

Jeremy said, 'How are you doing?'

I shrugged.

'This is a really great hospital,' he said. 'You know that, right?'

I wanted him to tell me that Rosie wouldn't get meningitis or a blood clot in her brain, but I also didn't want to speak the words *meningitis* or *clot* aloud. And really, anxious heart had made the rest of my body into a large, vacant, silent house; my limbs, even my head, were rooms that had been closed off for the winter.

After a minute, Jeremy said, 'Will you say something? I can't tell what you're thinking.'

It was hard to use my tongue to form words, but finally I said, 'I just want her to be okay.'

We looked at each other, and Jeremy said, 'She will.'

Another doctor, a different one from Dr Mittra, said they were keeping us overnight. This was after we'd been in the little exam room for six or seven hours. The room they took us to then – they pushed me in a wheelchair with Rosie on my lap, because they didn't want to let me carry her on foot – had a crib with a mattress more than four feet off the floor and a double set of stainless steel bars covering both the top and bottom halves. I rocked Rosie to sleep and deposited her gently on the mattress. Jeremy then went to close the two sets of bars, and they met with a great clanging lock that awakened Rosie, and all at once, she was crying, reaching for me, and I heard myself shrilly saying, 'Jeremy, open it! Open them! Get her out!' Because it was my dream: My dream of Rosie in a prison cell had come true, except that it wasn't a prison cell, it was a hospital crib.

Very quickly, he had unlocked the bars and I'd grabbed her, though she continued to scream, and Jeremy said, not accusingly but with concern, 'You scared her.'

'It was my dream!' I said. 'The baby bandit!' I was on the verge of hysteria myself.

'Okay,' Jeremy said. 'That's fine. She doesn't have to sleep in there.'

'But it means I knew this was going to happen!'

'Kate, you have to calm down. Want me to take her?'

I shook my head.

'You didn't know this would happen,' he said. 'Whatever you dreamed of, you couldn't have prevented it.'

Rosie slept that night in my arms, and I lay on a foldout chair. It was all reminiscent, in a gloomily inverted way, of Rosie's birth just five months earlier: the three of us together in a hospital room, but instead of feeling like Jeremy and I had pulled off the miracle of making a new person, this time everything just felt sad and scary. It was quieter at night, though there were still frequent visits from nurses and less frequent visits from doctors;

the worst part was when they appeared together and tried, with a kind of oversized wooden Q-tip, to pry Rosie's eye open.

Rosie wouldn't nurse, and early in the morning on the second day, someone brought me a pump because my breasts were engorged. Around us, we could hear the intermittent cries of other sick children. Jeremy went home to shower and get us new clothes, though I didn't bother to change, and he also brought back a sandwich and a box of granola bars, which I didn't eat. We spent a second night in the hospital, and everything that wasn't Rosie was still suspended. Her eye remained swollen, she continued to have a temperature when the acetaminophen wore off, and she was uninterested in the little stuffed cat that usually delighted her. Vi called my cellphone, and I didn't check the message. Jeremy and I had told no one, neither of our families, because what could they do? We were alone in this, I thought. No one loved Rosie as much as we did.

The second night, around eight P.M., when she was asleep on the foldout chair between my body and the wall, I looked down at her – she was wearing miniature hospital scrubs with turtles on them – and as her chest rose and fell, her swollen eye appeared to be a mistake, a thing that needed to be undone, though it also was hard to imagine her without it; it seemed that the prior months of her life had been a period in which we'd been naïve, even careless. We had worried, it turned out, insufficiently. Jeremy was in his own foldout chair, which faced ours, reading, and I said without looking up, 'If she doesn't get better, I think I'll kill myself.'

'The antibiotics will start working,' he said. 'By the morning, I bet.' Then he said, 'Look at me, Kate. This wasn't your fault.'

Had my own mother killed herself? Usually I believed she hadn't. But in the hospital, I thought the only reason I'd commit suicide was if something happened to my daughter, and what kind of person had my mother been if she'd done it even though she hadn't had to? The great concerns of her life – they weren't us.

Jeremy was wrong, and in the morning, Rosie wasn't better; she was worse, the most lethargic she'd been yet. Dr Mittra returned and told us in a somber voice that her lack of progress concerned him and he was ordering a CT scan. He left and came back with another doctor, and they speculated about whether Rosie was dehydrated, and instructed a nurse to give her dextrose solution through her IV, and it was perhaps an hour later – forty-eight hours after we'd entered the hospital – that at last she came around; she did, for the first time, start to improve. She wanted to pull my hair, and she wanted to look at the pictures in her book about jungle animals, and she wanted to nurse. It was hard to say exactly when the swelling went down, but her eye became visible, just a crack and then more, and Dr Mittra saw her eye move. 'This is very good news, Mom,' he said in his serious voice, and he patted my shoulder.

That afternoon, I took a shower in the bathroom adjacent to Rosie's room, and when I emerged in clean clothes, with wet hair, Jeremy was holding Rosie and talking to Vi, who sat on my foldout chair. 'Hey there, hot stuff,' Vi said. 'Sorry about everything.'

'She's doing much better now.'

'That's what Jeremy said. You should have called. I knew something was going on.'

'How'd you figure out we were here?' I asked.

'I called him.' Vi gestured at Jeremy.

'If you two want to walk around the block and get some air, Rosie and I will be fine,' Jeremy said.

'That's okay.' I extended my arms, and he passed Rosie to me.

'That's some eye,' Vi said. 'Will she have any scarring?'

This thought hadn't occurred to me. 'I don't know why she would,' Jeremy said.

'It's not contagious, is it?'

'Not unless you have an open cut that you rub against her eye,' I said.

'Maybe I won't hold her anyway, just to be safe.' Vi gestured to the box of granola bars. 'Can I have one?' As Jeremy nodded, Vi said to him, 'Was your mom wowed by me?'

'It sounds like she had a great time,' Jeremy said.

'You should come some night.' Vi glanced at me. 'It wasn't nearly as woo-woo as you imagined, right, Daze?'

I didn't, of course, hold Vi responsible for Rosie's infection, but I definitely wished I hadn't attended the session. I said, 'That stuff's not Jeremy's cup of tea.'

'Wow.' Vi laughed. 'Don't censor yourself.' She pointed at Rosie. 'Does Dad know?'

'I haven't had a chance to call him.'

'We never went to the ER when we were kids, did we?'

What was she implying? 'Not that I remember,' I said.

Vi said, 'Every time I look at her, you know what I think of? I think of *In the land of the blind, the one-eyed man is king.*'

If Rosie hadn't shown signs of improvement, I wouldn't have had the courage to fight with my sister; I wouldn't have wanted to release bad will into the world when I needed the world's beneficence. So perhaps it was a reflection of my confidence in Rosie's restored health that I said, 'Vi, if you're under the impression that you're making things better by being here, you know what? You're not.'

We stayed in the hospital one more night, and the strange part was that when they finally discharged us, I felt the return of anxious heart; it had gone away when Dr Mittra patted my shoulder, but it came back. Having a child in the hospital was, in most ways, awful, and yet I believed in the competence of the nurses and doctors more than I believed in my own; it was like turbulence on an airplane, how it could be both terrifying and out of your hands.

This was the time when, each night at home, I began putting the diaper bag by the front door, making sure that my wallet with my health insurance card was in it, when I'd charge my cellphone in the outlet closest to the diaper bag, and when I switched from sleeping in pajamas with silly patterns of monkeys or gnomes to sleeping in black yoga pants and plain T-shirt. I also kept wearing a nursing bra at night long after I'd stopped leaking milk, and in this way, I always knew that if I had to leave for the ER in the middle of the night, I could do so quickly.

Rosie didn't return to day care. We'd already paid the month's tuition, but I kept her home, and I quit my job effective immediately; I went back only to clean out my office. I'd thought my supervisor would be disappointed in me – she was a forty-eight-year-old divorced mother of three named Sue – but when I told her I was leaving the agency, she said without rancor, 'It's hard, isn't it? I envy you that you have the option of staying home.'

Which I did, but barely. The day Rosie was discharged from the hospital, when I told Jeremy I wanted to quit my job, he said, 'I ran the numbers and we'll be okay on just my salary, but we need to be more careful. For instance, no more ordering Rosie fifty-dollar Norwegian organic pajamas.'

'They're thirty dollars,' I said. 'And Swedish.'

'Her clothes fit her for a month,' he said. 'Just buy her stuff at Target.'

In the weeks and months after Rosie was in the hospital, I worried all the time: When she sneezed, I worried that she was getting a cold that would turn into cellulitis again, or perhaps pneumonia. I worried when I heard reports about resurgences in whooping cough, and when she started eating solids, I worried about her choking, and when I cut her pinkie while trimming her fingernails, I worried that she'd develop a staph infection. One afternoon while Jeremy was teaching, when she threw up five times in an hour for no obvious reason, I was so frantic that I had to make myself breathe in the way recommended by the teacher in the birthing class we'd taken.

It wasn't that I no longer took pleasure in Rosie's company; it was just that the joy of, say, watching her lie on her back and kick at the parrot hanging above her play mat was accompanied by a thrumming undercurrent of dread so constant and all-encompassing that it seemed hard to believe I'd lived without it for as long as I had. I had thought that I'd become a parent when Rosie was born, but now it seemed my true initiation had occurred during her return to the hospital.

When panic seized me – as when she threw up or I held a thermometer under her armpit and watched the digital numbers jump – I'd tell myself, *Be calm. It's completely normal for children to get sick.* But all during that first summer of Rosie's life, my heart would clench and clench.

I knew my anxiety was hard for Jeremy, too, less for what I said than the jittery waves I emanated, my reluctance to participate in activities without Rosie – to go to a movie, for instance. Even after I agreed to hire Kendra to babysit one morning a week, instead of leaving the house, I lurked, under the pretense of doing laundry and straightening up.

It was the double aspect of my anxiety, I think, that made it bad: First I worried that terrible things would befall Rosie, then I worried that I was right to worry because I was psychic. Like all new mothers, I'd been told repeatedly, by doctors and nurses and friends and strangers and advice books, to trust my instincts. But my instincts had betrayed me; they'd gone haywire.

The week before Rosie was eight months old, on a warm afternoon in late September while she was napping, I wrote *Having senses* on a piece of paper I'd torn from a notebook we kept by the phone. I folded the paper and dropped it into our clear salad bowl, along with a box of kitchen matches; I tucked Rosie's monitor under my arm and carried the bowl into the backyard.

I was too embarrassed to speak aloud before I struck a match against the strip on the box, but inside my head, I thought, *Please. Please, please let this work*. Then I lit the paper on fire. I felt ridiculous standing there in the sun as the paper burned; surely this brief rite would not be enough to eliminate a lifetime of premonitions. And in many ways, of course, it wasn't: I still sometimes dreamed of the future, and I still had hunches about people (the new dental hygienist at the practice Jeremy and I went to – she was being beaten up by her boyfriend, and I knew it the minute she called me back to the exam room). But burning that piece of paper *did* give me something, something that it's possible no one else had ever aspired to, which was grounds for doubting my own intuition. It gave me, inside the confines of my brain, plausible deniability. When a frightening thought about Rosie lodged itself in my head, I could say, *Maybe. But maybe not*. Perhaps I was still psychic, and perhaps I wasn't.

And soon there was evidence that both my senses and my anxiety were waning. A week after I burned the paper, I was driving on Delmar between Hanley and 170, Rosie in the back, when a cop pulled up behind me and turned on his lights and siren; once I realized what was under way, I was thrilled, which surely was a reaction the cop hadn't previously encountered. He was my age, a white guy who, when he saw Rosie, seemed almost apologetic. Nevertheless, because I'd been going forty-two miles an hour in a thirty-five-mile zone, he proceeded to issue me a speeding ticket.

That same week, when Kendra came, I left the house; I went to the Galleria and bought a new pair of jeans and a macadamia nut cookie. I also signed up to take a music class with Rosie, though surely such a class, with a dozen other babies and toddlers in it, would mean the exchange of many germs.

For a while after Rosie's eye infection, I thought I'd never have another child, because who would take care of the second one if the first was hospitalized? But over time, I became less preoccupied with this scenario; I almost forgot it. And really, this was the ultimate sign that my anxiety, in its severest form, had passed: that eight months after I burned my senses, I was pregnant with Owen.

CHAPTER 16

On the afternoon of October 15, after Jeremy had left for the airport, his absence didn't, at first, feel abnormal; after all, he was always gone on weekdays. I'd calculated that the time between when he departed for Denver and when Vi's earthquake prediction expired, assuming it expired at midnight, was thirty-three and a half hours.

Rosie and Owen both woke not long after Jeremy left, and following their snacks, I texted Hank: *Park?*

Coffee first, he texted back.

I still felt self-conscious about Rosie's banged-up lip, but after three days, it looked much better. And getting our coffee from Kaldi's, hanging out in the park – it was a regular afternoon. Perhaps Jeremy had been right.

Around five, as I was pushing Owen in a bucket swing and the girls were chasing each other, I said to Hank, 'Do you guys want to come over for dinner? We could order Chinese.'

'I told a mom at Amelia's school we'd go to the thing in Forest Park tonight.'

'The earthquake thing?' I'd received an email about this event through a playgroup Rosie and I hadn't attended in a year, and without fully reading it, I'd managed to absorb that the Science Center was sponsoring an evening for kids called 'EducationQuake!' If Vi Shramm weren't my sister, it was conceivable that we'd have gone.

'I might as well tell you now,' Hank said. 'We also got invited to an earthquake party tomorrow night.'

'What's an earthquake party?'

'I'm guessing it's an excuse for parents of young children to drink cocktails. You've heard of hurricane parties?'

'Are you staying overnight at their house?'

'God, no.' He paused then. 'Let me put it this way: Maybe some people are. *We're* not.' I gave Owen a push with the heel of my hand, and Hank said, 'Are you and Vi still in your *Today* show fight?'

'It looks that way.'

'I wonder if she's going on TV by herself.' I shrugged, and he looked amused. 'Don't try to tell me you're not planning to watch.'

'Honestly, I've seen enough of Vi on television.'

Hank grinned. 'Touché.' For the last several days, he had seemed to be in a good mood; he hadn't mentioned the abortion, so neither had I. We'd talked about my having run into Courtney and Jeremy at Blueberry Hill – Courtney had told him about it – and he'd treated it as a pleasant coincidence, an impression I hadn't corrected. He'd said, 'So you finally got busted for not leaving Owen with the sitter, huh?' and I'd said, 'No, I pretended it was a one-time thing.'

Rosie wandered over to the swing set. 'Rosie wants toast.'

'If we can't lure you with Chinese food, we should probably start heading back so I can get her dinner ready,' I said to Hank.

'You want to meet up with us later at Forest Park?'

'I don't think I have it in me.' I felt a clinginess then, a wish not to separate from Hank, as if nothing bad could happen to any of us in his presence. But this was childish, and I needed to be a grown-up.

'Hang in there.' Hank flicked my cheek with his thumb and middle finger. 'Okay?' There was something both odd and pleasing in the flicking gesture, though it wasn't until I was at home, waiting for the water to boil for the macaroni and cheese Rosie and I would eat, that I was able to pinpoint what the oddness was: It had been flirtatious. And Hank and I didn't, I was pretty sure, flirt.

After I drained the noodles, I heard my phone ding inside my vest pocket, and when I pulled it out, thinking it would be Jeremy, I saw that the text was from Hank: *Found out what yr famous sister is doing tmrw,* he'd written, and he'd pasted a link I couldn't resist clicking on. It was an article from the *Post-Dispatch,* with the headline EARTHQUAKE

PSYCHIC TO ATTEND PRIVATE VIGIL. The vigil would be at the Mind & Spirit Bookstore, I discovered as I continued reading, and it was closed to the public. So she'd be on the *Today* show in the morning, and then she'd embrace privacy and discretion? She was ridiculous.

By seven-thirty, I'd applied Rosie's Neosporin, put Owen to bed while Rosie danced and shouted around us in her nightly frenzy, and then put Rosie herself down, and the night ahead felt almost unsettlingly free. All my earthquake preparations – removing the wall hangings and storing the china; organizing the emergency supplies in the basement; even consolidating our important family documents, like birth certificates and Social Security cards, into a Ziploc bag – were complete. I wondered if I ought to organize the junk drawer in the kitchen, which barely closed, or if this was the moment to catch up on the last two and a half years' worth of emails, at least the non-earthquake-related emails, or if perhaps I should finish reading the novel I'd started over the summer. What usually happened when an unanticipated chunk of time presented itself was that I spent ten minutes pondering the possibilities available to me, at which point either Owen or Rosie woke up or else I realized that something demanded my immediate attention – poop-stained pants, milk pooling on the kitchen floor. And it was almost a relief to remember what it was I needed to attend to; otherwise the choices were bewildering.

Sure enough, as I descended the stairs, I realized that I ought to call my father. Jeremy's suggestion to the contrary, my father wouldn't help me with Owen and Rosie, but for his own sake, I wanted to offer him the option of staying at our house the following night. Because what else would he do with himself on this strange day, a day that could be momentous or ordinary? Did he believe that Vi's prediction would come to pass? It was such a basic question, yet it was unthinkable that I'd ask him. And even if I could have, he wouldn't have answered.

When I reached him and told him he was welcome to come over anytime the next day, from the morning on – 'We're up around six,' I said – he said, 'Maybe I could stop by in the afternoon.'

Something in his tone told me that he meant he'd be willing to do us a favor, not that he thought we'd be doing him one.

'Just if you want company,' I said. 'If you'd rather stay put in your own house, I don't blame you.'

'Well, Vi's event doesn't start until five, if I'm not mistaken.'

My father was attending Vi's bookstore vigil? 'Did she ask you to drive her?' I said.

'I don't mind. I'll sit out back and listen to the radio in the car.'

'Dad, she can get a ride with a friend who's going anyway. I'm sure it'll run really late.'

'I truly don't mind.'

You might not, I thought, *but how about the other people sharing the road with you when you can't see at night?*

'Let's touch base in the morning,' my father said.

I had, while talking to my father, been dimly aware of a rattling in the kitchen; I'd even walked in there from the living room, carrying the phone, but the kitchen was silent until I walked back out, at which point the rattling resumed. It wasn't an earthquake – it was much too small, and it kept starting and stopping.

I returned to the kitchen, and this time the rattling continued. I took a step toward the oven, which seemed to be its source, and it stopped, but when I waited a minute, it started again. I reached for my cellphone and texted Jeremy: *I think we have a mouse.*

As he had promised, no more than thirty seconds passed before our home phone rang.

'Where'd you see it?' he said. In the background, I could hear the buzz of many voices – the hotel bar, presumably, where he was busy placing articles in journals.

'I didn't see it yet, I only heard it under the stove. Isn't that where we had one last year?'

'Sorry this had to happen tonight. We have some traps in the basement, on that shelf where you keep the Christmas decorations.'

'Lovely,' I said.

'The traps are in a plastic bag.'

'Do I have to put cheese in it? Is that something people do in real life?'

Jeremy laughed. 'Has my princess never set a mousetrap? No, you don't need to put any food in. Just be careful with the spring, and you might want to put out more than one, but make sure you move them before Rosie's up in the morning. If you do catch a mouse, what I always do is just roll it up in newspaper and take the whole thing out to the trash bin.'

'It won't still be alive, will it?'

'No, but don't feel too guilty. Mice spread diseases. How'd things go tonight?'

To reveal that they hadn't gone badly would be to concede in a way I wasn't yet ready for. I said, 'About how you'd imagine.'

'The baloney's holding up in my absence?'

'You'll have to ask Rosie.'

'All right, then.' He wasn't going to let himself be pulled toward rancor. 'Call back if you have trouble with the trap, and call either way before you go to bed.'

Setting a mousetrap, it turned out, wasn't harder than applying antibiotic ointment to a squirming two-year-old. In fact, it was easier. I set three, washed my hands, and was opening the refrigerator door to reward myself with a beer when my cellphone rang.

'We're in the car leaving the park,' Hank said. 'I have a confession, and I need you to absolve me.'

'Is it Mommy?' I heard Amelia say, and Hank

443

said, 'It's Kate.' Then he said, 'The family that had us over for dinner served lasagna with M-E-A-T in it, and I ate it.'

'Should I call the cops?' I asked.

'Probably, because there's more. It was delicious. It was like an old friend giving me a big warm hug.'

I laughed. 'Did Amelia have any?'

'Maybe a bite. Not really.'

'Speaking of killing animals, I think we have a mouse. I just set my first traps.'

'Congrats.'

'Do vegetarians set mousetraps?'

'You'd have to ask one.'

'Ha,' I said. 'Where are you guys, by the way? You're welcome to come over.' Hank was quiet, and I said, 'Amelia probably needs to go to bed.' Already, it seemed a little weird that I'd invited them.

'We're on Skinker right now.' His voice sounded completely normal. 'Yeah, we'll come and say hi.'

'Rosie and Owen are asleep,' I said, which felt like a retraction of my invitation, but all Hank said was 'We'll be quiet.'

I waited for them in the living room and opened the front door before they knocked or rang the bell. 'Where's Rosie?' Amelia said. 'I want to see Rosie.'

'Owen and Rosie are sleeping,' I said.

'I want to wake them up.'

As they entered the living room, Hank said, 'At the rate you're going, you will.'

'Kate, can I have some milk?' Amelia asked.

I looked at Hank, who said, 'Sure. Why not?'

Because they needed to get home so Amelia could go to bed was why not, though it occurred to me that maybe Hank didn't want to leave any more than I wanted them to. This, I supposed, was the reason people had earthquake parties. 'You need a beer?' I asked, and Hank said, 'Nah, I'm good.'

Rosie still used a sippy cup, but Amelia had graduated to a regular glass, which I filled halfway and carried out to the living room. Hank and Amelia were side by side on the couch, and Amelia was turning the pages of *Frog and Toad All Year*. I set her milk on the table, and as I sat in the armchair, I said to Hank, 'So how long had it been since you last ate you-know-what?'

He looked up toward the ceiling, calculating. 'A really long time. Ten years?'

'And you never even had a bite?'

'Once at Courtney's parents' house, her mother was all proud for having made vegetable soup. If you know her mom, she was really stretching herself – first her daughter marries a black dude, then she stops eating meat. We're all at their dining room table, and Courtney says, "This is delicious," and her mom says, "It's so easy. I just cut up some carrots and celery and zucchini, added a little chicken stock –"' Hank smiled, shaking his head. 'So it was a cheat, but not even a satisfying one. And her mom was trying so hard.'

'Someday I might join the vegetarian club,' I said. 'When you least expect it.'

'We'll be honored to have you as a member.' He made a self-mocking expression. 'If I haven't been kicked out by then.'

They stayed for only about fifteen minutes, by which point Amelia's eyes were fluttering. Hank lifted her into his arms, and as I opened the front door for them, I said, 'You're sending Amelia to school tomorrow, aren't you?'

'Kate, if I kept Amelia home because of Vi's prediction, Courtney would file for divorce.'

I was glad then that Rosie wasn't in school yet, that this was an argument I didn't have to have with Jeremy. I said, 'Well, here's to things being uneventful,' and as I spoke, I again had that wish for Hank to stay, that sense of us as safe in his presence.

'You're okay, right?' Hank was looking at me with unusual seriousness.

What would he say, what could he do, if I told him no? He was holding a half-asleep child; we both were married to other people. Really, there was no room for me to not be okay. 'I'm fine,' I said.

Hank nodded his chin toward the staircase. 'Tell O to let you get some sleep tonight.'

The reason I went down to the basement after they were gone was to get Jeremy's sleeping bag, but I paused to survey the supplies I'd amassed: the gallons of water, the diapers and wipes, the crank radio and propane stove and first-aid kit. There was a peculiar pride I took in this collection, which might have been a sign that I had more in common than I'd ever realized with members of the survivalist movement.

I shoved a flashlight into my back pocket before pulling Jeremy's sleeping pad and sleeping bag from the closet; taking these items wasn't a spontaneous decision. Upstairs, I unrolled them both on the hardwood floor in the hall, right outside Rosie and Owen's rooms, and I pulled the pillow I normally used from our bedroom. I still needed to brush my teeth, but when I lay down, my head would be next to Owen's door and my feet next to Rosie's.

On a typical night, I slept approximately twenty-five feet from my children; on this night, I'd sleep, or not sleep, five feet from them. Which was perhaps ridiculous – Jeremy would have thought so – but I didn't see the harm. If shaking started, my plan was to grab Owen first, take him with me into Rosie's room, get her out of her crib, and sit on the floor holding them both, my back against the interior wall of Rosie's room. I'd sleep with the flashlight and my cellphone next to me. I was ready, insofar as it was possible to be ready for something completely amorphous.

And whether or not my behavior was ridiculous, Jeremy wasn't home to witness it. He had gone to Denver and left us behind.

*　　*　　*

It was raining when I awakened in the morning, and I thought, *Vi's wrong.* There wasn't going to be an earthquake. I knew because I'd never heard Vi mention rain, because it had never occurred to me that October 16 would be rainy, and yet the rain had that murmuring, all-day quality, as if it were pacing itself. But even as I felt relief, even as I thought about how removing the wall hangings and putting away the china had been a waste of time, I still wanted the day to be over.

It was five after six when I climbed out of Jeremy's sleeping bag and went downstairs to check the mousetraps, all of which were empty. When I returned upstairs, I could hear Owen and Rosie making noise in their separate rooms, neither of them sounding displeased, so I took a three-minute shower, then nursed Owen, changed him into clothes, and carried him with me to get Rosie. By the time we'd made it through breakfast and post-breakfast cleanup and settled to play in the living room, it was seven-twenty. Which was, of course, still punishingly early; there was still so much day to get through. But Rosie was in an excellent mood – she kept tapping my face with her index finger, saying, 'Mama's nose is friends with Mama's mouth' – and not one but two dogs walked past our house with their owners, making Owen squawk with delight when I held him up to the window.

Jeremy called as Cinnamon the schnauzer was disappearing from view. 'My cousin Joe in

Minneapolis just texted to ask if Matt Lauer is really in Vi's living room right now.'

I grabbed the remote control. And sure enough, there they were, sitting on chairs about two feet from each other. With Jeremy still on the line – it was an hour earlier in Denver, meaning Vi wasn't on there yet – I turned up the volume on the TV and put him on speaker so he could hear it, too. So distracting was the fact of Matt Lauer in Vi's house that it took me a few seconds to focus on Vi herself; she looked exhausted. She was wearing, I noted, the navy blue short-sleeved sweater I'd picked out for her to try on at Lane Bryant, which fit well, though she'd paired it with a somewhat tacky necklace of interlocking silver circles. 'I wonder who did her makeup this time,' I said.

'Will you be embarrassed if you're wrong?' Matt Lauer was asking.

'I'll be thrilled,' Vi said. 'That's what I've been telling people all along.' She knew, I thought. She, too, knew already that an earthquake wasn't going to happen.

'But your credibility will be undermined,' Matt Lauer said.

'Do you think I'd put thousands of people's lives at risk just so I don't look bad?' Vi said. 'Shame on you, Matt.'

Jeremy laughed. 'You gotta love her self-righteousness.'

'I want to ask you a question a lot of our viewers have asked since you and I last spoke,' Matt Lauer said. 'If you have the ability to see the future, why don't you take advantage of it by, for example, playing the lottery?'

'I wasn't given this gift to use for my own gain,' Vi said. 'I'm sure some mediums do that, but I've always wanted to help others.'

'One last question: What are your plans for today and tonight?'

'I'll be attending a low-key vigil with old friends,' Vi said. 'This is the kind of day you want to spend with people you're close to.'

'Wow,' Jeremy said. 'The irony.'

'She's roped my dad into driving her to the bookstore tonight.'

'He could have said no.' We were both quiet – it seemed we'd missed Vi and Matt Lauer's final exchange, and the interview had wrapped up – and I muted the TV and said, 'You think Matt Lauer used her bathroom? I hope she cleaned it.'

'If he did, she should install a plaque. Did you get Mickey Mouse, by the way?'

'Not yet.' I could have told Jeremy that in spite of Vi's latest appearance on TV, I felt the calmest I had since she'd made her prediction – that the day felt ordinary and not like the occasion of something terrible. But again, to reveal my own calmness would have been a kind of olive branch I still wasn't ready to offer. Yes, Jeremy had been right about the earthquake, but that didn't mean he should have gone to the conference. *He* hadn't known he was right. Instead, I said, 'I wonder if our family should stop eating meat.'

'But mice are so delicious! They're so tender.'

'Seriously,' I said.

'We can talk about it when I get home,' he said. 'I'd be up for cutting it out at least a couple days a week. You think Rosie would deign to say hi to me?'

I held the receiver toward her. 'Want to say hi to Daddy?'

Rosie took the phone and said, 'Hi, Rosie.'

'Hi, *Daddy,*' I said.

'Mama cleaned pee-pee on Rosie's pajamas,' Rosie said.

'Say, "I miss you."' Then I realized that without deciding to, I'd acquiesced, because surely Jeremy could hear me coaching her. 'Say, "Rosie misses you."'

'There's no more pee-pee on Rosie's pajamas,' Rosie shouted.

'Rosie misses you,' I repeated.

'Mommy misses you,' Rosie said.

If Vi was wrong, then I was wrong, too – after all, I'd thought the earthquake would occur on October 16 before she had. And yet hadn't I been wrong before, over and over? Wrong in believing that Scary Black Man would attack me; wrong that I would adopt Chinese girls; wrong that I would marry Ben Murphy or David Frankel and, on our first date, that I wouldn't marry Jeremy.

451

Confirmation bias was what Jeremy had called the tendency to pay greater attention to the times I was right, so what was its opposite? Because considering the many errors of my past was oddly comforting. Though I wouldn't have believed that anything other than an emergency could have induced me to take Rosie and Owen on an outing on what I'd imagined to be the most anxiety-provoking day of my life, it felt increasingly ridiculous to stay cooped up. As the rain continued, as seven forty-five became eight-twenty and eight-twenty became nine-twenty, as Owen went down for a nap, woke, ate, and it wasn't yet eleven, it just seemed silly for us to stay inside. And perhaps all I'd ever wanted was this – not the assurance of permanent, unbreachable safety for my children, because that was impossible, but the ability to distinguish between anything less than extreme caution and tempting fate. Because I *didn't* think I was tempting fate as I said, 'Hey, Rosie, want to go look for a Halloween costume?' I felt that I was doing what a normal parent, a normal person, would do.

Besides, I meant at Target, which would not be, by most people's standards, a bold journey. The store was two miles away, and though we'd drive, I'd have the stroller in the trunk so we could walk home if necessary – if the highway cracked open, say.

Before we left, I called Hank and said, 'I did end up watching Vi on TV this morning, and I can tell she doesn't believe her prediction anymore.' If I couldn't offer this gift to Jeremy, at least I could share it with Hank. I added, 'And I'm feeling so brave that we're going to Target to look for Halloween costumes. You need anything?'

In a surprisingly serious tone, Hank said, 'There were so many kids out at Amelia's school this morning that I had a moment of wondering if I shouldn't leave her.'

'I really don't think so.'

'Now I keep watching the clock till it's time to go back.'

'You're welcome to come with us to Target if you want a distraction.'

'Mmm—' I could tell he was considering it, but then he said, 'I was about to fix the leak in our tub. I promised Courtney I'd do it while she's gone.'

Rosie, Owen, and I were in the car but still in the driveway when my phone rang: *Dad cell*, the screen said. Which was an identification that had never shown up; Jeremy had entered a few numbers into my father's cellphone, but my father called me only at home. When I answered, it wasn't my father's voice on the other end. It was a woman.

'Your dad fainted, but he doesn't want to go to the hospital,' she said. 'You need to come get him.'

'Who is this?'

'He's at Relax Massage. Can you come get him? He says he's fine, but he's still out of it.'

'My father was getting a massage and he fainted?'

Since when had my father gotten massages? My heart was tightening the way I'd thought, when I'd awakened to rain, that it wouldn't.

'Can you come get him?' the woman said.

'Is he conscious?' I asked.

'Yeah, yeah, he's drinking a pop. He didn't want us to call you, but it's like, "We're calling an ambulance or your family. Take your pick."'

'Can I talk to him?'

I heard her say, 'Your daughter wants to talk to you,' and after a few seconds, there was a beep that I was pretty sure was my father inadvertently pressing the keypad of his phone, and then he was saying, 'Kate, I'm perfectly fine.'

'What happened? Do you need to go to the hospital?'

'I stood up too quickly, but I'm fine.'

'And you're getting a—' I almost couldn't say it; it seemed intimate in an unsavory way. 'You were having a massage?'

'When she was finished, I stood up too quickly,' my father said. 'That's all.'

'Your daughter come get you,' said a female voice in the background, a different voice – this one was accented, perhaps Eastern European or Russian, and more forceful. 'She get you or we call ambulance.'

'Will you pass me back to the person I was talking to before?' I said.

'Truly, I'm fine,' my father said, and it seemed that the second woman grabbed the phone

454

because she said, 'You come get father now. We are on Olive Boulevard. Relax Massage.' Then she hung up.

I glanced in the rearview mirror at Rosie and Owen before calling Hank. 'I just got a really weird call. This woman who doesn't identify herself says my dad was having a massage, he stood up and fainted, and I need to come get him.'

'Has he come to?'

'Yeah, I actually talked to him. He sounded normal, I guess.' I paused. 'I should go out there, right?' Without waiting, I said, 'Yeah, of course I should. You don't think they, like, kidnapped him, do you?'

'Did they say anything about money?'

'No.'

'You want me to go with you?'

The air of embarrassment around whatever was happening – I knew that for my father, it would be bad enough to have me witness it without Hank present, too.

'At least let me come over and watch the kids,' Hank was saying. 'But if you're worried it's unsafe, call the police.'

In fact, as I thought about it, it was like the opposite of a kidnapping – these women seemed intent on getting rid of my father.

I said, 'The whole massage thing – isn't that code for prostitution?'

'Not always.'

'No, I know there are legit places, but I just got this feeling—'

Hank laughed, before saying, 'Sorry. But if at his age, he's still – well, more power to him.'

'Yeah, if he's not your dad.' I looked once more at the backseat and made a decision. 'If you really don't mind, maybe I'll leave Rosie with you and keep Owen. Hopefully, I'll be back by the time Amelia's school lets out.'

'Come on over,' Hank said.

It is tempting, in retrospect, to assign a starting point to the sequence of events that unfolded on this day – tempting as well as futile – and when I do so, this is the obvious moment. Because surely, if I had decided to keep Rosie with me instead of handing her over to Hank, everything would have gone a different way. And I did feel a fleeting uneasiness about separating myself from my daughter, rain or no rain, but this was Hank, who was practically a third parent to Rosie, whom I trusted far more than Vi or my father as a care-taker. Plus, dealing with whatever situation I was about to enter at the massage place would be considerably easier without Rosie running around, grabbing things, and shrieking.

I pulled into the Wheelings' driveway, where Hank was waiting, and as he opened the back door, I said, 'You swear this is okay?'

'Don't even think about it.'

'I'll fix your tub later,' I said, and he grinned.

'Yeah, right.'

'Rosie, you get to stay with Hank while I run an errand,' I said. 'Maybe you can play with Amelia's grocery cart.'

She was looking at me with suspicion in the rearview mirror, and as Hank unbuckled her car seat, she yelled, 'Rosie wants a costume!'

'We'll get the costumes this afternoon,' I said.

'Rosie wants a costume now!'

Hank and I made eye contact in the mirror, and he said, 'If you trust me to help her pick something, I don't mind going to Target.'

How I wish that I'd said no and just let Rosie whine. Instead, I said, 'That would be awesome, if you're up for it. Just nothing S-L-U-T-T-Y.' I unfastened my own seat belt and climbed out of the car, taking Hank's place in extricating Rosie, and as I did, I said, 'You get to go with Hank to look for your costume. Isn't that nice of him? So please be his helper in the store and do what he tells you.'

When Rosie was standing in the driveway in the rain, the little green hood of her raincoat pulled up, Hank extended his hand, and somberly, Rosie took it. I could tell that she was confused in ways she couldn't express. I bent to kiss her forehead. 'I love you, little pumpkin,' I said.

Relax Massage was in a strip mall, and after I'd inserted Owen into the carrier and crossed the small parking lot, I almost collided with a man as

I stepped from between two parked cars onto the sidewalk in front of the stores. He stopped, gesturing for me to go first; I did, smiling apologetically, and as I walked the remaining few feet to the door of Relax Massage, I could feel him walking in after me.

The waiting room couldn't have been more than fifty square feet, a dimly lit space with tan walls and an opaque sliding window that was open onto an interior hall. A bell waited on the window ledge. None of which was that suspicious, but there was a musky smell in the air that wasn't at all like the minty scents of the spas I'd been to.

As I was wondering whether I ought to ring the bell or let the guy behind me ring it, a door next to the window opened and a middle-aged woman with dyed red hair emerged. She said, 'You are the daughter of Mr Earl?' When I nodded, she said, 'You come with me.' Looking at the man, she said, 'You sit down, Mr Nathan, and Alina, she is ready for you one minute.'

She led me to a room about the size of the waiting room, also dimly lit, where a tape player emitted classical music and my father sat with his legs hanging off what looked like a doctor's exam table except longer, and covered by a sheet rather than paper. He was – thank goodness – fully dressed, and drinking 7UP from a can; he wasn't visibly injured. 'Daisy, I didn't mean to trouble you,' he said. Leaning against a wall, her arms folded in front of her, was a young woman I assumed to be Alina, an unsmiling figure with light brown hair that fell almost to her hips, wearing black leggings, a black tank top, and dark red lipstick. She had large breasts beneath the tank top, and I tried to suppress the question of whether she'd recently given my father a hand job.

In a voice that was accent-free and neither friendly nor unfriendly, she said, 'Don't forget his raincoat.' She pulled it from a hook and passed it to me, even though my father had made no motion toward standing. When she spoke, I saw that behind the lipstick, she had a dead front tooth.

'Dad, you're well enough to walk to the car? Because I can call an ambulance.'

'I'm fine.'

As if my father were not present, the older woman said, 'You take him to doctor. Could be problem of—' First she tapped her chest, over her heart; then she said, 'Or here,' and tapped her head.

'Dad, why don't you lean on me to get up?' Even as I positioned myself beside him, Owen attached to me in the carrier, I thought my father would decline my assistance. When he didn't, I thought one of the women would offer to help, which also didn't occur. And so with one arm set around my shoulders, my father slid off the table into a standing position, and he continued to lean on me heavily as we made our slow progress out of the room. From the carrier, Owen turned his head to look at my father with curiosity. 'Say, "Hi, Grandpa,"' I said as we retraced our route through the little hall and back into the waiting room, where I intentionally didn't make eye contact with the next man waiting for Alina. Just before I reached for the handle of the door leading outside, the middle-aged woman said, 'Your father, he not pay.'

With my left hand, I pulled my wallet from the right pocket of my vest and shimmied out a credit card.

'No,' the woman said. 'Is cash only.'

Right, I thought. *Because you're prostitutes.* Aloud, I asked, 'How much?'

'I wouldn't think of having you pay.' My father passed his entire wallet to the woman. I watched her take what I thought was eighty dollars before passing it back.

'You go to doctor, Mr Earl,' she said.

In the parking lot, there was no discussion of my father driving his own car; after I'd helped him into the front seat of mine, I said, 'Want me to fasten the seat belt?'

'No,' he said.

When all three of us were finally settled in, I said, 'Did you eat breakfast this morning?'

'I did. I had a boiled egg.'

'Dad, I want to take you to the hospital. I'm sure you're fine, but I just want to hear it from a doctor.'

'That won't be necessary.'

'I'd rather be safe than—'

'Take me home, Daisy,' my father said. 'I'm liable to pick up an infection at the hospital when all I'd like to do right now is rest. And you can bet they'd keep us waiting for hours.'

I backed out of the parking space and pulled onto Olive, and when we were stopped at a red light, I said, 'How about if you come to our house? I'll take you home to pack a bag, and you can spend the night with us.' Which was pretty much what I'd suggested before, under different circumstances.

'I'd like to go home, and I'd like you to be on your way,' my father said. 'Don't treat me like a child.'

Again, I was silent, this time for several minutes, until at last I said, 'I still want to call Dr Gilmore and make an appointment.' When my father didn't respond, I said, 'I'll call and see what he has open.'

At his apartment, I escorted my father to the living room couch and, with Owen back in the carrier, rummaged around in the refrigerator, tossing a bag of deli turkey with a sell-by date from ten days earlier and setting a frozen chicken pot pie in the microwave.

I shouldn't have left Rosie with Hank, I thought. I should have brought her with me and we could have stayed with my father for the afternoon. Would it be too much to ask Hank to drive her out? I glanced at my watch and saw that there were fewer than forty minutes before he was due to pick up Amelia, which meant he couldn't drive Rosie here. Besides, Rosie would never nap at my father's.

'We'll come eat dinner with you,' I said. 'A really early dinner. How does that sound?'

But saying it, I felt afraid of the earthquake for the first time that day. The unexpectedness of the rain had pushed away the earthquake's likelihood, but the unexpectedness of my father's fainting had canceled out the unexpectedness of the rain.

'Let's see how the afternoon goes,' my father said.

I set Owen on the floor in the living room and gave him the star rattle to play with while I used my cellphone to call my father's internist's office. I was standing between the kitchen and the living room, still on hold – Owen was saying, 'Ba-ba-ba-ba,' and my father was saying nothing in return – when I saw that Hank was calling. Worried that the internist's office would pick up while I was on the other line, I didn't answer. After a minute, Hank called again, and this time, I answered immediately. 'Is everything okay?' If the earthquake had occurred, it seemed impossible that I wouldn't have felt it.

'Rosie's fine,' he said, but as he spoke, I could hear a crying child.

'Is that her?'

'She's not hurt, nothing like that, but I need you to come meet us. We're still at Target and we've been' – he paused, and when he spoke again his voice contained a fraught acidity I'd never heard – 'detained. The security guard here is concerned about Rosie.'

'I thought you said no one was hurt—'

'No. Kate. Rosie's fine. He's concerned about – about me. Because Rosie isn't my daughter.' Hank seemed to be selecting each word carefully, perhaps even speaking in code – obviously, he was being listened to – and all at once, I understood. Still in that weird, clipped way, he said, 'He's worried that you don't know Rosie's with me.'

'This is insane,' I said. 'Put me on the phone with the guard.'

'Rosie's mother is glad to talk to you,' I heard Hank say, leaning away from the receiver.

A male voice said, 'Sir, we'd like the child's mother to come here in person.'

'Should I call a lawyer?' I asked.

'Not yet, but can you come now? Is your dad—'

'Yeah, I'll leave in a second. Jesus. I'm so sorry.'

'We're in the office, which is after you pass the pharmacy.' To the security guard, he said, 'Should she come in the main entrance or a different one?' Then, to me, he said, 'Come in the main entrance and go right.'

Early on in my friendship with Hank, we'd taken the girls for a walk in their strollers on one of the semi-gated loops off Wydown, a neighborhood of enormous houses looming over enormous lawns – not the loop Mrs Abbott, my former employer, had lived on but the one just east of it. I'd suggested walking back there because there was little traffic, which meant it was safe to be in the street instead of jamming our two strollers together on the sidewalk. At some point, a golden retriever approached us, and Amelia, who was about eighteen months, waved at the dog while Hank petted her head. The dog stayed with us as we continued around the bend, and I said to Hank, 'See that thing on her collar? I wonder if she got out of her electric fence. I'm almost positive I've seen her before in the yard of that brick house back there.'

Hank turned toward the dog. 'You making a break for it?'

'Does her collar have a name on it?'

Hank bent over, peering into the dog's neck. 'No name or address,' he said.

'I feel like we should take her back and ask if she's theirs. I don't want her to get hit by a car.' I glanced at Hank. 'Do you mind?'

He seemed hesitant, and it crossed my mind that he was deciding I was too annoying to be friends with. But then he said, 'Sure, sure.'

When we reversed directions, the dog did, too. At the bottom of a long driveway leading up a massive lawn to a house with four two-story Ionic columns in front, Hank stopped. 'You're planning to go knock?'

I nodded.

'You should go by yourself. Or you and Rosie.'

'Do you think I'm being really weird?'

On Hank's face was an expression of what I initially thought was amusement. He said, 'The people who live in these houses – if they see a black man coming up their driveway, they'll call the police. Unless I'm here to do yard work, they don't want me on their property.' Then he smiled a little and said, 'Just a guess.'

I was mortified. The whole walk had probably been a mistake, I realized; I must have seemed to Hank like an insensitive moron.

'I'm sorry,' I said. 'I didn't—'

'Don't sweat it.' He still was looking up the sloped lawn. 'You and Lassie go do reconnaissance, and I'll wait here.'

As it turned out, the person who opened the door was a woman who I felt sure was a housekeeper even though she wasn't wearing a uniform, and who said, without much conviction, 'Ginger, you're a very bad puppy.' She didn't seem like she'd have called the cops if she'd seen Hank approaching, though I understood his point.

From that day on, we rarely spoke of race, but I tried to be careful. Once in the fall of 2008, when we were walking to Kaldi's with the girls, we passed a house with lots of Halloween decorations – oversized inflatable ghosts and witches, cottony cobwebs spread over the bushes – as well as a McCain-Palin yard sign, and Hank pointed to the sign and said, 'All the effort they went to, and that's the scariest thing of all.' The night Barack Obama won, we were watching TV at

Hank and Courtney's – Rosie was asleep in a portable crib in their bedroom, I was pregnant with Owen – and when the networks called the election around ten o'clock central time, Hank got choked up, but so did I; even Courtney seemed the tiniest bit misty.

There were plenty of moments when I forgot, though. I was, after all, a white woman who'd grown up in St Louis, now shepherding around my white children, seeming harried and harmless, reminding people of themselves. I forgot in a way that Hank, presumably, never could.

Since the time I'd received a ticket while Rosie was in the backseat, I'd been careful not to speed, but heading east – I had to take Manchester Road because of the ongoing highway construction – I drove ten miles over the limit. Owen had begun to cry as soon as we'd turned out of the parking lot of my father's building, and I had no idea where any of his pacifiers were. My father had seemed relieved by our departure; if he'd overheard my conversation with Hank, he didn't ask about it.

'I know,' I said as Owen wailed. 'You're ready to eat, aren't you?' I turned on the radio, hoping it might distract him, and after a Christina Aguilera song ended, the DJ said, 'No sign of an earthquake, but just got a report of an accident on Hanley south of Litzsinger Road.' Which wasn't far from Target, though I was pretty sure if I came in on Brentwood Boulevard, I'd be okay.

I'd learned from experience not to be too ambitious in the Target parking lot, but I had my pick of spaces; apparently, there was a way to keep people away from Target, and Vi had discovered it. I parked at an angle sufficiently awkward that I'd have reparked under different circumstances, turned off the engine, ran around to get Owen, and hurried with him toward the entrance.

The first set of automatic doors parted as we approached, then the second set, and inside the store, we walked quickly by the holding area of large red carts, turned right, passed the intra-Target Starbucks and the pharmacy, and then I spotted red double doors I'd never noticed, with a keypad by their handles and a small red rectangle that said the word PRIVATE. Through the narrow windows in the doors, I could see a hallway with a white linoleum floor and several rooms off it. I knocked loudly.

A trim white man in a black uniform came to let me in; on his right arm was a badge that said Target Asset Protection, and on his left an American flag. I followed him to a small room, and as I entered, I could see Hank's back, his close-shaved haircut from behind. He sat in a chair that faced a desk, and the guard took the seat on the desk's far side. From a chair next to Hank's, Rosie popped up on her knees and said, 'Rosie wants Mama!'

My sweet, pathetic daughter – she wasn't actively crying, but tears were pooled below her eyes, and snot clung to the cut above her mouth. Still holding Owen, I scooped her up so that each of my children was balanced on one hip, which was a position that wasn't sustainable for long. I looked at the security guard and said, 'I don't understand what's going on here, but this man' – I nodded toward Hank – 'is a very close friend and I asked him to look after my daughter.'

The man appeared unruffled. 'Ma'am, our foremost goal is safety.'

'Hi, Kate,' Hank said glumly.

'And you think you can decide better than me who my daughter is safe with?' I sounded shrill, I knew, but who did this security guard think he was? Already, my anxiety had shifted to anger.

'Another customer heard her say, "This man is not my father,"' the security guard said. 'You can see why we were concerned.'

That man's not Daddy. That's what Rosie would have said, as she had about Marisa Mazarelli's boyfriend at the acorn park and as she said every day about other men we passed. She wouldn't have said, *This man is not my father.* And I already knew, too, what Hank said next. He said, 'But she wasn't talking about me anyway. She was saying it about an old man.'

Perched on my left hip, Rosie reached up and twirled my hair. 'Rosie wants to eat.'

'We're about to leave.' I turned my gaze back to the security guard. 'Is there anything else you need?'

The man pointed to Rosie. 'She's your daughter?'

'Obviously!' As I snapped at him, I felt an awareness of how I could be outraged in a way Hank couldn't. Did that mean that being outraged was my duty? Or that it was humiliating to Hank?

Calmly, the security guard said, 'Can I see some ID?'

I glared. 'What will that prove? You don't even know my daughter's last name.'

'If I'm not mistaken, it's Tucker.' The guard was matter-of-fact, not gloating.

'Just show him your ID, Kate,' Hank said, and his voice was still tightly controlled, which seemed evidence that I was probably humiliating him.

I hadn't previously realized that I didn't have my driver's license on me; I'd been protesting on principle. But as I tried to think how I'd reach for my wallet with a child in each arm, it occurred to me that its saggy weight was absent from the pocket of my vest, which must have meant – I hoped – that the wallet had fallen out while I was driving. Aloud, I said, 'My license is in my car.' I made my voice polite, which probably just sounded like sarcasm, as I said to the guard, 'Would you like to walk out with us and I'll show you?' There was no way I was letting Rosie or Owen out of my sight.

The man curled his lower lip in and chewed on it. 'What's your home address?'

I recited it, thinking, *This is bullshit. This is bullshit, and we should sue.*

'Date of birth?' he asked.

I gave that as well.

'And the child's date of birth?'

Was this anything other than a face-saving exercise for him, the pretense that he'd release us because we'd provided the information he requested rather than because he'd screwed up by bringing Hank and Rosie back here in the first place? But I told him Rosie's date of birth, and I was not surprised when he said, 'All right then. I'm going to let you folks go. In the future, you need to watch that your children don't make statements that raise concerns.'

He led the four of us to the door that opened onto the store proper, and he stayed behind as we walked out. Immediately, the store's humming normality enveloped us: the rows of cosmetics and soaps and lotions, the ignorance of the other customers. 'Rosie, you can walk,' I said, and I slid her down my side. 'But hold my hand.' None of us spoke again until we were outside, when Hank said, 'I need to get Amelia.' There was a distance to his tone, as if we scarcely knew each other better than either of us knew the security guard.

'That guy was nuts,' I said. 'He had no grounds—'

Hank shook his head. 'Let's forget about it.'

At home, I had fed Rosie and Owen and gotten them down for their naps when my cellphone rang. Was Hank prepared now to talk about the weirdness of what had just happened? Had my father changed his mind about going to the hospital? But no, neither – it was Jeremy.

'I saw on CNN about the day care, and I don't know,' he said. 'Maybe you were right and I was wrong.' He sounded rattled, and unlike himself.

'What are you talking about?'

'Have you not heard?'

'Today has been crazy. But heard what?'

'An eighteen-wheeler crashed into Rosie's old day care. You remember that playroom in the front with the huge windows? It went right through there. There's pictures online, although you probably shouldn't—' Hastily, he added, 'Sorry, I should have said this already: No one was injured besides the driver. There was hardly anyone there today, because so many people kept their kids home.' Jeremy was quiet in an odd way, and when he spoke again, I was shocked to realize he was crying. He said, 'I just keep thinking, what if we hadn't pulled Rosie out of there, what if Vi hadn't made her prediction? I know I've been dismissive, but if Rosie had been—' Then he had to stop.

'Jeremy,' I said. 'Sweetheart. It's fine. We're fine. Those are really big ifs.' He said nothing, and I added, 'Rosie and Owen are asleep right now. Honestly, I don't think there's going to be an earthquake anymore. I'm not worried, and if I'm not worried, you definitely shouldn't be.'

He sniffed loudly (Jeremy had not cried at our wedding or at his aunt's funeral – in fact, the only time I'd ever seen him cry was watching the movie

Brian's Song, and even that had been more like watery eyes than tears) before saying, 'I'm thinking I should come home today.'

'We're fine,' I said. 'Forget everything I said before. You need to stay and deliver your paper and schmooze with people.' How had we arrived at this point, with him lobbying to return early and me trying to convince him not to? But it was, in a way, unsurprising; wasn't our marriage a series of flip-flops in which we alternated the stances either of us took? And, even if he didn't realize it, wasn't the reason he was suggesting coming home that he knew I'd talk him out of it?

Jeremy sniffed again. 'What did you mean about it being a crazy day?'

After I'd filled him in on my father's fainting and what I mistakenly referred to as Hank's arrest – no, no, I had to quickly say, not arrested, just detained – Jeremy said, 'Jesus Christ. Has Hank never had Rosie without you before?'

'I guess not,' I said.

'I wonder if Courtney knows yet. Her panel was this morning.'

'I assume Hank called her.'

'And you did or didn't make a doctor's appointment for your dad?'

'I didn't. I was on the phone with the office when I heard from Hank.'

'Your dad should definitely be checked out. It could be a head rush or it could be something serious.'

'I realize that,' I said. 'Believe me.'

'I'm not trying to stress you out.' He himself sounded more normal, not shaky like before. He said, 'Part of me wants you to see the pictures of the day care and part of me thinks you definitely shouldn't.'

'I'm not planning to look at them.' As if I needed a reminder that scary things could happen. On the contrary: I yearned to be a person stunned by misfortune.

'I checked the times for if I try to change my flight, and they're all bad,' Jeremy said.

Of course they were. And of course I'd told him not to bother, meaning that by staying in Denver, he was merely obliging me.

'Don't worry about it,' I said.

Rosie hadn't yet awakened from her nap by four – apparently, the drama of Target had worn her out – at which point I knew we wouldn't be returning to my father's apartment for dinner unless he outright asked us to. Which he wouldn't, though when I called him, he showed none of the morning's irritability. When I mentioned that I'd made a doctor's appointment for him for the following Monday, he even thanked me, and then – this was my true victory – I managed to extract a promise that he wouldn't drive Vi to the vigil. 'I've tried calling her a few times today, but it says her phone is full,' he said.

'I'll text her for you.'

473

'Will you tell her I'm sorry not to help?'

'I'm sure she'll understand.'

'I hope being wrong about the earthquake isn't a terrible blow.' He seemed to be in a musing sort of mood, as if he were talking to himself as much as to me, and he added, 'I suppose it still could happen, but when I woke this morning and it was raining, I thought it was awfully unlikely. Violet's picking up on something, there's no doubt about that, but I don't think it's an earthquake.'

So the weather had convinced him, too; this was amusing, coming from my not-exactly-intuitive father.

And then he said, 'I didn't have a sense one way or the other in advance. I certainly couldn't rule it out. But the rain made me think, *Not today.*'

There was no one except Owen to see it, and he was busy with a toy car on the living room floor, but my jaw literally dropped. *I didn't have a sense one way or the other?* Since when had my father – my *father* – had senses? And he was as casual as if this was not only an established fact between us but one we'd agreed was no big deal.

Trying to sound equally casual, I said, 'Yeah, the rain made me have doubts, too.'

I waited for him to reveal more, but instead he said, 'I hope it didn't disrupt your day to come get me this morning.'

'I'm just glad you're feeling better. Why don't I pick you up tomorrow morning and we'll get your car?'

'That's not an inconvenience?'

'Not at all. What if we come around eleven?' Then I said, 'Will you promise that you'll call if you feel faint again? I really mean it, Dad. Even if it's the middle of the night.'

After I hung up, I texted Vi: *Dad asked me to tell u he can't drive u tonight.* It wasn't that I was surprised when she didn't text back, but still, it was hard not to feel like I was waiting for a response. Because Vi and I weren't speaking, and because the topic of senses had gone sour between Jeremy and me, there was no one I could talk to about my father's revelation. To distract myself, I took a picture of Owen and his car with my phone and sent it off to Jeremy.

Around five, I texted Hank: *Have fun at eq party!* Though I still hadn't heard from Vi, Hank replied immediately: *Decided to skip. Want us to bring over chinese?*

Twist my arm, I wrote.

At our house, as Hank unloaded white cartons from a brown paper bag and set them on the kitchen table, he seemed subdued, the way he'd been in the days before and after Courtney's abortion. He didn't mention Target, and neither did I.

The children were seated, Owen in his high chair, and Amelia was chanting, 'I want noodles! I want noodles!' Rosie pointed at the pile of chopsticks still in their paper sleeves and said, 'Mama gives Rosie that.'

'Those are for grown-ups,' I said.

I set beers out for Hank and me and spooned rice onto a paper plate so that it would cool; the fact that we were eating takeout seemed to conceal the weirdness of my having put away our china. After Hank had opened the flaps of all the cartons – he'd ordered vegetable pot stickers, vegetable lo mein with tofu, broccoli with garlic sauce, and Szechuan eggplant – I thought of making a joke about how he'd become a vegetarian again, but I didn't want to risk offending him.

He prepared a plate for Amelia, and I made one for Rosie. Owen was having a jar of pears.

As Hank and I served ourselves, he said, 'I know you said Vi's wrong, but I'm still waiting for the ground to start rumbling.'

'Well, there's been so much hype.'

'You never had premonitions?'

His question had a making-conversation quality to it, or even a postfight quality, as if we'd quarreled but were now trying to get along. How could he know what a loaded topic he'd stumbled onto? It wasn't impossible that I'd have told him the truth under different circumstances, but it seemed unfair to dump my life-defining secret on him when he was just filling the silence. So I said, 'Not like Vi.' Then I said, 'Did you hear about the daycare place on Hanley?'

'Wow, I didn't even realize until right now – that's where Rosie went, huh?'

'Only for about five weeks. But Jeremy told me not to look at the pictures.'

'They were saying on the radio the driver fell asleep after being on the road for fifteen hours.'

'What's Mommy and Hank talking about?' Rosie said.

'A man who was driving a truck.' Glancing at her plate, I said, 'You're doing a great job eating broccoli.'

'How's your dad?' Hank asked.

'If you ask him, fine.' I sighed. 'He has a doctor's appointment for Monday.'

'Did you tell Vi he fainted?'

'That would involve speaking to her.' This wasn't even true – it could merely involve texting her – but presumably the day was chaotic enough for Vi without the addition of my father's health problems. Anyway, the thing I really wanted to talk to her about, even more than the fainting episode, was his astonishing mention of having senses.

'If you're interested in going to that vigil, I'll stay here,' Hank said. 'Amelia can go to sleep in your bed.'

'Honestly, the vigil sounds awful. Would *you* want to go?'

'She's not my sister.'

'You think I'm being unsupportive?'

'I think however things play out, this has to be an insanely weird night for her.'

I hadn't seriously considered attending the vigil, and for about thirty seconds, I thought, *Okay, if*

I put Owen and Rosie down first, and if Hank stays here with Amelia, and then I thought, *But it's closed to the public. And my name won't be on any list. And there'll be media camped outside. And Vi said I'm turning my children into clingy little wimps.* So no. She was on her own.

I said to Hank, 'You and Amelia are welcome to hang out here as long as you want, but I'm not going to the vigil.'

'Mama.' Rosie tugged on my shirt. 'This broccoli is tasty and wonderful.'

Hank and I both laughed, and as I said, 'I think so, too,' I felt that the awkwardness from Target had dissipated; things were normal again. After we finished eating, Hank distracted Rosie by singing 'Bingo' while I applied Neosporin to her cut, and then he watched all three children in the living room and I cleaned up the food and set out the mousetraps. When I rejoined them, I called Jeremy so Rosie could say good night, and when I carried Owen upstairs, Rosie and Amelia were taking turns holding Hank's hands, walking up his legs, and doing backward somersaults. If no one ended up puking, I thought, I just might have to conclude that the evening had been a success. Vi and I had indeed been wrong about what would happen on October 16.

Hank did put Amelia down to sleep in our bed, after I'd taken Rosie up to her room, and finally there was that moment, familiar to me from nights with Jeremy, when Hank and I could both relax. I'd turned the television to CNN, which was the only channel with live coverage of St Louis, though even on CNN it wasn't continuous. Anderson Cooper, who was in the studio in New York, was interviewing the surgeon general about subjects that had nothing to do with earthquakes, and then he'd get periodic updates from the ground in St Louis, where the correspondent was standing with the Arch behind him. 'You want another beer?' I said.

'Are you having one?' Hank asked.

He knew about my one-beer-and-one-coffee-per-day policy. 'I will if you will,' I said. 'But only because it's earthquake season.'

I sat in the armchair and he sat on the couch, and we flipped among various stations. On MSNBC, the host of the show was talking to a FEMA engineer, and Hank said, 'I thought all geologists were in Denver right now.' Later, when they showed a clip of Vi's first interview with Matt Lauer, Hank said, 'How weird is this for you?' and I said, 'Very.' Eventually, during a commercial break on CNN, we ended up watching a competitive cooking show and didn't change it.

Sitting there, I became conscious of a strange – an inappropriate – tension between Hank and me. The longer the stretches lasted when neither of us spoke, the more I felt like we were in a romantic comedy about two single parents trying, after years off the dating market, to get up the

479

nerve for a first kiss. Except that, obviously, having a first kiss was the worst thing Hank and I could do.

Just before ten, as the head chef berated a contestant, Owen let out a cry, and I said, 'I've been summoned' and went up to feed him. Usually after his ten o'clock nursing, I didn't go back downstairs – I went to bed, where Jeremy joined me after he'd closed down the house – but sitting in the glider in Owen's darkened room, I was completely awake. And what I was thinking about wasn't the countdown to the end of this bizarre day, this whole bizarre period; I wasn't thinking of Owen, even as I burped him, changed his diaper, and set him back in his crib. I was thinking of Hank, and what I realized was at once shocking and unsurprising: I wanted to have sex with him. I had never felt this way before. Had I? I was pretty sure I hadn't. Clearly, I needed to get him out of the house as quickly as possible. (I wanted to take off my clothes and I wanted him to take off his clothes, and when we were both naked, I wanted – well, any number of scenarios would work. I could get on top of him, or he could get on top of me, or he could enter me from behind, with me pressed against the couch cushions. I didn't generally love that position, but in this case, I'd take it. I'd take any of it.)

As I descended the stairs, my heart pounded, and this was not anxious heart; it was something else entirely, something familiar, though I hadn't experienced it for years. There was a pressure in the roof of my mouth, and even my saliva had thickened. Surely when I saw Hank sitting there, regular Hank, the friend with whom I discussed diaper rash and preschool admissions, surely this anticipatory alertness in my body would correct itself. Surely.

He turned his head as I entered the living room, and nothing was corrected; I felt deranged with lust. How had I managed, for the last two years, to ignore how good-looking he was, his eyes and his smile and his smooth, dark forearms? He patted the couch next to him and said, 'Come on over,' and still, we both might have pretended this was all just friendliness – maybe on his part it was – as I foolishly, foolishly sat beside him. Not as close as I'd have sat to Jeremy, not touching, but not far enough away.

The local news had come on – the anchor was describing a bank robbery in Fenton – and I said, 'Did they mention Vi yet?' My voice sounded oddly normal.

'Are you kidding? She was the top story.' His tone was normal, too.

'Of course she was.' I reached for the beer I'd left on the table and took a sip. (I wasn't drunk; I can't use that as an excuse.) I tried to make myself think of Jeremy, but he seemed like an idea and not a person; instead of being a body next to me, his name was just a word, and the body next to mine was someone else's.

The local news turned into *The Tonight Show*. It had been fifteen minutes since either of us had spoken, and I was afraid that if I did speak, it would be to beg Hank to touch me. Then, at the same time, we both started to talk. Hank motioned for me to go ahead, and I said, 'I was just going to say we should go to the zoo tomorrow. I'm driving out to my dad's at some point, but we're free besides that.' (Really, I was the dullest person on the planet. No wonder I irritated Vi.)

'Sure. We'd be up for the zoo.' There was another full minute of silence, then Hank said, 'See, I've gotten used to people seeing me out with Amelia during the day and assuming I'm her deadbeat dad – that she's one of the seven children I have with my five different baby mamas, and she's just the one who's with me while her mom is off, you know, collecting welfare.'

'Hank,' I said. 'No one would ever think that.'

'Trust me,' he said. 'They would and they do. That's not even my point. I'm used to it. It's just that, the idea that I'd kidnap this little white girl – it's like, okay, assume I'm a deadbeat, but seeing me as a child molester – that's where I draw the line.'

'Hank, I'm not just saying this to make you feel better. I swear to God I can't imagine anyone ever in a million years thinking you're a child molester.'

'Besides the security guard who thought exactly that? And the responsible Target shopper who turned us in?' He was quiet before saying, 'You want to feel like you're above all these prejudices and stereotypes. Like, hey, it's 2009! We can chart our own path! But me being the stay-at-home parent, it's not just other people who still don't get it. With Courtney, our deal was that this setup would give me more time to paint, and she's like, "I don't see any paintings." Not even from the perspective of generating income – she just wonders how I can have any self-respect doing nothing besides hanging out with a three-year-old all day.'

Of course Courtney would wonder this. 'I think anyone who's ever stayed home with a child knows how hard it is,' I said.

'She's right, though,' Hank said. 'I mean, what the fuck am I doing with my life? You wouldn't think it to look at us now, but there was a time when Courtney and I were considered equally promising. In our separate fields, we were both going to light the world on fire. Do you even know that I have a master's in painting?' Before I could respond, he said, 'Not to mention the whole traitor-to-the-race thing. First I squander my Harvard education studying art, then I marry a white girl, then I let her support me. When I could be a hedge fund manager in Manhattan, making big donations to my church, grooming my daughter for Jack and Jill.'

'I think you're being way too hard on yourself.'

Hank half-smiled. 'I'm sure you do.' He took a sip of beer. 'When Courtney was interviewing at Wash U, a friend of ours who'd done his postdoc at Mizzou told us Missouri is the northernmost southern state.'

'And the southernmost northern state,' I said. 'And the easternmost western state, and the westernmost eastern state.'

'But it was the southern part that got my attention – I was picturing good old boys waving Confederate flags.'

I said nothing; I did sometimes see Confederate flags, mostly in the form of bumper stickers.

Hank said, 'What happened after Wash U offered Courtney the job was almost the opposite. People were overly excited to find out I'm black. I'd been teaching at a prep school in Boston, but when Courtney put out feelers about whether Wash U could help me find a job here, the two schools I was interested in said they didn't need an art teacher. They'd meet with me for an informational interview, but they weren't hiring. So Courtney and I make a trip out anyway, I go to the schools, and from the minute I introduce myself, they're falling all over themselves, and what do you know? It turns out they *do* need another art teacher. Both schools! It was like they'd never met a black man who knew how to hold a paintbrush.'

'But you took one of the jobs, didn't you?'

'I did, and my co-workers were nice, for the most part. There wasn't an admissions tour in my three years there that didn't stop in my classroom, but they were nice.'

'For what this is worth,' I said, 'that Target

security guard doesn't represent everyone in St Louis.'

'Granted. But no matter how many liberal professors we know, there are certain realities. And then I think about Amelia, and were we selfish to have her? Like, "Yeah, the world is a fucked-up, racist place, but let's make our little half-black, half-white baby anyway because we're in love and she'll be so cute!"'

'I think every parent wonders some version of that,' I said. 'I definitely wonder what I've saddled Owen and Rosie with.'

'Maybe Courtney was right,' Hank said. 'Maybe being biracial and retarded would have been too much for one kid.'

'That wasn't her reasoning, was it?'

Hank shrugged.

'You know how earlier you asked if I'd ever had premonitions?' I said. 'Well, I lied. Vi and I started out exactly the same, when we were little, but as we got older, I decided being psychic was creepy and embarrassing. Before I met Jeremy, I was sure I wouldn't have biological children because I was afraid they'd be psychic, too. I wanted to be a mother, but I was planning to adopt.'

'Holy shit,' Hank said.

'I'm barely psychic anymore,' I said. 'Although today, when it was raining in the morning I knew Vi was wrong about the earthquake. I just knew.'

'And *have* your kids shown signs of ESP? I guess Owen wouldn't yet, but has Rosie?'

485

I shook my head. 'And now I can't imagine my life without them. But sometimes I feel like I'm waiting for the other shoe to drop.'

'I can't believe you've been holding out on me all this time.' Hank gave me a mischievous look.

'I'm telling you that I'm fourth-rate now. At best. Please don't put your hand behind your back and ask how many fingers you're holding up.'

'Oh, I'm planning to exploit you for far bigger gain. Investments I should make on the Tokyo Stock Exchange and that kind of thing.' Then he said, 'I know you feel really burned by Vi right now, but she completely looks up to you. You realize that, don't you?'

'Vi thinks I'm a shallow, boring housewife.' I laughed. 'And she's right.'

'We all need someone in our lives to keep us honest.' Then he said, 'That's not really how you see yourself, is it? Because you have everything going for you: your happy marriage and your cute kids, and you're all nice and pretty—' There was a weird way his voice caught on *nice* and again on *pretty*, like he was preemptively making fun of his own sincerity. Even so, these were by far the most generous things anyone had said to me in a long time. Jeremy and I were too tired to give each other compliments.

Simultaneously, I felt the impulse to point out the reasons Hank was wrong – and really, he of all people knew how messy our lives were, how narrow and repetitive our days – and the impulse to bask in this version of myself, to pretend that everything he said was true.

'You forgot organized,' I said. 'How well-organized I am and what a tidy housekeeper and that's why there are never any mice in our kitchen.'

We looked at each other, and he said, 'If I kissed you right now, it would probably be a really bad idea, huh?'

This was the final opportunity to avoid the evening's outcome. Deflecting his overture would be awkward, but surmountably so. We wouldn't have transgressed in any explicit way.

And so I did the opposite of deflecting: I lunged forward, I pressed my mouth against his, and we were kissing in a way Jeremy and I hardly kissed anymore – it was like Hank and I were trying to consume each other. Again I wondered, had we been waiting all along to do this? The idea that because he was a straight man and I was a straight woman, there would therefore be sexual tension between us seemed so clichéd that it had never been difficult for me to dismiss.

And then I wasn't wondering anything; his hands were all over me and my hands were all over him, and there was that good smell Hank had, like cloves and soap, a smell that I'd always been faintly aware of and now felt drugged by Jeremy did not, of course, exist in this moment (if he existed, how could I have done what I was doing?), yet even so I was conscious of Hank as Not Jeremy: Hank's torso was bigger, his shoulders were broader, his biceps harder. I had not held a man other than Jeremy for seven years; to me, sex meant sex with Jeremy. But here was a reminder that the narrowness of my life, the repetition of my habits, were choices I made.

We'd shifted so his back was against the arm of the couch, his legs out in front of him, and I was on his lap, and without much difficulty Hank managed to get his hand past the waistband of my jeans, into my underwear, and to touch me in a way that made me twist and moan above him, a way that made it seem extremely urgent that I unfasten his pants and pull them off, past his knees, that I then pull off his briefs – so Hank wore briefs; they were gray Calvin Klein – and I held his erection (again, in a fleeting not-thinking way, I did note that, consistent with the racial stereotype, his penis was larger than Jeremy's, though not dramatically so) and with my thumb I rubbed the exposed underside of the tip, this rubbing motion being something my husband who didn't exist liked, and something Hank apparently did, too, and then I guided Hank into me; I was slick and he glided right in.

He stayed inside me as he moved into an upright sitting position with his back to the couch cushions, as if he were watching television. And in fact the television was still on, but instead of following *The Tonight Show,* we were naked from the waist down, grinding against each other, both of us breathing quickly, and he was pushing up my shirt, pulling down the cups of my bra without bothering to unfasten them, and rubbing his face between my breasts, sucking my nipples, which was something I hadn't let Jeremy do since I'd given birth to Rosie, because it was too confusing to have my nipples in the mouth of more than one person. But with Hank – and I was wearing one of my usual threadbare nursing bras, and it was possible that I'd start leaking milk – I didn't care. Hank's tongue on my nipples was the least confusing part of what was happening, but I didn't care about any of it. I just needed him to keep jamming up into me, I needed to feel his warm skin under my hands, his solid body, which offered a comfort I had been unable to find elsewhere for the last several weeks. And then the good feeling tipped over and spread, I was shuddering with it, and when I moaned, he bounced me against him faster, gripping my hips, and a minute passed, and another minute, another minute after that, and he was still going. First, enough time elapsed for the woozy glow inside me to dissipate. Then I began to wonder how long it would be until he finished – was this intentional on his part, or was there a problem. Or neither; was he just not efficient but didn't see a need to be? And then I was officially waiting for him to be done, and then, perhaps seven minutes after I'd come, I heard from the other room a clacking sound, a single snap, and I knew immediately that the mouse had been caught. This was the moment when Jeremy reentered my consciousness, and I understood that I had betrayed him in an irreversible way.

Because if a mousetrap had snapped while Jeremy and I were going at it, we'd have started laughing. Or at least we'd have acknowledged it, whereas with Hank, as well as I knew him in other contexts, he was sexually a stranger to me. Had he even heard the mousetrap? If he hadn't, I wasn't about to bring it to his attention and thereby risk prolonging the conclusion of this act. (Later, there would be opportunity to wonder why I hadn't done exactly this. Or not prolonged the conclusion but prevented it. But in the moment, the idea of not allowing Hank as much time as he needed would have struck me as bad manners, like clearing the plates at a dinner party while your guests were in the middle of their meal.)

After an endless stretch in which I had traveled across continents of disbelief and regret, over forests and fields and rivers, and he was *still* thrusting away under me, finally, finally, he sighed deeply – his eyes were closed – and stopped moving. He tilted his head back against the cushions, and his hands remained at my hips, though it seemed to be because he hadn't gotten around to moving them rather than because he was actively placing them there. My head was above his, and I felt an uncertainty about what to do next that was as complete as the comfort I'd derived from him such a short time before. What words would either of us now say? In what way was I to extricate my body from his? And surely I was the one who had to start the extrication, wasn't I, since I was on top? The moment when he'd open his eyes would be terrifying, I thought; if there were a way to permanently avoid it, I would.

And then he did open them. He opened his eyes and raised his head and smiled wryly, and it was the same smile he'd exchanged with me the week before at the Oak Knoll playground when Amelia had thrown not one but two apples into a muddy puddle, as if he were saying, *What can you do?* He patted my side in a friendly way that also, clearly, meant *Get up.*

I swung my left leg over his lap and turned until I was also sitting on the couch – I was bare-assed on the couch where Rosie and I read about the adventures of Frog and Toad – and I leaned forward to retrieve my underwear and jeans from the floor. In my peripheral vision, I could see that he, too, was pulling his clothes back on, and I heard him zip his pants.

He tapped me on the arm, and I turned my head.

'Hi,' he said. Again, his expression – it wasn't one of intense amusement, but it wasn't unamused, either. It wasn't horrified. He said, 'Are you okay?'

'Yeah, I'm fine,' I said.

I felt another way I hadn't for years, which was that I didn't want to be the girl who was lame after sex. Who took it, for whatever reason, too seriously. This seems odd in retrospect, given that

I might have just wrecked my marriage and that surely wrecking one's marriage was grounds for seriousness.

Hank stood. 'I'm gonna pee,' he said.

This time, I just nodded.

I could hear him in our downstairs bathroom, and I had no idea what to do with myself. Go to the upstairs bathroom and wipe away the semen leaking into my underwear? Throw away the dead mouse in the kitchen? Check on my children?

The toilet flushed, the faucet ran, and he came back into the living room and said, 'So I should get Amelia home to sleep in her own bed.'

Yes, this was exactly what needed to happen – they needed to leave. Which did not preclude me from feeling a sting of rejection at the hastiness of his departure. How was it possible to know already that this had been a mistake and still to be as sensitive to his every inflection as if we were dating?

As I stood, I said, 'Let me get the leftover Chinese for you.'

'Nah, you keep it. Rosie was going to town on the broccoli, huh?' We were both quiet for a second, and he said, 'I'll say goodbye to you now, because who knows what state Amelia will be in when I bring her down.' He stepped forward and set his palms against both sides of my jaw and kissed me on the lips, quickly but fully. In a strange way, this moment brought me back to him. My jangled, seething brain was busy thinking, *I would never leave Jeremy for Hank; I could never even have an affair with Hank, because he takes so long to come.* But when he kissed me, it was so much the gesture of a husband that I could, however briefly and misguidedly, imagine being his wife. Also, this time, the taste of his mouth was familiar.

While he was getting Amelia, I gathered their jackets and Amelia's pink backpack. He carried her down the stairs, and as far as I could tell, she was still asleep. As I let them out the door, he whispered – he said it not the way a single guy does to a single woman but the regular way he'd said it to me hundreds of times before, for play-date-scheduling purposes – 'I'll give you a call tomorrow.'

The first thing I did when they were gone was go into the bathroom myself, but sitting on the toilet, I was so churned up I couldn't pee. What – *what* – had I done? What had I been thinking? How could such a ruinous act be so easy? Its non-occurrence up to this point hadn't required restraint, so it seemed as if, conversely, there ought to have been more effort involved in its occurrence. And what now? Should I tell Jeremy? If so, while he was still in Denver? No, not while he was away. Definitely not. But whatever had happened between Hank and me was finished, I thought. It had to be. And then, having resolved something, I was able to pee. When I wiped, Hank's semen coated the toilet paper.

After I'd washed my hands, I dried them on an orange hand towel, which was one of two Halloween-themed towels Rosie and I had picked out the year before at Target; the orange one was embroidered with a little spider, and the other was purple with an orange pumpkin on it. As I dried my hands, I experienced the first bout of nostalgia – there would be many – for the person I had been before this evening, the person who'd bought these silly towels, who hadn't cheated on her husband. The person who had felt guilty when she hid *The Berenstain Bears Go to Camp* because she was sick of reading it to Rosie or when she forgot to put sunscreen on Rosie and Owen before leaving for the playground. In the past, those had been the kinds of sins I committed against my family.

In the kitchen, while averting my eyes as much as possible, I slid the poor dead mouse in the trap into a plastic bag; I walked out the back door, deposited the bag in the garbage bin, and washed my hands again at the kitchen sink. Then I filled a glass with tap water and gulped it down. It was somehow reassuring that I'd already cleaned up from dinner; it was one less way that my life was squalid.

Back in the living room, I changed the channel from NBC to CNN. It was eleven twenty-three. Was there any point in watching the final half hour of a nonevent? I'd shower before bed, I decided, then return downstairs to hear them officially say on TV that nothing had happened.

I carried both monitors up to the bathroom and had just pulled back the shower curtain when the doorbell rang. I looked at my own face in the mirror, as if for guidance, and the bell rang again. Who would it be at almost midnight? Had Jeremy decided to come home after all? And Jesus, what if he'd arrived an hour earlier? But no, Jeremy would have a key. My father? It seemed doubtful. Marisa Mazarelli, attempting once more to pry her romantic future out of me? But she was traveling too. The likeliest possibilities had to be Hank or some reporter who wanted to interview me in the moment of my sister's prediction not coming to pass. Either way, to ignore the doorbell would keep me from getting in the shower out of worry that whoever had rung was still lurking.

I had failed to consider one person, and when I peered through the window at the top of the door, even though the glass was beveled and the porch light was off, I recognized her immediately. I opened the door and said, 'Hi, Vi.'

She held up both hands, as if in surrender. 'Just me – no paparazzi. Although I swear I understand now how Jennifer Aniston feels.' I let her in, and as she shrugged off her cape and tossed it toward the living room couch, she said, 'Is Jeremy asleep?'

'He's out of town.'

'He left you here to hold down the homestead while he fled for higher ground?'

'He's at a conference in Denver that was planned way before all this.'

'That makes more sense. I mean, I couldn't imagine he ever believed me.' She sounded nonchalant, not bitter, as she added, 'Which means that now he gets to say I told you so. I just wish Courtney Wheeling the self-righteous prune didn't get to say it, too.'

Courtney. So focused on my betrayal of Jeremy had I been that I hadn't yet considered her. And though she wasn't my favorite person, she was – she had been – a friend. Really, what had I done? What was my justification? That the past few weeks had been stressful or that Jeremy had let me down by going to Denver? These were not adequate, as justifications went. I pointed to the TV and said, 'Aren't you supposed to be at the vigil?'

'The whole vibe was bugging me, so I said I had to go to the bathroom and snuck out the back. I could tell that when midnight came, they were going to offer me condolences like someone had died while secretly gloating.' She added, 'I thought I'd feel humiliated, I know I'm *supposed* to feel humiliated, but I really and truly feel relieved. I had a nightmare this week of, like, this falling-down church with dead bodies in front of it, and it was so gruesome. And maybe it was just some slum in Nigeria or somewhere like that. Maybe it was the country I was supposed to go to for the Peace Corps, and not even an earthquake but normal life. Matt Lauer interviewed me again this morning—'

'I saw.'

'I think he thought I was lying when I said I wanted my prediction to be wrong – that I was putting on a good front. But it's true. Sometimes it's good to be wrong.' She paused. 'Do you think I should feel humiliated?'

I didn't answer right away, and then I said, 'I don't know what to think anymore.'

'Ha,' she said, but she still didn't seem offended. 'Nice dodge.'

'Dad fainted today,' I said. 'That was the reason he couldn't drive you. He – well, he was getting a massage, and he stood up afterward and passed out.'

'Dad was getting a *massage*? Like a *massage* massage or a happy-ending massage?' Already, I felt the relief of sharing this information with the one person in the world who'd feel exactly the way I did about it: just as concerned and just as squeamish. 'Is he okay?' she said.

'I think he's fine. He was super prickly when I went to get him. I wanted to take him to the hospital, and he insisted I take him home, although I did make a doctor's appointment for him for Monday. But here's the really bizarre part: Later, on the phone, he basically confessed that he has senses.'

'Dad? *Our* dad?'

'I know. He said he hadn't known before today if there would be an earthquake, then he woke up this morning and saw the rain and knew there wouldn't. And he said it very matter-of-factly, like he wasn't dropping a bombshell. I kind of wonder if he'd taken pain medication and was loopy.'

Vi's expression was one of uncertain and excited interest, as if she were trying to remember the details of a very odd but pleasant dream. At last, she said, 'Wow. I mean, holy crap, Dad, what else have you been hiding from us, you mild-mannered lighting salesman from Omaha, Nebraska? Besides your massages with hookers, that is.'

'I always thought senses were hereditary,' I said. 'I just didn't think they were from his side. Anyway, don't ask him about it. Or about the massage.'

'Why not?'

'Because it's none of our business.'

'Was the masseuse Asian?'

I shook my head. 'Maybe Polish.'

'It wasn't a tranny, was it?' It was hard to guess whether Vi wanted the answer to be yes or no.

'There was an older woman and a younger one, maybe a mother and daughter, and I think the daughter was the one who'd given him the massage. I mean, she looked over eighteen. And they were both real females. It was at a place in Olivette.'

'But it obviously skeeved you out, so what aren't you telling me?'

'I'm just not sure if it was a sexual thing.' Though, really, who was I to pass judgment? 'Let's not talk about it anymore.'

'Remember when you thought I should give Dad a gift certificate for a massage for his birthday and I said he'd hate it?' Vi laughed. 'Well, I stand corrected.'

And then on the television screen, there appeared

footage of the truck smashed into the day care, an aerial shot followed by a close-up of brightly colored plastic balls and a flattened teddy bear and shattered glass, and I could understand why Jeremy had warned me against looking at the images.

I said, 'Do you know this is where Rosie went?'

'Really?' Vi seemed more interested than I'd have expected, though I myself was preoccupied by trying to figure out why, in the last minutes before the clock ran out on Vi's prediction, CNN was showing this accident. I didn't yet understand that the accident at the day care would become a central part of the earthquake narrative – it would become the part that redeemed Vi, at least in the eyes of St Louisans. The logic was similar to Jeremy's when he'd told me about the accident: If not for Vi's prediction, then the front room of the building would have been filled with children when the truck crashed into it; ergo, Vi had saved the children's lives. And maybe the reason Vi wasn't humiliated when there was no earthquake on October 16 was that at some level, she already knew – she had a sense – of this public redemption.

Personally, I never bought into this version, and my view, it turns out, is shared by people outside St Louis, which I know because I no longer live in St Louis myself. It was only in the city of Vi's prediction that the prediction justified itself. The proximity of the accident made people nervous, left them feeling grateful for what hadn't happened, and their gratitude needed a recipient. That recipient became my sister. So she was wrong about the earthquake; she was right about something else, and her rightness allowed her to be forgiven.

In that moment when Vi and I were still watching TV, when it still wasn't quite midnight – we were standing just inside the front door because we'd never sat down – Vi said, 'You haven't asked how I got over here.'

'I thought you snuck out the back of the bookstore.'

'I did,' Vi said. 'But after that.'

'How'd you get over here?'

Vi beamed. 'I drove,' she said.

CHAPTER 17

osie's music class met in the basement of a temple in Clayton, and what I first noticed – this embarrasses me now – was that the parent in one of the other parent-child duos was a black man. Then I noticed that he was a fit black man wearing a Wash U T-shirt. Then I noticed that he was Hank Wheeling, the husband of Jeremy's colleague Courtney. Across the circle of children and moms – all the other parents were white mothers, and there were twelve adults total – I made eye contact with him, patted my chest, and mouthed, *Kate Tucker.* He nodded and smiled. We were waiting for the first class to start, and in my arms, Rosie squirmed in her flowered onesie. Amelia, who was then almost one and a half, though I knew neither her name nor her age, stood in front of Hank, clapping and yelling, 'Bubbles! Bubbles! Bubbles!' She was exceptionally cute – so cute, in fact, that she could have been a model for the Swedish organic cotton baby clothes I had told Jeremy I'd stop ordering. Her skin was light brown and her eyes were dark brown and she had ludicrously long eyelashes and curly, wiry hair that was pulled into a fluffy ponytail on top of her head. I happened to know that her striped T-shirt and pink skirt were *from* the Swedish organic clothing company because I recognized the outfit from the most recent catalog.

When the teacher arrived, toting little drums and bells, she had us introduce our children but not ourselves, after which we sang and danced for the next forty minutes. The class culminated with a conga line that snaked around the room as the adults shouted the lyrics to 'I've Been Working on the Railroad.' A few weeks later, when I convinced Jeremy to come with me to a class so he could see how adorable Rosie looked while pounding a drum, I asked him afterward what he thought, and he said, 'It was fine.' 'You didn't like it?' I said. 'No, it was cute,' he said. 'It was just kind of tedious.' Which made it clear, given that the class was a weekly high-water mark in entertainment for Rosie and me, that Jeremy could never have been a stay-at-home parent.

During that first class, as we moved around the room, reconfiguring ourselves, Hank and I exchanged general pleasantries of the sort I was also exchanging with the mothers – as Rosie reached for a bell, he'd say, 'Almost got it!' and I'd say, 'So close and yet so far,' and we'd chuckle warmly. It seemed to me there was a slight charge in the classroom, the surprise of the other mothers at Hank's presence. After all, at a parent-child music class in Clayton, a man was rare enough and a black man was basically astonishing. And then there was the fact of his defined biceps and flat abdomen – I'd seen it when he'd lifted Amelia onto his shoulders and his shirt had risen – while most of the mothers, even the skinny ones, were still lumpily post-pregnant.

And then, while everyone sang 'Goodbye to Rosie, we'll see you next time,' I patted my daughter's bottom and realized, touching wetness, that she'd had a blowout. The next thing I realized, after I'd quickly gathered up my diaper bag and carried her to the bathroom, was that I had no clean diapers with me.

I looked down at Rosie lying on the changing table totally naked, smiling impishly, and I considered pulling the dirty diaper out of the trash and putting her back in it, but the thought of rewrapping her in that warm mustard-colored sludge was just too disgusting. So I sat her up, guiding her arms into a clean onesie, snapping it over her chest, while the onesie's legs hung behind her bottom like the tails of a tuxedo. I lifted her and opened the door of the bathroom, and in the hall, walking by, were Hank and Amelia.

'Sorry to bother you, Hank, but do you have a spare diaper?'

'Sure,' Hank said. 'Threes okay?'

Rosie was still in size 2, but I said, 'Perfect. I feel so dumb.'

'It happens to all of us.'

As he passed me the diaper, I thought of asking

if he and Amelia wanted to go to the smoothie place where I was planning to get lunch, but it felt a little weird to issue this invitation to a man instead of another mom.

Then he said, 'Hey, you guys want to come with us to the Bread Company? Amelia is very into their mac and cheese right now.'

'We'd love to,' I said.

The diaper alone would have been enough to make me like Hank, but it was about ten minutes after we'd sat down with our food that I knew I could be true friends with him. First the name of Jeremy and Courtney's department head, Leland Marcus, came up, and with no hesitation – and this was before either of our spouses had tenure – Hank said, 'I don't think he's a bad guy, but the one I can't stand is his wife.'

'I know!' I said. 'She's so rude.'

'I swear, at the potluck at the Vogts' I saw her spit a bite of food on the floor. Intentionally, I mean. And we weren't outside.'

'Before Jeremy and I got married, she basically told me that no woman can be a good worker and a good mother.'

Hank laughed. 'Classic.'

After we'd moved on to talking about what solids Rosie was eating and how old Amelia had been when she'd learned to walk, a John Mayer song began playing over the speaker system, and Hank gestured toward the ceiling and said, 'Can I just say that I knew from the start this guy was all wrong for Jessica Simpson? It was so obvious he was going to leave her heartbroken.' My surprise must have registered on my face because Hank said, 'You disagree?'

'I just can't believe you know that Jessica Simpson and John Mayer dated.' I was pretty sure Jeremy didn't know who either Jessica Simpson or John Mayer was.

'Courtney leaves copies of *Us Weekly* lying around the house,' Hank said. 'What can I say? Resistance is futile.'

'Really, Courtney reads *Us Weekly*?'

'Are you kidding? She subscribes.'

'And do you open them up or just look at the covers?'

In a good-natured voice, Hank said, 'Kate, that's a very personal question.'

'Didn't Courtney just win some major science prize?'

Hank grinned. 'I know, right?'

I said, 'So are you a full-time stay-at-home dad?'

'Funny you should ask. That's a topic of debate in the Wheeling household. I used to be a high school art teacher, and after Amelia was born, we decided, okay, I'll hang out with her during the day, and I'll work on my painting during her naps.' He rolled his eyes. 'Which has mostly resulted in me not setting foot in my studio from one month to the next, but I do know all the words to *Hop on Pop*.'

'"Up pup"?' I said. '"Pup is up"?'

Hank smiled. 'The truth is that Courtney comes home at four, so I could go to my studio then, which is just in our attic, but at that point in the day, all I want to do is drink a beer and chill out.'

'I hear you.' Then I said, 'Wait, Courtney comes home at four?'

'Am I getting Jeremy in trouble?'

'He comes home at five-fifteen, which isn't terrible. But he's pretty strict about not keeping different hours from nonacademics. He leaves the house every day at eight forty-five.'

'Well, there you go. Courtney leaves at seven.'

My motherly judgmentalness – different from but overlapping with other kinds of judgmentalness I'd harbored during my life – snapped on. Courtney had a five-minute commute but was away from Amelia for nine hours every weekday? Then I thought, *Don't be like Xiaojian Marcus.* 'Did you guys consider sending Amelia to day care?' I asked.

'We checked some out, and Courtney was okay with them, but I was the one who resisted. So Courtney said, "Then why don't *you* stay home with her?" She was half-kidding, but the more we talked about it, the more it actually made sense.'

'We sent Rosie to that place on Hanley for about a month,' I said. 'Then she got an eye infection and ended up in the hospital, and I quit my job after that. Not that the infection was the day care's fault, but I just didn't know I'd worry about her so much.'

Hank and I looked at each other, and he said, 'You love them more than you ever imagined, right? And it's terrifying.'

And so our two families became friends, then good friends, and eventually best friends. The next week, following music class, Hank and Amelia and Rosie and I returned to the Bread Company, and as we were heading back to our cars after lunch – Amelia was going home to nap, and Rosie had already fallen asleep in her car seat – Hank said, 'Hey, you guys should come for dinner this weekend.' Which we did, walking the half block from our house to theirs, and we sat in their backyard and they grilled; they made vegetarian shish kebabs, a bean salad, and a loaf of bread with black olives in it. For dessert, I'd baked brownies from a mix, which I hadn't thought twice about beforehand but by the end of dinner had the impression the Wheelings wouldn't have done. Bake brownies, sure. Just not from a mix.

We left at seven-thirty, before either of the girls could have a meltdown, and as we were leaving, Courtney called out, 'Come back tomorrow morning, and I'll dig up some of Amelia's old clothes for Rosie.' This was what I would come to most appreciate about our friendship with the Wheelings – that our interactions had a frequency and logistical casualness I hadn't experienced since college with anyone besides Vi. Because of how close the Wheelings lived to us and because our families were similarly structured, we didn't have to plan in advance the way I'd learned you did in adulthood; I could avoid those multiday email exchanges with the wife in the other couple over which restaurant or whose house, kids or no kids, what time, what could we bring? Then I'd look for a sitter, whom we'd pay twelve dollars an hour, or, if our friends were coming to our house, I'd spend two days cleaning and grocery shopping and cooking, all the while questioning whether getting together with these people was more enjoyable than Jeremy and me just ordering takeout and watching TV. When I expressed my doubts aloud, Jeremy would say, 'Is this one of those situations where I'll get in trouble for *not* disagreeing with you?'

But with Courtney and Hank, one family could call the other at five-fifteen and say, 'Do you guys want to come here for pizza?' Or sometimes, that fall, the three of them would walk over after we'd eaten our separate dinners and I'd put Rosie to bed and the rest of us would watch *American Idol*. Soon Hank and the girls and I were meeting up nearly every weekday. We'd walk across Skinker Boulevard to Forest Park and push the strollers around the zoo, or just unfold a blanket above Art Hill and let the girls play in the grass; this was where Rosie took a step for the first time. At Thanksgiving, the Wheelings came to our house along with Vi and my father.

Meanwhile, Jeremy and Courtney started getting

coffee in the afternoons, though apparently they only went to buy it together before returning to their separate offices. 'You're allowed to drink your coffee with her,' I said. 'I won't think you're on a date.'

'It's not that,' he said. 'It's that neither of us has time.'

Before getting to know her, I'd been intimidated by Courtney – the night I'd met her, at the Marcuses' long-ago department holiday party, I'd heard her explain her research using about seven words I didn't know in just two sentences – and my intimidation didn't disappear. But that first time we had dinner at their house, there was a moment when she and I had carried plates into the kitchen and we could see in the backyard that Jeremy and Hank were trying to get Rosie and Amelia to give each other five, and Courtney said, 'Look at those daddies' girls.' I felt then that she and I were sharing the double luckiness of not only having good husbands but knowing we had good husbands.

A few minutes later, when we were back on the deck eating brownies – the Wheelings were polite enough to pretend they were delicious as opposed to merely adequate – Courtney said, 'Do you run, Kate? I'm looking for a running partner.'

'Not for a while.'

'But that means you *have* run in the past. What was your pace?'

'I don't even remember. It wasn't impressive.'

'I go to Forest Park at five Monday, Wednesday, and Friday mornings, so if you change your mind—'

Jeremy laughed. 'I don't think Kate would get up at five if our house was on fire.'

'Thanks,' I said. To Courtney, I said, 'How far do you go?'

'Around the park, which is what, six miles and change?' She wasn't bragging; she said it so matter-of-factly that it was as if she didn't realize it was worth bragging about. She added, 'It can be a little sketchy down by Kingshighway, so that's why I was thinking, safety in numbers.'

'I'll think about it,' I said, which was a lie that I wished were the truth. I was slightly surprised to hear Courtney refer to the sketchiness of the Central West End; the comment seemed racially fraught, or at least easily enough interpreted as such that I myself wouldn't have made it in front of Hank.

The next morning, when I went back to their house to collect Amelia's hand-me-downs, Courtney had three canvas bags from science conferences waiting by the front door. She said, 'I promise there are no tank tops that say *Princess* in sparkly letters. Don't you hate that shit? As if the kid is even literate.'

I saw that she'd separated the bags into shirts, pants, and dresses; I also saw that all the visible clothes were the same brand of organic Swedish cotton. 'Is Amelia's name in them?' I asked. 'Or I can just write down what everything is so we remember to—'

Courtney waved a hand through the air, cutting me off. 'It's all yours to keep. We're done.'

'Are you sure?'

She nodded. 'My uterus is closed for business.'

When Jeremy and I had walked home from the Wheelings' after shish kebabs and brownies, I'd waited until we were two houses past theirs and said, 'I really like them.'

Jeremy said, 'Someone has a friend crush.'

'On him or her?'

He laughed. 'Either way. They're an attractive couple.'

'The whole interracial thing is interesting,' I said. 'Don't you think? I wonder how much they're aware of it on a daily basis.'

'If you mean does Hank know he's black and does Courtney know she's white, I suspect the answer is yes.'

'Ha ha.'

'I'm sure they get comments from time to time. I mean, we're not living in Brooklyn. But they've been together since college.'

'Where'd they go?'

'Harvard.' Jeremy hadn't said it in a particularly meaningful tone – his best friend from high school had gone to Harvard – but it was a reminder of some of the differences between us. 'Hank paints, I think,' Jeremy said. 'Has he mentioned that?'

'A little.' Then I said, 'How about this? I promise not to fall in love with Hank if you promise not to fall in love with Courtney.'

We were one house away from ours, and I was pushing Rosie in the stroller; she had just gotten a second wind and was making high-pitched squeals. Jeremy was walking slightly behind me, and he patted my rear end. He said, 'How could I ever fall in love with Courtney when I'm married to this?'

CHAPTER 18

The night of Vi's prediction, we watched TV until twelve o'clock, at which point the world didn't end and my sister announced that she was hungry. In the kitchen, she went for the leftover lo mein first, eating it from the carton, still cold. After she'd polished it off, she moved on to the eggplant, which she heated in the microwave. She tilted the plate toward me and said, 'You really don't want any?'

'I ate dinner about six hours ago.'

'Exactly.'

'I'm okay. Oh, what the hell?' I pulled a pint of caramel ice cream from the freezer.

'Now we're talking,' Vi said.

'It's fine if you want to spend the night,' I said as I scooped ice cream into a mug. 'You can sleep upstairs with me.' The invitation wasn't entirely unselfish – as long as Vi remained in our house, the night was about her. If she left, what would distract me from what I'd done?

'Driving tonight was weird,' Vi said. 'Or weird in how not weird it was. It was like when you want to put someone out of your mind and you're like,

513

I haven't thought of the person in two whole days, but right then you *are* thinking of them. I was driving on Big Bend, thinking, *I'm not freaking out! And then I'd wonder, Or am I?'* After she'd swallowed a bite of eggplant, she said, 'The roads were really empty, though. Some lunatic predicted a huge earthquake, and everyone was staying home.'

'It's midnight in St Louis,' I said. 'Everyone is home anyway.'

She scoffed. 'You just think that because *you're* always home. Don't forget it's a Friday.'

'Well, it's great you drove. Whose car did you use?'

'Patrick's. Which, to give credit where credit is due, Patrick can be a pain in the ass about his Audi, but he didn't blink when I asked if I could borrow it.'

'Do you want any before I put it back in the freezer?' I held up the pint of ice cream, and Vi leaned forward, dipped her index finger in, and licked it.

'I meant in a mug,' I said.

She smirked. 'You offered.'

Upstairs, Vi used the bathroom while I checked on the children, and she was already under the covers when I climbed into bed. I turned off the light on my nightstand, and as I did, Vi bolted upright, frantically waving one hand in front of her face. 'Oh. My. God. You *reek* of sex.'

'What are you talking about?' I tried not to panic; at least in the dark, Vi couldn't see my face.

'Are you having an affair? Who'd you have sex with if Jeremy is out of town?'

Wasn't the answer to this question obvious? Presumably, a person could not be psychic at all and still get it on the first guess. But I wasn't admitting to anything; even if I wanted to, and a part of me did, doing so would be a further betrayal of Jeremy. I said, 'If you think I smell bad, feel free to sleep on the couch downstairs.'

'You don't need to be defensive just because you had sex.' Vi had laid back down, and she pulled up the sheet and bedspread. 'I forgot how nasty semen smells. There's a reason to be a dyke, huh? Remember when you were saying there's no good reason?'

'That was never what I said. You have to let that go, Vi.' But she had given me an opportunity to change the subject, and I said, 'So how's Stephanie?'

'I don't know. You'd have to ask her.'

'You're not an item anymore?'

'If you really want to know, this South African radio station interviewed me, and when they asked if I was single or married, I said I was in a relationship, and a few minutes later, the interviewer said, "So how does your beau feel about this prediction?" and I said, "It's not a big deal with us." Stephanie was listening online, which I had no idea she could even do, and she freaked out that I hadn't corrected him. And I was like, how was I supposed to know *beau* can only refer to a dude? I'm not fluent in French.' Vi turned her

515

head toward me in the dark. 'Oh, come on. You're not going to gloat over the irony?'

'I bet if you apologize to Stephanie, she'll give you another chance,' I said. 'She seemed super into you.'

'I did apologize.'

'You said you were sorry?'

'I said excuse me if I haven't been out and proud since I was a freshman in college, but not all of us arrived at the lesbian party as early as she did.'

'That's not an apology.' Then I said, 'Not that this is any of your business, but Jeremy and I had sex before he left town yesterday, and I haven't had a chance to take a shower. It's kind of hard with Rosie and Owen.'

'Wow, two young kids and you guys are still at it like rabbits.'

Oh, to have been telling the truth! To just be able to undo the act, to rewind the evening.

'By the way,' Vi said, 'I can't believe you shelled out fifteen grand for Emma Hall. I'd have guessed three thousand, five thousand tops, but fifteen thousand – too bad we can't all be publicists.'

'Is she still helping you?' I said. 'I assume she arranged the *Today* interview this morning.'

'She's good at what she does, don't get me wrong. But fifteen thousand is a lot of bones.'

'Did you end up getting any licensing-fee payments?'

'*Today* wanted to show family pictures, and I knew you wouldn't like it, so I said no. Aren't you impressed by my integrity?'

Not that she was wrong – I'd have hated for images of me or our parents to appear on television – but it seemed so frustratingly fitting that my sister alone among insta-celebrities was managing not to make money off her newfound fame.

'Do you really think I should call Stephanie?' she asked.

'Yes.' I turned onto my stomach. 'Just so you know, Owen will wake up in two hours, and I'll have to go feed him.'

'He doesn't sleep through the night yet?'

'Vi, if you're going to start—'

'Don't get your panties in a wad. Your disgusting-smelling panties, that is.'

We both were quiet for a long time, and I felt myself falling toward sleep when I heard Vi say, 'Now that I was wrong about the earthquake, do I have to move to a different city? Should I change my name?'

'No,' I said.

'Or dye my hair?'

'You don't need to dye your hair.'

'I could henna it.' She sounded chipper. 'I've always wanted to try that. Are you still awake?'

'Barely.'

'You could do it, too,' she said. 'Henna doesn't have chemicals like regular hair dye.' I didn't respond, and she said, 'I did know that *beau* means boyfriend. I pretended like I didn't, but I did.'

'Call her tomorrow,' I mumbled.

And then Vi didn't say anything more, and I didn't either, and the silence of the night stretched and stretched until it swallowed us; it pulled us down together, and my sister and I slept, as we had not done for many years, in the same bed.

I awoke at five-fifty and decided to shower. By the time I was dressed, Owen was stirring, and by the time I'd gotten both children downstairs, I'd received a text from Hank, adding to the two texts and two voice mails from Jeremy I hadn't responded to the night before, all of them saying variations on the same thing. *You ok? Going to bed, connect in a.m.* Hank's text said, *C coming home at noon. We should talk.*

Vi slept through the chaos of breakfast, and I left a note for her at the bottom of the stairs: *Taking kids for a walk. Help yourself in kitchen.*

When we joined Hank and Amelia in their back-yard, Hank was sitting on the step between the deck and the grass, drinking coffee from a stainless steel thermos, looking tired. As we approached, Amelia called out, 'I'm making porridge!'

I set my hand on Rosie's shoulder and said, 'Want to help Amelia?'

At breakfast, Rosie had held up a Cheerio and said, 'It looks like the baby's belly button,' and Owen had played peekaboo by setting his palms on his forehead and peering out from under them, as if we couldn't see him that way. What if Jeremy wanted a divorce and we had to split custody? No,

I could never tell him. After breakfast I'd texted, *Things fine here. Call u soon.*

The weather was nice again – it was a windy, sunny morning in the high fifties – and the day might, under different circumstances, have seemed like the coda to Vi's prediction. 'So no earthquake,' Hank said.

'No earthquake,' I repeated.

'And still no word from Vi?'

'Actually, she came by last night. She ended up staying over.'

He raised his eyebrows inquiringly, and while there were several possible questions he might have been asking – you made peace? how's she doing? – the one I answered was the one I suspected he felt most curious about. I said, 'I didn't tell her anything.'

Hank was still Hank, though – that was the confusing part. He still looked like the person I'd been friends with these last two years, he wore jeans and a long-sleeved orange T-shirt I recognized, but now I also knew about his gray Calvin Klein briefs, I knew the sigh he made when he came.

The grass was too wet with dew to set Owen in, and I hadn't brought a blanket, so I left him in the stroller, wheeling it around so that he'd be facing me when I joined Hank on the deck – when I joined him at a distance of several feet. I had a hunch we wouldn't be staying long and that Owen would be our excuse, because he'd recently started to get impatient if I left him in the unmoving stroller.

Hank was quiet for a full minute, and then, his tone lowered so that Amelia and Rosie wouldn't hear, he said, 'I'm assuming you know that I think you're great. I'd be lying if I claimed I can't imagine a parallel life of us together. But in this life, it'll explode in our faces.'

I wondered if he was waiting for me to persuade him otherwise, though at the same time I felt a little like he was breaking up with me. This idea seemed darkly funny; it seemed funny because I didn't understand how literal it was.

'I agree with you,' I said.

'I hope Courtney and I make it, that this is a rough patch and we come out stronger, or whatever the bullshit is people say about their marriages. But I need to keep trying. And I think you and Jeremy have a good thing going. I don't want to be involved in fucking it up.'

This morning, you don't, I thought, but Hank was no more accountable for what had happened the night before than I was. Though again, I wasn't sure if he expected me to disagree, to announce that Jeremy and I were secretly miserable.

Hank continued, 'So our options are tell Courtney and Jeremy or don't tell them. I know which one I vote for, but you and I have to be on the same page. It's too messy otherwise, if one knows and one doesn't, or if one tells the other.'

'I'm guessing you think we shouldn't tell them.'

'It might seem like confessing is honorable, but ultimately, who's the confession for? We unburden ourselves, and they both have to second-guess their whole lives. And I can see Courtney wanting a D-I-V-O-R-C-E. Just being furious at me, and going scorched earth.'

Would Jeremy leave me if he knew? I wasn't sure. The biggest reason he wouldn't, of course, was that he wouldn't want to live apart, even half the time, from Rosie and Owen; he wouldn't want them to be children of divorce like he'd been. If our days often felt relentless, how devastating to have them free – to inhabit an uncluttered apartment in which he could spend a Saturday afternoon reading a dense academic journal without interruption, in which he could set a glass of water on a table and not assume it would immediately be knocked over. How could he go back to such order after the shrieking exuberance of Rosie in bright pink pants and a yellow shirt, jumping on the sofa, shouting, 'Daddy likes to eat crocodile cheese!' No, I didn't think Jeremy would initiate a divorce; he was likelier to remain unhappily in the marriage I had poisoned. But again, I wasn't sure. And was there a way to explain to him, to convince him of, the insignificance of what I'd done – the impulsivity of it – and to thereby earn his absolution? Could I make him understand that having sex with Hank hadn't been the result of a mutual attraction simmering for years but, rather, a mistake born of loneliness and stupidity?

'Okay,' I said. Hank looked at me, and because of how we were positioned, he had to hold a hand up to his eyes to block the sun. 'Okay, we don't tell.'

What would our other selves, our before-last-night selves, have done at this moment? Pinkie-sworn, maybe, or some other joking kind of physical contact. *Had* an attraction between us been simmering for years? Not really, not exactly. We liked each other, sure, but only because something had happened had the attraction retroactively taken on the air of inevitability. I wanted to ask Hank if he'd ever cheated on Courtney before, but I couldn't. I could have if he hadn't cheated with me, but I couldn't now.

He said, 'Let's keep the conversation open, in case one of us changes our mind.'

'I won't change my mind,' I said. 'But okay.'

When Owen began to fuss, I explained that we ought to get going, that I wanted to check on Vi anyway, and Rosie climbed willingly into the stroller, though we'd barely been there fifteen minutes. As I pushed my children out of the Wheelings' backyard, I had no idea that I was walking away from the last moments of my friendship with Hank.

At our house, Vi was frying eggs. 'I was thinking about it, and now I get why October sixteenth was looming so large to you', she said. 'I mean, if that day care place is where Rosie went, then no shit you'd be tuned in. But here's what I still can't figure out: Where's my earthquake? Because I just can't see Guardian misleading me.'

'You thought October sixteenth, too,' I said.

'Well, I trusted you.'

'Wait, you *didn't* think October sixteenth?'

'I never got a firm date. But two heads are better than one, right? That's how we figured out Brady Ogden, with teamwork.'

I was the one – I alone – who had determined that the earthquake would be on October 16? Which meant – well, the implications were almost too awful to consider. That I, not Vi, had set the hysteria in motion. That I had agitated an entire city because I'd had a sense of something big happening on a certain date, but that, in the ultimate act of narcissism, I had failed to understand that the something big had only to do with me. And the event I'd sensed was not – I wished it had been – the accident at the day care. I said, 'But if I'm the one who said when the earthquake would be, who said where? Did Guardian? Did you? Did you get a vibe about St Louis, or was it just that Channel 5 newscaster with the huge boobs who assumed it?'

Vi looked stricken. 'You think?'

I wanted to tell her that she and I should never speak of this again, that we should permanently hide the enormous error we'd made together, but surely such a suggestion would result in Vi leaving my house and calling a press conference. She might call one anyway, to warn the world that her earthquake was still at large.

On the stove, I could see that the yolks of Vi's eggs had turned solid and pale, the way she didn't like them, and I said, 'You might want to take those off.'

And then on Sunday, Jeremy was home; his time away had been both endless and the blink of an eye, excessively eventful but without real meaning.

I met him at the door – how would I possibly be able to keep my secret from him? – and I said, 'They're both asleep,' and he said, 'Awesome. Let's go upstairs.'

'Really?' I said.

'Why not?'

I had thought he'd be emotional, as when he'd learned of the accident at the day care, but he was cheerful again; I was the emotional one. And indeed, after we'd gone up to our room, after we'd stood on opposite sides of the bed pulling off our clothes (for my part, I was less overwhelmed with desire than desperate to accommodate him), after I was lying on my back and he was on top of me, after we both came within roughly three minutes – after that was when I burst into tears, a profusion of them falling from my eyes, making me shake beneath Jeremy. He kissed where the salt water ran down my face. He said, 'Sweetheart. Oh, Katie. I know.' What had I done, what had I done, what had I done? And still he was kissing me, the kindest man in the world, and still I was crying uncontrollably.

'I know,' he kept saying. 'I know. I know.' But of course he didn't.

CHAPTER 19

When Kendra came over to babysit the next week, I left both Owen and Rosie at home, picked up my father, and drove with him to Hacienda to meet Vi; after lunch, my father and I would go to the grocery store. Vi had suggested inviting our father, and she was – this still seemed remarkable – driving herself to the restaurant.

It turned out there was a reason she wanted our father there. She was already waiting when we arrived, seated at a table for four with Stephanie next to her. As we approached, she said, 'Dad, this is my girlfriend, Stephanie. I've been wanting to introduce you.'

Stephanie smiled broadly. Without batting an eye – also, presumably, without understanding that Vi meant *girlfriend* girlfriend – my father shook her hand and said, 'How nice to meet you.'

I leaned in and hugged Stephanie. 'Good to see you again,' I said, and she said, 'Likewise.' As if the world hadn't gone topsy-turvy since we'd last crossed paths, as if this were just an ordinary Wednesday in October. Which, if I hadn't known better, I might have believed it was: Already, there seemed to be few references to the non-earthquake on the radio or in the *Post-Dispatch*, and certainly the national media had left the story behind. Hank and I hadn't communicated since Rosie, Owen, and I had left his backyard four days earlier, which felt deeply strange – I'd have the urge in my fingers to text him before remembering why I couldn't – and I hadn't told Jeremy what I'd done. This meant that I was buzzing with a constant guilt, which, like cicadas on a summer evening, would sometimes surge in volume until I was able to hear nothing else. But apparently the sound was inaudible to others. If anything, Jeremy was more doting than usual, repeatedly offering to watch both children if I wanted to take a nap or run errands alone, as if he were the one who needed to atone.

Two days before, my father had told me over the phone that he'd received a clean bill of health from the doctor. At the restaurant, Vi said she'd drink to that and ordered a Corona, then Stephanie said she'd have one, too, then my father said he thought he'd join them. Before I requested one as well, I had a fleeting, unpleasant recollection of my lunch at Blueberry Hill with Jeremy and Courtney.

My father asked where Stephanie was from, and it turned out he'd been to Cave City, Arkansas, more than once back when he'd sold carpet. 'If you were ever there in the summer, I hope you tasted our famous watermelon,' Stephanie said, and after that, the conversation never really lagged; she was as warm and patient with our father as Jeremy was.

When we'd finished eating, Vi followed me to the bathroom, and from the next stall she said, 'Are you impressed that I listened to you about Stephanie?'

'I knew she'd take you back.'

Vi was peeing. 'Did you hear I was mentioned on *Letterman*? Patrick said Letterman didn't say my name, but the joke was about how Congress should get economic advice from the psychic in St Louis.'

So references to Vi's prediction hadn't gone away entirely; that was too much to hope for. And undoubtedly Letterman had been mocking her, though Vi seemed pleased rather than offended. The dismantling of her prediction, its erasure, was more gradual than I wanted. I wanted it to be immediate and complete, but there were lingering reminders, like scraps of trash after a festival. And surely I wanted it all done away with as soon as possible because the faster and further we moved from her prediction, the faster and further we'd also be moving from my complicity in it and from my betrayal of Jeremy. But later, when I looked back, those weeks immediately after the earthquake hadn't happened still seemed to be such a raw time, so close to the day itself. It had been unrealistic of me to be impatient.

When we'd left the restaurant and my father and I were in the dairy section of Schnucks, I said, 'Dad, I think Stephanie is Vi's girlfriend as in they're dating.'

'Is she?' My father's tone was as mild as if I'd said, *I think Stephanie is a Cardinals fan.*

Had he still not understood? How could he not have, unless it was intentional? And even if it was, it seemed that the time had arrived to get this over with; I had the impression that Stephanie could be around for a while. 'I'm pretty sure Vi's gay now,' I said. 'And Stephanie is her partner.'

My father was lifting a tub of cream cheese from the shelf, and he looked over at me briefly and nodded. His tone remained mild as he said, 'Stephanie seems like a nice woman. And what a coincidence that she's from Cave City.'

And then – for assuming my father harbored the same prejudices I did, for imagining he was several steps behind me when the reverse was true – I felt humiliated. There was nothing for me to do but point down the shelf and say, 'You need eggs, right?'

Perhaps it was because I'd already dispensed with my dignity for the day that I asked the question I did as we were in the car waiting to turn out of the grocery store parking lot. I said, 'Dad, do you have senses?' *It's none of our business* – that was what I'd told Vi.

'Oh,' my father said. 'Well, sometimes, sure. Sure I do.' He motioned left and said, 'Be careful,

529

because some of the drivers come around there awfully quick.'

Had this been part of what frustrated my mother, his indirection? But no, if anything, she'd shared the tendency.

As I pulled onto Manchester Road, I said, 'You're psychic – you have psychic abilities?'

'Don't tell your sister, but I've never been fond of that word. It's cheap-sounding.'

'What kinds of things do you have senses about?'

'Oh, the same as you girls – this and that.' He laughed in a small way. 'Some things I want to know, some I'd prefer not to. I was sharper when I was a younger man, as with everything.'

How bizarre it was to be on the other side of this conversation, to hear another person say he had this ability and for the admission to prompt in me curiosity and disbelief.

My father's tone was still casual as he said, 'But I was always more like you than Violet, not encouraging it. It can be quite a double-edged sword.'

'And Mom knew?'

'She didn't care for it. She thought it was voodoo.'

All of this – simultaneously, it was astonishing and it explained so much. Vi and I had probably frightened our mother: her unexpected twins, with our creepy powers.

'Did you tell Mom before you were married or after?'

'Now, that's hard to recall. It's been so long,

hasn't it?' And I thought, *You told her after.* Our poor, ignorant twenty-three-year-old mother, abruptly surrounded on all sides by freaks of nature.

I said, 'When Mom was pregnant, did you know we'd be twins?'

What a strange expression there was on my father's face. It was as if he'd at last been caught for a petty crime committed decades earlier but also as if he'd wanted to be caught; the energy it took to outrun the past had become greater than the punishment he'd receive.

He said, 'I did bring it up. Wouldn't it be something if there were two babies? But she was firm about only wanting one. She was already worried about the delivery.' When there *had* been two of us, had that been when she realized he was prescient? And after he'd played along as she'd decorated a nursery for a single baby – she must have felt deceived by him, manipulated. But maybe he'd doubted his own foreknowledge.

'You were wonderful girls,' my father said. 'So lively and happy.'

Yeah, right, I thought, though after a few seconds, it occurred to me that his statement wasn't necessarily untrue. I'd let the onset of my mother's gloom cast itself backward over the years prior to my awareness of it, I'd let the shades she drew when we were eleven be drawn over everything before. But there was all that time when Vi and I had danced and sung, the afternoons we'd spent

531

hanging from the mulberry tree in the yard, the games we'd invented. 'The first time I saw your mother,' my father said, 'when she was standing behind the front desk at the hotel, I had a sense about you and Violet. I could see you at three or four, in your red bathing suits. You probably don't remember those.'

I didn't remember, but there was a photo of Vi and me in matching bikinis, and the familiarity of the photo was almost like a memory.

'I had been a bachelor for such a long time,' my father was saying, 'and suddenly I understood that it wasn't my fate to live alone after all.'

Did he mean to imply that he'd married my mother so we could exist? That it hadn't simply been my mother's beauty that attracted my father to her but the life he'd envisioned with all of us?

'I always believed things would get better for Rita,' he said. 'I knew it would be hard in the beginning, when you were babies, but I thought as you got older, she'd enjoy being a mother.'

The implication that she hadn't – it was nothing I didn't know, but it still stung.

'She just couldn't forgive herself, though,' my father said. 'If she had, I imagine things wouldn't have been as tough.'

'Forgive herself for what?'

This time, instead of looking caught, my father looked so lost in the past that it was as if I wasn't in the car. 'She took some money from her parents,' he said. 'Before she left home. Not a great deal, maybe forty or fifty dollars. And she repaid it after she was on her feet in St Louis, but when she sent it home, her mother wrote back saying Rita was no longer their daughter. They didn't approve of her moving away, living in a city.'

Sixty dollars – she had taken sixty, and I knew this because of my last night at Mrs Abbott's house, when she had called me Rita and told me to take that amount from her pocketbook. Which surely meant the Universe had absolved her, even if her family hadn't. And my poor mother, estranged from her parents and sister until she died over such a pittance. Or maybe the money hadn't been the real reason, just the excuse to punish her for other choices they disapproved of.

My father still seemed preoccupied when he spoke next, so much so that at the time, I wasn't even sure he was talking to me. He said, 'We all make mistakes, don't we? But if you can't forgive yourself, you'll always be an exile in your own life.'

I arrived home just before Owen's second nap and Rosie's first one. As I paid Kendra, I said, 'Did they torment each other?'

'They did great,' she said. 'Right, guys?'

Kendra and I were standing by the staircase, and we both turned toward the living room, where Owen sat on the floor and Rosie knelt in front of him. 'Hi, Owen.' She was gripping his left hand with her right one. 'Hi, baby. It's nice to meet you.'

★　　★　　★

For a few days after Hank and I had slept together, I'd avoided our usual parks anytime I knew Amelia wasn't in school, but when Rosie burst into tears as I turned the stroller into the acorn park for the fourth afternoon in a row – besides being the site of her split lip, since healed, the acorn park had no climbing toy – I turned around and walked to Oak Knoll; the next morning, we went to DeMun. (That its nickname was MILF Park now seemed, even if just in my own head, more cringe-inducing than funny.) Surprisingly, though, and despite Rosie's many queries about them, we never ran into Hank and Amelia. Either they themselves were avoiding these parks or they were going when Hank knew Rosie and Owen would be napping. As the days passed, I stopped anxiously scouting for them.

On Thanksgiving morning, I woke wondering if the Wheelings had really ended up going to Hawaii. After Jeremy had set our turkey in the oven, I realized we had less than a cup of sugar left and I hadn't yet made the cranberry relish or the pumpkin pie. I took Owen with me to Schnucks, and I hadn't decided ahead of time to buy a pregnancy test – I still hadn't gotten my period since Owen's birth, and I hadn't consciously thought about it – but as I passed the pharmacy, I abruptly turned the grocery cart down the aisle where the tests were and grabbed one. In the checkout line, after I'd paid, I jammed the box into the inside pocket of my coat.

At home, in the upstairs bathroom, I sat on the toilet and stuck the wand between my legs, peeing onto its tip. Then, so as to keep the wand horizontal – I no longer needed to read the instructions for a pregnancy test – I set toilet paper on the tile floor and placed the wand on top of the toilet paper. We had begun potty training Rosie in the beginning of November, and the only reading material in the bathroom for the three minutes I had to wait to get the results was a copy of *Everyone Poops,* which I had memorized weeks ago. ('Some stop to poop. Others do it on the move . . .')

I sat on the floor against the tub, crossed my legs, and closed my eyes. From downstairs, I could smell the turkey cooking and hear Jeremy building a fort with the children.

Please, no, I thought. *And I'll never tempt fate again. I'll always be good, for the rest of my life.* Because if I was pregnant yet again and Jeremy was the father, it would be bad enough; I doubted I had more to give, additional reservoirs of patience or attention beyond what Rosie and Owen depleted every day. But if I was pregnant again and Hank was the father, it would be unimaginable; it would be cataclysmic.

It's impossible, of course, to remember every moment of every day, impossible sometimes to remember *any* moment of a particular day. Certain instants come to stand in for whole swaths of time, and these three minutes, sitting on the bathroom floor on Thanksgiving, my back to the tub, Rosie laughing downstairs, is what I now remember when I think of being pregnant with Gabe. These moments were the last ones in which I didn't yet know that I was pregnant, or didn't know for sure, when I still felt a terrified wishfulness. It was when my third pregnancy seemed like an extremely unpleasant hypothetical condition rather than the start of a new life.

When I leaned forward to check the window on the wand, it said PREGNANT. I swallowed, and I didn't cry; who did I have to blame but myself? To be pregnant and not to know who the father was, for his identity to be revealed when I delivered either a white baby or a black one – this was a situation from a soap opera.

Before I went downstairs, I peed on the second wand in the package, and the word PREGNANT also appeared in its window. Then I returned both wands and their caps to the box, put the box inside an empty package of diapers I found in Owen's room, put the diaper package inside a plastic bag from Target, tied the handles of the Target bag, and carried it downstairs to the kitchen, where I inserted it in the only trash can in the house that had a lid. I mashed down the Target bag with my hand, letting other garbage rise over it – potato peels and wadded paper towels and a soggy piece of toast – and then I joined my husband and children in the living room.

Would this be our last Thanksgiving as a family?

I felt as if I were watching Jeremy and Rosie and Owen underwater. Though already, the suspense of my secret had shifted, the belief that being pregnant was the worst possible outcome. Now the worst possible outcome was that Hank was the father. Jeremy and I could deal with a third child that was ours; it would be hard, but plenty of people had three children, and we'd figure it out. If Hank was the father, however, it was not at all clear that Jeremy and I could figure it out, at least not together.

Making the cranberry relish, I vacillated between considering the logistics of our impending meal and wondering if I'd wrecked my life. If I set the table ahead of time, would Rosie grab the utensils? Was it possible to find out who the father was before you gave birth? I'd put out everything except the silverware, I decided.

I set Owen on the dining room rug and pulled the place mats and cloth napkins from the sideboard. Rosie was in the living room watching an episode of *Olivia,* and Jeremy was in the kitchen checking the turkey. 'Maybe you should carve it before my dad gets here,' I called to Jeremy. 'I feel like he's been shaky lately.'

Jeremy came to stand in the doorway between the kitchen and the dining room. 'Sure, if you think that's better. I can do that.' He didn't move right away – *he* hadn't guessed that I was pregnant, had he? – and then he said, 'I understand why you threw in the towel on Courtney. And I'm not

537

saying you should change your mind. But I kind of miss hanging out with the Wheelings.'

One could, while still pregnant, learn the identity of the father by two means, depending on how far along the pregnancy was: chorionic villus sampling, or CVS, if you were between your tenth and twelfth weeks – this was, coincidentally, the same procedure that had revealed that Courtney was carrying a baby with Down's – or amniocentesis after. Both procedures carried a small risk of miscarriage, with the risk being slightly higher with CVS. To confirm paternity, you needed a DNA sample – a swab from inside the mouth, a hair with the follicle still attached – from one of the candidates or their first-degree relatives. In other words, I could root around on Jeremy's pillow or I could take Rosie or Owen to a lab, options that all seemed treacherous and sordid.

I discovered this information on the Internet at the Richmond Heights library, where I'd gone during Kendra's babysitting hours the week after Thanksgiving. I could have found out sooner, I could have looked it up on my phone the minute my pregnancy test came back positive, but I didn't want Jeremy stumbling across my search history. Not that he used my phone, but I didn't want to worry that this would be the one time he did. Anyway, to not take action on my pregnancy was like not telling Jeremy I'd cheated in the first place: if it meant I had to bear the burden of guilt alone, it also meant my pregnancy wasn't real to anyone besides me.

From the parking lot of the library, I called Vi, and it was obvious that I'd awakened her. 'I have a favor to ask,' I said. 'Can I come over?'

When Vi opened her front door, wearing plaid flannel pajama bottoms and a red T-shirt under which she had on no bra, I said, 'I'm in a hurry, but I need you to do a reading for me. I'm pregnant again—'

'Good Lord, Fertile Myrtle!'

I shook my head; I wasn't sharing good news. 'Remember the night of your prediction, when you told me I smelled like sex? Well, I'd had it with Hank. And I'm not sure if the baby is his or Jeremy's, and that's what I need you to tell me.'

For a full ten seconds, Vi gawked at me, speechless. Then she said, 'Holy crap.' After thirty-four years, I had completely shocked my sister, but there was no satisfaction in the achievement. 'I mean—' She blinked several times. 'Just – wow. Wow.'

'I know.' Because I couldn't help myself, I said, 'It was only that once. I've never cheated on Jeremy besides that, with Hank or anyone else.'

'Does Jeremy know?'

'I've gone back and forth about whether to tell him, and it just seems selfish. Or more selfish than not telling.'

'He'll know if a black baby pops out of your cooter.'

'Well—' I paused. 'That's why I'm here.'

As I followed her into the living room, she said over her shoulder, 'If you and Jeremy split up, my faith in heterosexuality will be destroyed.'

Unexpectedly, my eyes filled with tears, but I willed them away. 'Maybe it should be.'

Before she sat in her lounger, she said, 'I'll help you, but why don't you just do a reading for yourself?'

'I'm not psychic anymore. You know Nancy's New Year's Eve party when we wrote down things we wanted to get rid of and burned them? I did that with my senses.'

Vi looked skeptical but not hostile. 'When?'

'After Rosie was in the hospital with her eye thing. Every time a thought came into my head, I didn't know if it was a normal new mom anxiety or a premonition. I couldn't live like that.'

'And it worked?' Vi said. 'You don't have senses anymore?'

'For the most part. I mean, apparently, I was wrong about October sixteenth.'

'Well, yes and no. There may not have been an earthquake, but it turns out something huge happened in your own life that night.'

'Yeah, because I *made* something happen.'

'But if you hadn't sensed you'd cheat, think of how things could have gone with the day-care accident.'

I had groped for this justification in my own mind, but I remained unconvinced. Because really, wasn't the opposite just as likely? After all, the roads had been less crowded on October 16, which meant the driver of the eighteen-wheeler reached Hanley Road earlier than he otherwise would have, which was why, when he fell asleep, he crashed into the front room of the day-care center. Under normal circumstances, he'd have been twenty miles back, or ten, or seven; he'd have crashed into a field of grazing cows, or an empty office space for rent, or a sandwich restaurant.

I said, 'I think if I want to put the senses to rest, I have to put them to rest. If information comes to me, I can't exactly stop it, but I shouldn't try to be psychic.'

'I can't believe you didn't tell me.'

'I thought you'd disapprove.'

'I do.' She looked admiring, though, as she added, 'I had no idea you were so good at keeping secrets.'

She settled herself in her lounger, and I sat in the folding chair just to her right. She closed her eyes, and they'd been closed for thirty seconds when she opened them and said, 'This'll be easier if – I know you don't like this, but is it okay if I ask Guardian?'

I nodded, and she closed her eyes again. This time only two or three seconds passed before she opened them. 'How can you be pregnant when you're still breast-feeding all the time?'

'This is you talking, right? Not Guardian.'

'Yes, this is me.'

'You can ovulate before you get your period. And Owen doesn't always nurse for that long. He's eating more and more solid food.'

'Okay, sorry.' She closed her eyes again, then opened them a third time. 'Have you told Hank?'

I shook my head. 'He and I don't hang out now.'

'And here I thought they weren't at Thanksgiving because of me. You think Hank told Courtney you guys did it?'

'I hope not.'

Vi cackled a little. 'Oh, you'd know if he had. She'd come to your front door and shoot you.'

'Thank you,' I said.

Vi leaned forward and swatted my arm. 'Lighten up, Daze. I'm kidding.'

This time when she closed her eyes, she was quiet for several minutes, a peace overtaking her features. She didn't speak aloud – I had wondered if she would, and she didn't – but I still knew when she'd made contact with Guardian. I felt the presence in the room, and Vi was right, it was a presence entirely different from the one that had been there when Marisa Mazarelli and I had used the Ouija board. This was a compassionate presence, a protective one – it was wise and calm, like an older relative or a boss who has great affection for you while recognizing that the calamities in your life aren't as significant as you believe them to be. I had never imagined I'd think so, but abruptly I was glad that Vi had had this companionship all these years; it meant that even when we'd grown apart while I was at Mizzou, even during our fights, even when I'd married Jeremy and she hadn't yet met Stephanie, she had never, I understood now, been alone.

When she finally looked at me again, her expression was so carefully composed, so sympathetic, that I knew immediately.

Gently, she said, 'If you got pregnant on October sixteenth, you're not that far along.'

'I can't get an abortion,' I said. 'I just can't.'

'I could go with you. I once went with Nancy.'

'Nancy had an abortion?' Then I shook my head. 'I can't.'

'Jeremy is as supportive as they come, but if you say to him—'

'I know.'

We both were quiet, and she said, 'Some mixed-race people have really light skin. Remember that guy Kent I used to work with at Trattoria Marcella?'

'Believe me, I've been telling myself that.'

She squinted. 'Are you pro-life?'

'You know how Courtney Wheeling miscarried? Well, she didn't miscarry. They found out the baby had Down's, and she had an abortion. And at the time, I thought that I wouldn't have done it if I were her, so how can I live with myself aborting a healthy baby?' After a few seconds, I said, 'Is this a healthy baby?'

'Guardian didn't give any indications to the contrary. But, Daze, it's totally normal to disapprove of what other people do until you're in the same situation.' Vi grinned. 'It's one of my hobbies. And it's not like you rented a billboard and publicly declared that Courtney is a bad person.'

'I just can't.'

'But will you share custody with the Wheelings? Half the week at your house, half at theirs?'

'I don't know.' I stood up. I hadn't even removed my coat. 'I should go. Thanks for this.'

'Hold on.' Vi was still sitting. 'Want to know the sex?'

This seemed such a peripheral piece of information at that moment, so inconsequential, but when she told me, it started to make the baby real.

She said, 'It's another boy. Hey, it's not too late to finish that blanket I started for Owen.'

I read to Rosie before bed, and she sat on my lap. When I was turning a page, she pointed to my left hand and said, 'What's those on Mama?'

'They're my knuckles.' I held up my right hand, making a fist. 'I have them on my other hand, and you have them, too.'

Her plump little toddler hands – they would soon vanish. They'd vanish along with her fixation with the baloney puzzle piece, her pronunciation of lion as 'nion' and bathing suit as 'babing suit,' her fondness for holding up individual strands of spaghetti at dinner and making them dance. Rosie wasn't yet three, and already her babyhood was forever irretrievable.

She wiggled her fingers. 'Rosie have knuckles.'

'That's right.'

'And Mama have knuckles.'

'I do.'

'Mama and Rosie are having knuckles together.'

I kissed the top of her head. 'We're very lucky.'

Downstairs, Jeremy was sitting on the couch, the TV turned to ESPN. He was eating ice cream from a mug, and a second mug waited for me on the table. He said, 'We ran out of chocolate chip, so I supplemented with lemon sorbet.'

What would I have said on a night on which I wasn't planning to announce that I was pregnant with another man's child? I might have said *God forbid*. Or *I think I can manage*. Without touching the mug, I sat in the armchair. 'What are you doing all the way over there?' Jeremy said.

'I have to tell you something.' My heart was beating rapidly.

'Something bad?' His eyes were warm and crinkly, his tone light.

'Yes,' I said.

'Really?'

'Yes, really.'

He started to speak again, and I held up one hand and said, 'Let me just say it.'

His expression changed – he was beginning to understand that I wasn't kidding, that what I would tell him would not be that I'd been in a fender bender in the parking lot of Schnucks, or that I'd gone online and ordered four-hundred-dollar organic mattresses for our children. Regarding me seriously, Jeremy said, 'Okay.'

After I said it, I would never be able to take it back. Even if we stayed married – *please,* I thought, *please let us stay married* – the information would always exist between us. But what was the alternative? The alternative was to have an abortion and shut the fuck up for the rest of my life, and these prospects, especially in tandem, felt impossible.

I said, 'No matter how mad you are, please remember this: I love you so much, Jeremy. You're the best thing—' My voice cracked, but it would be unfair to make him comfort me. I swallowed. 'You're the best thing that ever happened to me. Our life together – I think we have a really good life. And I don't know why I did what I did. I mean, I can come up with reasons, but they're stupid.'

He had to know, I thought; at this point, surely he could guess. But he simply watched me in an unfamiliar, unsmiling way, and there was nothing left to do but tell him. I said, 'When you were in Denver, I had sex with Hank, and now I'm pregnant and it's his.' I had decided ahead of time that both parts had to be in the same sentence, a one-two punch, because it would be too terrible if he thought I had finished delivering the bad news when I was only halfway through it.

I'd let my gaze wander toward the fireplace as I

spoke, but I made myself look at him, and he was blinking rapidly behind his wire glasses.

'I'm sorry,' I said. 'I can't explain how sorry.'

A minute passed without him saying a word, and finally, in a tone I had never heard – it was so cold yet also so small, much too intimate for him to use with a stranger – he said, 'You're sure you're pregnant?'

'Yes,' I said. 'I'm sure.'

'How do you know it's Hank's?'

'Well, you can do a procedure called CVS or else if you're past twelve weeks you can have an amnio, but you still need a DNA sample from—' I hesitated. 'From the guy. So instead I had Vi do a reading for me.'

This was the first moment since I'd told him that Jeremy's face revealed any real emotion, and the emotion it revealed was scorn. 'Seriously?' he said.

'I know you think it's all nonsense, but this is the kind of thing Vi is really good at.' Of course I had considered that she could be wrong, but at the moment when she'd opened her eyes, it had felt like she was confirming what I already knew.

'You need to get tested,' he said. 'Have you told Hank?'

'No.' We were both quiet and I said, 'I hope you believe that I've never – I've never done anything like this. I've never considered it. I realize I've messed up really badly.'

He was silent, and I thought how in the past

there wouldn't have been a conversation between us in which he didn't protest when I said, *I've messed up really badly*. Finally, because I couldn't stand it, I said, 'You're surprised, right? I hope you don't think – it wasn't something—' Fair or not, I was asking him to comfort me after all; seeking his comfort was such a habit between us that I didn't know how not to.

He still was blinking. 'Yes, I'm surprised.'

'You're just not – the way you're reacting – I can't tell what your reaction is. You can yell at me if you want to.'

Again, there was an incredibly long silence before he said, 'You're telling me that you fucked Hank once?' I had never, I was pretty sure, heard Jeremy use *fuck* to mean *have sex with*.

'It was definitely only once.'

'But you got pregnant?'

Did he think I was lying? 'I haven't gotten my period since having Owen, but I guess I was ovulating already – I don't – Jeremy, I'm sorry. I'm so, so sorry.'

He said, 'And then you fucked me when I got home from Denver, right? So Vi's reading notwithstanding, there should be a fifty-fifty chance it's mine.' That *fucked* again – I didn't like it, though certainly I had no grounds for objecting. 'And you're what, nine weeks along?'

I said, 'Even if it's Hank's, which I'm sorry, Jeremy, but I think it is – even if it is, I would rather not have an abortion, but if you want me to, I will.

If I'm choosing between staying married to you and having the baby, I'd choose you.'

'But you want both?' Again, in his otherwise impassive face, there crossed that scorn. He made my wish to keep the baby seem greedy, not humane. But he didn't need to convince me of my own venality. If in fact I was willing to terminate the pregnancy, why hadn't I done so without telling him anything? Did I hope to make the termination his decision, his responsibility? Either to absolve myself of guilt or to use it as currency, expressing my aversion so that when I went through with it, he'd understand I was making a sacrifice and be likelier to forgive me? So thoroughly did I distrust myself that it was hard to remember that my desire not to have an abortion was sincere.

I said, 'Courtney's abortion – I just – I found it really sad. And then to turn around . . .' I trailed off.

'After Courtney and I ran into you at Blueberry Hill and I told you I wasn't having an affair with her, did you not believe me?' A confused and tentative hope flickered across Jeremy's face. He was broaching a possible explanation, and he was a person who liked explanations. He said, 'Do you think I've been cheating on you?'

Maybe it would have been wiser or kinder to lie, but it felt like the time for lying had passed. 'No,' I said. 'I don't think you've cheated.'

The clouds collected in his face again; what he'd

been offering, he rescinded. He said, 'If you don't want to have an abortion, what happens when you give birth to a biracial baby? People aren't idiots.'

I'd had time to consider the question since Vi had asked it earlier that day, and I said, 'I think we do nothing. We don't try to explain it. We have a son with dark skin – Vi said the baby is a boy – and so what? Family members can have different complexions.'

'*We* have a son with dark skin?' His tone of coiled but unconcealed anger made me understand how completely I had, prior to this conversation, stayed within Jeremy's good graces; from the time we'd met, even when we'd quarreled, he'd never directed any hostility at me, and I had assumed it was because such hostility didn't exist within his personality. But I had been wrong.

I said, 'Jeremy, I already told you that I'll do whatever you want.' I looked down at my lap – my knuckles – and he said, 'I need some air. I'm going out.'

I looked up. 'Are you coming back tonight?'

'Maybe.'

'If you don't, will you just text and let me know you're fine? You don't have to say where you are.' Had I surrendered all my rights as a wife this abruptly? It appeared I had.

His voice was sarcastic as he said, 'I appreciate your concern.' And then he'd stood and was putting on his coat, and my back was to him, and I didn't turn; neither of us said anything as he let himself out the front door, and I heard him locking it from the other side. A minute later, his car started. I leaned forward then, held my palms up to my forehead, and sobbed and sobbed.

Was he driving to a bar? His office? A hotel? Was he about to kill himself, or sleep with an undergrad, or go tell Courtney Wheeling? No, he probably wasn't telling Courtney – for that, he could have gone on foot. But we had no script, and I couldn't imagine where he was; I couldn't follow him in my mind.

I cried for a while, and then I started to get that itchy feeling, even given the circumstances, of wasting time, so I put the ice cream mugs in the sink, picked up toys from the living room floor, and replaced books Owen had pulled off the shelf. It was while setting the lunch puzzle pieces back in their slots – sans baloney, because that was upstairs in Rosie's crib – that I had an awful thought: Jeremy could remarry. He could re-create our life, a second version of it, with someone else. It would be easy for him to find another wife – he was cute and nice and had a good job – and that wife would probably be younger than I was. She'd like Rosie and Owen but want children of her own. Would I be able to find another husband? Depending on whom I'd settle for, maybe, but I wouldn't have my pick – a single man with two young kids was sympathetic and endearing, while a single woman with three was needy and baggage-laden. And no matter what, I'd never find a husband like Jeremy, as easy to be around, as kind and calm and unpretentiously smart. All of which raised the question – but, no, I'd just start crying again if I went down that path. I had long believed that my own mother had made our lives unnecessarily hard when I was growing up, but it now seemed I'd done the same to my family. And then I thought, was my notion of Jeremy remarrying a fear, or was it a sense?

If he left me, I'd definitely need to return to work. Should I, I wondered, send an email to my former boss at this very moment? Would they take me back, in light of the economy, and even if they would, would they take me back pregnant? I'd have to put this baby in day care when he was three or four months old, though with three children, wouldn't a nanny be cheaper? But it made no sense to return to work only to pay another woman to take care of my own children in my own house. Did any divorced mothers who didn't get huge settlements from rich ex-husbands not have jobs? Oh, to be able to undo that moment when I'd sat too close to Hank on the couch, to have just said yes when he'd asked if it would be a bad idea if he kissed me. Yes, it had been a bad idea, it had been a terrible idea, and I had recognized it as such at the time; that had been part of its irresistibility.

Jeremy hadn't returned home, nor had he texted me, by the time I nursed Owen at ten. I brushed my teeth and got into bed without setting the

552

security alarm. I didn't think I'd be able to fall asleep, and first I was right, but eventually I was wrong; I realized I was wrong because it was after midnight, and I was waking up as Jeremy climbed into bed. There was something bad between us, I remembered, before I remembered what the bad thing was. Normally, he'd have rolled toward me or I'd have reached out and patted his thigh, but we didn't touch each other or speak. He lay on his side, facing away from me.

In the morning, our routine was the same as usual except undergirded by our mutual awareness of my betrayal, and Jeremy's distance; he barely met my eyes and spoke to me only when necessary. When I came downstairs after showering and said, 'What did Owen eat?' Jeremy said, 'Oatmeal and pears,' and he didn't say anything else to me for more than twenty minutes. Was it always going to be like this, from here on out? Because life with young children – it was hard enough without him hating me. Maybe divorce *would* be preferable to this punitive domesticity. But no, I needed to be patient, to let him absorb what I'd known for weeks.

Rosie was drawing on construction paper, and she passed Jeremy a green crayon and said, 'Daddy wants to draw Mama making a happy face.'

'I'll draw a turtle,' Jeremy said.

Before he left for work, I asked, 'Are you coming home for dinner?'

After a pause, he said, 'I guess.' Then, not in a mean way, just in a businesslike way – that was, in its dispassion, almost worse than meanness, he said, 'Call today and schedule a CVS.'

That night at dinner, while I fed Owen a jar of squash and Jeremy, Rosie, and I ate pizza that Jeremy had told me via text he'd pick up, Rosie said, 'Rosie's birthday is coming up.'

'That's true,' I said. 'In January. How old will you be?'

'Is Mama coming to my birthday party?'

'Of course,' I said. 'You'll be three.'

'Is Daddy coming to my birthday party?'

Jeremy said nothing, and I said, 'Of course he is.'

'Is the baby coming to my birthday party?'

'Owen would love to come to your birthday party,' I said.

'Is a purple cake coming to my birthday party?'

'We can make a purple cake.'

Jeremy set the slice of pizza he'd been eating on his plate, stood, and walked into the dining room. Rosie said, 'Is a balloon coming to my birthday party?'

I stood, too; when I looked into the dining room, I saw Jeremy by the windows, his back to me, his shoulders heaving. There was a noise coming from him, an almost imperceptible squeaking. 'Is a balloon coming to my birthday party?' Rosie asked again. I had no idea whether Jeremy would want me to comfort him or leave him alone. Since I was the source of his unhappiness, it seemed safer to assume the latter.

'Is a balloon coming to my birthday party?' Rosie asked for the third time, and as I returned to the kitchen table, I said, 'Yes, a balloon is coming.'

A few minutes later, I heard Jeremy leave the house. Again, he didn't get home until I was asleep.

The CVS was nine days later, performed not by my obstetrician but by a red-bearded maternal-fetal-medicine specialist, and Jeremy wasn't there. Though I'd mentioned when the appointment was, it had seemed wrong to ask him to accompany me, and he hadn't offered. A technician did an ultrasound first, to confirm that I was right about being ten weeks along, and the technician stayed, the view of my inhabited womb in blurry black and white remaining on the computer screen, while the doctor used a needle to extract the tissue sample. On the screen, I could see a shrimp shape with little limb buds, and just before the doctor inserted the needle, fear gripped me that the CVS would cause a miscarriage. If this happened, it would simplify everything, but still – I wanted the baby to be okay.

The procedure was more uncomfortable than truly painful, and when the doctor was finished, they observed the baby's heartbeat for several minutes; then he left and the technician helped me stand. 'Do you have someone to drive you home?' she asked, and I nodded, which was a lie. But I'd hired Kendra until five-fifteen, when Jeremy would return from work. I walked slowly to the parking garage, climbed into my car in the semi-darkness of the winter afternoon, then put the key in the ignition. At home, I texted Kendra from the driveway to tell her to take Rosie and Owen to the kitchen. Just before I opened the front door, I noticed outside it a brown paper lunch bag. My name was on it in Vi's handwriting. Inside was a thumbnail-sized shiny red gemstone flecked with black, and a scrap of paper on which Vi had written, *Jasper – for balancing emotional energy/stress – wear in your auric field (i.e., on you or carry) – can't hurt!* I slipped the stone and note into the pocket of my coat and went up to bed.

The CVS didn't cause me to miscarry; I was still pregnant in the days after. I could tell because, besides not cramping or spotting, I was usually either queasy or ravenously hungry, and some-times I was both at once.

I didn't know exactly when Jeremy had his DNA sample drawn, or how he directed the information to my obstetrician's office, but eight days after the CVS, while the children were having their after-noon naps, I received a call on my cellphone from my obstetrician, a tall, merry, middle-aged Jewish woman who had delivered Rosie and Owen and whom I adored. 'So I've got your results in front of me, and Jeremy's DNA doesn't match baby's,' she said. Shame surged through me, and after a few seconds, she said, 'Is that a surprise for you?'

'No,' I said.

'I hope you're taking care of yourself,' she said. 'Eating well and getting plenty of rest.'

'I am. Thank you for calling.'

'Kate, if you'd like to talk to someone, I know a fabulous therapist in Clayton.'

So Dr Rosenstein, cheerful, frank Dr Rosenstein with her dark, curly hair and her bright, unfashionable, vaguely ethnic wardrobe – I'd once seen her wearing a Hawaiian-print shirt under her white coat – Dr Rosenstein now knew I was a slut who'd cheated on my husband.

'That's okay,' I said. 'But thanks.'

After I'd hung up, I texted Jeremy: *CVS test results back. Your DNA does not match baby.* I had no idea if sending this information in a text was an act of cowardice or mercy. At home, for the past few weeks, we'd been sleepwalking. After Owen and Rosie were down at night, Jeremy would read or grade in the living room, with the television turned to sports and muted. Once I said, 'Do you want to watch *Saturday Night Live*?' and he said, 'No, but if you do, I can go to the kitchen.'

After that, I began getting into bed myself as soon as Rosie was asleep, even though it was seven-thirty. I ended up finishing the novel I'd started in June, and then I started and finished a memoir by Michael J. Fox. Jeremy never came to bed until after I'd nursed Owen at ten and gone to sleep. It occurred to me to try to get him to have sex, either to stay awake upstairs or just throw myself at him downstairs, but would I throw myself at him on the same couch where I'd thrown myself at Hank? Did Jeremy suspect that the couch was where Hank and I had had sex? Anyway, if Jeremy rebuffed me, it would be mortifying; it would be unbearable. What was it I'd thought that night with Hank about Jeremy not giving me compliments – that we were too tired for it? Which was true enough, but what I'd overlooked was how Jeremy's daily kindnesses, the way he pulled me onto his lap, the way he washed the dinner dishes, were their own compliments, their own reassurance. In their absence, I could feel the corners of furniture more sharply, the drafty windows and cold floors.

A minute after I'd sent him the text with the CVS results, Jeremy texted me back: *Let's talk tonight.*

There wasn't ice cream this time around; because Jeremy and I no longer ate it at night together in front of the TV, I'd taken to consuming ice cream alone, in the afternoon, when Rosie and Owen were napping. Sometimes I ate it while crafting the email to my former boss, though I still hadn't sent her anything.

As during our last real conversation, I sat in the armchair and Jeremy sat on the couch. This time he was the one who spoke first. He cleared his throat. 'When you told me we should just raise the baby and not explain to anyone why he has dark skin, I thought that was ridiculous, but I haven't been able to come up with a better solution.'

'You don't want a divorce?' The words had leapt from my mouth; although they probably sounded pathetic, I didn't care.

Matter-of-factly, he said, 'It's not that I haven't considered it. But the way you feel about an abortion is how I feel about a divorce. Everyone pretends like if it's in the parents' best interest, then it's in the kids', too. Or, you know, kids are resilient, they get over it. But plenty of kids *don't* get over it.' He made a wry expression, an almost smile – oh, how I missed Jeremy's smile – and said, 'Plus, you'd marry Hank.'

'Is that what you think?' The suggestion was weirdly flattering, the implication that marrying Hank was an option available to me, but even more so, the implication that Jeremy could still feel jealous – that he didn't loathe me completely.

He shrugged. 'Except I don't know how you'd support yourselves.'

'I'm not going to marry Hank,' I said. 'I promise.'

'Anyway.' Jeremy pressed his index finger to the bridge of his glasses, pushing them up. 'For about a minute, I was thinking we could tell the baby he's adopted, but it's too fucked up for him to believe his real mom gave him up. And then he's sixteen or eighteen and wants to find her and – it's just not fair to him. Plus, Rosie's probably old enough that she'd understand you'd been pregnant. So then I thought that we say we went to a fertility clinic and they mixed up the sperm, but that's way too much detail, and who'd believe we were going to a fertility clinic when we had a six-month-old? So I thought, okay, we tell people the truth. Too bad if it embarrasses Kate. But you'll be relieved to hear that I decided telling the truth would create its own set of problems. If anyone ever gets to learn the truth, it's him – the child, when he's older. But we don't tell anyone else anything. People are so rude that I'm sure they'll ask, and we'll just say there's Greek blood on my side.'

'Is there?'

'No. But Greek blood, Italian, whatever – we pick an ethnicity and stick with it.'

'Not black blood?'

Jeremy shook his head. 'It's too close to the truth.'

'What do we tell your family?'

'That there's Greek blood on your side.'

My heart was thudding. 'Thank you, Jeremy.'

'There's more,' he said. 'We leave St Louis. We move away. Because if you think you can hide this baby, you're crazy. The minute Hank sees him, he'll know. And the idea of getting into some custody battle with the Wheelings—' Jeremy made an expression of distaste.

'I doubt Courtney would want anything to do with the baby.'

'Sure,' Jeremy said. 'Courtney wouldn't.'

We both were quiet, and finally I said, 'Not that I want to tell Hank, but is it legal not to?'

'I have no idea.'

We were quiet again. 'Where would we go?' I asked.

'I emailed Lukovich, and the deadline for that Cornell job was December first, but he's willing to slip my application in. And it's not guaranteed, obviously, but I have as good a shot as anyone.' Jeremy looked at me, and it wasn't a warm look – he was telling, not asking. He said, 'If we can, we'll go to Ithaca.'

So this was to be my punishment: Not divorce. Not abortion. Just a move. A move of almost a thousand miles, to a part of the country where I'd never spent time, in a state where I knew no one, where I'd be looking after three young children. We'd need to find a new house, new parks, a new pediatrician. And what of my father and Vi? Could I train them to look out for each other? Vi would have to learn which brands our father liked to buy at the grocery store, and she'd have to be patient when he passed his coupons to the checkout person.

No, a move wasn't ideal. It was what I'd thought I could count on not happening as long as my father was alive. But still, comparatively, I'd be getting off easy. I swallowed and said, 'Okay.'

Many times, starting as soon as later that night, I have recalled this conversation and marveled at our naïveté, all the possibilities we failed to consider. Would we never again send out a Christmas card? Even if we didn't, did we think we could prevent a friend from taking a picture of our son at a birthday party and posting it on Facebook? And whether or not Jeremy worked in the same department as Courtney Wheeling, he'd see her regularly at conferences; they'd always know countless people in common. Two and a half years have passed since our decision, and Jeremy and I have not yet been caught, or at least we have not been confronted; most important, we have not been confronted by the Wheelings. What others might suspect, I can only guess. But surely – like an impending earthquake – our unmasking awaits us. And maybe we knew at the time we were being unrealistic; maybe it was a situation in which being unrealistic was the only way to proceed.

'This is the last thing,' Jeremy said in the living room. 'For all intents and purposes, I'm the baby's father. It's my name on the birth certificate. There's no asterisk. He's my son.'

'Okay,' I said again. 'Okay for all of it.' Then I said, 'I know it won't be now, but I hope that someday you'll be able to forgive me.'

He didn't stand to hug me; he didn't motion for me to join him on the couch. We weren't about to watch TV together, apparently, or to have sex. He merely said, 'I hope so, too,' and then he leaned forward and lifted a stack of papers from the table.

* * *

But then we did have sex; later that night, we did. He got into bed while I was nursing Owen at ten (now that I was definitely having this baby, definitely not terminating, I would have to wean Owen before he turned one, I thought; even if it was biologically possible, I couldn't see nursing him atop my pregnant belly). When I re-entered our room, Jeremy was sitting up, shirtless, the covers pulled to his waist. He wasn't using his phone. I'd already changed into my pajamas and had been reading before I nursed Owen, and I'd left the book open and facedown on my nightstand. I hadn't yet closed the door behind me when Jeremy said, 'Come here.'

I approached his side of the bed instead of mine and stood a couple feet from him.

'Take off your pajamas,' he said. I hesitated only briefly before pulling my T-shirt and then my nursing bra over my head; I hooked my thumbs into the sides of my underwear and pants and pushed them both down at the same time. The light on Jeremy's nightstand was off, and the light on mine was on. He appraised my body. I was already gaining pregnancy weight again around my midsection, having never completely lost it since delivering Owen, and I couldn't remember when I'd last shaved my bikini line, but some rite of penance was occurring, I understood, and debasing myself was part of it.

Jeremy said, 'When you were fucking Hank, did you think about me?'

I bit my lip. 'I was upset with you for leaving town. But, Jeremy, I only love you.'

'Did you enjoy fucking him?'

I wanted to defend myself, to explain, but I needed to answer his questions succinctly and carefully; after all, we were constructing the narrative we'd live with. I said, 'The way you touch me – nobody else knows how to touch me like you.' Jeremy could say Hank's name, but I couldn't; I was pretty sure that was one of the rules of this exchange.

'Did you come?'

'You know what to do to make me come.' I stepped toward him, reached for his hand, and brought it down between my legs, where it was already wet. 'See?' I said. And then I climbed onto the bed, onto him, my naked body on his, and I pushed down the covers, and he gripped my ass. I'm not sure it was a decision on his part so much as habit or reflex.

When he was inside me, I said it again: 'I only love you, Jeremy. I only love you. I only love you.' Even when his breath broke against my ear, he didn't say anything back.

Things were better in the morning – not completely, but a little, and I understood that this was the most I could hope for. After breakfast, playing in the living room, Rosie said in an excited tone, 'There's chocolate in Mama's diaper!'

'I don't wear diapers,' I said. 'I use the potty.'

'But if she did wear diapers,' Jeremy said, and though he was ostensibly speaking to Rosie, there was something in his voice for me, too, 'she would definitely have chocolate in them.'

At Christmas, which we hosted – Jeremy's father and stepmother flew out for three days, and my father, Vi, and Stephanie joined us for Christmas dinner – Vi dried serving dishes as I washed them after the meal, and she said, 'I dreamed last night of the earthquake again. Did I ever tell you that in my dreams, it's all black people?'

No, Vi, I thought. *No more of this.* I passed her the bowl that had held the sweet potatoes and said, 'Yes, you've mentioned that.' After a few seconds, I said, 'Dad is really quiet tonight.'

'Dad's always quiet.'

Surely my recent nervousness about my father was nervousness about the prospect of moving. But I hadn't yet brought up the job at Cornell with Vi because Jeremy had asked me not to, in case he didn't get it. Even though I was certain that he would, I'd complied with his request. 'I wonder if Dad's been driving at night again,' I said.

'Well, you don't have to worry about that tonight.' Vi and Stephanie had picked him up. Then Vi said, 'I just wish I knew where my earthquake is.'

Was this never going to be fully behind us? No, it wasn't. Even then, as I was washing dishes at the sink, my belly was swelling again; it wouldn't be long before people other than Jeremy and Vi knew I was pregnant.

'Maybe your earthquake was never an earthquake,' I said.

Three weeks later, on the afternoon of January 12, 2010, as the children and I were driving home from the shoe store after buying Rosie a pair of purple sequined sneakers, I received a text from Jeremy: *So sad about Haiti.* I turned on the car radio and learned that a magnitude 7 earthquake had struck just west of Port-au-Prince, killing and injuring countless people, blocking the roads with rubble, and cutting off electricity and phone service.

As I was turning into our driveway, my cellphone rang, and when I answered, Vi was sobbing. 'It's awful,' she said. 'It's awful.'

In the backseat, Rosie reached out, plucked Owen's pacifier from his mouth – her arms were getting long – and stuck it in her own. To Vi, I said, 'Do you want to come over?'

'Maybe.' Vi sniffed. 'Isn't Haiti already really fucked up without this?'

'I'm sorry,' I said.

Jeremy and I didn't watch any news until the children were in bed, and even then, I couldn't take much at a time. I'd get up to put laundry in the dryer or to carry a water glass from the living room mantel to the kitchen sink, and I was sorting the mail that had accumulated recently when Vi called.

'I'm going down there to volunteer,' she said.

I had already heard someone on CNN say that you'd be better off just sending money, but there were so many steps between Vi expressing her plan and boarding a plane to Port-au-Prince that it didn't seem like I needed to dissuade her.

'Come over,' I said. 'Seriously.'

'Stephanie will be here soon.'

'She's welcome, too.'

'I'm not talking to reporters, if that's what you're worried about.'

'Are reporters calling you?'

'Well, I heard from Emma about ten seconds after the quake. The ground might still have been shaking. But I'm done with the media.'

'Really?' I tried to conceal my relief.

'When I was doing all those interviews, it seemed fun, but the thought of talking to some newspaper columnist now – I mean, they all ask you the same questions over and over, the questions are dumb to begin with, and then they either take what you say out of context or just straight-up misquote you.'

May you always feel exactly as you do now, I thought. Aloud, I said, 'I can see that.'

After I hung up, there was footage on-screen of a collapsed hospital, and a weeping woman outside it was being interviewed, a translator speaking over her in French-accented English. I gestured toward the TV. 'I guess this explains why Vi was so insistent about her prediction, if that's what she was picking up on.'

Jeremy gave me a dubious look. 'You're really convinced her ghost guide mixed up Haiti and St Louis? The poorest country in the Northern Hemisphere and a declining midwestern city?'

'I don't think Vi would lie. She doesn't have much to gain at this point.'

Jeremy was silent, and then he said, 'I hope those godforsaken people down there get a fraction of the attention your sister did.'

I hadn't yet embarked on my plan, with regard to my father, to train Vi as my replacement – the first step would be to have Vi come along to the grocery store – but it turned out that I never needed to. Two days after the earthquake in Haiti, my father was having lunch at home when an aneurysm in his brain ruptured, causing him to double over with a searing headache. Though he was able to call an ambulance, he wasn't conscious when the medics arrived, and they had to break down his locked front door. Early that evening, when Jeremy went to my father's apartment so that neither Vi nor I had to, he found the door hanging from the hinges, a splattering of vomit on the dining room rug, and the uneaten remains of a turkey sandwich at the table. My father had died five hours earlier, in the ambulance en route to the hospital.

It's hard to say what would have been a preferable way for him to go, but the lunch alone, the vomit, the fact that he called his own ambulance, then died in pain and among strangers – if I had

568

been choosing for him, certainly I'd have chosen something else. We used the same funeral home he'd used for our mother, and though I initially didn't want a graveside service – I feared no one would come – Jeremy and Vi persuaded me. Fourteen people showed up, including Jeremy's mother; we hired Kendra to watch Rosie and Owen. Vi had said she'd write a poem about our father, but as Jeremy and I turned in through the gates of the cemetery, she called my cellphone and said, 'I started something, but it seemed really cheesy, so I'm reading the poem Jackie O's boyfriend read at her funeral.'

'That's fine.'

'You'll like it,' Vi said. 'It's classy.'

More irritably than I meant to, I said, 'I already told you it's fine.'

The service lasted ten minutes, during which I thought about how my father had been lonely before meeting my mother, then lonely in a different way after marrying her. But wasn't I filled with sorrow less for the quiet futility of my father's life than out of fear that my own children would judge me as harshly as I judged my parents? Was I enough different from my mother and father? I tried to be, but hadn't I just messed up in other ways?

We hadn't arranged to have a reception afterward, which felt inhospitable but not inhospitable enough to spontaneously invite everyone back to our house. Instead, we made small talk by the casket, then drove home with Jeremy's mother, followed by Vi and Stephanie. Jeremy's mother had come to the cemetery in a taxi from the airport and was flying out the next morning.

No one at the grave site had said anything about Vi's prediction. Or at least no one had said anything to me.

The following weekend, Vi and I cleared out our father's apartment. He wasn't someone who'd held on to much, which was part of why it was a surprise to find, in the drawer in his bedside table, a letter from a neurosurgeon I'd never heard of dated August 24, 2009, confirming that he had been diagnosed with a cerebral aneurysm and that against the doctor's advice and in spite of the risks of rupture, including but not limited to subarachnoid hemorrhage or intracranial hematoma, he did not at this time wish to seek further treatment.

I took the letter into the kitchen, where Vi was emptying cabinets. She pointed to a large flat cardboard box on the table. 'That's a really nice skillet, and he never even opened it.'

'Jeremy and I gave it to him.'

'Does that mean you have dibs on it?'

'Keep it. Look at this.' I passed the letter to her and waited while she read it. 'Why wouldn't he have wanted treatment?'

'He was seventy-four, Daze. Maybe he didn't want to use his remaining time being poked and prodded by doctors.'

'But to not even try – you don't think he was, like, depressed—'

In a skeptical voice, Vi said, 'Do *you* think he was depressed?'

'Not that I noticed, but—'

She shook her head. 'Dad was fine. He had all those sexy massages to live for.'

'You never said anything about that, did you?'

Vi rolled her eyes. 'No, I didn't say anything.' She set the letter on top of the skillet box. 'Although now I wish I hadn't let you talk me out of asking him about having senses. You know how he hardly asked us questions about our lives? Do you think it's because he didn't need to? Like, he just knew?'

I thought, for the first time in years, of that evening the summer after Vi and I had been in eighth grade, when my father had taken me to get ice cream and told me how he hadn't enjoyed junior high. 'You know what?' I said. 'I think he did. Did he know we were the ones cooking dinner all that time? He must have.'

'Did he know I'd grow up to be a big fat dyke?'

'Believe it or not, I think he knew that, too. Did he know Mom would die so young? Or what an unhappy marriage they'd have?'

'They had good times together, Daze. You don't believe it, but they did. Did I ever tell you that a couple months before she died, I went to Steak 'n Shake one day for lunch and saw them? I walk in, and there the two of them are. I couldn't hear what they were saying, but they were definitely talking.'

'Mom was up that early? And eating?' I tried to picture them, my father in a short-sleeved plaid polyester shirt, my excessively skinny, once-pretty mother.

'I decided not to say hi. They looked like they were having a nice lunch, and why disturb them? So I left.'

'Do you think it's not true that Mom didn't like Dad?'

Vi puffed out her cheeks, considering the question, then exhaled. 'I think Mom didn't like Mom.' Then she said, 'But she didn't kill herself. Despite what that douchey boyfriend of yours claimed. Wow, I can't even remember his name.'

'Ben,' I said, and at the same time, Vi said, 'Don't tell me. He doesn't deserve the space in my brain.' Vi reached for the letter from our father's doctor and, as I watched, folded it into a paper airplane. When she launched it, it hit the refrigerator before bouncing to the floor. She said, 'The fact that he wasn't jumping for joy all the time doesn't mean he was miserable. It's not one or the other. Mom had problems, yeah, but I really don't think Dad was depressed. He was just a grown-up.'

Although Vi didn't end up traveling to Haiti, there was a child, a ten-year-old girl named Ginette who was written about in an Associated Press article that ran in the *Post-Dispatch*, whom Vi became preoccupied with. After losing her mother in the earthquake, Ginette was living in a donated tent with five other children, the youngest of whom was eleven months and the oldest of whom was fifteen. They were sleeping on carpet scraps and foraging for food, and they had intestinal parasites. A pastor checked on them erratically; the baby lay in filth, covered in flies, and when he fussed, Ginette sang him lullabies.

For a few days, Vi wanted to adopt Ginette; then she wanted to make a donation to the pastor so that he could buy the children uncontaminated food. One afternoon while Rosie and Owen were napping, Vi and I looked online together, trying to figure out how to find the pastor, or at least the reporter who'd written about Ginette and the pastor, but when Jeremy got home, he said what I already knew, what Vi probably knew, too – that it was better to give money to an aid organization. This was what he and I did.

Vi kept tracking Ginette, she told me – she meant through either visualization or communicating with Guardian, not through the newspaper, because no other articles about Ginette ran – and she thought that a distant family member had come to collect her, then sold her as a servant. After that, Vi couldn't locate Ginette anymore. She said, 'What do I do now?'

It was an unusually warm February day, and we were in our yard; I was blowing bubbles, which Rosie was chasing, and Owen, who had begun walking the week before, took halting steps across the grass. I dipped the plastic wand back into the jar of soap. 'I don't know,' I said.

Six weeks after the earthquake in Haiti, there was an even stronger one – magnitude 8.8 – in Chile, and though it caused serious damage, there were far fewer fatalities and much less destruction because the quake's epicenter was in a small town. Later in the year, major earthquakes occurred in Indonesia, China, and Turkey. In March 2011, a magnitude 9 earthquake killed more than fifteen thousand people in Japan. Did this mean that in fact there *had* been a kind of earthquake season that started in September 2009? A geophysicist – Courtney Wheeling – would say no. On average, an earthquake of magnitude 6 or greater happens somewhere in the world every three days. Mostly, they happen underwater, and we hardly take notice. It is only when the earthquakes come to us, upending the streets and houses and trees we think of as ours, that they command our attention. But the earth, as Courtney once told a local TV reporter, is always busy.

Jeremy had been offered and accepted the Cornell job at the end of January. During his spring break, we flew out with the children to look at houses, and I met with the obstetrician whose name Jeremy's adviser's wife had passed along. My due date was July 3, and we'd move in May, as soon as Jeremy finished teaching. What we didn't say, what we didn't need to, was that it seemed wiser for me to have the baby outside St Louis.

Jeremy's accepting the job – our shared understanding of the move as my punishment – was another thing that eased the lingering tension between us. Though we didn't acknowledge such distasteful facts, the earthquake in Haiti had also made things better between us, as had my father's death. These global and personal tragedies made us glad not to be alone, glad to still be moving forward together as a family. Even so, I sometimes thought of what Jeremy had said to me the night we first slept together – *There's nothing you need to be sorry for* – and of how it was no longer true. It would never be true again.

We saw Vi and Stephanie frequently that spring. In their presence, it could almost seem as if I hadn't fucked up as colossally as I had. The irony was that the two of them – I assumed Vi had told Stephanie – were the only people other than Jeremy and me who knew that the baby I was carrying was Hank's. But maybe we nevertheless found them comforting because Stephanie hadn't been part of our lives before Vi's prediction and was therefore a change for us, but not a bad change; enjoying her company didn't represent pretense or loss.

Stephanie moved in with Vi in March, and when Vi told me she was about to, she said, 'Don't even make the joke.'

In April, at Owen's first-birthday celebration, for which we invited over only Vi and Stephanie, Vi declined both cake and ice cream, and I was incredulous. 'If you must know,' Vi said, 'I'm doing Weight Watchers. And no offense, but that cake doesn't look good enough to be worth the points.'

'You know, I was thinking you were thinner,' I said.

'Really?' Vi looked unabashedly thrilled. 'I've lost six pounds.'

The next weekend, when they came over on Sunday so Stephanie and Jeremy could watch the Cards play the Cubs, I said, 'Do you guys want to stay for dinner? It's vegetable stir-fry, so it's healthy.'

'Thanks, but Vi has promised to make me her famous herb-encrusted salmon tonight,' Stephanie said.

'Herb-encrusted salmon?' Jeremy turned to my sister and said, 'She has you by the balls, Vi.'

There was a silence, and I wondered if Jeremy's remark, which he'd meant as a teasing compliment to Stephanie, had come across as equating lesbians and men. And then, with complete aplomb, Stephanie said, 'Jeremy, my hands aren't that big.'

This wasn't the only time I thought it, but it was the first time: that it was all right for me to leave St Louis, because now there was someone there who loved Vi as much as I did. Before they went home that day, I said to her, 'I think you'll be okay after we're in New York.'

'No shit I will.' Vi looked amused. 'Please don't

tell me you're getting sentimental about moving. Don't you remember what you wished under the Arch? It's finally coming true.'

'Well, not quite like I pictured.'

'Of course not.' Vi shrugged. 'Not for me, either. No Peace Corps and no' – she held up her fingers – '"husband."' Then she patted my hand. 'But don't worry, Daze. It's not like you can escape me. Whatever happens, wherever you go, you'll always still be living in Sisterland.'

One Saturday morning when Jeremy had taken the children to the zoo and I was running errands alone, I stopped at the Schnucks on Manchester, which I hadn't been to since my father's death. The store was crowded, and I didn't realize until I was loading my food onto the conveyor belt that the cashier was an older woman with heavy makeup who'd helped us many times before.

She gestured toward my belly. 'Honey, you've been busy!'

I smiled sheepishly. There was an embarrassment I now felt when Owen and Rosie were with me, which was most of the time, as if people were thinking, *Why doesn't that woman stop having children?* Perhaps they assumed I was a member of a religious sect determined to build its population.

'Your dad's not with you today?' the woman said.

I shook my head.

The woman smiled. 'What a nice man he is.'

* * *

577

On a Monday in mid-April, in the middle of story hour at the Richmond Heights library, I received a text from Hank: *Heard you're expecting again. Congrats!* I was by then in the beginning of my third trimester, and I was huge. I was standing behind the group of children at the librarian's feet, following Owen as he toddled among the shelves.

Just as jarring as this unexpected contact with Hank was the realization, as evidenced by the time stamp on the screen of my phone, that six months had passed since his previous text. He'd sent that one the morning after we'd had sex: *C coming home at noon. We should talk.* And to think that there had been a time I'd felt impatient on the mornings Amelia attended preschool; those few hours had seemed too long to wait before reconnecting with Hank. All this time later, Hank as a notion, an idea, made me feel a reflexive queasiness, as I might if thinking of Marisa Mazarelli, but when I actually recalled the hours we'd spent together at parks and in each other's yards, it was hard not to miss him.

In the library, I was preoccupied enough, caught off guard enough, not to be gripped by nostalgia. I texted back, *Thanks.* He could ask, but I wouldn't initiate the topic.

His next text didn't arrive for several minutes: *Just want to confirm there's nothing we should discuss.*

Thank God for texting, I thought. Because how capacious, that single line in its invitation to lie without officially lying.

Nope, I wrote, *nothing to discuss.*

Wow three kids, he wrote back.

I know! I wrote. *Hope you guys are well.* Which was as bland, as innocuous, as what I might have told a former co-worker or a person I'd known distantly in college. Five weeks later, on the day we left St Louis, I still hadn't seen Hank again.

For the most part, the movers packed us. I insisted on transporting only our most fragile items: the antique perfume holder Vi had brought to the hospital when Rosie was born, a platter Jeremy's brother and sister-in-law had given us that was painted with our names and the date and place of our wedding. The week before departing from St Louis, after Jeremy did due diligence with *Consumer Reports,* we traded in both our cars and bought a minivan, a purchase Jeremy had mentioned first. We'd use it to drive to Ithaca, where it would become mine, and Jeremy would buy a sedan with snow tires.

Gabriel – Gabe – was born four days before his due date, on June 30, and we gave him the middle name Earl, after my father. Gabe's skin at birth was only the slightest bit darker than Rosie's and Owen's had been, though he definitely had more hair, and even a few curls, to the delight of the nurses. He's over two now, and he does have a different complexion than the rest of us; perhaps I think this only because I'm his mother, but I'd describe it as a golden glow. I can honestly say that he reminds me less of Hank than of Owen and Rosie when they were toddlers – Owen is now three, and Rosie is five – though sometimes Gabe makes an expression that causes me to gasp with recognition. At such moments, I wonder about my obligation not just to Hank but to Amelia as well. But I still believe that, at least for the time being, it's best to do nothing. It would be foolish, too, for me not to realize that the older Gabe gets, and the further he ventures into the world without us, the more likely he is to be perceived, accurately, as half black. I think, of course, of Dr Jeff Parker – Scary Black Man – and I worry for Gabe; there are so many large and small uglinesses around race, and how can I realistically expect other people to be better than I myself have managed to be?

But for now, Gabe is just a toddler. He loves singing 'The Itsy-Bitsy Spider.' Outside, he passes me leaves and says, 'Thank you.' In one of his books, there's an illustration of a scarecrow, and he always points at it and says, 'It's Mama.'

Around Jeremy, I've always been more careful with Gabe than I was with Rosie or Owen – careful not to complain, mostly. Sometimes when Rosie and Owen were really tiny and waking up eight times a night, if I couldn't take it anymore, I'd pass them off to Jeremy, telling him to go down-stairs with them, or anywhere – I just needed to sleep. I never did that with Gabe, even when he and I were both in tears. When he was a newborn,

I slept with him in my arms – not between Jeremy and me but between my body and the mini-crib we'd pushed up against our bed. I knew Jeremy didn't consider this safe, so I did it without mentioning it to him, though surely he must have noticed. But Gabe was soon a better sleeper than Owen had been, and when Gabe was six months old, we moved him into his brother's room. Jeremy is warm with Gabe, he is patient and silly and boisterous, and perhaps the fact that I detect the slightest withholding on Jeremy's part, the absence of a reflexive rather than a decided love, is only my imagination; perhaps I am seeing what I've primed myself to see.

I wondered if Jeremy would want us to have another child, if he'd decide it could be a further means of chipping away at my infidelity, re-inforcing the balance of our family as our family. I didn't think I could stand it, but what could I say if he insisted? And so at my six-week post-partum appointment, I requested an IUD. But Gabe was only four months old on the autumn evening when Jeremy said he'd been thinking that over Christmas break, he should get a vasectomy.

This past spring, while I was changing Gabe's diaper, he looked up at me, smiled, and said, 'Mama's other name is Daisy.' Vi and Stephanie have visited us a few times, so it's not impossible that he'd heard Vi call me Daisy, but I don't believe this is how he knew; when he spoke, my heart clenched. 'Mama's other name is Kate,' I said firmly. 'It used to be Daisy, but now it's Kate.' And then, a few weeks later, while the children and I were in the playroom off the kitchen, he turned to me and said, 'Daddy is Rosie's daddy.'

'That's true,' I said.

'And Daddy is Owen's daddy.'

'That's true, too,' I said.

He said, 'Who's my daddy?'

I swallowed. 'Daddy is your daddy. Daddy is all of your daddy.' I didn't say anything to Jeremy about this specific comment or its larger implications – time will tell if I'm overreacting, though again, I don't think I am. If it were to be only one of them, I'd have guessed Rosie, maybe because she's a girl like me. But I have guessed wrong about many things

My father had left no will, and after his estate went through probate, Vi and I received nineteen thousand dollars each. I had indeed ended up paying Emma Hall with a credit card – two credit cards, actually – and I used the money from my father to pay off the balance. I suspect Vi would have chipped in if I'd asked her to, but it felt like another kind of penance, given my complicity in everything, not to ask.

When people here in Ithaca learn where we moved from, they often mention Vi's prediction, not knowing that Vi is my sister. They don't remember her name, but they say something friendly and derisive, like 'Ah, St Louis, where the earth didn't shake.' And though it feels slightly cowardly or dishonest, I merely nod and change the subject. I feel that Vi's prediction is past and has concluded; I don't want to mock or defend or explain it, not to anyone, not ever again.

How peculiar, that morning we pulled out of our driveway on San Bonita Avenue for the last time, to think that Rosie and Owen wouldn't remember living in this city, this house; if Rosie did remember, it would be only vaguely. There are, I have learned, so many gifts of motherhood, and so many sadnesses, and one of the sadnesses is the asymmetry of the family experience: that in spite of all the daily nuisances, and in spite of the unforgivable way I transgressed, these years of the children being little are the sweetest time in my life. And yet, for Rosie and Owen and Gabe, these won't be their best years. They'll grow up and go away, they'll find spouses and have sons or daughters, and no matter how much we loved them, they'll probably recall their childhoods as strange and confusing, as all childhoods are. The happiest time in their lives, if they're lucky, will be when they're raising their own families.

Shortly before we left St Louis, the day Jeremy cleaned out his office at Wash U, he came home from campus and passed me an envelope, saying, 'I took this from your dad's apartment that day.' He meant the day my father had died, and I must have made an alarmed expression because Jeremy added, 'It's nothing bad – just pictures.'

My father had put my name on the front of the envelope, spindly letters in blue ballpoint, and I felt a little ache seeing his handwriting. The envelope wasn't sealed, and inside were three photographs, all taken by my father on the evening of his birthday the previous September: one of Rosie, blurrily running across the grass; one of Vi sitting in a not particularly ladylike way in our recliner, Owen on her lap; and one of just Jeremy and me, standing side by side. It had been a while – longer than Rosie had been alive, I was pretty sure – since I'd seen a picture of Jeremy and me together and no one else. Usually, one of us was the photographer.

As I held the edges of the picture, I had an intimation – perhaps I mean a sense – of our children looking at it years in the future, when they themselves were adults: Rosie at thirty, say, and Owen at twenty-eight and Gabe at twenty-seven. Who would Jeremy and I be by then? Would we still be married, would we even still both be alive? I hoped so, I hoped it desperately, but the future (this is true for all of us) is opaque.

Our children, our grown-up children, who might or might not know the secrets of their parents but who'd surely possess secrets of their own – would they regard us with affection or resentment? The answer, presumably, is both, but still, it is hard not to wonder in what proportions, hard not to yearn, as I did at my father's burial, for those proportions to be favorable. As little girls, Vi and

I studied an image of our parents at the Arch, our mother in her belted orange wool jacket and matching beret, our father with his dark sideburns. And surely the clothes Jeremy and I wore in this picture, the haircuts we had, would seem as amusingly outdated to our children as the Arch photo had seemed to Vi and me, the year 2009 as faraway to them as 1974 had been to us.

And then one of my adult children speaks; I imagine it being Rosie. She and her brothers are clustered around the picture of Jeremy and me, examining it with the combination of disdain and curiosity we all feel when confronted with evidence of a world that dared to exist before our consciousness of it. 'I can't believe how young they were,' Rosie says.